Humphrey Prideaux, John Ellis

Letters of Humphrey Prideaux, sometime dean of Norwich,

to John Ellis, sometime under-secretary of State, 1674-1722

Humphrey Prideaux, John Ellis

Letters of Humphrey Prideaux, sometime dean of Norwich,
to John Ellis, sometime under-secretary of State, 1674-1722

ISBN/EAN: 9783337018313

Printed in Europe, USA, Canada, Australia, Japan

Cover: Foto ©Raphael Reischuk / pixelio.de

More available books at **www.hansebooks.com**

LETTERS

OF

HUMPHREY PRIDEAUX

SOMETIME DEAN OF NORWICH

TO

JOHN ELLIS

SOMETIME UNDER-SECRETARY OF STATE

1674-1722.

EDITED BY

EDWARD MAUNDE THOMPSON

BARRISTER-AT-LAW AND ASSISTANT-KEEPER OF MSS. IN THE BRITISH MUSEUM

PRINTED FOR THE CAMDEN SOCIETY.

M.DCCC.LXXV.

WESTMINSTER:
PRINTED BY NICHOLS AND SONS,
25, PARLIAMENT STREET.

[NEW SERIES XV.]

PREFACE.

HUMPHREY PRIDEAUX was born at Padstow on the 3rd of May, 1648. He came of an ancient Cornish family, being the third son of Edmund Prideaux of Padstow, a gentleman of good position and of influence in the county.

After some schooling at Liskeard and Bodmin, Humphrey was sent to Westminster in 1665, and remained there for three years as King's scholar under Dr. Busby. From thence he went up to Oxford, obtaining a studentship at Christ Church in December 1668; and took his B.A. degree in 1672.

At this time Dr. John Fell, Dean of Christ Church and soon afterwards Bishop of Oxford, was diligently urging on the work of the University press. He forthwith engaged Prideaux to assist in an edition of Lucius Florus, and, when that book was finished, set him to make notes for the work which afterwards appeared as the "Marmora Oxoniensia," and at the same time placed in his hands the History of Joannes Malala to edit. Prideaux was "groaning under the oppression of these two heavy burdens" in 1674, but soon threw off the second one, "a horrid, musty, foolish book," "stuffed with foolish and incredible lies," and devoted himself to the "Marmora," which was published in 1676.[a]

---

[a] John Evelyn has the following entry in his Diary, under date of 28th April, 1676: "The University of Oxford presented me with the 'Marmora Oxoniensia Arundeliana;' the Bishop of Oxford writing to desire that I would introduce Mr.

CAMD. SOC.   *b*

To this work Prideaux owed his introduction to his patron the Lord Chancellor Finch, who appointed him his chaplain, placed one of his sons with him as a pupil, gave him a sinecure in Wales, and in 1679 presented him to the rectory of St. Clement's, Oxford.

Meanwhile, he had taken his M.A. degree in 1675,[a] and became tutor and Hebrew lecturer in his college, in which last capacity he published two tracts of Maimonides with a Latin translation in 1679. That he was a disciplinarian may be easily imagined after reading his letters; and loss of popularity—the lot of most reformers—naturally attended his efforts in correcting abuses.

In 1681 Prideaux became Prebendary of Norwich, a preferment which he again owed to the Lord Chancellor, now Earl of Nottingham, and early in 1683 he was presented to the rectory of Bladen-cum-Woodstock by Lord Keeper North. His appointment to Norwich, where, with his usual activity, he at once began to busy himself in the affairs of the cathedral, weakened his connexion with Oxford. He was tired of college life, his generation had passed away, and his chance of succeeding to the Hebrew professorship and a canonry at Christ Church seemed but a poor one; so he took a decisive step: "yielding to the circumstances of his present condition" he married a wife, though "he little thought he should ever come to this," and, exchanging his living of Bladen and his sinecure for the rectory of Saham-Tony in Norfolk, he bade farewell to Oxford in 1686, and settled down to the duties of his cathedral and parish. As if to sever the last tie that bound him to the University, the death of his old friend, Bishop Fell, took place just at this time.

Prideaux, the editor (a young man most learned in antiquities), to the Duke of Norfolk, to present another dedicated to his Grace, which I did, and we dined with the Duke at Arundel House, and supped at the Bishop of Rochester's, with Isaac Vossius."

[a] He became B.D. in 1682, and D.D. in 1686.

From this period the letters become less regular and fewer in number. Oxford gossip gives place to county politics, and criticism is transferred from heads of colleges to the Bishop and the Dean of Norwich, not always to the advantage of the latter.

Prideaux became Archdeacon of Suffolk at the close of 1688; but resigned his living of Saham in 1694, and retired to Norwich. In 1696, however, he took the small vicarage of Trowse near that city, and continued to hold it until 1710. During this quiet period of his life he had spare time to devote to literature, and produced, in 1697, his " Life of Mahomet," which was well received. And now the time was come when he was to receive his last promotion. In 1702 Dean Fairfax passed away after a reign of thirteen years, too long if the character which Prideaux has drawn of him with no sparing hand be a true one. Prideaux was installed Dean of Norwich on the 8th of June in the same year, having been recommended for the place by Daniel Earl of Nottingham, Secretary of State, the son of his old patron. He was now fifty-four years of age, his constitution was unusually good, and he had every prospect of a long and useful term of years before him. But seven years after he was overtaken by the "calamitous distemper" of the stone, which soon reached a critical stage. " My case grows worse and worse " he writes, " and there is noe remedy for me but by cutteing; and, on full advice had upon my case, I am told I cannot bear that operation, but that in all likelyhood I must dy under it. If soe, to put myselfe upon it is nothing lesse than selfe murder, and for that I cannot answer to God who gave me my life, and therefore I must be content to bear my burden as it is, and it is heavy enough." However he did undergo the operation, and not only survived it but would in all probability have thoroughly recovered, had he not been carelessly treated afterwards. Yet, in spite of the doctors, he rallied, and was soon at work again. During his confinement he composed the book by which he is best remembered, "The Old and New Testaments connected," and published the first part in

1715. Three years later his health began to break; his hands were affected with a palsy; and his life was surely though slowly drawing to its close.

The last letter in this volume is dated two years before his death, and shows no lack of mental vigour; but his body soon gave way, and, after a year of lingering helplessness, he died on the 1st November, 1724, aged 76.

The following sketch of his character, which appears in his "Life," published in 1748,[a] will be recognised by the reader of these letters as in most particulars a faithful portrait: "Dr. Prideaux was naturally of a very strong robust constitution, which enabled him to pursue his studies with great assiduity; and, notwithstanding his close application and sedentary manner of life, enjoyed great vigour both of body and mind for many years together, till he was seized with the unhappy distemper of the stone. His parts were very good, rather solid than lively, his judgment excellent. As a writer he is clear, strong, and intelligent, without any pomp of language or ostentation of eloquence. His conversation was a good deal of the same kind, learned and instructive, with a conciseness of expression on many occasions, which to those who were not well acquainted with him had sometimes the appearance of rusticity. In his manner of life he was very regular and temperate, being seldom out of his bed after ten at night, and generally rose to his studies before five in the morning. His manners were sincere and candid. He generally spoke his mind with freedom and boldness, and was not easily diverted from pursuing what he thought right. In his friendships he was constant and invariable; to his family

---

[a] "Life of the Rev. Humphrey Prideaux, D.D., Dean of Norwich, with several Tracts and Letters of his upon various subjects never before published." London, 1748, 8vo. The outline of his life contained in this book seems to have been drawn from information supplied by his son, Edmund Prideaux, in a letter to Dr. Thomas Birch, dated 26 Aug., 1738, and now preserved in the British Museum, Add. MS. 4223, f. 155.

was an affectionate husband, a tender and careful father, and greatly
esteemed by his friends and relations, as he was very serviceable to
them on all occasions."

Of the constancy of his friendship the letters printed in this
volume are a visible testimony, being the result of a lifelong
intimacy with one who, his senior by a few years, still outlived
him. Such series of letters, requiring as the condition of their
existence the happy combination of long lives and unchanging
friendship, are rarely met with, and when found have a peculiar
interest. A man of Prideaux's rough vigour of mind could not
well be free from prejudice; too ready, perhaps, to condemn his
opponent as a " pragmatical rascal," and to declare his friend to be a
" very worthy gentleman," he was nevertheless perfectly honest in his
contempt of anything bad or mean, sensible in his opinions, social or
political, and thoroughly practical in daily life; but in sentiment his
nature was sadly wanting, witness the very mercantile way in which
he lays before his friend his arrangements for marriage, and, though
he was young at the time, his very unpoetical estimate of Sir Philip
Sidney, " so high in esteem among women and fools."

As an Orientalist he enjoyed some reputation among his contem-
poraries, though he does not seem to have cared much for oriental
studies. When, in 1691, the Hebrew professorship at Oxford was
offered to him, he declined it, because, as he tells Ellis, he " nau-
seates that learning " and is " resolved to loose noe more time upon
it." He gave his oriental books, before his death, to Clare Hall,
Cambridge.

A contemporary's opinion of Prideaux—an unfavourable one—
which has been handed down to us by Hearne, may be here quoted;
but it should be received with caution. There appears to have
been a mutual dislike; for it will be noticed that Prideaux speaks
disparagingly of Aldrich in certain passages of these letters.

" The late Dr. Henry Aldrich, Dean of Christ Church, had but
a mean opinion, and used to speak slightingly, of Dr. Humphrey

Prideaux, Dean of Norwich, as an unaccurate muddy-headed man. Prideaux's chief skill was in Orientals, and yet even there he was far from being perfect in either, unless in Hebrew, which he was well versed in. In 1677 he was preparing for the press an edition of Dionysius Halicarnasseus, to be printed at the Theatre, but it came to nothing, I know not for what reason, unless it was found that 'twould be as incorrect as his *Marmora Oxoniensia*, and that he would do little or nothing to it, besides heaping up notes; and yet from a letter in his own hand I gather that he intended to be short in them, and to make them consist only of references to other authors, where the several stories were also told. As for MSS., I perceive from that letter that he would not trouble himself about any, but rest wholly upon what had been done to his hands by former editors."[a]

Prideaux left a son, Edmund, the ancestor of the present representatives of the family.

A few words as to Prideaux's correspondent. John Ellis was the eldest son of a father of the same name, the Rector of Waddesdon, in Buckinghamshire, a puritan divine of some repute in his day. John was the eldest of a family of six sons and two daughters, and was born in 1645. He was educated at Westminster, and elected student of Christ Church in 1664, and had therefore left the school before Prideaux entered it. Their friendship was probably formed afterwards at Oxford. He did not take a degree, but entered the public service at an early age, and was first employed in the Secretary of State's department. In 1674, the year in which the letters commence, he was under Sir Joseph Williamson in the Paper Office, but was thrown out of employment by the promotion of his chief to be Secretary of State. After some months' idleness, however, he was appointed secretary to Sir Leoline Jenkins, one of the plenipotentiaries proceeding to the Conference

---

[a] Reliquiæ Hearnianæ; ed. P. Bliss. Oxford, 1857, p. 844.

at Nimeguen, and set out thither in December 1675. Three years later we find him acting as secretary to the Earl of Ossory, and in 1683 as secretary to the Commissioners of the Revenue of Ireland, a post which he continued to hold till the Revolution. It seems to have been his own fault that he lost this appointment, for, having come over to England, apparently to watch how the game went, he was supplanted by some one on the spot, and remained idle for nearly a year. However, he fell back upon his interest with the Butlers, and became secretary to the Duke of Ormonde towards the end of 1689. Two years after he was one of the Commissioners of Transports, and at length Under-Secretary of State from 1695 to 1705. His resignation of the last appointment took place on some misunderstanding with Secretary Hedges. After this, he was again for a short time in office as Comptroller of the Mint in the reign of Queen Anne.

Ellis represented Harwich in the parliaments of 1705 and 1707, and became a justice of the peace for Middlesex. He is represented as having grown exceedingly wealthy, probably from making good use of those opportunities by which, in his time, it was considered quite fair for a public man to benefit. He died, unmarried, on the 8th July, 1738, having reached the extreme age of ninety-three years.[a]

Judging by the large collection that he has left of letters addressed to him on both public and private matters, Ellis must have been

* Of Ellis's five brothers, all of whom were educated at Westminster, three rose to some distinction, though in very different careers. William became secretary to the Duke of Tyrconnel, Lord Lieutenant of Ireland, was knighted, and was subsequently Secretary of State to James II. at St. Germains, and treasurer to the Old Pretender. Philip was kidnapped by the Jesuits and brought up at St. Omer; became chaplain to Mary of Modena, consort of James II., and eventually Bishop of Segni. Welbore was Dean of Christ Church, Dublin, a Privy Councillor, and successively Bishop of Kildare and Meath. His son Welbore was the first Lord Mendip. Two of the brothers are mentioned in these letters.—See Welch, *Westminster Scholars;* and the account of the Ellis family in *The Ellis Correspondence,* ed. Hon. G. Agar Ellis, 2 vols. London, 1829, which, however, is incorrect in some details.

both industrious and obliging, if not of much ability. And one who could hold for ten years the office of Under-Secretary to three successive Secretaries of State must needs have had temper and good business habits. With his more intimate acquaintances he was certainly a favourite, as their letters sufficiently prove. Unhappily for his private moral character, an intrigue with the Duchess of Cleveland has been made by Pope the occasion for his name to appear in verse along with certain disreputable company.[a]

The letters published in this volume form part of Ellis's papers, which were purchased in 1872 by the Trustees of the British Museum from the Earl of Macclesfield. They are now numbered Additional MS. 28,929; and extend from the year 1674 to 1722, but unfortunately with many gaps. They proceed with some regularity to 1686; thence, they belong to the years 1688 (one letter only drawn from another collection), 1691-1693, 1696-1700, 1705, 1707-1710, and 1722.

The letters written during Prideaux's residence at Oxford present to us an amusing, and in many points an instructive, view of University life some two hundred years ago. Fell, as Dean of Christ Church, naturally takes a prominent place, busy with his building, and busy with his printing; with autocratic indifference altering paragraphs in Wood's " Antiquities," or inventing a spelling of his own for a new edition of the Bible; " dealeing in most vile small businesses " rather than be dealing in none at all; urging on his editors, watching his press with jealous care, and once surprising a surreptitious impression of scandalous engravings—a private enterprise of the men of All Souls, whose discomfiture Prideaux, their sworn enemy, narrates with no small satisfaction.

[a] In " A Sermon against Adultery," an imitation of the Second Satire of the First Book of Horace.

The men of Balliol "bubb" beer at a "dingy horrid scandalous alehouse," conveniently placed over against their gate, whilst those of Trinity affect the "Split Crow." Dull sermons were as common then as now; college tutors were not unknown to beat their pupils; and authors sometimes encountered each other with fisticuffs. The respected name of Anthony Wood is connected in our minds rather with literature than with boxing, yet we find the author of the "Athenæ" standing firm against the assaults of his formidable adversary Dick Peers and not coming off worst in the encounter.

Van Tromp is entertained at Christ Church, but will have none of their degrees, calls for salt junk, and in fact proves himself "a greazy drunkeing Dutchman." But Dr. Speed with well-seasoned head comes to the rescue, and the admiral strikes to the superior drinking powers of the gownsman. There is poor Byram Eaton, the head of a hall bereft of undergraduates, hard put to it to pay the accumulated chimney-tax of tenantless rooms; Woodroffe, the Christ Church tutor, making himself ridiculous in pulpit and in hall, till Prideaux himself—who never tires of abusing him—cries "enought of a fool;" Bodley's Librarian beaten by his wife; and the Principal of Hart Hall eating himself into madness. As to college matters, the elections to All Souls' fellowships require much management, and the report of a mandamus in favour of the son of the King's cook has naturally a disturbing influence; nor are New and Magdalen free from charge of selling places, the latter college too getting into further trouble by internal squabbles.

Nor does Prideaux spare the townsmen. Among other things, their struggle for the formal admission of their town-clerk is a principal subject in many of the letters, and Mayor Pauling, "a rank phanatique," and factious Alderman Wright are prominent figures.

We have also passing glimpses of some of the more notable men of the day; of Pocock the orientalist, of Bathurst, and of Busby;

of Hobbes, of Burnet, the " troublesome knave" of the Rolls, and of Trelawny, vehement almost to madness.

But, amongst all, the most interesting notices are those which refer to John Locke. Senior both to Ellis and Prideaux, he had passed through Westminster and had taken his degree long before their time; their interest in him was therefore political rather than personal. Knowing as we do that Prideaux was aware that information contained in his letters often reached the Secretary's ears, there can be little doubt that his references to Locke's movements were as much for the benefit of the Government as for Ellis's amusement. Nor would Prideaux feel compunction that he was playing the spy ; as an enemy to " republicarians" he naturally looked on a friend of Shaftesbury with no kindly eye. Under the date of the 7th February, 1675, Locke " hath wrigled into Ireland's faculty place," the studentship of which Fell afterwards received the royal command to deprive him. Early in 1682 he " lives a very cunning unintelligible life here, beeing two days in town and three out, and noe one knows where he goes or when he goes, or when he returns . . . . not a word of politics comes from him, nothing of news or anything else concerneing our present affairs, as if he were not at all concernd in them. If any one asks him what news when he returns from a progresse, his answere is, ' we know nothing.' " " Sometimes he himselfe goes out and leaves his man behind, who shall then to be often seen in yᵉ quadrangle to make people beleive his master is at home, for he will let noe one come to his chamber, and therefore it is not certain when he is there or when he is absent."

This account of Locke's watchful reserve is repeated in Fell's well-known letter of the 8th November, 1684, to the Earl of Sunderland, wherein the Bishop says, " I have for divers years had an eye upon him, but so close has his guard been on himself, that, after several strict enquiries, I may confidently affirm there is not anyone in the college, however familiar with him, who has heard him speak a word either against or so much as concerning the government; and although very frequently, both in public and in private, discourses have been purposely introduced, to the disparagement of his master, the Earl of Shaftesbury, his party and designs, he could never be provoked to take any notice, or discover in word or look the least concern; so that I believe there is not in the world such a master of taciturnity and passion."[a]

After Shaftesbury's escape Prideaux has a good word for Locke, who now "lives very quietly with us, and not a word ever drops from his mouth that discovers anything of his heart within. Now his master is fled, I suppose we shall have him all togeather. He seems to be a man of very good converse and that we have of him with content; as for what else he is he keeps it to himselfe, and therefore troubles not us with it nor we him." The circumstances of his withdrawal from Oxford may be read under the date of the 12th November, 1684, and his expulsion is announced in the following letter.

With Prideaux's change of residence to Norfolk we are at once carried into county politics. He had already, in 1681, made acquaintance with Norwich, and had found it "devided into two factions, Whigs and Torys," the former the more numerous, the latter the governing body, and both contending with the utmost violence. Under the fostering care of successive Tory mayors, brewers by trade, "this town swarms with alehouses." Prideaux has something to say about papists, and more about Jacobites, he holding both in abhorrence as a staunch supporter of William's government. We hear something too of cathedral matters, of Bishop Moore who loves London life better than his diocese, and of the "horrid sot we have got for our Dean." In truth Dean Fairfax is not painted in bright colours. The scene in which, pipe in mouth and swallowing alternate draughts of claret and "nog," he chuckles over

[a] Lord King, *Life of John Locke*, 1830, vol. i. p. 279

Don Quixote with Mr. Prebendary Hodges, is at once ludicrous
and woeful. " Certainly ye preferments of ye Church were never
designed for such drones," cries Prideaux; yet the preferments of
the Church were convenient shelving-places for troublesome people.
Here is Drelincourt, tutor to Lord Ossory's son, unable to manage
his pupil, and in a word " this Frenchman is intolerable in ye eyes
of every on y^t hath any respect for ye honourable family " to which
he belongs. But there is the vicarage of Bradworthy vacant, "faln
into ye King's disposal," and " one word from My Lord will easyly
procure it for him, and therewith his utmost deserts and the greatest
service he hath don My Lord will be more then abundantly
satisfyed." And again, " We have another man y^t wants preferment, one Mr. Charles Allestree, who hath marryed the most
scandalously bad that any fellow hath don, I beleive, for these
many years, his wife being one Mother Yalden, an old alewife
with an house full of children." Comment is needless.

No correspondence or memoirs of this time would, I suppose, be
complete without the introduction of some of Charles the Second's
many mistresses. Accordingly, two anecdotes will be found in
these pages, characteristic enough of the silly vanity of the Duchess
of Cleveland, who sits in her carriage in the streets of Oxford for
all the world to admire, and of the free and easy manners of Nell
Gwyn as she accosts Charles in the public fields of Newmarket.

After the courteous fashion of his time Prideaux always addresses
his correspondent " Sir," and signs himself " your most faithful
humble servant," " your affectionate friend and humble servant,"
and even " your most affectionate friend and faithful humble
servant." In printing a series of letters from a single individual
it did not seem necessary to give these recurring formalities.

I may here state, with regard to the letter of the Duke of
Ormonde to his grandson, printed at page 71, that I accidentally

overlooked it in print in the Appendix to Carte's Life of the Duke
of Ormonde, where it is entered under a wrong date. As, however,
it is now printed with the original spelling, and free from a few
inaccuracies which have crept into Carte's impression, its insertion
in this volume may not be unwelcome.

In conclusion, I take this opportunity of thankfully acknow-
ledging the assistance of my friend the Rev. J. R. Bloxam, D.D.,
Vicar of Upper Beeding, in supplying some of the information
which is embodied in the foot-notes.

E. M. T.

CORRIGENDA.

Page   19, line   2, *for* plate *read* pate.

„   39,   „   14, *for* I have translated it *read* I have it translated.

„   40, note *d*, *for* on the side of *read* on the site of.

„   52, line 15, *for* Barthurst *read* Bathurst.

„   137, note *b*, *for* Peirce *read* Pierce.

„   211, line 36, *for* letter to Southwell *read* letter on Southwell.

LETTERS

OF

HUMPHREY PRIDEAUX

TO

JOHN ELLIS.

LETTERS

OF

HUMPHREY PRIDEAUX TO JOHN ELLIS.

Oxf[ord], July 28th, [16]74.

. . . . Here is now come out of our presse a booke of
Dr. Coles,[a] Fellow of Winchester, against the Papists, writt in
dialogues : I suppose the old tale tould over again. There is
nothing in the presse at present but a catalogue of the books of
Bodleian Library,[b] and a Greeke Testament[c] with the various
lections (which at the same time is now performeing in Holland
and will be out before ours), and an English Bible in qu[to].[d] Dr.

---

[a] Gilbert Coles, D.D., educated at Winchester, Fellow of New College 1637, and
afterwards Fellow of Winchester College. Successively Rector of East Meon, co.
Hants, of Easton, near Winchester, and of Ash, in Surrey. Died 1676. The book
referred to is "Theophilus and Orthodoxus; or several Conferences between two
Friends, the one a true Son of the Church of England, the other faln off to the
Church of Rome." Oxf. 1674, 4to.

[b] "Catalogus impressorum Librorum Bibliothecæ Bodleianæ in Academia Oxon-
iensi. Curâ et operâ Thomæ Hyde è Coll. Reginæ Protobibliothecarii." Oxon.
1674, fol.

[c] "Novi Testamenti Libri Omnes. Accesserunt Parallela Scripturæ Loca, necnon
Variantes Lectiones ex plus 100 MSS. Codicibus, et Antiquis Versionibus Collectæ."
Oxon. 1675, 8vo.

[d] "The Holy Bible, containing the Old Testament and the New; Translated out
of the Original Tongues, and with the former Translations diligently compared and
revised, by His Majestie's Special Command." Oxford, 1675, 4to.

CAMD. SOC.   B

3 5

Dorrel and Dr. Hawkings [a] are the Bishop of Winchester's [b] Commissioners to visit his colledges. In town, on of their inquirys is whither any of the schollars of those colledge[s] weare pantaloons or periwiqnes, or keep dogs, but which is most materiall is their inquiry wither any buy or sel places. If he can rectify this abuse which is crept in at Magdalen's and New Colledge, to the notorious scandall of the University, he will doe us a considerable kindnesse and gain himselfe much credit; but I thinke not that he is able soe far to provide against this in such manner as those which have found out soe many tricks to cheat God Almighty and their own consciences will not likewise have store of them to evade all his provisions, especially since they have the old politician Satan to helpe them out, and their damd averice to entice them to harken to his counsel. But the Bishop on farther deliberation is ashamed to own that which first put him upon the humour of risking his designes, beeing then to show his power and indignation on Corpus Christi, for that the fellows with contempt rejected his letters which he wrot to them, whereby he enjoyned them to transfer on of those two places, which the founder entaild on Hampshire, on Jersey and Garnsay; but he beeing since informed that it is not within the limits of his or the colledge's power to alter a clause which is inserted in their charter, or deprive a county of their right which will not tamely be parted with, the gentlemen thereof beeing resolved to commence a law sute if any such thing should be enacted, he hath wholely omitted the mention thereof by his Commissioners, and excuseing his attempt to others by alledgeing he was compeld thereto by the King's command on the instigation of Sir George Carteret. [c] But, however, that he may come of with credit, it is talked that he himselfe will make provision for those place[s] by

---

[a] Walter Dayrell or Darrell, D.D. of Christ Church, and William Hawkins, D.D., Prebendaries of Winchester.

[b] Dr. George Morley, formerly Dean of Christ Church and Bishop of Worcester.

[c] The distinguished Royalist who held Jersey for the King. After the Restoration, Vice-Chamberlain of the Household and Treasurer of the Navy.

some new settlement of his own on some colledge or other in the
University; but I suppose it will be hard for him to find on that
will receive his donation except Pembroke, the fittest colledge in
town for brutes. Mr. Dean[a] was yesterday taken with a violent
fit of the stone, but he is now again abroad. At the end of the
Antiquitys you will find an answer of his to a pamplet of Hobs,[b]

[a] John Fell, son of Dr. Samuel Fell, Dean of Christ Church, was born at Sunning-
well, near Abingdon, and became student of Christ Church in 1636, when eleven
years old. Took arms in the Royalist cause in garrison at Oxford, and became
ensign. At the Restoration he was made Canon of Christ Church, and soon afterwards Dean. He was a great benefactor to his college, adding considerably to its
buildings. Vice-Chancellor, 1666-9. Wood gives him the character of a good disciplinarian, and reformer in the cut of caps and gowns. " He likewise advanced the
learned press, and improv'd the maunfacture of printing in Oxford in such manner
as it had been designed before by that public-spirited person, Dr. Lund, Archbishop
of Canterbury. . . . . . He was also a person of a most generous spirit, undervalued
money, and disburs'd it so freely upon learned, pious, and charitable uses, that he left
sometimes for himself and his private use little or nothing.
" He caused also at his own proper charge the *Hist. and Antiq. of the Univ. of
Oxon.* to be translated into Latin, and kept two men in pay for doing it, besides
what he did himself, which was considerable, and the author, which was less. And,
being so done, he caused it, at his own charge also, to be printed with a good
character on good paper; but he taking to himself liberty of putting in and out
several things according to his own judgment, and those that he employ'd being not
careful enough to carry the whole design in their head as the author would have
done, it is desired that the author may not be accountable for anything which was
inserted by him, or be censured for any useless repetitions or omissions of his agents
under him."
He was made Bishop of Oxford in 1676, but was still allowed to hold his deanery.
Died 10 June, 1686, " leaving behind him the general character of a learned and
pious divine, and of an excellent Grecian, Latinist, and philologist, of a great
assertor of the Church of England, of another founder of his own college, and of a
patron of the whole University."—*Ath. Oxon.* iv. 193-199.
[b] Thomas Hobbes, of Malmesbury, born 1588. Educated at Malmesbury and
Magdalen Hall, which he entered in 1602. After taking his degree, in 1607, he
became tutor to Lord William Cavendish, son of Lord Hardwick, afterwards Earl of
Devonshire, with whose family he was intimate all his life. On the outbreak of the
Civil War he retired to Paris, where he wrote his " Leviathan." Died in 1679 at
Hardwick, the house of the Earl of Devonshire.
His quarrel with Fell, referred to in the text, is an amusing instance of the Dean's
overbearing temper, and arose out of the unhappy translation of Wood's " Anti-

which he set forth against him. If you use to read before
you sleep, there is a booke put forth last term of the Imposters of
Muscovy,[a] which will be very proper to be read at such times. It
containeth a very pleasant story and true; only you must pardon
the ill stile, which is some places bombast. I assure you it kept me
awake last night longer then I was willing; but I repent not of it,
since it gave me very pleaseing diversion and informed of a good
tale. I cannot learn where Bernard lodgeth in London, or know
not how to come to the knowledge of it, without enquireing of that
fellow who was with him at the Castle[b] with us, who I fear hath
been already instructed not to let any on know. Without takeing
farther trouble on you, the best way when he cometh next to town

quitles." " The Deane of Christ Church, having the absolute power of the presse
there, perused every sheet before it was sent to presse, and after, and maugre the
author, and to his grief and sore displeasure, expunged and inserted what he thought
fitt. Among other authors, he made divers alterations in Mr. Wood's copie, in the
account he gives of Mr. T. Hobbes of Malmesbury's life." In self-defence Wood
told Fell that he must inform Hobbes of these alterations, to which he replied, " Yea,
in God's name, and great reason it was that he should know what he had done; and
what he had done he would answer for." In the early part of 1674 Hobbes was
accordingly told of what was going on, and he thereupon, having got the King's
leave to vindicate himself, wrote an epistle to Wood, which was sent down in MS. to
Oxford for the purpose of being shown to the Dean. The latter, however, treated it
with scorn, read it over carelessly, and bade Wood tell Hobbes " that he was an old
man, had one foot in the grave, that he should mind his latter end, and not trouble
the world any more with his papers." But the epistle was then printed, the Dean
gave it more attention, and, " upon the reading of it, fretted and fumed." The title
was " Epistola ad dom. Ant. à Wood, Authorem Historiæ et Antiq. Univ. Oxon;
29 Apr. 1674." Fell took a mean revenge by printing, at the end of the "Antiquities," a savage attack, in which he denounces " irritabile illud et vanissimum
Malmesburiense animal," and takes some credit to himself for being so forbearing
as "ut Viro pessime de Deo, hominibus, literisque merito, locum inter literatos
relinqueret." Hobbes gave the best answer to this extravagance by his contemptuous
silence.—See John Aubrey, *Letters written by eminent Persons*, Lond. 2 vols. 1813.
Ath. Oxon. iii. 1214

[a] "The Russian Impostor, or the History of Muskovie under the Usurpation of
Boris, and the Imposture of Demetrius, late Emperors of Muskovy." London,
1674, 8vo.

[b] Windsor Castle.

is to send a processe to the law beadle, which will make him bring
in his mony with a vengance or commit his corps to the dungeon.
The players parted from us with small gains, not haveing gained so
much as after al things payed to make a dividcnt of 10[1] to the chiefe
sharers; which I hope will give them noe encouragement to come
again. Neither, I suppose, will the University for the future permit
them here, if they can be kept out, since they were guilty of such
great rudenesses before they left us, going about the town in the
night breakeing of windows, and committeing many other unpardonable rudenesses. . . . . .

———— ... -　　-　... ——.

[Oxford.] Aug. 18th, [16]74.

　　I am got again to Oxford, but had such miserable bad company
in my journey here, that, were it not that at London I had yours,
it would be sufficient to make me repent my journey thither. I
had a whore on on side and a pitifull rogue on the other; and
two schollars in the opposit seat violated my ears with such horrid,
dissolute, and profane discourse, as I scarce should have thought
the divell himselfe dared either use or teach others, were it not that
I was soe unfortunate as to have this miserable experience thereof.
On of them was a dull rogue, and only sordidly affected debauchery
to be thought brave, and by his discourse only seemed to arrive to
the beastly part thereof, and appeared through his industry and
continuall excercise to be, in spight of plegme, soe miserably versed
therein that I believe he equalleth any whose affections better
spirits doe more violently incline thereto. His name is Fincher,[a]
son to on Major Fincher, who liveth not far from this place, and
pretendeth to a great deal of sanctifyed piety, but hath given very
bad demonstration thereof in the education of his son. The other
seemed to be a lad of very iugenious parts, much younger then the

* Perhaps James Fincher, of Trinity College, B.A 1674, M.A. 1677.

other, and I believe his pupil; but having better abilitys hath gon
infinitely beyond him, and in his discourse expressed such a violent
affection to vice that he seemed to me to be mad therewith and in a
frenzy all the while I was with him. His name is Daniel,[a] and son
to on Col[l] Daniel of Lancashire, a gentleman of good account and
wealth in those parts, by whome he was sent to the University
about last Christmas; but his designes beeing after another sort of
education, he hath not yet put on a gownd, that he may not be
obstructed therein by the disciplin of the University; and truely I
thinke he hath imployed his time soe well as not to remain ignorant
of anything that his own vile nature can incline him to or the divil
teach him. It greived me to thinke soe dissolute a person was to
be planted in a papist county, to give scandall to the religion by
which he is named, and make the adversarys thereof rejoice; but,
considering his course of live, I thinke I may without much un-
certainty expect, and without uncharity hope, he may never live to
it. This ill company made me very malancholy all the way.
Only once I could not but heartyly laugh to see Fincher be sturdyly
belaboured by five or six carmen with whips and prong-staves for
provokcing them with some of his extravagant froliques. I must
beg your pardon for beeing soe impertinently tedious in this relation.
These two gentlemen beeing persons of quality and heirs to considerable estates, I thought fit to give you this account, that, if
hereafter by chance you have anything to doe with them, you may
from hence learn what kind of men they are. As soon as I came
here, I went to All Souls to inquire of Dr. Bourcher[b] concerneing
your businesse, but found him not there, he beeing absent from
the University and not expected here till October. On Sunday
morneing I went to hear on Bayly[c] of Maudlins preach, who is
esteemed the mightiest man amongst his own, but made a very

---

[a] This name does not appear among the Oxford graduates of the period.
[b] Thomas Bourchier, LL.D. Regius Professor of Civil Law, Principal of St.
Alban's Hall 1678.
[c] Thomas Bayley, D.D. of Magdalen College.

sorry peece, and was guilty therein of severall absurd blunders; for
he proved the frailty of man's nature in that by the weekly bills it
appeared more always dyed then were born, as if all those that dyed
were not born but dropt from the skys, to be mortall here, and afford
him an argument that wanted better sense. He repeated a long
sentence out of Tully to prove the same thing, which he sayd he
learnt from the Academy or Porch, as if the Academiks and Stoiks
were the same, or Tully ever inclined to the later. If he had ever
read his oration " pro Murena," he might sufficiently from thence
be informed what opinion Tully had of that extravagant sect.
Severall others I omit to tell you, because I will have rome enough
to write those your tutor Woodruffe [a] was guilty of in a sermon
preached the same day at the funerall of Alderman Harris, whom
he observed to have been buryed in the sheet that was given him at
his christneing, after haveing kept it eighty years; and thereon
gave advice to every on to give their godsons such giftes as might
put them in mind of their mortality. He likewise observed that he
catchd a cold by lyeing on the ground thirty years agoe in the
King's service; that the last time he received the Sacrament was
on his birthday; that beeing a taylor he got his estate by his
honest imployment, which is an epithet which I thinke doth not
belong to that trade. He contradicted the Psalmist for sayeing
that man's life is but threescore and ten, Alderman Harris liveing
eighty years. Some of the choicest things I cannot tell you, not

[a] Benjamin Woodroffe, born at Oxford, 1638. Scholar of Westminster, and
Student of Christ Church, 1656; B.A. 1659; M.A. 1662; D.D. 1673. "After he had
taken the degree of master of arts he became a noted tutor in the college." In 1669
he became chaplain to the Duke of York, and was present, on board the "Royal
Prince," at the battle of Southwold Bay in 1672. Canon of Christ Church, and
Vicar of Piddleton, co. Dorset; then Vicar of Shrivenham, co. Berks, and chaplain
in ordinary to the King. Prebendary of Lichfield in 1678, and Rector of St.
Bartholomew's, London; nominated Dean of Christ Church in 1688, but was not
installed. He became Principal of Gloucester Hall in 1692, on the resignation of
Dr. Byrom Eaton, and "bestowed several hundreds of pounds in repairing it and
making it a fit habitation for the Muses; which being done, he, by his great interest
among the gentry, made it flourish with hopeful sprouts."—*Ath. Oxon.* iv. 640.

beeing his auditor; and those that were refuse to give as good an
account as I would have, out of a consciousnesse perchance that
they themselves cannot make better. This same sermon, as far as it
was applicable, was formerly preached on the Duke's [a] coachman.
Squib [b] hath succeeded in his contest for his living and carryed it
from his antagonist. The Bishop of Winchester hath suspended
Byfeild,[c] of Magdelen Coll., for sayeing that the Bishop did more
hurt then good by his visiteing their colledge; which hath appeared
very true, haveing only spent the colledges money without doeing
them any good those two times he hath been with them, not at the
least endeavoureing to compose their difference and remove faction
from among them, by which they are almost undon. If the old
man had not lost his prudence, he would not have been so passionate
a judge in his own case. At New Colledge he pretended to take
great care for the prevention of resignations, but unluckyly, while
his commissioners were there, a fellow cometh to the colledge with
a letter from the Bishop himselfe for a fellowship by resignation,
which he procured for 160 ginnys from on Bigs, which hath by the
same Bishop been admitted into orders, and instituted and inducted
into a liveing of 300^l per an., not beeing yet graduate or exceeding
the 21 year of his age. Peers [d] is very angry that he is not men-

[a] The Duke of York.
[b] Arthur Squibb, elected from Westminster to Christ Church 1656; B.A. 1659;
M.A. 1662.
[c] Richard Byfield, B.A. at Corpus Christi College 1649; Fellow of Magdalen
College 1650; M.A. 1652; B.D. 1663; Curate of Horspath 1666; presented to Sel-
borne 1678; died 1679.
[d] Richard Peers, born in Down, in Ireland, was, according to Anthony Wood,
intended by his father to be trained a tanner; but, running away from home to a
relative at Bristol, he was sent to Westminster School, where he became a favourite
of Busby. By another account he is said to have been also a pupil of Jeremy
Taylor, at Newton, in Carmarthenshire. In 1665 he was elected a Student at Christ
Church, Oxford, "where, making a hard shift to rub out (for 'twas usual with him
to make the exercise of idle scholars, either for money, or something worth it from
the buttery book), he took the degree in Arts, and, afterwards, being elected superior
beadle of that faculty and of physic, in the place of Franc. White, deceased, on the

tioned in the Preface to the Antiquitys, and hath, to give the worlde
an account, printed a paper to inform us of his worke and how
much he did of it.

———————

Ox[ford], Aug. 23, [16]74.

. . . . I must beg your pardon for beeing the cause
of a trouble which will be cast upon you by Dic Peers. As
soon as I returnd, I informd him of Busby's[a] desire to have his

21st of Sept. 1675, he, instead of prosecuting his studies, took to him a wife, and
enjoyed the comforts of the world. In the latter end of the reign of King James II.
he applied his mind to the study of physic, having been secretly informed that his
beneficial place was to be bestowed on a person more agreeable to those times; but,
fearing his bulk and fatness, which he had obtained by eating, drinking, and sleeping,
would hinder his practice, he quitted that project."

Among other literary work he was employed "in the translating from English
into Latin *Historia et Antiquitates Univers. Oxon.*, but in the beginning of his
undertaking, he being much to seek for such a version that might please Dr. Fell,
the publisher of that history, that doctor therefore did condescend so far as to direct
and instruct him in it (while the author, being made a tool, was forced to stand
still); and not only so, but to correct with great pains what he had done, so much
sometimes that that doctor's handwriting being more seen in the copy than that of
the translator, the copy was sometimes transcribed twice before it was fit to go to
the press. At length the translator, by his great diligence and observation over-
coming the difficulties, became a compleat master of the Latin tongue, and what he
did was excellent, yet always to the last 'twas overseen and corrected by the
publisher, who took more than ordinary liberty to put in and out what he pleased,
contrary to the will of the author." Peers died at Oxford, 11th August, 1690.—*Ath.
Oxon.* iv. 290, 291.

Wood further adds, in regard to the translation of the *Antiquities*, "Peers was a
sullen, dogged, clownish, and perverse fellow, and, when he saw the author concerned
at the altering of his copie, he would alter it the more, and studie to put all things
in that might vex him, and yet please his deane, Dr. Fell."—*Life*, lxviii. This
matter of the translation was a sore subject with Wood, and certainly the Dean had
peculiar views of the rights of authors.

[a] Richard Busby, the famous Master of Westminster, was born in 1606; Scholar of
Westminster, and elected to Christ Church in 1624; B.A. 1628; M.A. 1631. Pro-

booke,[a] and that I was imployed to get on for him, which hath put him upon a designe of presenting on to him, as likewise to the Bishop of Rochester,[b] out of a conceit that his presents will be rewarded with very considerable returns, the schoolmaster's place at least. Little Penny[c] beeing againe upon his journy to Rome, he was designed for the presenter of them; but, I convinceing him of the absurdity of imployeing any other in that businesse then those which are known unto him, especially his children, he hath altered his resolution and pitched on you; and, I suppose, accordingly about Tuesday or Wednesday the bookes will be left with you, with direction how to dispose of them. In the third page of the preface, towards the end of the page, you will find two paragraphs, to which are prefixed 1[o] and 2[o], which are omitted in all other copies. In the first of them there is given an account of the translator and how much he translated, which Peers is very willing everybody should know, that, as he saith, he may not be accountable for the improprietys and other unexcusable faults committed by Reevs,[d] who

visionally appointed Master of Westminster in 1638, and confirmed in 1640; Rector of Cadworth 1639. After the Restoration he became D.D., Prebendary of Westminster and Canon of Wells. "He was a person eminent and exemplary for piety and justice, an encourager of vertuous and forward youth, of great learning and hospitality, and the chief person that educated more youths that were afterwards eminent in the church and state than any master of his time." He died 6 April, 1695, aged 93. *Ath. Oxon.* iv. 417. Welch, *Westminster Scholars*, 95.

[a] Wood's "Historia et Antiquitates Universitatis Oxoniensis duobus voluminibus comprehensæ." Oxon. 1674, fol.

[b] John Dolben, elected Student of Christ Church from Westminster School in 1640. He served in the Royalist army, and rose to the rank of major. Canon of Christ Church in 1660, Dean of Westminster in 1662, and Bishop of Rochester in 1666; translated to York in 1683.

[c] James Penny, of Christ Church, B.A. 1669; M.A. 1672.

[d] Richard Reeve, Servitor at Trinity College in 1661, and Head-Master of Magdalen School in 1670. In 1667 he joined the Church of Rome, and in 1674 went to Douay and became a monk. Returning to England in 1687, he was re-established at Magdalen School, and thence removed to the mastership of Sir T. Rich's hospital at Gloucester. At the Revolution he was imprisoned for eight months. "He had a considerable hand in the translation of the *Hist. et Antiq. Univ. Oxon.*, which he took upon him at the desire of Dr. John Fell." Died 1693.

translated the rest; in the second Woods[a] accuseth the Dean and Peers for altercing his copys, and calleth God to witnesse that whatsoever harsh or derogateing expression be found in any part of his booke he is not the author of it. The later beeing put in without the Dean's consent, at his beeing at the Bath, and the former without the author's, by Peers himselfe, made both angry, and was the cause of much contention between Woods and the Dean, the Dean standeing for the former paragraph and the expungeing of the second, and Woods for the second and the expungeing of the first; neither could there be any end put to the contention till each party receeded something from their pretentions. There was an agreement made at last by omitteing both, and the preface printed o'er again without makeing any mention of Peers, which exceedingly greiveth him. But he, haveing got the former prefaces into his hands, taketh great care to disperse them about, and I doubt not but that this will be bound up with all the bookes he presenteth. I suppose that you have heard of the continuall feuds and often battles between the author and the translator; they had a skirmish at Sol. Hardeing,[b] another at the

---

[a] Anthony Wood, the antiquary and biographer, born at Oxford 1632. Educated at Thame and Merton College; B.A. 1652; M.A. 1655. He resided all his life at Oxford, and devoted himself to the history of his University. He began to write his "History and Antiquities" in 1663; published in Latin in 1674. The original English was published by John Gutch, 1792-6. His great work, the "Athenæ Oxonienses," containing biographies of all writers and bishops bred at the University from the year 1500, was first published in 1691. Having in this book stated that Judge Glynne obtained his promotion at the time of the Restoration " by the corrupt dealing of the then Chancellor," he incurred the displeasure of the Earl of Clarendon, who, in 1693, brought an action against him for defamation of his father's character. Wood was severely punished; he was sentenced to banishment from the University until he should subscribe a public recantation, and his book was burnt. This attack upon him was from a quarter where he might least expect it, his partiality to the High Church party, and even to Romanism, being most conspicuous. He died in 1695. His life is prefixed to Bliss's edition of the "Athenæ."

[b] Soladell or Soladin Harding, cook, who kept a house of entertainment in All Saints parish.

printeing house,[a] and severall other places; but Peers always comeing
of with a bloody nose or a black eye, he was a long time afraid to
goe anywhere where he might chance to meet his too powerfull
adversary, for fear of another drubbeing, till he was pro-proctor;
and now Woods is as much afraid to meet him, least he should
exercise his authority upon him; and, although he be a good bowzeing
blad, yet it hath been observed that never since his adversary hath
been in office hath he dared to be out after nine, least he should
meet him and exact the rigor of the statute [b] upon him. However
Die hath not forgot his old fears, but, although armed with an office,
yet, by reason of his former drubbeing, fears his adversary as much
as formerly; soe that, both partys beeing affraid of each other, each
liveth in peace; but however each forgetteth not his enmyty to each
other, and [I] suppose it was only an effect of this that Woods
would not let the translator's name be inserted in the preface, I not
beeing able to immagin any other cause why he should be against
it, then that he was unwilling thereby to gratify his adversary in
that which he knew he did most vehemently desire. Busby hath
lately given 50[l] to Baliol College, on the account of his acquaintance
with Dr. Good,[c] the head, who is a good honest old tost, and under-

---

[a] The Sheldonian Theatre.

[b] " Statutum est quod omnes scholares cujuscunque conditionis, quos occasione
quacunque extra collegia sua vel aulas vesperi agere contigerit, ante horam nonam
(quæ pulsatione magnæ campanæ Collegii Ædis Christi denunciari solet) ad collegia
et aulas proprias se recipiant." — *Statuta Univ. Oxon.*

[c] Thomas Good, Scholar of Balliol in 1624, when fifteen years of age; B.A. 1628;
Fellow 1629. He obtained the cure of Coreley, in his native county, Shropshire, in
1658; at the Restoration, D.D. About the same time he became Canon of Hereford
and Rector of Wistanstow; Master of Balliol in 1672. " He was in his younger
years accounted a brisk disputant, and, when resident in his college, a frequent
preacher, yet always esteemed an honest and harmless Puritan. A noted author
[Richard Baxter] of the Presbyterian persuasion tells us that he was one of the
most peaceable, moderate, and honest conformists of his acquaintance, and subscribed
the Worcestershire agreement for concord, and joyned with the Presbyterians in
their association and meetings at Kedirminster, and was the man that drew the
catalogue of questions for their disputations at their meetings, and never talked then
to them of what he afterwards wrote in his book called *Dubitantius and Firmianus;*

stands businesse well enough, but is very often guilty of absurditys, which rendreth him contemptible to the yong men of the town. He hath lately, out of a desire to be a fool in print, set forth a dialogue between a Protestant and new converted Papist, whom he calleth Dubitantius and Firmianus.[a] If you will be pleased to be acquainted with their talke, I doubt not but that they will make you good sport, for I assure you they dispute the case most sturdyly. Not long since he preached at St. Mary's, and in the mist of his sermon, in a queer tone, bauld out that about fifty years agoe he remembred he read such a passage in a booke De Anima, and then, after a long pause, recoll[ect]eing himselfe, cryed out, " Ah, 'tis to let, 'tis to let," which made us then all laugh and ever since call him " To let." There is another ridiculous story of him, which I doe not well beleeve; but however you shall have it. There is over against Baliol College a dingy, horrid, scandalous alehouse, fit for none but draymen and tinkers and such as by goeing there have made themselfes equally scandalous. Here the Baliol men continually ly, and by perpetuall bubbeing ad art to their natural stupidity to make themselfes perfect sots. The head, beeing informed of this, called them togeather, and in a grave speech informed them of the mischeifs of that hellish liquor cald ale, that it destroyed both body and soul, and adviced them by noe means to have anything more to do with it; but on of them, not willing soe tamely to be preached out of his beloved liquor, made reply that the Vice-Chancelour's men dranke ale at the Split Crow, and why should not they to? The old man, beeing nonplusd with this reply, immediately packeth away to the Vice-Chancelour,[b] and informd him

by which, when published, he lost his credit among them, and was lesser esteemed by Mr. Baxter, the pride and glory of that party." Died 1678. *Ath. Oxon.* iii. 1154.

[a] "Firmianus and Dubitantius : or certain Dialogues concerning Atheism, Infidelity, Popery, and other Heresies and Schisms," &c. Oxon. 1674, 8vo.

[b] Ralph Bathurst, D.D. distinguished wit and Latin poet, was born at Howthorpe, co. Northampton, in 1620, being one of a large family, of which six of the sons fell in the King's service. He entered at Gloncester Hall, but removed to Trinity, where he became Scholar and B.A. in 1637, and Fellow 1640. He was ordained in 1644 ;

of the ill example his fellows gave the rest of the town by drinkeing ale, and desired him to prohibit them for the future; but Bathurst, not likeing his proposall, beeing formerly and [sic] old lover of ale himselfe, answared him roughly, that there was noe hurt in ale, and that as long as his fellows did noe worse he would not disturb them, and soe turnd the old man goeing; who, returneing to his colledge, calld his fellows again and told them he had been with the Vice-Chancelour, and that he told him there was noe hurt in ale; truely he thought there was, but now, beeing informed of the contrary, since the Vice-Chancelour gave his men leave to drinke ale, he would give them leave to; soe that now they may be sots by authority. I must beg your pardon for troubleing you with soe ridiculous a tale, and desire not to thinke me an idle fellow in spendeing my time to insert it. When it was first told me it made me heartyly laugh, and I hope it will you to; only this inconvenience it hath, that I, haveing spent so much of my paper informeing you this, have not enough left to write unto you what better deserveth your knowledge, you shall have in my next.

[P.S.] I desire you to inform Dr. Busby that I was again to wait on him before I left the town, but found him not at home, beeing gon to Chiswick. My businesse was to talke with him concerneing the task I have imposed on me by Mr. Dean, of makeing notes on the monuments,[a] and to beg his directions. I desire you to mention as much to him and write me what he sayeth.

---

but during the Civil War he practised as a physician in the navy, and then at Oxford. He was one of the founders of the Royal Society. President of his college 1664; Vice-Chancellor 1673 and 1675; Dean of Wells 1670. The last appointment he is said to have owed to the Earl of Devonshire, whose notice was attracted by his copy of Latin Iambics prefixed to Hobbes's "Human Nature." He refused the Bishopric of Bristol in 1691. It was during his presidency that the buildings of Trinity College were reconstructed or improved. He died in 1704, being blind during the latter years of his life.

[a] In preparation for the "Marmora Oxoniensia," which he published in May, 1676.

[Oxford], Aug. 30th, [16]74.

I have yours from Windsor of Aug. 21, by which I perceived
my last was not then come to your hands. I suppose now you
have it, and in this expect that I should give an account of those
things which then I tould you my paper beeing filled too full with
a ridiculous tale would not afford me rome to insert. I was then
goeing to give you an account of our presse, and what bookes
here are designed for it. There is nothing now printing there but
a booke of Brevints,[a] of the ridiculousnesse of the Roman devotions,
wherein I suppose we shall have the old tales of St Francis, of
worshippeing the Virgin Mary, and such like over again. I fear
his booke will inform us of nothing else but that he is ridiculous in
writeing of it. If such designes could anyway advantage the
Protestant cause it would be worth the while of some observing
and judicious person to be at Rome this year of Júbele, where he
may se the whole mistery of their devotion, not again to be seen in
an age. But till he doth first convince them of their errour in
buildeing their faith upon the tradition of the Church, and receiveing whatsoever it delivered to them thereby with the same
undoubteing assent they receive the word of God itselfe, as beeing
with it upon the same testimony of the same infallible truth, he
may as well tell them of the ridiculousnesse of the jawbone of the
asse wherewith Sampson kild the Philistins, or the well that sprang
from thence, as of the tales of St Francis, since they built the beleife
of both upon the same foundations. Our printers will doe a more
acceptable worke in speedyly putteing those bookes into the presse

---

[a] "Saul and Samuel at Endor, or the New Waies of Salvation and Service, which
usually temt men to Rome and detain them there, Truly Represented and Refuted.
By Dan. Brevint, D.D." Oxford, 1674, 8vo. The writer was a native of Jersey,
and was the first holder of the French fellowship founded in Jesus College by
Charles I. Ejected in 1648, he went into exile in France. At the Restoration he
became Prebendary of Durham, and, in 1682, Dean of Lincoln. Died in 1695.

which they now designe and are preparcing for it. They are Guildas and other of the most antient British and Saxon authors,[a] several of which have never yet been printed, which beeing all bound togeather will make a folio about the bignesse of our Antiquity booke. They are likewise upon a designe of princeing Johannes Antiochenus Malela,[b] a booke of great antiquity, and very usefull for cronologers; the copy whereof is noewhere extant but in our publick library. The B. of Armagh[c] first tooke notice of it and perswaded the University to print it; and in order thereto Mr. Chilmead[d] was imployed to transcribe it and make a Latin interpretation of it, but the war comeing on, the worke was interrupted and never since thought of, till of late, it being made use of by severall of our cronologers and antiquarys, we are continually pestered with letters from forrain parts to set it forth, out of a conceit that rare things ly hid therein, wereas more then halfe the booke is stuffed with ridiculous and incredible lys; and, although there be something of good use contained therein, yet they are not of such number or value as to make any recompense for the rest of his booke, which is intolerable. It was writ about 400 years after Christ by an Antiochean, in Greeke. The copy is very much moth-eaten and extremely difficult to be made perfect. Some on must be forced to cast away his time in the unprofitable worke of repaireing it. I fear mine will not be much better, which is to be

---

[a] This reference is probably to the work, published later, "Historiæ Britannicæ, Saxonicæ, Anglo-Danicæ, Scriptores xv. by T. Gale." Oxon. 1691.

[b] "Joannis Antiocheni cognomento Malalæ Historia Chronica. E MS, Cod. Bibliothecæ Bodleianæ nunc primum edita, cum Interpret. et Notis Edm. Chilmeadi. . . . . . Præmittitur Dissertatio de Autore, per Humfredum Hodium, S. T. B. Coll. Wadham Socium. Accedit Epistola Richardi Bentleii ad Cl. V. Jo. Millium S. T. P." Oxon. 1691, 8vo.

[c] James Usher, Archbishop of Armagh, 1624-55.

[d] Edmund Chilmead, born at Stow-in-the-Wold, co. Gloucester, entered Magdalen College in 1625; M.A. 1632, Minor Canon of Christ Church. He was ejected in 1648, and was forced to get a living by a weekly music meeting, which he set up at the Black Horse, Aldersgate. He was accounted a good mathematician and Grecian. Died 1654.—Ath. Oxon. iii. 350.

imployed in makeing notes on the marbles; however, next Munday
I intend to set about the work, and hope again you come here to
have made a good progresse therein. Trouble not Busby unlesse
you have businesse unto him (that which Peers designed for you to
him is cast upon Crespion [a]), and then mention my businesse only
by the by; and, if you can hansomely doe it, draw to give his
judgement what is most fit to be don in this worke, especially
concerneing the Parian Cronicle,[b] which is an account of time from
the beginncing of the Athenians and the reigne of Cecrops till the
time of Alexander. There is a translation of Procopius's Secret
History [c] set forth, which containeth the history of Justinian's
Court. I doubt not but that the relation he giveth of the founder
of your civil law will surprise you. It is a booke writt with much
malice, which in many places he sufficiently discovereth, when he
suffereth his judgement to be soe much perverted as to make many
of the actions of that Emperor the objects of his calumny, which in
themselves were good and commendable. But he is most weakely
folish in on place, when, without beeing metaphoricall, he would
needs perswade us that Justinian was a reall devil; and truely,
though he were, I can scarce thinke him able to be guilty of all he
layeth to his charge. If you should be pleased to read the booke,
in my next I will farther give you my judgement of it; it hath
some relation to your faculty and may be worth your reading.
Tony Wood, our antiquary, having pored so long on old monkish
storys, at last dotes on them and is turned Papist.[d] When a man

---

[a] Stephen Crespion, Westminster scholar, and of Christ Church; B.A. 1670; M.A.
1672; Prebendary of Bristol 1683. Died 1711.

[b] One of the Arundel Marbles, published by Prideaux in his "Marmora Oxoniensia," p. 157.

[c] "The Secret History of the Court of the Emperor Justinian. Written by Procopius of Cesarea; Faithfully rendered into English." London, 1674, 8vo.

[d] Wood took particular care, on his deathbed, to deny such rumours. "He himself particularly ordered that it should be inserted in his will, which was made three
or four days before his death, that he died in the communion of the Church of
England as by law established." *Life, Appendix*, cxxxiii.

maketh this his only study, and his utmost reputation is founded on
the knowledge of such tales, it is hard not to believe them, since
otherwise he must cast a disrepute on his own profession, and
acknowledge in himselfe a great deal of folly in spending his time
in rakeing togeather such dotages; and this is Dugdale's[a] case,
who on the same account hath imbraced the same religion. Mr.
Horsman,[b] on of our best scollars in the University, haveing
streined his brains by ingageing them in too deep contemplation
after they had been much weakened by a long sicknesse, it is feared
he hath soe far disturbed them that he will speedyly be mad, if he
is not soe already, which his actions doe make every on mistrust
that is acquainted with them. The Chancelour of Danemarke[c]
hath sent by Ambassadour Henshaw[d] a present to D^r Ba[thurst];
. . . .[e] he desireth him to receive his picture, to be put
in mind thereby of the great freindship was between when [sic]
when he lived in Oxford, and likewise the present annexed, as a

---

[a] William Dugdale, the herald and antiquary, at this time Norroy. Appointed
Garter and knighted in 1677. The report of his having joined the Church of Rome
may have had its foundation in the publication of his great work, the "Monasticon
Anglicanum;" it being noticed in his Life, prefixed to the "History of St. Paul's"
(London, 1716, fol.), that some looked suspiciously upon that work as a means to
further the restoration of the monasteries, preparatory to the re-establishment of the
Romish religion.

[b] Nicholas Horseman, B.D, Fellow of Corpus Christi. In 1669 he, "after going the
college-progress, became crazed by an unseasonable journey (late at night) through
certain marshes in Kent, and so continued to his dying day, with an allowance from
his college in consideration of his fellowship."—*Ath. Oxon.* iv. 616.

[c] Peter Schumacher, Count Griffenfeldt, the able minister of Christian V. He was
"a sojourner this [1657] and several years after in Oxon, purposely to obtain
literature in the public library. . . . . . Afterwards he became a man of note in his
own country, and, tho' the son of a vintner, Chancellor of Denmark, &c. He hath
lately sent his picture to the University of Oxon, and it now hangs in the school
gallery."—*Fasti Oxon.* ii. 213.

[d] Thomas Henshaw, of University College, F.R.S. French Secretary successively to
Charles II., James II., and William III. In 1672 he was sent as Secretary to the
Duke of Richmond on his embassage to Denmark, and succeeded as Ambassador on
the Duke's death in the same year. Died 1700.

[e] Mutilated.

testimony how firmely he retaineth it still on his part. This letter
the Doctor keepeth with as much care as he doth his plate, and is
sure to show them both to every on that cometh to his house. I
am sorry you are soe far disappointed as to be forced to betake
yourselfe to another imployment; however, I will not yet dispair of
Williamson's [a] provideing for you some way or other, and I would
advice you not to omit any way whereby he may be drawen to it,
especially since I fear you will find but a poor refuge at D[rs]
Commons.[b] . . . .

———

Oxf[ord], Sep. 17, [16]74.

Had I been in town, you should sooner have had the account of
Dr. Compton's [c] Secretary you desired in your last, but, haveing
made an excursion to talke old storys with S[r] Richard Willis,[d] I
was not here sooner either to receive you[r] letter or inquire concerneing that you would know. Since my return they tell me his

[a] Sir Joseph Williamson, son of Joseph Williamson, Vicar of Bridekirk, in Cum-
berland, was educated at Westminster, and afterwards at Queen's College, Oxford,
of which he became Fellow, and a benefactor in after-years; B.A. 1653. He is
said to have taken deacon's orders. After the Restoration he was made Keeper
of the Paper Office, Whitehall; Under Secretary of State, 1665; Plenipotentiary for
the Treaty of Cologne, 1673-4; Secretary of State, 1674-78. President of the Royal
Society, 1678. Died in 1701. For fuller particulars of the subject of this note, see
vol. i. of " Letters addressed from London to Sir Joseph Williamson," published by
the Camden Society in 1873, p. xiv. of the Introduction.
[b] Ellis had been lately engaged in the Paper Office, under Sir Joseph Williamson.
He was now thinking of becoming a proctor.
[c] Henry Compton, a younger son of Spencer Earl of Northampton, entered
Queen's College in 1649. After the Restoration he became a cornet in the regiment
commanded by Aubrey Earl of Oxford. He then went to Cambridge, took the
M.A. degree, and was ordained. Master of St. Cross, Winchester, in 1667; Canon of
Christ Church in 1669; Bishop of Oxford, 1674; Dean of the Royal Chapel, and
translated to London, and Privy Councillor, 1675. He was suspended by James II.
in 1686, "for having behaved cross to him." An active promoter of the Revolution.
Died 1713.
[d] Sir Richard Willys, a Royalist officer, was Governor of Newark, and was created
a baronet by Charles I. in 1646. Died 1690.

name is Parker, and that he was cornet to that troop in the Earle of Oxford's regiment of which the Dr. was liuetenant, and is someway related to him. I inquired farther of Sʳ Richard concerneing the Mercurio Italico,[a] and receive this account thereof from him, that at his beeing in Italy they were set forth each year by a select committee, choosen out of the Senat, to manage the intelligence and each year give an account of all the transactions of Europe; which he assureth me is the best he ever met with. I have writ to Peny to inquire after them when he cometh into Italy, and send me the ten last tomes. He showed me among his Italian bookes that out of which Sandys [b] had his travels. I compared both togeather and found the cuts in each to be exactly the same, and therefore I was easyly perswaded to beleive what Sʳ Richard assured me, who had farther compared them, that the matter is the same to, and that Sandys travelled no farther for his observations then into a bookeseller's shop in Italy, where he met with this booke, out of which he transcribed them. He likewise showed me an Italian romance, called Archadia De Sanizara,[c] to which Sʳ Philip Sidny was beholdon for his, that beeing as he assured me only a bare translation of this. Accordeing to my judgement of his peice, I thinke it could not have been much worse if he had made it himselfe, although it hath the luck to be in soe high esteem among women

<hr>

[a] "Il Mercurio, overo Historia de' correnti Tempi," by Vittore Siri. Casal. 1644-82, 15 vols. 4to.

[b] George Sandys, younger son of Edwin Sandys, Archbishop of York, and probably of Corpus Christi College. In 1610 he set out on his travels, and in 1615 published an account of them with the title, "A Relation of a Journey begun An. Dom. 1610. Foure Bookes. Containing a description of the Turkish Empire, of Ægypt, of the Holy Land, of the remote parts of Italy, and Ilands adioyning." London, 1615, fol. Whatever the Italian book may be, the fact is that many of the plates in Sandys's work also appear in "Le Tresdevot Voyage de Jerusalem, avecq les Figures des lieux sainets, et plusieurs autres, tirées au naturel. Faict et descript par Jean Zuallart." Antwerp, 1608, small 4to. See Ath. Oxon. iii. 97 note.

[c] Sir Richard could hardly have taken the trouble to compare more than the titles of the two books; he would otherwise have found Sidney's "Arcadia" a very different work from that of Sannazaro.

and fooles, who know not how better to bestow their time then in reading such like foolish trash. As for my part, I must confesse myselfe to be utterly ignorant on what account Sr Philip Sidny hath soe great repute among us, I knoweing nothing of him that may in the least deserve it, only the world conceived great hopes of him, which, if he had lived, perchance he would never have satisfyed, and bee er this as little remembred as other men.

Tuesday night the Dutchesse of Cleveland ^a lodged here in town, and sent for Mr. Dean to her lodgings, whom she treated with much civility, and desired him to take her son ^b into his care, whom she will send here next weeke, and leave the whole disposal of him to Mr. Dean, as for the appointeing of his tutors, lodgeing, allowance, and all other things whatsoever. Her [thir]d son ^c was with her, who beeing, she told Mr. Dean, born in Oxford among the schollars, shall live [som]e considerable time among them, especially since he is far more apt to receive instructions then his elder brother, whom she confesseth to be a very kockish idle boy. The morneing before she went she sate at least an hour in her coach, that every body might se her.

[Oxford], Sep. 27th, [1674].

This beeing now the criticall time in which you are to expect your doom, I long to hear how you have succeeded, that I may rejoice with you if you have got any advantage by Williamson's

---

^a Barbara Villiers, daughter of William Visconnt Grandison, and mistress of Charles II.; created Duchess of Cleveland in 1670. Died.1709.

^b Charles Fitz-Roy, created Duke of Southampton, 10 September, 1674; succeeded his mother in the dukedom of Cleveland, 1709. Died 1730.

^c George Fitz-Roy, Earl, afterwards Duke, of Northumberland, was born within the walls of Merton College, 28 December, 1665; the Court being then at Oxford, on account of the plague in London. He died in 1716.

preferment,[a] or share with you in greiveing for your ill fortune if
you still remain as you were. Al the information I could possibly
get conccrnceing D[rs] Commons I have already sent you, which I
hope hath come safe to your hands, although in your last letter
you mentioned nothing thereof. I am now groaneing under the
oppression of two or three heavy burdens which Mr. Dean hath layed
upon me. After what rate I shall rid my hands of them I know not.
John of Antioch,[b] of which I formerly wrot unto you, is got into
my hands to be prepared for the presse. Whatever I wrot to you
of him formerly, I now sufficiently know him to be a horrid musty
foolish booke, and many degrees below the worst of authors that I
ever yet met with. I wish I were rid of him; and, if my opinion
were to be harkned to, instead of goeing to the presse, he should
be condemned back again to the rubbish from whence he was taken,
and there ly till moths and rats have rid the world of such horrid
and insufferable nonsense. However I promise myselfe this happynesse from it, if you come hither this winter, to have your good
company at a fire to be furnished from hence with subjects sufficient
to make you laugh heartyly whensoever you are disposed thereto;
for I assure you he is a pleasant rogue and tells his lys not after an
ordinary manner. But conccrnceing the marbles it is not agreed
what shall be don. That which is y[e] best we have is the Parian
Cronicle, a marble which containeth an epitome of all the Greeke
cronology till the time of Alexander. My designe is, if they would
approve thereof, to doe something thereon which should be profitable
and usefull to the understandeing the Greeke historys; for I propose
to make first a table of all the Greeke cronology, to which I will
likewise annex all necessary syncronismes, beginning it from the
very first plantation of that country and endeing it in the end of y[e]
Greeke Empire at the battle of Actium, which I will call "Crono-
logia Græca ad epochas marmoris conformata," and endeavour to

---

[a] Sir Joseph Williamson succeeded the Earl of Arlington as Principal Secretary
of State, 11 September, 1674.

[b] See above, page 16, note [b].

make it the most methodicall and correct of any that have been yet
set forth. To it I will annex notes, in which I will determin all
cronologicall controversys which have been ever moved in the Greeke
history, and explain whatsoever else may be necessary to the understandeing of the antiquitys, customs, and historys of the Grecians,
and call them " Notæ ad Tabulum Cronologicam in quibus continetur
quicquid Philologicum quicquid Cronologicum ad intelligendos Græcos
Authores videatur necessarium." [a] You have here a full account of
my designe; I desire your judgement of it in your next. It is not
approved of by Mr. Dean, because he thinketh the worke will require
more time then he is willing to allow me; he beeing desirous that
his booke should be out speedyly, whereas my worke would at least
require a whole year to make it full and compleat, as I designe it
shall be, if it ever come forth. I confesse I am for[ce]d to bestow
my labour hereon, and am resolved again to move it to Mr. Dean,
if I am encouraged by your good opinion and approbation hereof.
I have likewise, besides this which is imposed on me by my superiors,
another designe of myne own goeing on, which would er this be in
a good measure finished, had [not] those other businesses come in
to interrupt it. Of this I will talke with you when we next meet.
Our town affordeth nothing worth informeing you; only Woodruffe
dayly exposeth himselfe to contempt by his ridiculous actions.
Last night he had Madam Walcup [b] at his lodgeings, and stood
with her in a great window next the quadrangle, where he was
seen by Mr. Dean himselfe and almost all the house toyeing with
her most ridiculously, and fanneing himselfe with her fan for almost
all the after noon. A little before, he put the D[rs] men out of
commons for havoing the victualls on their table before he came in.
It is a custom [obser]ved by the servants, that if the canons come
not before an half hour past 6 to take their victualls and fall to.
Wodruffe comeing in at the third quarter and findeing the meat on
their table, raged most furiously, which not beeing tuched by the

---

[a] Prideaux did not entirely carry out this plan.
[b] Probably one of the family of Warcupp, of Oxfordshire.

servants was carryed back again to the canons' table for Woodruffe
to cat thereof if he had pleased; but he, beeing exceeding offended
at their insolence, as he calld it, in bringeing victualls to his table
which had been defiled by haveing been on theirs, commanded his
man to carry it to the prisoners, at which the rest of the canons
were exceedingly angry, and sufficiently rebuked him for it the
next day, and commanded their men not to let their victualls goe
soe patiently another time; by which they have been encouraged
since to affront [him] to his face, and he forced to take it patiently.
Die Pierce telleth me Busby hath his booke, and promised Crispion [a]
to send him three ginnys for it. He is now on a very ridiculous
designe, in which, if he proceedeth, he will get as little credit thereby
as he did by his musty ballads [b] he formerly set forth. Some seaman's journall of the Streights of Magelan hath fallen into his hands,
which he is furiously about to print, and intendeth to prefix a map;
but I have demonstrated to him the folly of his designe, and how
much it is beneath a scoller to deal in tarpaulcings writings, as likewise his own inabilitys of doeing therein that which will signify
any thing, businesse of that nature not beeing to be don by specula-
tion, but the experience of those which have been versed in sea
affairs. Besides, the terms of forelands, rifs, and others such sea
terms may be well supposed not to be understood by on which was
never any thing else but an Oxford schollar; beside, I showed him
the description of Captain Narborow,[c] put out but last year, of the

[a] See above, page 17.

[b] "Four small copies of Verses made on sundry Occasions." Oxon. 1667, 4to.

[c] This edition of Sir John Narborough's voyage is not noticed in the bibliogra-
phical manuals. However, it is quoted by Seixas y Lovera (Descripcion de la
Region austral Magallicana. Madrid, 1690, p. 59) as a work printed by John
Templeman, one of Narborough's companions, and is referred to by Burney (Discoveries in the South Sea. London, 1813, vol. iii. p. 317), who, however, had never
met with a copy. It must have soon become a scarce book, for it is stated in the
Introduction to "An Account of several late Voyages and Discoveries to the South
and North " (London, 1694, 8vo.), in which Narborough's Voyage appears, that it is
there for the first time published. Narborough was sent out on this voyage by the
Government, and was engaged in it from May, 1669, to June, 1671.

same place, in a fuller and better manner then we can expect from
Dic. But, however, the conceat that he shall get mony by this
foolish designe prevaileth more then anything I can say against it.
Beside, the fool would willingly be in print, that in the preface of
something he might let the world (*sic*) know that it was he that translated Woodses booke. I desire you to inform me whether I shall
still direct my letters to the Paper Office, or reather at the Secretarys
Office. I hope speedyly to hear from you.

[P.S.] We have had here news of the finisheing of the
Royall Cittadal.[a] I desire you in your next to inform me what
it meaneth.

[Oxford, 27 October, 1674.]

By reason of the multiplicity of businesse Mr. Dean hath at
present cast upon me, I have only time to tell you that if you
intend to take your degree[b] this term it is full time you were
already here; and that yesterday, at 10 in the morneing, David
Whitford[c] was found dead in his chamber, haveing been the night
before and that very morneing at 8 very well. He had not on

---

[a] This seems to be the name of a ship; but no such vessel was in the fleet.

[b] Ellis did not graduate. The Duke of Ormonde applied to the University in
favour of his being admitted M.A. by a letter of 31 May, 1674; in which it is stated
that his engagements in the public service had prevented his taking his degree at
the proper time.—Brit. Mus. Add. MS. 28,930, f. 43.

[c] David Whitford, son of Dr. Walter Whitford, Bishop of Brechin. Elected from
Westminster to Christ Church, 1642. He bore arms in the garrison of Oxford, and
was wounded and taken prisoner at the battle of Worcester. He afterwards
"became usher to James Shirley, the poet, when he taught school in the White-
fryers." Restored to studentship in 1660, and became chaplain to the Earl of
Lauderdale. He died " suddenly in his chambers in Christ Church, in the morning
of 26 Oct. in 1674 (at which time his bed-maker found him dead, lying on his bed
with his wearing apparel on him)."—*Ath. Oxon.* iii. 1016; Welch, 118.

farthing in his pocket, although he had received 9[1] within 10 days before; but all was spent in ale, he haveing been drunke almost every night since he came hither. He was found falln back upon his bed halfe dressed, with a brandy bottle in on hand and the corck in the other; he findeing himselfe ill, as it semeth, was going to take a dram for refreshment, but death came between the cup and the lips: and this is the end of Davy. Mr. Dean comeing into his chamber upon the noise of this accident, we searched to se what he had left; among his papers I by chance light on a bond ready drawn up to be sealed, by which Davy bound himselfe to give 500[1] for a parsonage by such a day or resigne it again. The horror of this crime joyned to the rest of his lude life hath made death appear very dismall unto me. Pardon my hast, and accept of the good wishes of, etc.

--- --- --- --- ---

[Oxford], Nov. 15th [1674.]

. . . . I have nothing new to tell you but that your tutor Woodruff last Sunday preached the most scandalous duncecall sermon that hath been preached before the University ever since the King returnd, as it is agreed on by all that heard it. I thought it not worth my labour to be his auditor. He maketh use of all indirect and sneakeing means to get the office of subdean, and already talketh what he will do in order to the reforming of the house when he hath this office; although the Dean hath declared publickly that he will make any shift reather then intrust him with it . . . .

[Oxford, 13 Dec. 1674.]

. . . . We have got a booke here to print against Hobs, writ by Chancelour Hyde.[a] It is much commended. When it cometh forth we shall se what it is. We call Churchills booke[b] here the Chancelours. I know not whence we had the information; but if it be worth the reading, as you write me, shure it cannot be Churchills, although it bear his name. I desire you in your next to inform me whither S[r] John Churchill[c] is like to gain any thinke by the late removall among the lawyers on the death of Vaughan.[d] We are likewise printceing here a comment on the Epistles,[e] writ by Mr. Walker,[f] which is to be a specimen of what we designe to doe on the whole Bible, severall men haveing been formerly imployed on the worke and don a great deal in order thereto. After Christmas Mr. Dean intendeth to begin to print the Greek fathers[g] in larg octavos, as the Dutch have printed Polybius, Arrian, and Appian. I perswaded him to it, and I doubt not but that it will be the most beneficiall work, as well for himselfe as others, that he can undertake; since I scarce thinke any divine will be without them, when they are printed in such volums that their price will not be above any on's purse or their own worth. Our Christmas booke will be

[a] "A brief View and Survey of the dangerons and pernicious Errors to Church and State in Mr. Hobbes's book entitled Leviathan. By Edward, Earl of Clarendon." Oxon. 1676, 4to.

[b] Perhaps, "Divi Britannici: being a Remark upon the Lives of all the Kings of this Isle, from the year of the world 2855 unto the year of grace 1660." By Sir Winston Churchill, Knt. London, 1675, fol.

[c] Master of the Rolls, 1685.

[d] Sir John Vaughan, Chief Justice of the Common Pleas.

[e] "A Paraphrase and Annotations upon the Epistles of St. Paul written to the Romans, Corinthians, and Hebrews." Oxford, 1675, 8vo.

[f] Obadiah Walker, Fellow of University College; Master, 1676. Declared himself a Roman Catholic 1685, and was deprived 1689.

[g] The works of St. Cyprian, printed in 1682, were perhaps the first result of this project.

Cornelius Nepos,[a] to the end of which, by my contrivancy, is added
the life of Aristomenes, a Greek heroe, taken out of Pausanias. I
doubt not but that when you read it you will acknowledge it to be
the finest story you ever met with in the Greek history. Our
Marbles are now printeing. I am now at worke makeing the notes,
but fear I shall be put to the necessity of inserteing in many things
which I shall after be ashamed of; especially since I have not time
sufficient allowed me either to collect things togeather or consider
what is to be deduced from them; but the best is, it is out of the
rode, and therefore few will perceive where I walke not right. I
coat a multitude of authors; if people thinke the better of me for
that, I will thinke the worse of them for their judgement. It beeing
soe easyly a thing to make this specious show, he must be a fool
that cannot gain whatsoever repute is to be gotten by it. If people
will admire him for this, they may; I shall admire such for nothing
else but their good indexs. As long as bookes have these, on what
subject may we not coat as many others as we please, and never
have read on of them? Mr. Dean hath long had a design of
makeing an English and Latin dictionary; the method he proposeth
is very good. He put Altham[b] upon it about five years since; but
he haveing brough[t] his books home to the Dean without haveing
on line of his businesse don, he hath utterly lost himselfe with him;
especially since, he beeing now forced to come to the publick test,
his exercise show him a very mean schollar, and therefore on that
account cannot deserve any great respects. I write you not this
out of any spleen to the man, we beeing now very good friends, but
that I may performe my promise of informeing you of our Christ
Church affaires. Die doeth nothing but drinke ale, his businesse
of translateing beeing over; and with it, I thinke, is ended his repute

[a] " Vitæ excellentium Imperatorum, collatione quatuor MSS. recognitæ. Accessit
Aristomenis Messenii Vita ex Pausania." Oxon. 1675, 12mo.
[b] Roger Altham, Scholar of Westminster, and Student of Christ Church 1668;
M.A. 1675; Senior Proctor, 1682; B.D. and Prebendary of York, 1683; Canon of
Christ Church and Hebrew Professor, 1691; D.D. 1694. He was Vicar of Finedon,
co. Northampton, 1688.

with the Dean as well as every body else. We have a strange story of an apparition at Malborough, which [has] been related here with all the circomstance imaginable to gain beleive. Were it not that I fear I should lose my dinner, I would tell it you; if I have time nex Tuesday you shall have it; but perchance it may be subject of a ballet and be cryed about the streets before that time, and then I shall save my labour. It is an excellent story for Dr Moor,[a] and must come in in his next edition of his booke of Atheisme . . . .

Oxf[ord], 24 Jan. [16]7$\frac{4}{5}$.

The death of Clarendon [b] hath brought Levet [c] again to our house, and with him is come the Lord Corenbury,[d] eldest son to the present Earle of Clarendon. His unkle [e] is come with him to the University, but since is father was of Magdalen Colledge he reather chooseth to be there under the tuition of his kindsman Dr Hyde.[f] I hope now, the Earle beeing dead, it will not be long till we have his history.[g] If you know anything of its publishing, pray impart it. I am informed it is already in the presse somewhere beyond sea. We have here a multitude of other reports; on tels us that there is a Vicar General to be made and that Ashly [h] is to be the man; another

[a] Henry More, D.D. " An Antidote against Atheism." London, 1656, 8vo.

[b] Edward Hyde, Earl of Clarendon, died in exile at Rouen, 19 December, 1674.

[c] William Levett, of Christ Church, D.D. 1680; Principal of Magdalen Hall, 1681; and Dean of Bristol, 1685. Died 1694.

[d] Edward Hyde, Viscount Cornbury, son of Henry second Earl of Clarendon, succeeded his father as third Earl.

[e] Lawrence Hyde, created Earl of Rochester, 1682.

[f] Prideaux has confounded the College with the Hall. James Hyde, M.D. sometime Fellow of Christ Church, Principal of Magdalen Hall,-1662-81. He was also Regius Professor of Medicine.

[g] The " History of the Rebellion " was first printed at Oxford, in 1702-4.

[h] Prideaux means the Earl of Shaftesbury, which title had been conferred on Anthony Ashley Cooper, Lord Ashley, in 1672. He would still be better remembered as the Ashley of the Cabal. In his letter of 3 February, 1674-5, addressed to the

that another declaration for indulgence is to be issued out; and that which I least beleive is that the French King hath sent over to know by what method Harry the 8th proceeded in the suppresscing of monestrys, and that severall people have been employed to search the records in the Tower for above these six weeks to give him satisfaction herein. A multitude of other lys are imposed on us here, and, were it not for your intelligence, perchance I might give some credit to them as other fools doe; but this beeing to me *regula recti et curvi*, I find I doe with good successe assent to whatsoever I find in your letters, and conclude all false of which you give me noe information. The presse hath often furnished me with something to tell you. You little thinke it hath been imployed about printeing Aretins postures.[a] I assure you we were like to have had an edition of them from thence were it not that last night the whole worke was mard. The gentlemen of All Souls had got them engraved, and had imployed our presse to print them of. The time that was chosen for the worke was the eveneing after 4, Mr. Dean after that time never useing to come to the theator; but last night, beeing imployed the other part of the day, he went not thither till the work was begun. How he tooke to find his presse workeing at such an imployment I leave it to you to immagin. The prints and plates he hath seased, and threatens the owners of them with expulsion; and I thinke they would deserve it were they of any other colledge then All Souls, but there I will allow them to be vertuous that are bawdy only in pictures. That colledge in my esteem is a scandalous place, and I cannot but be much offended at

---

Earl of Carlisle, Shaftesbury himself refers to this rumour: "I hear from all quarters of letters from Whitehall that I am coming up to town, that a great office, with a strange name, is preparing for me, and such like." *The Life of the first Earl of Shaftesbury.* Edited by G. W. Cooke. London, 2 vols. 8vo: vol. ii, p. 110.

[a] These famous, or rather infamous, engravings, executed by Marc Antonio from designs by Giulio Romano, were intended to illustrate the sonnets of Pietro Aretino; but most of the plates were seized and destroyed by Clement VII., who also imprisoned Marc Antonio and expelled Aretino from Rome. The impressions are extremely rare.

yᵉ behaviour of yᵗ Society in Morleys[a] businesse. . . . Mr. Nurse,[b]
which was formerly of University Coll. and is now a Roman Catholick,
we hear hath writ a booke in answare to Whitby.[c] I tould you in
my former letters that I thought our Sub-Dean[d] would afford me
many pleasant storys of his government to inform you; but his
follys I find are to many to be related, and he thereby renderd not
worth your consideration; his repeated follys makeing him not
worth a laugheing at. He came yesterday to the cannons mens
table, and findeing his not at the upper end of the table, he began
to be very outragious, and stormd very violently that any durst take
place of the Sub-Deans man. The other day Dʳ Pocock[e] and he
calld at the same time for a glasse of wind (sic); the man bringeing
it first to Dʳ Pocock he could scarce be diswaded from beateing him.
But enought of a fool. If you have a mind to hear some of his
nonsense you may have enough of it if you will hear him preache
on the 30th of January at the Temple. . . .

---

[a] Charles Morley, of All Souls College, B.C.L. 1677. Prideaux accuses him of immorality and his college of overlooking it.

[b] Timothy Nourse, Fellow of University College, 1658, was a noted preacher. "This person, who was a man of parts but conceited, changed his religion for that of Rome, and therefore was deprived of his fellowship, January, 1673[4]." He bequeathed a good collection of coins to the Bodleian Library. His book, mentioned above, if published at all, did not appear under his name.—*Ath. Oxon.* iv. 448.

[c] Daniel Whitby, D.D. of Trinity College, Rector of St. Edmund's church, Salisbury. He was a great writer against Roman Catholic doctrines. The work which provoked Nourse's answer was probably "A Discourse concerning the Idolatry of the Church of Rome, wherein that charge is justified, and the pretended Refutation of Dr. Stillingfleet's Discourse is answered." London, 1674, 8vo.

[d] Benjamin Woodroffe.

[e] Edward Pocock, D.D. Canon of Christ Church, the famous Orientalist, was born at Oxford in 1604, and educated at Thame. He entered at Magdalen Hall in 1618; Scholar of Corpus Christi College, 1620, and afterwards Fellow. In 1636, after travelling in the East, he became the first Landian professor of Arabic, and was appointed Hebrew professor in 1648. Died 1691.

[Oxford], 31 Jan. [1675.]

. . . . . . When I wrot to you concerneing Clarendons History
I meant not his life, but the history which he wrot of the late Civil
Wars, of which you must needs have heard the fame of it, haveing
been spred about everywhere long since, which maketh many have
strong expectations of it. I wish it may answare them. I have
been informed that on his death bed he commanded the speedy
publisheing thereof, and that in obedience thereto it is now printeing
at Rohan; but I fear this is only what people would have done
rather that what is really performeing. Van Trump [a] came hither
on Tuesday night and immediately waited on our Dean, by whom
he was treated at dinner the next day; he desired he might have
salt meat, he never useing to eat any other, which put M[r] Dean
much to it to find that which [would] please his pallet. He had much
respects shown him here, and the University presented him with a
D[rs] degree, but the seaman thinkeing that title out of his element
would have nothing to doe with it. He was much gazed at by the
boys, who perchance wondred to find him, whom they had found so
famous in Gazets, to be at last but a drunkeing greazy Dutchman.
Speed [b] stayd in town on purpose to drinke with him, which is the
only thing he is good for; and for fear he should loose soe commendable a quality he dayly exerciseth it, for wont of better
company, with Price out [sic, our] butler and Rawlins the plumber,
with whom he spendeth al the time he is here either in the
brandy shop or tavern. It was not all Aretine our gentlemen were
printeing here, but some of his more famous cuts for the private
use of themselfes and their friends. However, about 60 of them
had gon abroad before the businesse was discovered; but Mr. Dean
hath made them call them in again and commit them to the fire.

---

[a] Cornelis van Tromp, the Dutch admiral, visited England in 1675, and was
created a baron by Charles II.

[b] John Speed, of St. John's College, M.D. 1666.

I must desire you to let noe on know from whom you have such like intelligence. The All Souls men from on end to the other have all declared war against me already for sayeing they had noe famous man since Digs,[a] and that they lived on his credit ever since. If they should know this to they would hamstring me ; therefore you must be sure to keep secret for fear of the worst, for I assure you they are terrible fellows at some things. I am sorry such a knave a[s] Bredoc[b] should be made a bishop ; he is exceeding ambitious to have a student of our house to tutor to his children, and hath at last prevailed with Mr. Dean to send him Gascoigne.[c] We still talk here of an indulgence,[d] and say the meeting at Lambeth[e] is about it. What the secret is time will discover, and till then we must be content to be without it. . . . .

---

[a] Dudley Digges, son of Sir Dudley Digges, Commoner of University College, 1620 ; B.A. 1631 ; Fellow of All Souls, 1632. "Became a great scholar, general artist, and linguist." Died 1643.—*Ath. Oxon.* iv. 63.

[b] Ralph Brideoake, Bishop of Chichester. He entered Brasenose College in 1630; was afterwards of New College. As chaplain to the Earl of Derby he was in Latham House during the memorable siege. He afterwards got preferment by favour of Speaker Lenthall. Canon of Windsor, 1660 ; Dean of Salisbury, 1667. "In Feb. 1674[5] he was, by the endeavours of Lodovisa, Duchess of Portsmouth (whose hands were always ready to take bribes), nominated by the King to be Bishop of Chichester."—*Ath. Oxon.* iv. 859.

[c] Joseph Gascoigne, elected from Westminster to Christ Church, B.A. 1673 ; M.A. 1675.

[d] The famous Declaration of Indulgence, the original cause of such rumours, was published in March 1672, and withdrawn in February 1673.

[e] "Besides this, the great Ministers of State did in their common publick assure the partie that all the places of profit, command, and trust, should only be given to the old Cavalier ; no man that had served or been of the contrary party should be left in any of them ; and a direction is issued to the great Ministers before mentioned, and six or seven of the Bishops, to meet at Lambeth House, who were, like the Lords of the Articles in Scotland, to prepare their compleat modell for the ensuing session of Parliament."—*A Letter from a Person of Quality*, 1675.

[Oxford, 7 Feb. 1675.]

I have received your letres, and am sorry that for the good intelligence you weekely give me I cannot return you any that is worth your knowledge; but, since your good nature is pleased to put a value on the information I give you of our small occurrences here, you have enabled me thereby at least to expresse the acknowledgement of your favours, although I can return you nothing worthy of them. Dr. Jackson[a] is now giving up the goast, we each hour expecteing that Tom[b] should give us information of his death. Lock[c] and Hodges[d] are both here. Lock hath wrigled into Irelands[e] faculty place, and intendeth this act to proceed D[r] in physick, which will be a great kindnesse to us, we not being above four to bear the whole charges of the act supper. I would not have you discouraged by this from comeing to make on with

[a] Samuel Jackson, of Christ Church, M.D. 1671. Served in the King's army, and afterwards practised in the University for many years. He died 3 March, 1675—*Fast. Oxon.* ii. 331.

[b] The bell.

[c] John Locke, the famous writer and philosopher, was born in 1632. Elected to Christ Church from Westminster in 1652 : B.A. 1655 ; M.A. 1658 ; "but, rather than take orders and be a minister according to the Church of England, he entered on the physic line, and on a course of chymistry, and got some little practice in Oxon." B.M. 1674, and afterwards appointed faculty student of medicine, as referred to in the letter above. He had accidently been introduced to Lord Ashley, afterwards Earl of Shaftesbury, and became his secretary, receiving the post of Secretary of Presentations when the Earl became Lord Chancellor in 1672, and in 1673 being appointed Secretary of the Board of Trade. After Shaftesbury's death, in 1683, he retired to Holland. The next year he was deprived of his studentship. He returned to England in 1689, and was made Commissioner of Appeals in the Excise and of Trade and Plantations. Died 1704.—*Ath. Oxon.* iv. 638; Welch, *Westm. Scholars,* 140.

[d] Nathaniel Hodges of Christ Church, M.A. 1657 ; Proctor 1666 ; Professor of Moral Philosophy. He was chaplain to the Earl of Shaftesbury, who procured for him, in 1673, prebendaries both at Norwich and Gloucester .Died 1700.

[e] Thomas Ireland, elected from Westminster to Christ Church, 1649. Afterwards ejected, and took the degree of B.C.L. at St. Mary's Hall. In 1664 he was nominated to the newly-created faculty studentship of medicine at Christ Church ; Chancellor of Durham, 1674. Died 1676.—Welch, 132.

us; however I dare not except you since that doth seldom come to passe what is most earnestly desired. We got a greater victory over Van Trump here then all your sea captaines in London, he confesseing that he was more drunke here then anywhere else since he came into England, which I thinke very little to the honour of our University. Dr Speed was the chiefe man that encountred him, who mustering up about five or six more as able men as himselfe at wine and brandy got the Dutchman to the Crown Tavern, and there soe plyed him with both that at 12 at night they were fain to carry him to his lodgeings. We have a booke come over here from Holland writ by Curselæus[a] which giveth great offence here: it is a very hetrodox booke and containeth worse yn the doctrin of Socinus; but that which we have most reason to make exceptions against is that the editor therefore sayeth he set [it] forth to give satisfaction to the desires of the English devines, which will be very little to our credit abroad, especially in the Romish Church. Mr. Deans Bible[b] is now come forth; as soone as you here anything of it, pray give me information. Cold weather must excuse bad writing and everything else I wit.

[Oxford, 11 March, 1675.]

I must now thanke you for your good news, since that which you inform me of your speedy beeing here is soe pleasant and welcome unto me, I hope you will keep your word, unlesse businesse of more advantagious concern hinder you. I hope your goeing to Nimmegen[c] will neither put an end to or interrupt our corres-

---

[a] Etienne de Courcelles, Swiss theologian, 1586-1659. "Stephani Curcellæi Opera Theologica, Quorum pars præcipua Institutio Religionis Christianæ."—Amstelod. 1675, fol.

[b] See above, page 1, note [d].

[c] Ellis accompanied Sir Leoline Jenkins to the Conference of Nimegnen, as his secretary, at the end of this year.

pondence.   Dr Jackson is dead and buried, and Alestry ^{a} is admitted
into his place, soe that now all our faculty places a[re] filed with
tosts, and those which formerly had the learnedst and most eminent
men in the University are become the refuges of dunces and
knaves.   We have been for these eight or nine days in strange
consternation here by reason of a prophecy said to be by Lilly,^{b}
which fortold that on the 10th of March on part of the town should
be burned and the other swallowed up with an earth quake; but
the best is, the day is past and we are secure.   However, our people
did soe strangely beleive it here that most of our greezy townsmen
that had any love for their carcases or money tooke care to remove
both from this place; and by a decree of the mayor and his brethren,
after a long consultation, watches were set in every street to prevent
the mischeife fortold; but Dic Perse, executeing his office of
walkeing that night, clapt all my gentlemen into the castle; which
hath created a great deal of bussel, the townsmen accuseing us that
we have a mind the town shall be burned.   The country people are
likewise soe terrifyed with this, that few are soe hardy as to dare
yet to come to market.   I scarce thinke a prophecy from God
Almighty would have been able to have don quarter as much, or
that the town of Ninive did halfe as much fear the destruction
foretold by Jonas as our coxcombs this by Lilly.   At our assizes
five were condemned, but are all to be transported.   Wild^c fell
sick here, and therefore could continue the circute noe further, but
was forced to return, Thurland^d goeing the rest of the circute by
himselfe.   Our law case is not yet ended; four advocates come down
from Drs Commons to plead it next term.   If you be as good as
your word to be here, you will have the advantage of heareing the

---

^{a} Perhaps Charles Allestree; entered Christ Church, 1671; B.A. 1674; M.A.
1677.   Afterwards Vicar of Cassington, co. Oxon., and of Daventry, co. North-
ampton.
^{b} William Lilly, the astrologer.   Died 1681.
^{c} Sir William Wylde, Puisne Judge of the King's Bench.
^{d} Sir Edward Thurland, Junior Baron of the Exchequer.

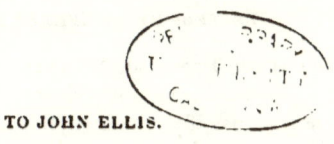

tryall. I wish this could be a temptation to you to be here. Many pleasant transactions have hapned concerneing this businesse since I first informed you of it, but they are too many to [be] inserted in a sheet of paper; when we next meet we will talk of them. The reason why I have not been soe constant in writeing to you as I could wish is, that I grone under the presse. I have been ashamed hitherto to tell you that I am comeing out in folio.[a] I am now at the 107 page; when it is don it must be exposed to your judge- ment, although I could have wished Mr. Dean had found out some on of more ability to undertake it. I fear he will suffer for it in the sale of his booke . . . .

[Oxford], March 20, [1675].

. . . . We have got another booke of Dr. Willises[b] in the presse. beside which nothing is to be expected from us that is worth the publicke vew, Mr. Dean at present dealeing in most vile small businesses. I must confesse most of his designes are shallow, and I am sure will conduce very little to the advancement of learneing and knowledge. We have scarce as yet set forth any booke of

---

[a] The "Marmora Oxoniensia."

[b] Thomas Willis, the most famous physician of his time, born 1621. Entered Christ Church in 1636. He bore arms in the garrison of Oxford, and, after taking his degree of B.M., practised there. He married a daughter of Dr. Samuel Fell, Dean of Christ Church. In 1660 he became Sedley Professor, M.D., and F.R.S. He removed to Westminster in 1666, where he had a large practice. "Though he was a plain man, a man of no carriage, little discourse, complaisance, or society, yet for his deep insight, happy researches in natural and experimental philosophy, anatomy, and chymistry, for his wonderful success and repute in his practice, the natural smoothness, pure elegance, delightful unaffected neatness of Latin stile, none scarce hath equall'd, much less outdone, him, how great soever." He died in 1675. The work referred to above is " Pharmacentice Rationalis: sive Diatriba de medicamen- torum operationibus in humano corpore." Oxon. 1674-5, 4to.—Ath. Oxon. iii. 1048.

worth, neither can I perswade Mr. Dean to attempt any, his answare
to all my proposals becing, it will not sell. A Bible hath lately
come forth from us; if you hear anything of it pray inform us. I
must confesse, since Mr. Dean hath taken the liberty of inventeing
a new way of spelleing and useing it therein, which I thinke will
confound and alter the analogy of the English tongue, y[t] I doe not
at all approve thereof; and I could hartyly wish that he would be
a looser by the experiment, that we may have noe more of it.[a] Our
prophecy and the effects thereof hath occasioned a great deal of
bussel in town; but your friend Die l'eirce hath got the worst,
beeing baffled by the townsmen in his contention with them, since
the Vice-Chancelonr though[t] not fit to joyne with him in his
zeal against them, but, on the contrary, dismist his prisoners without
suffercing them to pay their fees, and checked the yong man for
his over hasty, and in his opinion imprudent, act in committing
them.   Beside, the townsmen, haveing got information that after he
had finished his preamble he spent the residue of the night in the
tavern, have endeavoured to be revenged on him by spreadeing this
story to his disgrace.   Here is like to be a great contention between
the Hales and St. Johns Colledge about the next years proctorship.
The statutes, whensoever the Colledges do not present a man capable
before the time prefixed, that is before six a clock the first Wednesday
in Lent, give the election of the proctor that year to the Hals.   St.
John presented on Waple,[b] who is not full four years standeing
master, which is a standeing the statutes require to make a man
capable of that office.   The Hales therefore, claimeing the election
as devolved on them by the default of St. Johns in not chuseing
a statuteable man, hath choosen another man, and, as they say

<hr>

  [a] One of the Dean's peculiarities of spelling in this Bible, and that which
Prideaux had probably in mind, is the substitution of i or ie for y in all cases,
without regard to the ordinary rules of orthography, as cies, maiest, daics, slaieth,
alwaies, staied, &c.
  [b] Edward Waple, of St. John's College, B.A. 1667; M.A. 1671. He became
Prebendary of Wells, 1680, and Archdeacon of Taunton, 1682. Afterwards Vicar
of St. Sepulchre's, London.

(since the rest of the University utterly disapprove of their pretentions and are resolved not to allow them, if they are made judges
of the controversy), are resolved, in order to the establishing of him
in the office, to petition the King that they may not be deprived of
the right which they think the statutes give them; but Waple
beeing four years standeing in terms, the whole controversy is What
is an academicall year? whither it consist of quatuor terminos et
quatuor vacationes or only of 4 terminos; and this they say the
King, as beeing the supreme interpreter of our statutes, must
determine to decide the controversy. I have a letter here lately
sent from Samaria by the residue of the Samaritans there, wherein
they give a fuller account of their religion, customs, and manner
of liveing, then hath as yet been known in Europe. It was write
in Samaritan, from which I have translated it into Latin, and esteem
it a great rarity; and, if you doe so too, I shall take care to have it
transcribed for you, and will annext the history how it came here.[a]

---

[a] Correspondence has from time to time been maintained between the Samaritans
and European scholars, from a desire on the part of the latter to obtain information
regarding the ancient laws, rites, and history of that people and the Jews. Joseph
Scaliger was the first to open communication, in 1589. In 1671, Robert Huntington,
minister of the English Church at Aleppo, and afterwards Bishop of Raphoe, visited
the Samaritans of Nábulns, and so surprised them by his knowledge of their language
that they assumed that some of their brethren must have settled in England. Huntington encouraged the idea, and the result was that he at once received a copy of
the Samaritan Pentateuch, and soon after a letter, for the Samaritan brethren in
England. It is this letter that Prideaux refers to. An answer to it was written by
Dr. Thomas Marshall in 1674. The correspondence thus begun was kept up for
some years; and it has been re-opened early in the present century. A Latin translation of the letter, by Edward Bernard, who is, in all probability, the Mr. Bernard
that appears in Prideaux's next letter, was printed by Cellarius (Epistolæ Sama-
ritanæ ad Johnm Ludolfum) in 1688, and may be the very translation mentioned
above.—See *Correspondance des Samaritains de Naplouse, par S. de Sacy*, in
Notices et Extraits des MSS. de la Bibl. du Roi, tom. xii. Paris, 1831.

[Oxford], Aprill 13th [1675].

Our term beeing this day begun, I hope it will not be long till you will give us the happinesse of enjoyeing your good company here. I must confesse at present I have some reason why I should desire it, since Mr. Bernard,[a] to whom I have been beholden for revewceing all my papers before they have gon to the presse, beeing now about to leave us (beeing appointed to wait on [the] Earl of Southampton as his tutour in his travels), I shall hugely want such a freind as you to assist me with your judgement. I hope when we have got you here you will be soe kind as to give me this assistance, and therefore I am resolved to reserve the trouble for you. Mr. Dean hath been absent from us ever since Easter Munday, beeing gon to the Lord Leighs[b] to reconcile him and his wife if possible. In his return he taketh Worcester in his way, where he is buildeing a church to his hospital.[c] I suppose you remember in University Colledge there was on side of the quadrangle wanteing. They are now very busy in supplyeing that defect with a new buildeing[d] uniform to the rest, which will make that colledge looke very handsom, and not inferior in beuty to any other in the University. If you be here in the beginning of the term, you will have the happinesse of hearcing your tutor Woodruffe perform his exercise

[a] Edward Bernard, elected Scholar of St. John's College from Merchant Taylors' School, 1655; afterwards Fellow. M.A. 1662; D.D. 1684; Savilian Professor of Astronomy, 1673. Rector of Cheam, in Surrey, and of Brightwell, in Berkshire. "He is a person admirably well read in all kind of ancient learning, in astronomy, and mathematics, a curious critic, an excellent Grecian, Latinist, chronologer, and orientalian." Died 1696.—*Ath. Oxon.* iv. 701.

[b] Thomas, second Lord Leigh, 1672-1710.

[c] St. Oswald's Hospital, in the parish of Claines, in the city of Worcester, was founded in the thirteenth century. At the time of the dissolution of the monasteries it was given to the Dean and Chapter as a college or hospital for poor men and women. Dr. John Fell was appointed Master in 1660, in succession to his father.— Nash, *Hist. Worcestershire*, 1781-2, fol. i. 224.

[d] On the east side, on the side of the old refectory.

for his degree,[a] which he hath oughed us hitherto, and now for fear of the Terræ filius[b] beginneth to pay it. We have two or three small pidlcing things printeing here; on is an account of the Jacobits,[c] another of the kingdom of Golcondah.[d] They contain pretty storys, and therefore, to give you a night's diversion before you goe to bed, I intend to send them as soon as they are publick, unlesse you prevent me by your comeing here. . . . .

[Oxford]. Aug. 15, [1675.]

. . . . I know not here what is worth informeing you, but that the small pox have kild many more besides my brother.[e] Severall dy each day thereof. I suppose, since it first reigned here, near 200 have died of it, whereof about 50 schollars. Our house hath escaped the best of any in Oxford; we have only lost two servitors. You have, I suppose, seen our bookes lately set forth,

---

[a] Woodroffe had taken his D.D. degree as far back as January, 1673.

[b] The origin of the *Terræ filius* has never yet been properly investigated, though the office is provided for in the old University statutes. He was an officer appointed to take part in the Disputations at the Acts, and appears to have been allowed a certain licence of tongue, a statute providing for his punishment in case he should exceed proper bounds. Ayliffe (*Ancient and Present State of the University of Oxford*, ii. 134) says, " There is not that licence given for an impudentbuffoon, of no reputation in himself, called a *Terræ filius*, to sport and play with the good name and reputation of others; but the business of this *Terræ filius* is a solemn and grave disputation. And although this manner of sportive wit had its first original at the time of the Reformation, when the gross absurdities and superstitions of the Roman Church were to be exposed, and should have been restrain'd to things, and not have reach'd men's persons and characters, yet it has since become very scandalous and abusive." As early as 1591 a *Terræ filius* was expelled for his bitter satire. Nor did the mlucky speaker always escape with a whole skin; Wood (*Life*, xci.) tells us that More, *Terræ filius* of Merton, was cudgelled by Sir T. Spencer's son for some reflections on the father, 9 July, 1681.

[c] " Historia Jacobitarum seu Coptorum in Ægypto, Lybia, Nubia, &c. Opera Josephi Abudacio seu Barbati," &c. Oxon. 1675, 8vo.

[d] I have been unable to identify this book.—ED.

[e] Nicholas Prideaux, of Corpus Christi College, a younger brother.

Lydiat,[a] the Greeke Testament,[b] and Mr. Walkers Notes on S[t] Pauls Epistles.[c] We are now goeing to print Notes of D[r] Pococks on the Minor Prophets.[d] I have the manuscript at present in my chamber, the D[r] haveing thought me worthy to peruse it before it goe to the presse, and accordeing to my judgement I thinke it the best literal comment and the plainest I ever saw on any booke; although others, who are unacquainted with the learneing the D[r] is conversant in, will thinke it tedious, and many things inserted superfluous, although I am confident that men of better learneing will not thinke any thing in it ought to be omitted. We are setteing forth Quintilians Declamations,[e] to which Altham maketh notes. There is likewise a mathematicall booke of Mr. Oughtreds[f] in the presse, and Maximus Tyrius[g] in 12⁰. I believe it will be Christmas before I have don, especially since I am interrupted by this journey. I see many of your letters to Woodruffe, I would advise you by noe means to rely on him; how he will deal with you you may learn from how he served Dic Pears. The Ld Conway[h] had spoken to the Ld Keeper[i] in Peerses behalfe, and got a promise that he should have any preferment that he would give him notice of was vacant in his guift. A very good parsonage[k] not many miles distant from this place beeing void, and Dic, haveing notice of the incumbant's death the very day he dyed, posteth to Woodruffe, who

<hr>

[a] Thomas Lydiat. " Canones Chronologici, necnon series summorum Magistratunm Romanorum," &c. Oxon. 1675, 8vo.

[b] See above, page 1, note [e].

[c] See above, page 27, note [c].

[d] The Commentary on Hosea appeared in 1685, and that on Joel in 1691.

[e] " M. F. Quintiliani Declamationum liber, etc. quae omnia notis illustrantur " Oxon. 1675, 8vo.

[f] William Oughtred. " Opuscula Mathematica hactenus inedita." Oxon. 1677, 8vo.

[g] " Maximi Tyrii Dissertationes." Oxon. 1677, 8vo.

[h] Edward, Viscount, afterwards Earl of, Conway; Secretary of State, 1681-83.

[i] Sir Heneage Finch; Lord Finch and Lord Chancellor, 19 December, 1675; afterwards Earl of Nottingham.

[k] Shrivenham, co. Berks.

immediately promised him his service and deswaded him from goeing to London himselfe, assureing that he, beeing to be there the next day, would effectually doe his businesse for him; as accordingly he did in another sense, the next news we heard beeing that Woodruffe had got it for himselfe. From hence you may know the nature of the beast; you[r] own prudence will be sufficient to direct you how far he is to be relyed on.

[Oxford, 2 Sept. 1675.]

The letres you directed to me at Portledge I have sent for, and desire that you would be pleased to continue your correspondence with me in this place, I not designeing now to move from hence till my booke be don; since it will be a fortnight at least before I shall be able to ride, and then it will be to late in the year to begin soe long a journy, unlesse I should intend to keep my winter in Cornwall, which I will not be perswaded to doe, my father's house lyeing on the north sea, and open to all the wind and weather which come from thence, which I am not willeing to endure; especially since I thinke I can live much more comfortably here in the winter and there in the summer. I confesse it is a great disappointment unto me that I could not goe when I designed, but my greatest affliction now is the sicknesse of my worthy friend Dr. Pocock, who hath his old distemper returned upon him, which, if it doth prevaile, must necessaryly kill him and deprive me of the best freind I have in this place, and utterly spoile me for a linguist; since the greatest encouragement I have to follow those studys is the more then ordinary helpe which I hope to receive from him. However I have got all his comment transcribed, that that may not be lost with him. If he liveth, we designe great things, and I am resolved to labour hard to bring them to passe; but I fear the D^{rs} designes are above his strength, by reason of his age, which is great, he haveing gon chaplain to the ambassadour at Constantinople before our King was born; and you may easyly immagin he was

not then a yong man, beeing made choise of for that imployment
by reason of his eminence at that time in the Arabick tongue.
We have a yong man of All Souls, a Batchelour, who I confesse
is the greatest miracle in the knowledge of that I ever heard of,
he haveing made himselfe a perfect m^r of that copious and difficult
language. His name is Guise,[a] and is eldest son to a gentleman of
an estate of 500^l a year. I am sorry he is not yet grown up to be
old enough to succeed the D^r, if he should chance to march of.
Since I must return to my Marbles again, I must beg your assistance,
and desire of you that you would be pleased to walk through the
matted gallery at Whitehall and observe whither there be any
inscription on any of the pedestals of the statues that stand there,
and, if you find any such, to transcribe them with some smal dis-
cription of the statues to which they belong. I here there are some
inscriptions likewise at St Jameses; I desire the like favour from
you, that you would be pleased at your leasure likewise to transcribe
them. All that are in the privy garden I already have. If you
hear of any other inscriptions which are in noblemens gardens about
London you would be a very considerable benefactour to my booke
to assist me with them. I confesse the favour I beg of you will
put [you] to much trouble, but the confidence I have in your
freindship giveth me presumption to desire it of you, and I doubt
but that herein you will be pleased to satisfy the desires of your
most assured, etc.

[Oxford. 9-14 Oct. 1675.]

I informed you in my last of your freind Peerses preferment to
a beedles place.[b] He hath since behaved himself soe indiscreetly,

---

[a] William Guise, Fellow of All Souls, B.A. 1674; M.A. 1677. He was held "in
great esteem for his Oriental learning, but soon after [1683] cut off by the small
pox, to the great reluctancy of all those who were acquainted with his pregnant
parts."—*Ath. Oxon.* iv. 114.
[b] Peers was elected Superior Beadle of Arts, 21 September, 1675.

or rather knavishly, y^t he hath utterly lost himselfe in the esteem of our whole house. I formerly wrot to you that he was choosen grammar lecturer for the two ensueing years by our house. On his election to the beedles place, the halls, thinkeing his election inconsistent with that and therefore lapsed to them (they haveing right to choose as often as the colledges, to whose turn it came to elect, either omitt to elect, or choose a man not capable by statute), proceeded to an election and choose on Evans[a] of New In Hall. Great bussel was made to keep Peers in; the Dean tooke great pains in his behalfe, and soe likewise did several others, and carryed it for him. But, since he though[t] it not convenient to read in his beedles gownd, a deputy was appointed and an agreement made that he should have 6^l a year out of the place. However, that very same day all this was don for him, Evans, haveing tempted him with better conditions. prevailed with him to breake his former bargain, and immediately in favour of him, without consultceing any of his freinds whom he had soe much troubled, made a resignation of his place to the Vice-Chancelour; which hath soe much incensed the Dean y^t it is supposed he will turn him out at Christmas; and in that measure displeased all the m^{rs} of our house that none of us have ever since spake to him, unlesse it be to obbraid him with his knavery, we beeing cheifly concerned that he hath thereby betrayed the interest of our house, and made this a president for the halls ever after to challenge the lecture as lapsed to them on such occasions. Beside, this will be added to his affliction, that the man in favour of whom he resigned will not have the place, and consequently his bargain with him be nuld; for he beeing elected without the readeing of the Act of Parliament, which is to be read at all elections, his election is declared void and another appointed, wherein it is supposed another will be choosen; it is the endeavour of many of us that it may be soe. Last Thursday[b] we chose Dr Bathurst again our Vice Chancelour, at which time likewise was read in the Convocation house, to be approved by us, a letter which

[a] Henry Evans, M.A. 1661. [b] 7th October.

is to be sent from the University to the Duke of Tuscany; with which are likewise sent the catalogue of our library, the Antiquitys, Loggins Cuts,[a] and Morisons Herbal,[b] as a present from the University.[c] If my booke had been don, it had gon with it. The same present is designed likewise to be sent to Huelius,[d] the great astronomer, he haveing sent all his workes hither to be put in the library. Holder the keeper of the schools is dead. The disposal of the place belongeing either to the Chancelour or Vice-Chancelour, he that is first appointed by either hath the place. The Vice-Chancelour designed it for his man, and hath accordeingly given it him, although on appeared with the Chancelours letter as soon as the man was dead; but, the Vice-Chancelour haveing kept his gates locked all that morneing Holder dyed till he had confirmed his new officer by putteing the University seal to his patent, the other candidate, knockeing in vain for admittance, had it not till it was to late for him to get the place.

Our library keeper Hyde at present lyeth under heavy affliction. The story is pleasant and therefore I will relate it at full. I suppose you know he marryed an old whore here about four or five years since, who hath domineered over the poor fool most imperiously ever since, and, having lately found him too familiar with her mayd, began to mistrust him of makeing love to her, and challenged him for it. The poor man to appease his wife took a formal oath on the Bible he designed noe such thing with the mayd as he was accused of, but, this not beeing sufficient to satisfy the wife, she beat him

---

[a] "Oxonia Illustrata." Engravings of Oxford, by David Loggan. Oxon. 1675, fol.

[b] "Plantarum Umbelliferarum Distributio nova, per tabulas coguationis et affinitatis ex libro Naturæ observata et detecta. Authore Roberto Morison, Medico et Professore Botanico Regio." Oxon. 1672, fol.

[c] "This year also the same books were, by a decree of Convocation, presented to the most illustrious prince Cosmo de Medicis, Grand Duke of Tuscany; which present was accompanied with a Latin letter, written by the public orator, Dr. South, wherein a character of the books was given."—Wood, Life, lxxvi.

[d] Johann Hevelius, of Danzig, 1611-87.

soe basely that he hath kept his chamber these two months, and is now in danger of looseing his hand, which he made use of only to defend the blows and beg mercy. . . . .

[Oxford], Nov. 8, [1675]

. . . . . . Our town affords little news worth your knowledge; y' which is most talked of at present is what each colledge contributeth towards the rebuildeing of Northampton.[a] Our schollars are ridiculously liberal to this phanatical town. If all others should equall them in their contributions, North Hampton would get double what it lost by beeing burnt. Such ridiculous pride and emulation in giveing much haveing soe possesst all our schollars, y' poor rogues that are scarce worth 40s thinke themselfes undervalued if they give not 20. Most of our fellows of houses are in this humour; but I thought 5s as great an almes as I could give or that roguy town deserve. We shall from our University alone, althoug[h] now very thin, send above 500l; and this we doe to exceed Cambridge, which place we are informed hath given 300l. . . . . There is at present printeing in our theater an account of the Greek Church[b] as it is at this present, written by on Mr. Smith,[c] of Magd. Coll., who was formerly Chaplain to Sr Daniel Harvy at Constantinople, where he then made his observations; else we have nothing new, nor nothing y' I know designed, which is worth setteing forth. However, Mr. Dean is soe eager and busy

[a] Northampton was burnt down, 20 September, 1675, and was rebuilt by public subscription.

[b] "De Græcæ Ecclesiæ hodierno statu Epistola. Authore Thoma Smitho, S.T.B." Oxon. 1676, 8vo.

[c] Thomas Smith, of Queen's College, 1657; B.A. 1661; M.A. 1663; B.D. 1674: D.D. 1683. Fellow of Magdalen College, 1660; Master of Magdalen School, 1663; chaplain to Sir Daniel Harvey, 1668-71; and, about 1676, chaplain to Sir Joseph Williamson. Rector of Stanlake, 1684. Deprived of his fellowship by Dr. Gifford, the Popish President of Magdalen College, in 1688, and again in 1692, for refusing the oaths of allegiance. Died 1710.—Ath. Oxon. iv. 597.

at the presse, and soe far engaged to prosecute the worke thereof,'
that, although he should be nominated to London, he will not as he
hath declared accept of it, nor of the Bishoprick of Oxford, if
Compton[a] leave us, he beeing resolved as he sayth not [to] keep
pluralitys.[b] We are at present in great expectation of the Duke of
Southampton. Topham, his governour, hath already been here
and furnished his lodgeings. He would have been here er this,
had it not been for Peter Mews;[c] who putteing in for London, to
ingratiate himselfe with the Dutchesse and ingage her to befreind
him in his suit, hath carryed her the story of the small poxes beeing
here and diswaded her from sendeing him while the contagion is
among us; but Topham haveing been here and findeing our house
cleare of it saith this shal not retard his comeing, but will bring
him here about the end of this weeke or ye beginneing of ye next.
Harry Aldrich[d] is to be his tutour; what he will get by him I
know not. It is the generall desire among us that he come not.
I suppose you accompany the embassadours to Nimmegen,[e] although
you have not informed me thereof. If there [sic] departure be so
soon as is reported it will not be long I shall have the happynesse

[a] Henry Compton, Bishop of Oxford, translated to London, 18 December, 1675.

[b] Fell was elected Bishop of Oxford, 8 January, 1676, and got over his scruples so far as to retain his deanery.

[c] Peter Mews, or Meaux, educated at Merchant Taylors' School; St. John's College, 1637; afterwards Fellow. Served in the Royalist army. Archdeacon of Huntingdon and LL.D. 1660; Canon of Windsor, 1662; President of his college, 1667; Vice-Chancellor of the University, 1669-72. He became Dean of Rochester, 1670, and Bishop of Bath and Wells, 1672. Translated to Winchester, 1674. He served in the field against Monmouth. Died 1706 —*Ath. Oxon.* iv. 888.

[d] Henry Aldrich, Scholar of Westminster; Student of Christ Church, 1662; B.A. 1666; M.A. 1669; D.D. 1682. A noted tutor in his college. Canon of Christ Church, 1682; and Dean, 1689. Vice-Chancellor, 1692 and 1694. Besides being a theologian and scholar, he was fond of architecture, on which he wrote a small treatise. His name will be noticed in the next letter, in connexion with the building of St. Mary's Church. He is also said to have made designs for Peckwater and Canterbury quadrangles. Aubrey (*Letters by Eminent Persons*) adds that he was skilled in music, and that he indulged much in smoking.

[e] Ellis left England for Holland, 20 December, 1675.

of heareing from you soe often; however I hope you will not be soe much clogged with businesse but y* you will be able to find some time to let me know how you doe from thence.

[P.S.] New Colledge Tresury was robd last night, and out of it was taken in plate and other things to the value of 300¹. George Wall ª goeth to London on Monday in order to a journy into France. What is his businesse there I know not, unlesse it be to be John Locks chaplain, whom he accompanyeth thither.ᵇ On the 5ᵗʰ of November Tom Bennet ᶜ instructed us, who now oppenly acknowledgeth himselfe marryed, haveing taken a house in town, where he and his trul live togeather.

Oxf[ord], Aug. 6th, [16]76.

. . . . . . On my return I found Dʳ Trevor ᵈ and Mʳ Dobre,ᵉ fellows of Merton, Mʳ Warren,ᶠ fellow of Brasen Nose, Mʳ Owen,ᵍ fellow of All Souls, Dʳ Clayton,ʰ head of University Colledge, and Norton Bold,ⁱ on of the Esquire Beadles, to have dyed, and Dʳ

ª George Walls, Scholar of Westminster, and Student of Christ Church 1663; B.A. 1667; M.A. 1669; B.D. 1682; D.D. 1694. Prebendary of Worcester, 1694, and Rector of Holt, 1695. Died 1727.—Welch, 157.

ᵇ Locke resided abroad, for the benefit of his health, from December 1675 to May 1679.

ᶜ Probably Thomas Bennet, Scholar of Westminster and Student of Christ Church; B.A. 1666; M.A. 1669. After taking his degree he was appointed one of the correctors of the University press. Vicar of Steventon, and minister of Hunger-ford. Died 1681.—Welch, 154.

ᵈ Richard Trevor, M.D. of Padua. Incorporated 12 November, 1661. Died 17 July, 1676.—Fast. Oxon. ii. 251.

ᵉ William Dobrey, M.A.; Fellow of Merton, 1672.

ᶠ Edward Warren, M.A.

ᵍ Charles Owen, M.A.

ʰ Richard Clayton, D.D. Master of University College, 1665-76; Canon of Salis-bury, where he died, 10 June, 1676.—Fast. Oxon. ii. 291.

ⁱ Norton Bold, Superior Beadle of Divinity, 1671; formerly Fellow of Corpus Christi College.

Barlow[a] to have resigned his Margaret Professor's place in my absence. M[r] Walker[b] succeedeth D[r] Clayton, D[r] Hall,[c] of Pembroke, D[r] Barlow, and M[r] Minshow,[d] of New Colledge, Norton Bold. We have the sermon now every Sunday at Christ Church, a great deal of mony beeing now expendeing on S[t] Mary's to make it looke somewhat more like the Church of soe great a University; but, Harry Aldrich and Wheeler[e] beeing the cheife architects, I fear it will not be imployed at the best advantage. University Coll. is now all built up. At Trinity there are likewise new buildeings goeing on[f] At our presse I found printed an answare of the Earl of Clarendon to Hobbes Leviathan.[g] There are likewise in the presse an Historical Geographical and Philosophical Survey of Oxfordshire,[h] which will be a specimen of what the author D[r]

---

[a] Thomas Barlow, educated at Appleby; entered Queen's College in 1624; Fellow 1633; and eventually Provost, 1657. In 1646 "he sided with the men in power," and kept his fellowship during the Commonwealth. Keeper of the Bodleian Library 1652; D.D. 1660; and Margaret Professor of Divinity 1662. Archdeacon of Oxford 1664, and Bishop of Lincoln 1675. Wood makes him out a time-server, and adds that "he was esteemed by those who knew him to have been a thorough-paced Calvinist, tho' some of his writings show him to have been a great scholar, profoundly learned both in divinity and the civil and canon law." He died in 1691.—*Ath. Oxon.* iv. 333.

[b] Obadiah Walker. See above, p. 27, note [e].

[c] John Hall, D.D. Master of Pembroke College. Scholar 1647; M.A. 1653. He became a preacher during the Commonwealth, "but whether he was ordain'd by a Bishop, till the King's Restoration, I cannot tell." Elected Margaret Professor, 24 May, 1676; Bishop of Bristol, 1691. Died 1709.—*Ath. Oxon.* iv. 900.

[d] Christopher Minshull, B.A. 1661; M.A. 1665. Killed by a fall from his horse, 1681.

[e] Maurice Wheeler, B.A. of New Inn Hall, 1670; M.A. of Christ Church, 1670. Rector of St. Ebbe's, Oxford, and of Sibbertoft, co. Northampton. Afterwards head-master of Gloucester School.

[f] Very extensive buildings, including the new quadrangle, were carried on at Trinity College in 1675 and 1676, under the care of Dr. Bathurst.

[g] See above, p. 27, note [a].

[h] "The Natural History of Oxfordshire, being an Essay toward the Natural History of England. By Robert Plot, Doctor of Laws." Oxon. [1677] fol.

Plot[a] of Mag. Hall designeth of all England, and a Comentary
of D[r] Pococks on the Minor Prophets;[b] and those are the only
bookes of value which are at present to be expected from us . . . .

———— -- ——

. . . . I have little news worth sendeing you from this
place. We busy ourselfes still at the presse, but the London
printars are soe industrious to obstruct the sale of our bookes, that
I belcive they must of necessity breake us. We have since my
last put Jamblicus his workes[c] into the presse, beeing prepared
thereto by D[r] Gale,[d] schoolmaster of Paul's School. To contrive
the sale of our bookes we have set forth a proposal for subscriptions,
wherein we desire not paying any more before hand but only the
engageing of promise to buy such bookes as they like when printed.
I would put on of those proposals into this letter, but y[t] I remember
it is to goe a great way and therefore will be chargeable unto you.
Our bishop is likewise setteing forth another edition of Clements
Epistle to the Corinthians.[e] If you ever come hither again, you
will find S[t] Marys quite transmografyed; the old men, who are
always against innovation or alterations let it be ever soe much for
the better, exceedingly exclaim against it; how it will be for my
part I cannot tell till I see it finished. Glocester Hal is like to be

* Robert Plot, the celebrated naturalist, F.R.S.; entered Magdalen Hall, 1658.
He was the first keeper of the Ashmolean Museum. Historiographer Royal, 1688;
Mowbray Herald, 1694. Died 1696.
b See above, p. 42, note d.
c "Jamblicus Chalcidensis de Mysteriis. Epistola Porphyrii de eodem Argu-
mento, Gr. et Lat. ex versione Thomæ Gale." Oxon, 1678, fol.
d Thomas Gale, the famous Grecian, historian, and antiquary, F.R.S. Scholar of
Westminster; elected to Cambridge 1655; B.A. 1659; M.A. 1662; D.D. 1675.
Regius Professor of Greek, 1666; High Master of St. Paul's School, 1672; Prebendary of St. Paul's, 1677; Dean of York, 1697. Died 1702. His collection of
MSS. he gave to Trinity College, Cambridge.
e " S. Patris et Martyris Clementis ad Corinthios Epistola." Oxon. 1677, 12mo,

demolished, the charge of Chimny money [a] beeing soe great that
Byram Eaton [b] will scarce live there any longer. There hath been
noe schollers there these three or four years; for all which time the
hal beeing in arrears for this tax the collectors have at last fallen
upon the principal, who, beeing by the Act lyable to the payment,
hath made great complaints about the town and created us very
good sport; but the old fool hath been forced to pay the money,
which hath amounted to a considerable sum. We are now brought
to great extremity concerning the election of a new Vice-Chancelour,
we not knoweing whom to lay that office upon. D[r] Ironside [c] was
first designed, but, he haveing excused himselfe on the account of
his wont wherewith to support the dignity, it was put on D[r] Clark, [d]
head of Magd. Col., who hath likewise, pretendeing sicknesse,
excused himselfe; soe that it must on year more be conferred on
D[r] Barthurst, who seemeth willing enough to accept thereof,
hopeing y[t] it will at last get him a bishoprick, as it did his predecessor Mews. At All Souls there is great convascing against the
ensueing election, there beeing four dead places this year, the last
whereof was void by the death of Mr. Car, [e] formerly proctor, a
known boon blade of our town. Mr. Luzanzy, [f] of whom the bussle

[a] Chimney or Hearth-money, a tax of 2s. on every hearth.

[b] Byram Eaton, Fellow of Brasenose College; D.D. 1660; Principal of Gloucester
Hall, 1662-92; Archdeacon of Stow, 1677; and of Leicester, 1683. Died 1703.

[c] Gilbert Ironside, D.D. son of Gilbert Ironside, Bishop of Bristol, entered
Wadham College in 1649; Fellow, 1656; Warden, 1664; Vice-Chancellor, 1687
and 1688; Bishop of Bristol, 1689; translated to Hereford, 1691. Died 1701.

[d] Henry Clerk, M.D. He was Vice-Chancellor for this year.

[e] Alan Carr, M.A.; Proctor, 1671.

[f] Hippolyte du Chastlet de Luzancy, educated at the University of Paris, and
became a tutor and preacher for some years. He then came to England, and openly
abjured the Roman Catholic religion in the Savoy Chapel; and was consequently
violently attacked, a jesuit, named St. Germaine, threatening to assassinate him.
He was protected by the Bishop of London, and soon ordained. He went to Oxford,
and was allowed rooms and diet at Christ Church; and in 1676 was admitted M.A.
According to Wood he left Oxford in debt in 1679. He was afterwards Vicar of
Dovercourt, and in 1702 of South Weld, co. Essex. Died 1713.—*Fast. Oxon.*
ii. 350.

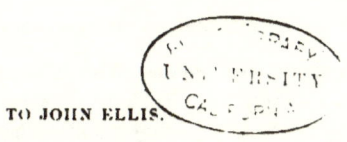

was last Session of Parliament, liveth still with us, and as far as I
can judge he is a very prudent sober man and a good schollar, but
exceedingly hated by the French Protestants at London as well as
by the Papists. The former have printed pamphlets against him,
wherein they horriblely asperse him. If he be an hypocrite, he is
an exceeding cunning on, haveing for all the time he hath been
here, which hath been for three-quarters of an year, soe behaved
himselfe as not to give the least occasion for any on to suspect his
reality or soundness of manners and integrity of life. Your tutor
is like to be marryed speedyly to Sr Blewet Stonehouses[a] sister,
with whom they say he is to have two thousand pounds. He is
very troublesom here, especially to me. The Lord Chancelour
haveing desired me to take his son[b] into my tuition, Woodruff
continually interposeth, and thereby creates me soe much trouble
and the yong lad soe much losse of time, that I se I must of
necessity quarrel with him, unlesse his marriage findeth him other
businesse. Publick news I will not trouble you with, since you
cannot but have much better intelligence thereof in the Ld.
Ambassadors house then any I can give him. Pray present my
service to Mr Morice,[c] Mr Morley, and as many as I know y^t are
with you.

— -

[Oxford.] Oct 31, [16]76.

I have yours, and humbly thanke you for the trouble you have
been pleased to take on yourselfe in sendeing to Amsterdam for

[a] Sir Blewet Stonehouse, of Amberden Hall, co. Essex, Bart.; died 1693.

[b] Charles Finch, fourth son of Lord-Chancellor Finch, of Christ Church; B.A.
1678; afterwards Fellow of All Souls; B.C.L. 1683; D.C.L. 1688. He died young.

[c] Henry Maurice, of Jesus College; B.A. 1668; M.A. 1671; B.D. 1679; D.D.
1683; Margaret Professor of Divinity, 1691. Early distinguished as a contro-
versialist. He accompanied Sir Leoline Jenkins to Nimeguen as his chaplain.
He was also chaplain to Archbishop Sancroft, 1683-91. Rector of Chevening, in
Kent; of Llandrillo, in the diocese of St. Asaph; and of Newington, co. Oxon.
He was also Prebendary of Worcester. Died 1691.—Ath. Oxon. iv. 326.

those bookes I writ you for.   The Misna of Caph Nachad [a] edition
I would willingly have, as likewise Juchasin.[b] If these 2 come to
above 16 or 18 shillings they are dear; however I would willingly
have them, although the price be greater; but, as for the other, I
now care not for them, we haveing got a very good collection of
Hebrews bookes in our library, where I can be furnished. We
bought them from the public library, out of which all duplicates
were lately sould to make more rome for other bookes.   The
Archbishop of Canterbury [c] beeing like to dy, we talk much here
as if S[r] Lionel Jinkings [d] were to goe into orders and succeed him.
If soe, I shall be glad of it on no other account then for your sake,
this beeing a designe layed by the Yorkish faction, who thinke S[r]
Lionel a complying man and therefore judge him the fittest for
their turn.   Your tutor D[r] Woodruffe is this week to be marryed
to on of S[r] Blewet Stonehouses sisters; they talk y[t] she is worth
3000[l]; if soe, I scarce think she would marry on with nothing,
especially beeing guided in this businesse by her father-in-law
Lental [e] and her mother, who are both to cunning to be cheated

[a] " Caph Nacath," commentary on the Mishna by Isaac Ibn Gabbai.
[b] The " Yuchasin " of Abraham ben Samuel Zacuto.
[c] Gilbert Sheldon, Archbishop of Canterbury, died 9 November, 1677.
[d] Sir Leoline Jenkins entered Jesus College in 1641; and became Fellow in 1660,
and soon after Principal and D.C.L.; Judge of the Admiralty Court, and of the
Prerogative Court in 1668.   He was sent on an embassy to France in 1669;
negociated the Treaty of Cologne, 1673-4; and was one of the Plenipotentiaries at
Nimegnen.   On the death of Archbishop Sheldon " all the report was that he was to
succeed to that See; " M.P. for Oxford University 1679-85; Secretary of State
1680-4. Died 1685. He was buried in Jesus College, of which he was a great
benefactor.—Fast. Oxon. ii. 231.
[e] John Lenthall, son of Speaker Lenthall, married, as his second wife, Mary,
widow of Sir James Stonehouse. Wood calls him " the grand braggadocio and lyer
of the age he lived in; bred in C.C.C. in this University, made early motions and
ran with the times, as his father did; was a recruiter of the Long Parliament,
consented to the trial of the King, was a colonel while Oliver was Protector, from
whom he received the town of Rutland on the 9 Mar. 1657, was one of the six
clerks in Chancery, and for a time Governor of Windsor Castle."   High Sheriff for
Oxfordshire 1672; knighted 1677. Died 1681.—Ath. Oxon. iii. 609.

by Woodruffe. I suppose 3000[1] may be promised, but Woodruffe
must get it where it can. Your old friend Peirce gets mony apace;
he made above 200[1] of his place last year. At Christmas he goeth
out. Christ Church is now altogether becom a stranger to you,
we beeing al almost your juniors. Cremer[a] and Keeling,[b] if you
know them, are lately cut of from us by marriage, and the later
since by death. Cremer hath marryed very wel, haveing above
2000[1] with his wife. I wonder how you have with patience
endured your long tarrying where you are. I scarce yet thinke
your treaty will come to any thing, but will, notwithstandeing the
States apointed a day for the opeueing of the assembly, breake up
without treateing till on side be well beaten; neither will hearken
to reasonable conditions. Our people here would fain have us goe
to war to. We shall see what will be don when the Parliament
meet. Old Cartret of Ano,[c] of whom you must have heard, is dead,
haveïng left behind him about an 120000[1] in mony and 8000[1] per
annum in land, a vast estate, which hath been collected togeather
by much thrift and niggardlynesse; but he that heaped it up had
not the power to dispose of it, he dying before he could make his
will, soe his mony is shared among his grandchildren, of which
2 little girles will have 25000[1] a peice, which before they are
marriageable will grow to a much greater sum. I suppose the
King may put in for some of his bastards. Y[t] which he hath here
with us[d] is kept very orderly, but will ever be very simple, and
scarce, I beleive, ever attain to the reputation of not beeing thought

---

[a] Acton Cremer, B.A. 1674: M.A. 1677.
[b] Venables Keeling, B.A. 1673; M.A. 1675.
[c] John Cartwright of Aynho, co. Northampton, twice Sheriff for Oxfordshire,
died 17 October, 1676. He married Catherine, daughter of William Noy, Attorney-
General, and had one son, William, who died before him. William Cartwright
married, first, Anne, daughter of Sir Roger Townsend, by whom he had two
daughters, Mary and Dorothy: and, second, Ursula, daughter of Ferdinando Lord
Fairfax, by whom he had surviving issue Thomas and Rhoda.—Bridge's *History of
Northamptonshire*, Oxon. 1791, i. 137.
[d] The Duke of Southampton.

a fool. If I can serve you in any thing here pray command me. I beleive there may now bee ougheing to you a pretty sum of mony from the College; if you soe order it, it shall be returned to you. My service to M[r] Morice, M[r] Morly, and M[r] Benson[a] if he be with you.

. . . . . You may tell Mr. Benson, in answare to his query, that M[r] Wal,[b] senior, is first of the junior m[rs] table (of which he is) and Penny last, and that his brother Jack is senior bachelor and prospereth mightyly here (to hear which I am sure will be a torment to him). Poor man! he is of a restlesse disposition, and in what station soever he be in he will never enjoy tranquillity of mind, but envy and discontent will perpetually be knawering there. Dr. South[c] and he are almost of the same disposition as to this point, perpetually discont[ent]ed. I suppose I have formerly given you an account that we sent a present to the Duke of Tuscany from the University[d] (Woods Antiquitys of Oxford, the Catalogue of the Library, Loggins Cuts of the Colledges, and D[r] Morisons Herbal), with a letter penned by D[r] South, and that we expected it would mightyly well be taken from us; but [we] have very much been

---

[a] One of Ellis's colleagues employed in the Secretary of State's Office.

[b] See above, p. 49, note [a].

[c] Robert South, D.D. Public Orator. Elected from Westminster to Christ Church 1651; B.A. 1655; M.A. 1657, when he was "Terræ filius;" D.D. 1663: Chaplain to the Earl of Clarendon, 1660; and to James Duke of York, 1667. Prebendary of Westminster, 1663; Canon of Christ Church, 1670; Rector of Islip, 1678. He was famous as a preacher, and, as such, called " the scourge of fanaticism." Wood gives an unfavourable character of him, that at Westminster " he obtained a considerable stock of grammar and philological learning, but more of impudence and sauciness," and that he trimmed to every party in turn. Busby is said to have remarked of him when at school, " I see great talents in that sulky boy, and I shall endeavour to bring them out." He died in 1716.—*Ath. Oxon.* iv. 631; Welch, 136.

[d] See above, p. 46.

deceived in our expectations, the Duke scarce takeing any notice of
it or showeing the least civility to the person that delivered it,
which is solely to be attributed to the D[rs] letter, which I thinke
the absurdest that was ever sent from any publick society where
learneing is professed; it containeing nothing else but hyperbolical
praises of the present sent, and those to very dull ons, without
passeing any complement to the person to whom it was sent, which
ought to be the whole subject of this letter; and this gave such
distast to the Duke that he tooke noe notice of the present but
seemed reather angry that we should accost him in soe rude a
manner. Great persons expect enconiums and complements to the
higth of flattery, especially in Italy where this art is soe much
practiced, and therefore the omission of it was accounted rudenesse,
and our present wrought a quite contrary effect to what we expected.
The Ld Mohun [a] my country man is, contrary to every ons expectations, recovered of his wound. When he lay at the point of death
he behaved himselfe very stupidly at in reference to his concern
for a future life, Ashley haveing been with him and infused his
principles into him. I thinke I told you in my last that he hath
wrot a booke against the eternity of hell torments,[b] a good step to
athisme. The next progresse we expect from him will be to deny
them altogeather, and the reather because he knows if there be any
such he is sure to goe to them; and this in effect my Ld of Anglesy [c]
told him, who is of late turnd of late a great divine, and hath wrot

---

[a] Charles, fourth Lord Mohun, father of the notorious duellist. He appears, after
all, to have died from the effects of his wound, the result of a duel, about Michaelmas
1677, if Wood is right in stating that "Casus Medico-Chirurgicus, or a most
memorable Case of a Nobleman deceased, by Gideon Harvey, M.D.," refers to him.
He was a zealous member of Shaftesbury's party. The Mohuns were a Cornish
family.

[b] No doubt "The Foundations of Hell Torments shaken and removed," a
pamphlet published at this time, to which an answer was written by the Rev. John
Brandon with the title "Everlasting Fire no Fancy," 1678.

[c] Arthur Annesley, Earl of Anglesey. "Truth unveiled on behalf of the Church
of England." London. 1676, 8vo.

a booke in defence of Dr Tully concerneing justification by faith,[a] but it is a very shallow on. Sr Charles Wosely[b] hath lately exceedingly well stated that point contrary to my lord's and Dr Barlow sense of it, which hath much offended them both. The Earles son[c] is in orders, and is on of our Lent preachers at St Peters this year; he seems to be a sober honest gentleman. Dr Floyd[d] hath a new booke come out containeing a project for suppresseing popery,[e] which he would have don by soweing divisions among them here by encourageing the seculars against the regulars, betwoen which there hath been a long controversy in England. My friend Mr. Bernard,[f] who went into France to attend on the 2 bastards of Cleveland, hath been soe affronted and abused there by that insolent woman that he hath been forced to quit that imployment and return. She driveth a cunneing trade and followeth her old imployment very hard there, especially with the Arch Bishop of Paris,[g] who is her principal gallant. At Trinity Colledge at Cambridge there are mighty doeings, they beeing there buildeing a library[h]

---

[a] Thomas Tully, D.D., Dean of Ripon, died 1676. His book, "Justificatio Paulina," was answered by Richard Baxter.

[b] Sir Charles Wolseley. "Justification Evangelical, or a Plain Impartial account of God's method in justifying a sinner." London, 1677, 8vo.

[c] Richard Annesley of Magdalen College, M.A. 1670; B.D. 1677; D.D. 1689; Dean of Exeter 1680. Succeeded his nephew as Lord Altham, and died 1701.

[d] An error for Lloyd. William Lloyd, D.D. entered Oriel College 1639; Scholar of Jesus College, 1640, and afterwards Fellow; B.A. 1642; D.D. 1667. Rector of Bradfield; Prebendary of Ripon, 1660; Vicar of St. Mary's, Reading, and Archdeacon of Merioneth, 1668; Dean of Bangor, 1672; Canon of Salisbury, 1674; Vicar of St. Martin's, Westminster, 1676; Bishop of St. Asaph, 1680; translated to Lichfield 1692, and to Worcester 1699. Besides being a good preacher, divine, critic, and historian, he was "a zealous enemy to Popery and Papists." Died 1717.—*Ath. Oxon.* iv. 714.

[e] "Considerations touching the true way to suppress Popery in this Kingdom . . . . on occasion whereof is inserted an historical Account of the Reformation here in England." London, 1677, 4to.

[f] See above, p. 40.

[g] François de Harlay de Champ-Valon.

[h] Trinity College Library was built from designs supplied gratuitously by Sir Christopher Wren. It was several years building.

which will cost 16000[1], and they doe this that there Colledge may without dispute be granted to exceed ours. I am glad their æmulation hath produced soe good effects. We shall goe on buildeing to, as soon as spring begins. Old Busby hath long talked to us of a benefaction he intends to bestow upon us for the erecteing of a catachist lecture [in] the University, but hath soe many cautions in his head and adjoynes such hard conditions with it that the University cannot receive it.[a] The old man a little before Christmas spit blood and thought he should have immediately dyed, but when I was with him I thought him as well as ever I saw him since I knew him. Knipe[b] hath quite ruined that school by his neglect to ly in the Colledge. Sprat[c] hath marryed the other sister after she had been his and the Duke of Buckingams whore many years. My service to Mr. Dolbin,[d] who you were pleased to mention in your last was soe kind as to remember me. I pray likewise remember me to what others of my acquaintance are with you.

---

[a] Busby gave to Christ Church a stipend of 30l. a year for a catechetical lecture to be read in one of the parish churches of Oxford.

[b] Thomas Knipe, Scholar of Westminster; elected to Christ Church, 1657; B.A. 1660; M.A. 1663. First an under-master, and afterwards successor to Busby as head-master of Westminster, his service as a teacher amounting in all to fifty years; D.D. 1695. Busby is said to have had a poor opinion of him, but he seems to have been esteemed by his pupils. He died 1711.—Welch, 147.

[c] Thomas Sprat, D.D. Entered Wadham College, 1651; B.A. 1654; M.A. 1657; D.D. 1669. He was chaplain to George, Duke of Buckingham; Prebendary of Westminster, 1668; Canon of Windsor, 1680; Dean of Westminster, 1683; and Bishop of Rochester, 1684. He made some attempts as a poet in his younger days, and was, according to Wood, known at Oxford as " Pindaric Sprat." The reference to his marriage will remind the reader of Macaulay's description, in his third chapter, of the state of the clergy under Charles the Second, and of their choice of wives. As far, however, as Sprat is concerned, we may presume that there was no truth in the scandal, as in his will he refers to his wife in terms of affection and esteem.

[d] This is perhaps John Dolben, second son of the Archbishop of York, and who appears to have been attached to the English embassy in Paris in 1680 and following years.

[Oxford, June or July? 1677.]

. . . . . Old Vernon[a] hath miscarryed, and the spirit of Tom Coriot[b] is extinct in him, he beeing kild at Hispahan in Persia by some Armenian merchants with whom he quarrcld about a knife they had taken from him. He had with him a huge bundle of observations, which are all lost.[c] His designe was for China. I fancy, if he had returned in safety, he would have given us relations of his travels which might have been very acceptable, but his ill nature was inconsistant with the designe he undertooke, and there-fore he miscarryd in it. Your tutor D[r] Woodruffe lives not with us here now, haveing taken an house at Knightsbridge, to be near the court, where he at present resides. We have here set forth the Philosophical History of Oxfordshire,[d] and are now on a designe of erecteing a Lecture for Philosophicall History to be read by the author[e] of that booke; to which end, as soon as we are agreed on the ground, we shall built a school on purpose for it with a

---

[a] Francis Vernon, Scholar of Westminster, and Student of Christ Church in 1654; B.A. 1657; M.A. 1660; F.R.S. 1672. In 1669 he was secretary to Ralph Montagu, Ambassador at Paris. He was a great traveller, and on one occasion was captured by pirates. In 1677, " being in Persia, arose between him and some of the Arabs a small quarrel concerning an English peaknife that Mr. Vernon had with him; who shewing himself cross and peevish in not communicating it to them, they fell upon him and hack'd him to death."—*Ath. Oxon.* iii. 1133.

[b] Thomas Coryate, " esurient of fame " and " a whetstone for wits of his time," was a commoner of Gloucester Hall, 1596. He was received into the family of Henry, Prince of Wales, " at which time falling into the company of the wits, who found him little better than a fool in many respects, made him their whetstone, and so became *notus nimis omnibus.*" In 1608 he travelled in Europe, and published his " Crudities hastily gobled up in five months' travel in France, Savoy," etc. 1611. In 1612 he set out again, and, making his way overland to India, stayed some time at Agra. He became very proficient in the native dialects. Wood tells an amusing story of his silencing " a Laundry-woman, a famous scold," in her own Hindustani. He died at Surat, 1617.—*Ath. Oxon.* ii. 208.

[c] Vernon's journal is, however, preserved in the library of the Royal Society.

[d] See above, p. 50, note [b].

[e] Robert Plot.

labratory annext and severall other rooms for other uses, whereof
on is to hold John Tredeskins[a] raritys, which Elias Ashmole,[b] in
whose hands they are, hath promised to give to the University as
soon as we have built a place to receive them. We have new
buildeings likewise goeing on in Christ Church, part of which will
be a tower for astronomical observations. To our library likewise
we have made a very considerable addition, so that now we have
room to receive 4000 volumnes more, if any on would be soe kind
as to give them to us. Baliol hath lately received a considerable
benefaction of this nature, on of the best private librarys in England
beeing given that colledge by legacy on the death of the gentleman
that owned it.[c] There is a booke of the L[d] Cheife Justice Hales[d]
come forth since his death. The subject is to prove the creation of
man against the different hypotheses of the atheists. Burnet hath
writ an history of the late rebellion in Scotland till Worcester fight,

---

[a] Hans Tradescant, botanist and traveller. He settled in England about 1600,
was gardener to Charles I. and owned some large gardens at Lambeth. He formed
a good collection of natural objects, coins, medals, etc. Some account of him is to
be found in "A Letter from Dr. Ducarel, F.R.S. and F.S.A. to William Watson,
M.D., F.R.S. upon the early cultivation of Botany in England." Lond. 1763, 4to.

[b] Elias Ashmole, son of a saddler of Lichfield, born in 1617. In his youth he was a
chorister in the cathedral. He went up to seek his fortunes in London in 1633, under
the patronage of James Paget, Junior Baron of the Exchequer, a connexion by marriage. In 1638 he became a solicitor with Chancery practice, but left London on
the outbreak of the Civil War. In 1644 he entered Brasenose College, and during
the wars lived at various places, studying as an astronomer, chemist, and antiquary.
In 1660 he was appointed Windsor Herald, and was called to the Bar; F.R.S., M.D.,
1669. In 1677 he offered to the University all his coins, medals, MSS. and the
rarities which he had obtained "of a famous gardener called Joh. Tredescant, a
Dutchman," if a building were raised to receive them; but lost many of them in the
fire in the Middle Temple, in 1678. The Ashmolean Museum was built in 1679-82,
and his collections were then removed thither. He died in 1692.—*Ath. Oxon.*
iv. 354.

[c] Sir Thomas Wendy, of Haselingfield, co. Cambridge, K.B. sometime gentleman
commoner of Balliol College, bequeathed to it, in 1673, his library, valued at 600l.,
which was removed to Oxford in 1677.

[d] Sir Matthew Hale. "The primitive origination of Mankind considered and
explained according to the light of Nature." London, 1677, folio.

which he calleth the Memoires of Duke Hamilton.[a] It is a large
folio, and to the composeing of it he was assisted with all the
papers of that Duke, and likewise those of his brother[b] who was
Secretary of State in Scotland through all those times.   D[r] Outram[c]
hath set forth a learned booke de Sacrificiis.   The subject of it is
in the first part to describe the ancient manner of sacrifices both
among the heathen and Jews, in the latter to prove the sacrifice of
Christ against the Socinians.   D[r] Cudworths[d] booke against Hobs
is expected, but as yet comes not forth.   There is a second pacquet
of advices to the men of Shaftsbury,[e] who take heart again now on
the late adjournment of the Parliament.   I am now goeing into
Wales to take possession of a sine cure[f] given me there on the
death of D[r] Barrow[g] by the L[d] Chancelour, soe that if you for a
while receive noe letters from me you must impute it to my
absence.

[Oxford], Dec. 12, [16]78.

. . . . I thanke [you] for your news but have not any to return
you; only we have left of here to pray for the Queen by the title of

[a] "Memoirs of the Lives and Actions of James and William, Dukes of Hamilton,
etc. in which an Account is given of the Rise and Progress of the Civil Wars of
Scotland, with other Transactions, both in England and Germany, from the year
1625 to 1652." London, 1677, folio.

[b] William, Earl of Lanark, afterwards Duke of Hamilton.

[c] William Outram, D.D. Canon of Westminster. "De sacrificiis libri duo:
quorum altero explicantur omnia Judæorum nonnulla Gentium Profanarum sacri-
ficia, altero Sacrificium Christi." London, 1677, 4to.

[d] Ralph Cudworth, D.D. Master of Christ's College, Cambridge, and Professor of
Hebrew. "The true Intellectual System of the Universe: wherein the Reason and
Philosophy of Atheism is confuted," etc. London, 1678, folio.

[e] "A second Pacquet of Advices and Animadversions. Sent to the men of Shaftsbury. Occasioned by several Seditions Pamphlets," etc. London, 1677, 4to.

[f] The Rectory of Llanddewi-Felfrey, in Pembrokeshire.

[g] Isaac Barrow, D.D. Master of Trinity College, Cambridge, died 4 May, 1677.

most gracious. It was the conceit of a foolish phantasticall fellow we have for on of our chaplings that the Queen, been faln from grace (as he concludes from Oats's accusation), was not to be prayed for by the title of most gracious; and therefore, yesterday, it beeing his turn to read prayers, he omitted that title; but notwithstandeing, the censor laying down his office last night, we made this gentleman at his chamber drinke her health by the title of most gracious . . . .

_____

[Oxford], Jan. 5, [16]7⅚.

. . . . . . As to the gentleman for whom you desire a method of readeing the Greek and Latin historys, he may receive better information from Degory Whears[a] booke, "de Methodo legendi Historias," then any that I can give you. If he be a gentleman, Dr. Hoels Universal History[b] in English will be sufficient for him; but if he be a schollar, and desires to read the best historians in the original, for the Greeke he must begin with Herodotus, wherein he will find a ful history of the wars of the Persians with that people in the time of Darius and his son Xerxes. Thucydides begins where he leaves of, and Xenophon continues Thucydides till the end of the empire of the Thebans, which was extinct with their captain Epaminandos, slain at the battle of Mantinea; after this the actions of King Philip and his son Alexander succeed in the order of time, and are fully related by Diodorus Siculus; but as to the life of Alexander, I judge it best written by Arrian; the wars of Alexanders captains about the division of his empire you have likewise related in Diodorus Siculus. What comes after are actions for the most part soe obscure as that they deserve noe historian, and I know none they have except Polybius, and his relations are reather of the Roman then

* Degory Wheare, Camdenian Professor of History at Oxford, died 1647. " Lectiones Hiemales de ratione et methodo legendi Historias Civiles et Ecclesiasticas."
b William Howell, LL.D. Chancellor of Lincoln. "An Institution of General History." London, printed for Henry Herringman, 1662, folio.

Greek affaires, Greece in his time beeing made a province of the Roman Empire. As to the Roman history, Dionysius Halicarnassensis must be begun with; if your gentleman would reather read it in Latin then Greek, the translation of Æmilius Porta is much the best, and the best edition is that of Geneva.[a] The original and first foundation of the Roman Empire is noe where better treated of then in this author, which I thinke to be much the best of any that relates the actions of ancient times and the most diverting. Livy may be read with him, and continues likewise the history where Dionysius leavs of, which is at the abolishing the government of the Decemviri. The second decade of Livy is wonteing, and with it likewise the history which he related in it, scarce any other author affordeing any narration of it, exceptceing some summary accounts which you will find in the Epitomy of L. Florus, and in the first booke of Polybius The third decade of Livy fully relates the second Carthaginian war, and the fourth those actions which followed with the Macedonians and other nations, of which likewise you have an account in those bookes of Polybius which are preserved from the injurys of time. From the time when Livy failes you, you must be contented with what Plutarch tels you in the lifes of Marius, Sylla, Lycurgus, and Cicero, till Dio Cassius comes in, who, from the piratical war till the death of the Emperour Claudius, gives you a full and most excellent history. The best edition of this author is by Leunclavius,[b] in Greek and Latin. I need not tell you that Salust, Cæsar in his Commentarys, Tacitus and Suetonius likewise treat of affaires within the same compasse of time, and that the 2 last continue their historys down farther. Appian is likewise to be consulted, particularly where he treats of the wars of Mitridates and the civil wars of the Romans with themselfes. The Mercurius

---

[a] "Dionysius Halicarnassensis. Antiquitatum Romanorum libri xi. ab Æmilio Porto et post aliorum Interpretationes Latine redditi." Geneva, 1614, 12mo.

[b] "Dion Cassius. Rom. Hist. libb. xlvj. Gr. Lat. partim integri, partim mutili, partim excerpti, Joannis Leunclavii studio tam aucti quam expoliti," etc. Hanov. 1606, folio.

Librarius[a] tells me that it is this term set forth in English.[b] For the ensueing times are to be read Xiphilin, Herodian, and the Historiæ Augustæ Scriptores, and, if you will goe farther down, Zosimus and Ammianus Marcellinus, which, although to his language is very barbarous, is however a most excellent author. In the readeing of both sort of historys, Plutarch is to be used, because he writes the lives both of Romans and Grecians. Simpsons Chronology[c] will be of exceeding use in directeing to the true order of time, and he that intends to have a full prospect of the Greek and Latin history cannot be without it. In reading the Roman history it is to be observed the faithfullest relators of it are the Grecians, and that more is to be learnt from them then the Roman writers themselfes, and therefore I judge Dionysius and Dio in those things they treat of are to be preferred to Livy and Tacitus. The hast I am in permits me not to give you a fuller account. If the gentleman desire a short account and an easy way to it, you cannot put a better booke into his hands then D[r] Hoels General History set forth by Haringman; but, if he be a schollar, give him M[r] Whears booke and bid him follow the method he prescribes; but, if you thinke not this sufficient, I shall be ready when I have more leasure, in an half-sheet of paper, to give him a full and ample account of all authors and their best editions which treat of those affaires he desires to inform himselfe in . . . . . .

Oxford, Feb. 23, [16]7$\frac{3}{4}$.

I am greatly in your debt for many letters and much kindnesse. Your designe of gaineing me to be tutor to the Earle of Ossorys

---

[a] The Mercurius Librarius must have been an ephemeral publication, which has not surrived to the present day.

[b] "Appian's History, in two parts . . . . made English by J. D." London, 1679, folio.

[c] Edward Simpson, D.D. "Chronicon Historiam Catholicam complectens. ab orbe condito ad annum Christi 71." Oxon, 1652, folio.

son [a] I esteem as great an obligation as if it had succeeded. His governour [b] brought me your letter, and I shall be very glad if I can be in any thing serviceable to him while he tarrys here. Two others of yours by the post I confesse to have received since I writ any; the busines of our election, in which I am particularly concernd for Mr Solicitor,[c] hath soe taken us all up here yt the obligation I tooke on my selfe of sendeing you a method of readeing the Greeke and Latin historians for the gentleman you desire is not yet performed, and on that account I deferred to write to you, hopeing dayly I should find time to satisfy your desires; but now despaireing to have it till this businesse be over I must beg your pardon that I send it not with this. Next Thursday will be the decideing day. Our candidates are Mr Solicitor, Dr Edesbury,[d] and Dr Lamphire;[e] I doubt not but that the former will be on; of the other two its not a halfepenny to chuse. A great deal of bussle and noise hath been made about it.[f] Williamson first stood, but found such opposition that he was forced to desist. As soon as I have leasure you shall again hear from me.

[a] James Butler, son of the gallant Earl of Ossory. He entered at Christ Church; M.A. 1680; D.C.L. 1683. He succeeded his grandfather as Duke of Ormonde and Chancellor of the University of Oxford in 1688.

[b] P. Drelincourt. Some of his letters are among the Ellis Correspondence (Brit. Mus. Add. MSS. 28875 *et seqq.*), and are sometimes endorsed " Dr. Drelincourt."

[c] Heneage Finch, second son of the Lord Chancellor.

[d] John Edisbury, of Brasenose, LL.D. 1672. Afterwards Master in Chancery and Chancellor of Exeter.

[e] John Lamphire, M A., Fellow of New College and Camden Professor of History. M.D. 1660; Principal of Hart Hall. Died 1688.

[f] " 19 Feb. 1679.—Convocation, wherein letters were read from the Chancellor on behalf of Mr. Heneage Finch, Solicitor-general, to be one of our burgesses to sit in Parliament, purposely to set aside Dr. Eadisbury. of Brazennose, who audaciously, and with too much conceit of his own worth, stood against the said Mr. Finch, Dr. Lamphire, and Dr. Yerbury; but a week before Dr. Yerbury put off his votes to Finch, for fear Eddisbury should carry it. Note that Dr. Eddisbury stood in 1675 against him and Sir Christopher Wren, but, being soundly geered and laughed at for an impudent fellow, desisted."—Wood, *Life*, lxxxiii. Edisbury and Finch were returned.

[Oxford], June 18th, [16]79.

We have now quite finished your businesse, your letter having passed the Convocation this afternoon, soe y^t now you have nothing else to doe but to come hither when your occasions will give you leave, and, on the performance of those exercises I mentioned to you in my last, take your degree. The Scotch businesse being over,^{a} I hope I shall have the happynesse of seeing you here this summer; but as to the businesse of your degree, y^t cannot be don but in term time, as your occasions will give you leave. I would advise you to provide your lectures and declamations; as to the other exercises, they are only form and will signify nothing to trouble you. I mus[t] beg your assistance in a small affair; from my sine cure in Wales I am charged with the arrears of 6 years tenths due in my predecessors time, and likewise with 19^s charges for each year, soe that the whole amounts to 9^l od mony, whereas in reality there is not above 4^l due. About 7 years since the knavery of some officers in the Exchequer had brought it to this, that if any incumbent should neglect his payments of tenths he was forthwith charged with 19^s for the neglect each year; but on complaint made this abuse was rectifyed, and an order made y^t noe commissioner for the collecteing of arrears shall charge on the under collector above 5^s 8^d, to be received by him with the arrears for how many years soever they were to be payd. But the diocese of St Davids beeing a great way of, those rogues of the Exchequer thinke they may play their old tricks there among the poor Welchmen without control. He that issueth out those commissions is on Pretyman, who keeps his office somewhere about the Exchequer; on enquiry you may easyly find him out, he beeing the cheife man concerned in receiving the Kings tenths and first fruits there. I desire y^t you would be pleased to talke with him

---

^{a} The rising of the Scottish Covenanters was finally quelled by Monmouth at Bothwell Bridge on the 22nd June.

about this affaire, and knowe from him what is due to the King for
the tenthes from the rectory of Landewy-belfry, in the dioccsse
of Pembroke and deanery of Carmarden, and what he demands for
charges. If he tells you 19ˢ each year, pray ask him wither there
was not an order lately made that noe incumbent on the payment
of arrears, especially such as were due in his predecessors time,
should be liable to pay above 5ˢ 8ᵈ for charges; and how comes it
to passe that that order is not observed in the dioccsse of Sᵗ Davids
as in all others, and particularly in this, where the collector (who is
the bishops man) assures me he never received above 5ˢ and 8ᵈ
ever since he managed that office for charges with arrears for how
many years soever. I am unwilling a rogue should cheat me of
5ˡ if I can helpe it. I have enterest with them yᵗ can doe me right,
and I am resolved I will complain, and desire, if your occasions
will give you leave to talke with this fellow, yᵗ you would tell him
as much. I beg your pardon for presumeing soe far on you, but
since Westminster Hall is soe near, and your other occasions soe
often call you there, I hope it may be noe great trouble to you
to talke with this fellow. I am concerneing more for the poor
Welch men then myselfe, who I doubt not imposed on on all
occasions with such knaverys, and I would willingly doe them
right; although as to myselfe my case is hard enough to pay my
predecessors arrears, and much more to pay charges likewise for his
neglect. Drelincourts weaknesse dayly appears more and more,
and I fear it is a great prejudice to the yong Lord that soe simple
a fellow should have the government of him; I fear he teacheth
him many mean silly trickes much misbecomeing a person of his
quality, but from wᵗ you told me in London I fear there cannot be
a remedy. I wish you all happynesse.

[Oxford]. July 10th, [16]79.

. . . . . . We are now ready for the Act; it begins next Friday and lasts till Tuesday. Our proceeders in divinity are D[r] Jane,[a] D[r] Ken,[b] and D[r] Hinkly,[c] your acquaintance M[r] Hinkleys ffather; but the heat of the weather haveing ill effects on me, I suppose I shall not be at any of their performances. Of D[r] Lockys[d] death and his successor I suppose you have heard; the old man dyed at short warneing, haveing been indisposed not above 3 days before he deceased. He was never sick before in his life, neither in this did feel much pain, but departed out of perfect decay of spirits, as a lamp that goeth out for wont of oyl. D[r] Killegrew[e] is his sole executor and its supposed will get 800[l] by him, if not more. The warden of Winchester, D[r] Birt,[f] beeing dead, our Vice-Chancelour[g] is to be translated from New Coll. to succeed him, that is from 200[l] per annum to 700[l] per annum. D[r] Beeson,[h] the schoolmaster of

[a] William Jane, Scholar of Westminster, Student of Christ Church 1660; B.A. 1664; M.A. 1667; B.D. 1674; D.D. 1679. Canon of Christ Church and Regius Professor of Divinity, 1680; Dean of Gloucester, 1685; Chancellor of Exeter, 1703.

[b] Thomas Ken, educated at Winchester, Fellow of New College; M.A. 1664; B.D. 1678; D.D. 1679; Bishop of Bath and Wells, 1684. One of the Seven Bishops. Deprived in 1690 for refusing the oaths of allegiance and supremacy. Died 1711.

[c] John Hinckley, of St. Alban's Hall; Vicar of Coleshull, co. Berks, of Drayton, co. Leicester, and of Northfield, co. Worcester; and Prebendary of Wolverhampton.

[d] Thomas Lockey, D.D., Canon of Christ Church. Formerly a celebrated tutor and antiquary, and Keeper of Bodley's Library. He died 29 June, 1679, aged 78. He was succeeded in his canonry by John Hammond.

[e] Henry Killigrew, son of Sir Robert Killigrew, of Christ Church, 1628; chaplain in the King's army; Prebendary of Westminster, 1642; Almoner to the Duke of York and Rector of Wheathamstead, 1660; Master of the Savoy, 1661. He was the father of Anne Killigrew, on whose death Dryden wrote an elegy in 1685.

[f] William Burt, D.D. Fellow of New College, 1627; master of the free school at Thame; Rector of Whitfield and Head-master of Winchester College, 1647; and Warden, 1658. Died 8 July, 1679.

[g] John Nicholas, D.D. Warden of New College.

[h] Henry Beeston, LL.D. Head-master of Winchester College, and Prebendary of Winchester. Warden of New College, 7 August, 1679.

Winchester, its supposed, will come hither to fill the place the
Vice-Chancelour leavs; but as to those affairs I suppose you are
not much concernd, and therefore I will trouble you noe farther
with them.

[Oxford], July 29th, [16]79.

. . . . . Pray in your next do me the favour to let me know on
w^t terms Oats stands since the last tryall, and how people are satisfied
with Wakemans^a escape. I much fear that this businesse at last
will appear very foul and render us odious and contemptible through
all Europe. I know not what to thinke of it. On Coll. Vernon ^b
comes hither to stand to be Parliament man, under the title of my
Ld of Ossorys friend; but that will not doe his businesse. We
laugh at him for a fool, and soe he will come of. He is a person
we never heard of or knew before his appearing here, and since,
on examination, we find y^t his wife and all his children are papists,
and therefore we much admire ye presumption of the man, y^t he
should thinke he must be regarded here. I know not whom we
shall choose, none as yet appearing worthy of our choice. Secretary
Coventry ^c and Sr Leonel Jinkings may be, if they will appear for
it, but y^t is left to their own discretion.

---

^a Sir George Wakeman, one of the Queen's physicians; put upon his trial for
designing to poison the King, and acquitted, 18 July, 1679.

^b Perhaps Colonel Edward Vernon, of North Aston, co. Oxon. on whom the
honorary degree of LL.D. was conferred in 1677.

^c Henry Coventry, Secretary of State. 1672-80.

[Oxford], October 19, [16]79.

I suppose you now begin to thinke of Spain, and since the Queen [a] is now arrived there it will not be long er my L[d] [b] carrys the complement after her. The yong L[d] James of late growing to hard for his governour, I perceive he hath made complaints of it, and that was the occasion of S[r] Robert Southwells [c] comeing

[a] Marie Louise, daughter of Philippe, Duc d'Orléans, married to Charles II. of Spain in August, 1679.

[b] Thomas, the gallant Earl of Ossory, to whom Ellis served as secretary from 1678 to 1680, was to have gone as Envoy Extraordinary to Spain on this occasion. This design was, however, thwarted by the intrigues of the Earl of Warwick, and a simple congratulatory letter was sent instead.—Carte, *Life of James Duke of Ormonde*, ii. 506.

[c] Sir Robert Southwell, Secretary of State for Ireland, 1690-1702. An original letter preserved in the British Museum (Add. MS. 28103, f. 70) from the Duke of Ormonde to his grandson "the young Lord James," so well illustrates Prideaux's remarks, and is withal so characteristic, that, in spite of its length, it is here inserted—

"Cornbury, 16 of Feb. '8⅔.

" Besides y[e] many casualtys that put an end to our fraile lives, and to w[ch] all ages and conditions of men are subiect, I have livd so many years already that I can not hope or wish to passe over many more in this world without falling into such a degree of folly and dotage as I hope God will keepe me from, and in y[e] other world I think time will hee no more measurd. Upon this consideration I have thought it to bee parte of my duty to leave you (who I hope will long survive mee and fill my roome) such usefull admonitions and instructions as so long a life in such times and in such imployments as I have had might inable mee to compose, if my education and talent had bin equall to my experience; but those defects will in some measure bee supplyd in that you may hee shure my advices will bee y[e] best I can give, and that they will have no obiect or designe but y[r] honour and compleat hapynesse.

" In y[e] discours I meane to leave you (if God gives mee time to perfect it) it is lyke I shall endeavour to give you y[e] best rules I can think of, how and by what markes and qnalifications you may most probably make good choyce of friends and confidents, I meane such as you may safly rely upon and open y[r] thoughts freely unto; and amongst those rules one will certainly bee that you shall take into y[r] confidence aud trust such as are of y[e] same principles I am, and have manifested them as I have done, tho in different coniunctures, times, and stations, and have

hither, for since the Monsr hath engaged with Aldrich in beateing his pupil, ye yong Bartlet, he and his mirmidons have made it their

faithfully discharged ye trusts I have reposed in them; and this brings mee, after perhaps too long a preamble, to y^r designe of this leter.

" It doth not allways hapen that ye posterity of Parents who have bin good and possibly intimat friends continue to bee so; but where it falls out to continue, there ye friendship aquires confirmation and increas by desent. Sr Robert Southwell's Father and Grandfather were very affectionat friends to mine. My Mother at her first comeing into Ireland was intertaind at his Grandfather's house, and that for a good whyle, for there my Sister Clancartie was born. His Father was well known to mee for above forty yeares; and some of them were yeares of tryall, in wch many fell not only from their obligations of loyalty to ye Crown, but from those of friendship and gratitude to mee; but Sr Robert's Father never swervd from loyallty, but, on y^r contrary, imployd his paines and his purs to serve ye King in times and things of danger when there was very small expectation of any return of profit or advancement; and tho hee performd this duty of a good subiect as such, yet I know hee did it ye more cheerfully for that ye Kings affaires of all sortes in that kingdom were then managed by and under me, for till his death, wch tooke him in a good old age, he continued his concernment for all things relateing to mee and my familly, and dureing my government and his life since his late Maties return hee has discharged what he had in comand and comission in relation to ye publick with great dilligence and ahillity.

" My acquaintance with his sonne Sr Robert is of about 23 yeares standing, and began upon his return from travell in foraigne partes, by wch he had so profited that I was extreamly pleased to finde in ye person of ye sonne and grandsonne of antient and usefull friends to mee and my familly one that I could with confidence recomend to ye late King my Ma^{rs} service, into wch hee was recev'd, and for 16 yeares discharged all ye partes given him with remarkable fidelity and successe, and with such indefatigable industry and aplication that, haveing almost distroyd his helth by that labour and ye variety of y^r climats hee was sent into, hee was compelld to retire from businesse with ye leave and ye favour of ye King. In y^r time hee serv'd ye King at home and abroad there hapened some changes in my condition, sometimes I was imployd and sometimes others in ye government of Ireland, and sometimes and in some things my credit at court seemd to bee more and sometimes lesse, as there hapened designes to bee layd and changes proiected, such as I was more or lesse thought fit to bee consulted in or to execute; but in all these changes I never found any in Sr Robert Sonthwell's friendship to mee, or for ye concerne hee formerly profest to have for my honour and for ye advantage of my family, but, on y^r contrary, his afection to mee and care of my interest appeard to hee more warm when others thought mee under a cloud and quit mee, then when ye sun shone more conspicuously upon mee.

" The paines he tooke to bring you ye hapynesse and my family the blesseing of

businesse to make him contemptable to his L^d, and have soe far
effected it as I see he hath little heed to be governed by him. This
is a wicked trick, but such as we must expect from such people.
I have some thoughts of goeing into Cornwall this winter; if they
hold, I shall see you before you leave England. I have of late had
a pleasant encounter with Coll. Vernon, wch I cannot but give you
an account of. On his standeing to be Parliament man for the
University, I, haveing occasion to visit a kinsman of mine that
lives near him, made enquiry of him concerneing the gentleman,
who in a passion immediately answered y^t he was a papist, that his
house was the greatest harbour of preists and jesuits in all the
country, that he sent a son to St Omers within these 2 years, and
y^t not long after the first discovery of the plot he, beeing a deputy
lieutenant, had complaint brought him of a meeting of papists held
at this Vernons house; whereon he, takeing another deputy lieutenant with him, went thither, and, accordeing as information was
given him, he found there Goring and Gage,^a wch are in the Tower,
ye Lady Abergenny,^b and severall other persons of quality of that
communion, as many as filld 7 coaches, there in close consultation
with their preists; and he told me that he did verily beleive their

<hr>

such a lady as you have maryd highly augments ye obligation wee are under to make
as proportionable returnes as wee can, upon all occasions, to him and his. I shall
perform my parte whylst I live. The conclusion of all is that you may, with all
imaginable security, open y^r self freely to him as to a faithfull friend; you may
depend upon ye fidellity and prudence of his advice; and yon ought upon all
opertunitys, and as well as you are or shall be able, to advance his good and his
familly's; and so God blesse yon.

" Y^r most affectionat Grandfather,
" ORMONDE.

" To my Grandsoune Ossory."

The lady referred to in the latter part of the letter was Anne, danghter of
Lawrence Hyde, Earl of Rochester.
^a Sir Henry Goring, Bart. of Burton, co. Sussex, and Sir John Gage, Bart. of
Firle, were connected by marriage.
^b Mary, Dowager Lady Abergavenny, widow of George, eleventh Earl, and
danghter of Thomas Gifford, of Dunton Walet, co. Essex.

businesse there was to contrive how farther to carry on the plot, and
that he suspected above 12 among them to have been preists. On
my return to the University I informed every on of this story,
which beeing noised abroad squelchd the Colls pretensions, and we
heard noe more of him; but ever since he hath been studying how
to be revenged on me. First he sent me word he would sue me
and that he would undoe me. I answered I was not soe easyly
undon as he imagind; perchance I might have as much mony to
spend as he had, and that I had sayd nothing but what I could
prove: whereon the Coll., findeing he could nothing with me this
way, came to the Bishop with a mighty complain against me, and
the Bishop I found was prepared to give the Coll. some satisfaction,
as far as his power would give him leave, but that, as soon as the
Bishop began to mention it, I musterd up my accusation with soe
many circumstances, named the 2 deputy lieutenants who were
ready to attest it, and added threats of putteing in an information
to the Secret Comitty against him of this and many other things
wch I could prove against him; whereon both the Bishop and the
Coll. pulld in their horns, and I have since been troubled with
neither of them concerneing this businesse, onlesse by a message to
perswade me to acquiesce. His greatest argument he made for
himselfe was y^t he was a friend of the Chancellors, but your letter
told me the contrary. I perceive the fellow to be a fool and I
beleive a beggar. The prorogation of the Parliament [a] to a farther
day seems to me a prelude to a dissolution. I beleive in March we
shall be again chooseing, and perchance it may be my lot again to
encounter the valiant Coll.

[Oxford], Jan. 13th, 1679[80].

I give you many thankes for the kindnesse of yours, and in return
to the news you impart unto me I have nothing else to send you

[a] The prorogation was repeated many times, till October, 1680.

but the enclosed paper concerneing a controversy between us and ye Kings printers now dependeing before the Councill and to be tryed next Fryday. I beleive it may be worth your while to be there and hear w^t is sayd on both sides. The short of the case is: when monopolys were in use we were limited in our right in favour of a monopoly of Bibles granted to the Kings printers by an order of Councill; but that not beeing sufficient to alter any mans property we have thought fit (especially now y^t monopoly granted the Kings printers, 1620, for 60 years beeing expired last Christmas day) to resume our right, wch ye common law will most certainly give us; and to that we will goe, if the cause be not determined in our favour at the Councill board. The petition* is got among our townsmen and they all subscribe like mad; the whole nation is bent upon it, and I thinke there is noe avoideing the Parliament must sit. The King seems to have staved of the evill day as far as he is able, and now I fear it will come upon him with the utmost calamitys we can apprehend. He seems to all ends and purposes to be an undon man. I wish I could please my selfe with but imagineing that it were possible for him to restore him selfe and the nation to any settled condition, but I can see noe hopes and therefore I give all for lost, and none will suffer more in ruin then we Churchmen, who are sure to be grinded, wither Papist or Presbyterians prevail, and I know not wch adversary most to fear. By the next post I will send you a bill for your mony; in the meantime I wish you a good new year.

The state of ye affair of Printeing in ye University of Oxford.

In the year 1672, several persons, members of the University of Oxford, namely, John Bishop of Oxford, Sr Joseph Williamson,

* For a parliament.

Sʳ Leolin Jinkings, and Dʳ Thomas Yats,[a] takeing into consideration yᵉ low estate of the manufacture of printeing in this kingdom, and particularly in the aforesayd University, depressed by the combination and monopolys of traders, and thinkeing yᵗ it might be a usefull service to the public and the interest of learneing, and in especiall manner of yᵉ University, to redeem yᵉ sayd manufacture from yᵉ ill circumstances under which it lay, tooke upon themselfes the charge of the presse in the sayd University, and at the expence of above four thousand pounds furnished from Germany, France, and Holland an imprimery with all the necessarys thereof, and pursued the undertakeing soe vigorously as in the short compasse of time which have since intervened to have printed many considerable bookes in Hebrew, Greeke, and Latine, as well as English, both for matter and elegance of letter and paper very satisfactory to the learned abroad and at home, and have at present in yᵉ presse several bookes of great and public concern. But the sayd persons, seeing themselfes under presseing difficultys by the spight and combination of bookesellers and printers against them, found it advisable to engage in their concerns some men of trade, and accordingly about an year and halfe since tooke to them Mʳ Moses Pitt and some other London booksellers, who, haveing among other things set themselfes to the printeing of Bibles, have actually brought down the price of quarto Bibles with Common Prayer, Psalmes, and Apocrypha, from 13ˢ 4ᵈ unto 5ˢ 9ᵈ, and octavos from 8ˢ 8ᵈ unto 4ˢ 2ᵈ; whereby they have soe provokd the Kings printers, who before had the monopoly of yᵗ booke and made an extravagant gain to themselfes by the public damage, that they now molest the sayd Mʳ Pitt and his partners, summoneing them by an order of his Maᵗʸˢ most honourable Privy Councill, as alsoe the Vice-Chancellor of yᵉ University of Oxford and all persons concernd in printeing there, to appear before yᵗ board on the 16ᵗʰ day of this instant January, upon suggestion that the sayd Mʳ Pitt

[a] Thomas Yate, D.D. Principal of Brasenose College. Died 1681.

and his partners have broken some orders of y^t board of the years
1623 and 1629, made with the mutual submission and agreement of
the Kings printers and the printers of the University of Cambridge;
unto wch orders the University of Oxford are noe otherwise partys
then y^t it is by a subsequent order declared y^t it was his Majestys
intendment y^t the benefit of the aforesayd orders should be extended
to them, which orders Mr Pitt and his partners are ready to make
appear that they have not broken, albeit that they conceive them
noe otherwise concerned in them then as a favour and advantage
wch they are at liberty to wave. For the cleareing of this matter
it may be usefull to take notice that the right of the University of
Oxford to the liberty of printceing stands upon a quite different
bottom from that of ye University of Cambridge, for, long before
the invention of printceing, the multiplying and encreaseing of
bookes by writeing was a privilege of the University of Oxford,
and all men and all trades employed therein were priviledged
persons of ye sayd University, as is accorded, 18th Edw. I., coram
ipso Domino Rege et ejus concilio ad Parliamentum. But when
the art of printceing was invented, Thomas Bourchier, Archbishop
of Canterbury and Chancellor of the University of Oxford, moved
King Henry the 6th y^t ye sayd art might be brought into this
kingdom, and contributeing 300 markes towards y^t purpose, sent
over 2 persons to Harlem, who enticed on Fr[e]deric Corsellis a
workeman there to goe into England with them, who beeing
conveyed to Oxford there set up printceing,ª and in ye year 1468
(within ten years after ye first invention) had finished St Hieroms
Tract on the Creed, and afterward several other bookes yet extant;
and ye sayd University continued in ye possession and use of the
sayd manufacture without interruption till ye 13th of Q. Eliz., at w^ch
time there past an act for the incorporateing the two Universitys,
wherein it is enacted, among other things, that *they may severally
have, hold, possesse, enjoy, and use all manner of libertys, priviledges,*

ª This "fabrication," as Dibdin calls it, has been long since disposed of.

and other things whatsoever they be, the wch either of the sayd corporal bodys of either of the sayd Universitys had held, occupyed, or enjoyed at any time or times before the makeing of this Act. And consequently it is by Act of Parliament granted to them y^t they might use, possesse, and enjoy their liberty of printeing. And therefore it is observable y^t when King Henry ye 8th gave charters to the two Universitys, y^t to Cambridge enabled them to have 3 printers, whereas noe such thing was granted unto Oxford in their charter, though it were most ample and obtained for them by Cardinal Wolsey in his greatest florish; that University beeing entitled before to the liberty of printeing by long usage, and never had it granted by charter till the time of K. Charles ye 1st, whose grant recites the sayd usage and thereupon confirmes the right of printeing omnes et omnimodos libros publice non prohibitos, and interpret the meaneing of that phrase to be only to restrain them from printeing bookes by law or public order prohibitid, not from those for the publisheing whereof a privilege was granted. It is likewise to be noted y^t ye before-mentioned charter of K. Charles ye 1st to the University was perpetual, whereas y^t to the Kings printers then on foot was temporal, and now is worn out; soe y^t if the University of Oxford depended intirely in their right of printeing on the sayd charter, and were to comport with ye privileges granted before to the Kings printers and the orders of the Councill board pursuant of them, this can only oblidge during ye date of the sayd patent to the Kings printers. But thenceforward the University will be at large to act according to the utmost extent of their charter, notwithstandeing that ye Kings printers doe renew their term; soe y^t upon all accounts ye Kings printers are injurious in ye molestation they at present give to those that print at Oxford.

It may be further considered that the Kings printers have never yet taken care to supply ye kingdom with Bibles, but in all times ye generality of sale has been made out from Holland, to the manifest

dammage of this nation, unto the importeing of wch from abroad y^e
unreasonable prices set upon Bibles by those who had ye monopoly
here gave abundant encouragement, notwithstandeing all restraints
layd upon the importation.   And this stoln trade, as it is a damage
to the nation in general, is a great injury to his Ma^ty, ye custom of
all prohibited bookes y^t are imported beeing certainly stoln; whereas,
if bookes be printed in England, the Kings duty upon paper, w^ch
is greater then that on bookes, is sure to be payd.   Nor doe y^e
Hollanders with their Bibles only fill the market in England, but
alsoe in Scotland and Ireland, and furnish entirely all our plantations
in the Indys, the ready cure of wch evills will be the takeing of the
present monopoly.   Beside, it is notorious y^t the sayd Kings printers
have had little regard to the letter, or paper, or correctnesse of what
they printed, beeing sure y^t while they had the monopoly whatsoever
their bookes or prices were they should make their market.   Whereas
for the future, if ye printeing in the Universitys do proceed, these
inconveniences must necessarily be removed, and all will be oblidged
to print well and sell cheap.   Lastly, ye University of Oxford, by
their printeing of Bibles and other saleable bookes, will be enabled
to goe forward with those other less vendible which they designe
and are in hand with, for the honour of the nation and ye benefit
of learneing.

[Oxford], Feb. 24th, 1679[80].

I am heartyly glad at your safe return and the successe of your
businesse,[a] of wch you are pleased to give me an account.   I beleive
you find a great alteration at Court since your departure, and a

---

[a] This probably refers to a journey to Holland which Ellis undertook about this
time, to lay before the States General the claims of the Earl of Ossory. The Earl
had received the commission of General from the Prince of Orange, but the appointment had never been confirmed by the States.   It was this confirmation on which
the Earl insisted, and which he now obtained.

greater will be on ye Dukes return.^a They have talked furiously since your absence y^t my patron ye Ld Chancellor was to be layd aside, but I suppose there is noe truth in it. I suppose my Ld of Ossory will now come in play again, for they say ye King hath declared y^t he will have a court of his own. We have gotten here a very od fellow mayor of the town,^b who seems to have been put into this office on purpose to serve ye Presbyterians, as there shall be an occasion. He was turnd out of the Corporation at the regulation after ye Kings return, and soe hath remained till about last Michaelmas, to his not small advantage, because, when any squabble was between the town and us, all repaired to him to be furnished at his shop, as beeing a fellow not concernd against us. He is one of the richest men in the town, and oweth it all to his not beeing of the Corporation, and therefore hath for many years refused all invitations of returneing among them. But last Michaelmas, one of ye 13 dying, he made use of all the interest he could to get himselfe choosen to succeed him, and was thereon choosen mayor of the town, in which office he acteth to the utmost folly of phanaticisme, molesteing both the University and town, talkeing against the King and Government with the utmost malice. Trenchard^c and Vaughan^d comeing here about the time of his

^a The Duke of York returned on this day from Scotland, whither he had gone the previous October.

^b "A.D. 1679, Robert Panling [or Pawlin], draper, chose mayor. This person walks in the night to take tradesmen in tipling houses, prohibits coffee to be sold on Sundays, ... hath been bred up a Puritan; he is no friend to the University, and a dissuader of such gentlemen that he knows from sending their children to the University, because that he saith 'tis a debauched place, a rude place of no discipline."—Wood, *Life*, lxxxvii.

^c John Trenchard; entered New College, but soon after went to the Bar. His early life was spent in continual turmoil. M.P. for Taunton, 1679. He was concerned in Oates's plot, and again in the Whig conspiracies of 1683. He passed many years in exile, and was excepted from the general pardon of 1686. Serjeant-at-Law and knighted in 1689; Secretary of State, 1693.

^d Altham Vaughan, son of the Earl of Carbery. He was M.P. for Carmarthen in the parliament of 1679, and, in company with Trenchard and other Members, assisted in drawing up the Exclusion Bill.

election, and beeing as I know in frequent conference with him, I believe it was by their influence y[t] he was choosen, as beeing a man very fit to be subservient to their designes. Those rogues have designes goeing on, but if the King will but put on a little rigour he may easyly quel them. I hope he will continue as he hath begun. Our Atlas[a] is now almost finished, of w[ch] Mr. Pit can give you an account.

———   — ——

[Oxford], Apr. 23, [16]80.

In my last I writ to you concerneing Drelincourt, and advised y[t] a liveing bee procured for him and some more deserveing and prudent person placed in his imployment. There is now in Devonshire y[e] vicaridge of Bradworthy faln into y[e] Kings disposal, worth above 100[l] per annum, the last incumbent dying but y[e] 16th of this instant.[b] I suppose it is not yet disposed of, and one word from my Lord will easily procure it for him, and therewith his utmost deserts, and the greatest service he hath don my Lord will be more then abundantly satisfyed. If this project be reguarded, pray let noe on know I had an hand in it; to say the truth this Frenchman is intolerable in y[e] eyes of every on y[t] hath any respect for y[e] honourable family you are in, and for your sake I cannot but have a greater sense of this then others have. All the company this yong Lord is accustomed to are Cap[t] Woods and his son, one Gibs a querester, an idle gentleman commoner, Mon[r] his Governour, and his dogges. The Cap[t] is a gentleman and a noted honest man, but poor, and therefore cannot bear y[e] charge my Ld constantly puts him to by frequenteing his house; and it is very dishonourable

[a] "The English Atlas; by M. Pitt, W. Nicholson, and R. Peers." Oxon. 1680-3, 5 vols. folio.
[b] Drelincourt did not get the living. He remained in the Duke of Ormonde's family for many years after this time.

to my Ld of Ossory y⁴ his son should be a burden to him. I write
freely to you what is proper for you to know, and leave it to your
prudence to make what use of it you thinke fitt.

Oxford, March 17th, 1680[1].

On my return hither from yᵉ country, where I have been absent
ever since Christmas, I received your kind letter, for wᶜʰ I thanke
you. I am sorry yᵉ Ld Lieutenant ᵃ keeps you still with him to
your disadvantage. I doubt not, had you been here, you might er
this have been on better terms. We have had yᵉ Court with us ever
since Monday last. You will see an account of the Kings reception
in yᵉ Gazet, and therefore I will not trouble you with it. He
knighted yᵉ Recorder ᵇ that made the speech to him in behalfe of
yᵉ town, beeing very much pleased with it, because of an argument
quite contrary to that of yᵉ Earl of Essex's speech wᶜʰ he made to
him on yᵉ presenteing of yᵉ addresse for yᵉ Parliaments not sitteing
at Oxford.ᶜ He likewise conferred the same honour on Capᵗ Bartue,ᵈ
brother to the Ld Norris, and on Mr. Pudsey,ᵉ a neighbour gentleman to this place, wᶜʰ by the directions of yᵉ Court hath appeared
three times here to be Parliament man and lost it. This day yᵉ
King is gon to Burford to be present at an horse race, and in his
return is treated at yᵉ Ld Clarendons house at Cornbury. The
Queen came hither with him, pretendeing she can be noo where
safe but where yᵉ King is present to protect her. Your old friend

ᵃ James Duke of Ormonde, Lord Lieutenant of Ireland. After the death of the
Earl of Ossory, in August, 1680, Ellis became secretary to the Duke.

ᵇ Sir Richard Croke.

ᶜ The Earl of Essex and other peers petitioned the King against the meeting of
parliament at Oxford, 11 March.

ᵈ Henry Bertie, brother of James Lord Norreys of Rycote, afterwards Earl of
Abingdon.

ᵉ George Pudsey, of Ellsfield; succeeded Sir R. Croke as Recorder.

Sr Jos. Williamson hath had a great losse, his house beeing robd by a German he intrusted with it to the value of 6000^l. I am afraid ye poor fool is quite undon. We have lately set forth here an account of ye late civil wars written by Sr William Dugdale,^a wch is much approved of. Burnet hath likewise published the 2^d part of his History of ye Reformation.^b Pamplets fly abroad in great numbers, but all tend to the breeding a dislike of ye present government; and it is not in ye Kings power to suppresse them. My humble service to your brother.

[Oxford]. May 21, 1681.

Whoever now is head of Magd. Hall must go to law for it, Magd. Coll. haveing revived some old pretensions to it, and this morneing elected one of their fellows into this headship,^c and are resolved to stand by him at a suit of law in defence of this right they have given him, wch you would doe well speedyly to acquaint the D. of Ormond with.^d But all their pretensions will signify nothing, there beeing against them a prescription of 120 years, and beside a statute of the University, to w^cb Magdalen Coll. as well as all others consented to in the body of ye University in full convocation. The Marmayd Tavern is lately broke, and we Christ Church men bear ye blame of it, our ticks, as ye noise of ye town will have it, amounteing to 1500^l. Pawlin, ye mercer, our grand adversary, they tell us is almost in the same condition, for on his

---

^a " A short View of the late Troubles in England; setting forth their Rise, Growth, and Tragical Conclusion. To which is added, A perfect Narrative of the Treaty of Uxbridge, in 1644." Oxford, 1681, folio.

^b "History of the Reformation of the Church of England." London, 1679-81, 2 vols. folio.

^c Francis Smith, of Magdalen College, elected to succeed Dr. James Hyde, in opposition to Dr. Levett of Christ Church. He afterwards served as a physician in King William's army in Ireland, and died there in 1691.

^d As Chancellor of the University.

late quarrells with us when mayor, y^r University haveing withdrawn their trade from him, his creditors have come faster upon him then he is able to pay y^m, which makes people suspect it is more then his estate is sufficient to doe to satisfy all. An addresse hath been agitated here this weeke to thanke ye King for his declaration,[a] but ye mayor beeing a rank phanatique violently opposeth it, and, that it may not passe by publick autority, refuseth to call a Common Councill; but when we have brooken him too it will [be] to late for ye fool to repent, for now this is the course we are resolved to take if any towns man be sawcy with us, to withdraw all trade from him, wch will more effectually right us then all the favour Westminster Hall can show us, and likewise save us a great deal of charges. When you remove to any other lodgeing pray let me be informed of it.

[Oxford], June 2d, 1681.

I haveing not of late heard from you I suppose you have been out of town, perchance at Windsor; but now ye Court is again returned I suppose this will find you at London. After all ye pretensions and braggeings of ye Maudlin men they have submitted and let Dr Levet[b] have peaceable possession. Till the day of his admission they kept guards, pretendeing if the Vice-Chancellor came thither to give any possession but to their own man they would oppose him by force of arms; but when the Vice-Chancellor came in earnest to doe his office in this particular they sneaked away, and not one appeared either to oppose Levets admission or

---

[a] A declaration of his reasons for dissolving the two last parliaments, to which addresses of thanks were presented from the country.

[b] See above, page 29, note ^c. Another claim to the election of the Principal of Magdalen Hall was set up by Magdalen College after Levett's death in 1693. The result was a trial, and a verdict against the College.

as much as to protest against it. For in truth ye President,[a] in whose absence they had made ye election, not approveing of ye folly and madnesse of their proceedings, refused to grant them ye colledge seal, and therby they beeing deprived of a foundation ye Maudlin principal had nothing to ground his right upon or any thing to show for his title to it, and therefore sneaked of with his foolish pretensions, and all that he is like to get by it is to be called Principal Smith as long as he lives in ye University. We have had great contest about an addresse to the King with thankes for his declaration. Y^e disaffected opposed it violently and had Sr Francis Winnington[b] with them here all ye Whitsunweek to give them assistance herein; but, notwithstandeing all they could doe, ye addresse past on Monday last, and yeasterday it was sent to y^r King by the hands of ye mayor of ye town and 2 others wch were ye most violent opposers of it, and ye Duke of Buckingham is desired to assist at ye solemnity, he beeing Steward of ye town. One Dr Luffe[c] is, as we hear, appointed our physick professor, a man of very obscure note, but noe other appeareing for it, unlesse one wch was utterly unfit for it, ye place is fallen to him for want [of] others to accept it. . . . . . .

--

[Oxford], June 25th, 1681.

I humbly thanke you for ye kindnesse you were pleased to doe me in talkeing with the Dean of Norwich[d] about my concerns. Your information you give me from him is full and satisfactory, and now I have considered it I am of ye same opinion with ye Dean, y^t he is actually prebend till he be made by instalment actually Dean; for ye King[s] patent is only of ye nature of a presentation, wch puts him in noe right but only gives him a title

[a] Henry Clerk, M.D. President of Magdalen College, 1671-87.
[b] Solicitor-General, 1675-9.
[c] John Luffe, of St. Mary's Hall, sometime of Trinity College; M.D. 1673.
[d] John Sharp, D.D. Dean of Norwich, 8 June, 1681; Dean of Canterbury, 23 September, 1689; and Archbishop of York, 1691.

to demand it, and, till he hath don soe and is possessed of that
right, his former is good to all pretences and purposes, and therefore
if my patent[a] be passed before his be vacated it will not be good in
law. M[r] Hodges[b] beeing now at Norwich I intend to write to him
for instructions concerncing my time of goeing thither. If it may
be noe disadvantage to me to defer my journy till y[e] time y[e] Dean
mentions, I shall put myselfe to noe more charge then need; but
I will loose nothing by tarrying here, since now, haveing nothing
to detain me in this place, I can be as well there as here. The
inclosed paper tells you of a new designe we have to support our
presse since y[e] death of D[r] Yates; I wish it may take. We [are]
now busy about y[e] election of a new Squire Beadle, Mr. Minshul,
one of y[m], haveing made himselfe top heavy by drinkeing too
much last Tuesday night fell of his horse and broke his neck.[c]
We are now here upon a designe de propaganda in fide (sic) in y[e]
East Indys, the East Indy Company haveing sent us very large and
good proposals to that end, beeing moved thereto by y[e] Bp. when
last in London.[d] Our great gate goes on apace; if y[e] Court comes
hither next winter they will find us all in rubbish.

Oxford, July 5th, 1681.

I have delivered both your letters; it seems Croon[e] is not yet
marryed, but is in a fair way to it, at least y[e] Bp. hath received noe
certain intelligence of it, but expects y[t] er long he shall; you may
be easyly informed in London. Whensoever y[e] place falls, his

---

[a] Prideaux succeeded Dr. Sharp in his prebend at Norwich, and was installed on
the 15th of August.

[b] Nathaniel Hodges, M.A. Prebendary of Norwich.

[e] Christopher Minshull; killed by a fall from his horse, between Abingdon and
Locking. See above, p. 50, note [d].

[d] See a paper on this subject written by Prideaux in 1694-5, and printed in *The
Life of the Rev. H. Prideaux, D.D. Dean of Norwich.* London, 1748. 8vo.

[e] Croon's name does not appear among the list of Graduates. It is evident that
he held a fellowship at Christ Church, which Ellis hoped to step into on Croon's
marriage.

Ldship tells me he shall remember you; he sayd he knew none could pretend to it that did better deserve it, and therefore you may be assured y^t as soon as this or any other place is vacant you shall be put in into it. We are much surprised here at ye news of Shaftsbury's commitment.[a] I hope now all ye roguery will come out I wish it be not more y^n will be to our advantage to know, for I mightyly suspect y^t old knave hath been gnilty of many subornations in ye management of ye Popish plot, which will be mightyly to our disgrace should it prove soe, and would give ye Papists such an advantage that they would carry all things before y^m. We are told here in our publick news letters y^t some of those which have deposed against Shaftsbury have accused him of suggesting all y^t was sworn against Plunket,[b] and y^t he subornd ye witnesses which appeared against him, and y^t some of them are since grown distracted and have confessed ye whole. If soe, it is a very bad businesse, and all English men y^t goe into popish countrys will be sufficiently told of it. We have 10 D^{rs} wch proceed in Divinity this Act, Dr Ratcliff[e] of our colledge; Dr Yonger,[d] Dr Pudsey,[e] Dr Smith,[f] and Dr Fairfax[g] of Magdalen Coll.; Dr Caswell,[h] ye Vicar of Bray, Dr Hoor[i] of St Mary Overy, and Dr Hearn,[k] of Exeter Coll.; and Dr Reinolds[l] and Dr Fowler[m] of Corpus X^{ti}. All happynesse to you.

--

[a] The Earl of Shaftesbury was committed to the Tower for high treason, 2nd July.

[b] Dr. Oliver Plunket, Roman Catholic Archbishop of Armagh, was put upon his trial, 3 May, 1681, charged with plotting a French invasion of Ireland and the destruction of the Protestants; he was found guilty, and was executed. Burnet (*History of his Own Times*, 502) says, " The witnesses were brutal and profligate men, yet the Earl of Shaftesbury cherished them much."

[c] Anthony Radcliffe, Canon of Christ Church.

[d] John Younger, Prebendary of Canterbury.   [e] Alexander Pudsey.

[f] John Smith.   [g] Henry Fairfax, Dean of Norwich, 1689.

[h] Francis Carswell.   [i] William Hore, Prebendary of Worcester.

[k] John Hearne.   [l] George Reynell.

[m] Edward Fowler, afterwards Bishop of Gloucester, 1691. He took the degree of M.A. at Trinity College, Cambridge.

[Oxford], July 20th, 1681.

What you write to me concerneing a protestation from our grand jury on their findeing y⁰ bill against Colledge ⁿ is news to every one I inquire of concerneing it. The jury indeed tooke a longer time then ordinary to consider yᵉ bill, but yᵗ there was any thing of a protestation made I can meet with noe one yᵗ ever heard of it. I will by yᵉ next soe far inform myselfe as to be able to give you a perfect account of the whole proceeding of yᵉ grand jury in this affair. Mʳ Croon is most certainly marryed, but I suppose he will not be put out of his place till Christmas. His wife is the Lady Heath, formerly widow to Dʳ Doughty,ʰ prebend of Westminster. You need not trouble yourselfe to sollicite yᵉ Bp. any farther, he haveing positively declared unto me you should have yᵉ place. I shall be in London on my way to Norfolk about yᵉ 13ᵗʰ of yᵉ next month, and then I hope I shall see you there.

——— ———

Oxford, [July] 1681.

I have since further informed myselfe concerneing yᵉ proceedings of our grand jury in Colledge's businesse, and am assured by one yᵗ very well knows it that the bill on yᵉ examineing witnesses was immediatcly found nemine contradicente. There were indeed some Monmuthians that would willingly have thrust themselfes on yᵉ jury, that they might have had opportunity to doe some such thing as you write of, but the Sheriffe would not admitt yᵐ, haveing

* Stephen Colledge, "the Protestant joiner," was arraigned for high treason, but the grand jury for Middlesex threw out the bill. The Crown, however, moved the trial to Oxford, on the ground that the plot with which he was charged was to have been carried out in that place; and, succeeding in the prosecution, obtained his conviction.

ʰ John Doughty, D.D. died 1672.

made up his pannel before. Therefore from what your Wiggs at London talke you may understand reather what would have been don then was really was [*sic*], supposeing their designe of makeing a jury of their men had succeeded. But it happens we have a very honest man to our Sheriffe,[a] who will not be subservient to such designes. Several of our factious justices were left out of commission last assizes, as S[r] John Cope,[b] M[r] Hoard,[c] Alderman Wright,[d] M[r] Taverner Harris,[e] and M[r] Clerke of Aston, with some others, w[ch] is a great affliction to them. We expected Shaftsbury and Howards[f] bills would likewise have been put before our grand jury. Had it been don they would both certainly have been found. We have a great noise here as if y[e] Duke were again turneing Protestant, and some men mightyly please themselfes in it, as if it were true; but to me it seems inpossible. The Bp. is gon into Wales and will not again return till after this weeke; his businesse there is only to give a visit to S[r] Thomas Middleton.[g] About 3 weekes hence I hope I shall see you.

Norwich, Aug. 17th, 1681.

I have here taken possession . . . . . . I am very well satisfyed with y[e] time of my residence, for I can bear travel much better in winter then in summer. The dean is at present with us, and we are very happy in his company. Judge Atkings[h] came hither at

[a] Edward Gregory.
[b] Sir John Cope, Bart. of Hanwell; M.P. for co. Oxon, 1680.
[c] Thomas Hoard, M.P. for co. Oxon, 1680-1.
[d] William Wright, M.P. for Oxford, 1679-81.
[e] Son-in-law of Alderman Wright.
[f] Edward, Lord Howard of Escrick, charged with complicity in Fitz-Harris's libel. He was concerned in the Rye House plot, and turned informer and appeared as witness against Lord William Russell and Algernon Sidney.
[g] Sir Thomas Myddelton, Bart. of Chirk Castle, co. Denbigh.
[h] Sir Edward Atkyns, Junior Baron, afterwards Chief Baron of the Excheqner.

ye same time with me, haveing taken Sr John Hubbards^a house and resolved to fix his family here; but as soon as he arrived the Kings orders came after him to be at London to direct in the Lord Shaftsburys tryal. This town I find devided into two factions, Whigs and Torys; the former are ye more numerous, but the later carry all before them as consisteing of ye governeing part of ye town, and both contend for their way with the utmost violence. I doe not beleive any place can afford of either part more vehement votarys to it then this town. I tooke Cambridge in my way hither, and find it a much meaner place then I thought; but when I again see you I shall have opportunity of talkeing farther of these things.

[Oxford], Sept 20th, 1681.

I had sooner written to you since my return, had I found any thing here worth informeing you. Yesterday was the election of our mayor, and the man choosen is one Alderman Bayly,^b whom they put up out of his order to be mayor that they might put by Mr. Harris,^c the only person in the corporation that is for the Kings interest; but this beeing an unpardonable crime among our Whiggish townsmen, they have set up this old blade, although more then halfe doted, because somewhat more agreable to their principles. The old Lady Lovelace^d is very busy at all businesses in the town to influence them her way, and she is now grown soc zealous a Whig that she goes every Sunday to the Lady Angleseys^e to make one of the holy sisters at her conventicle. By her and some other that come hither our Oxonians are made soc couragious

---

^a Sir John Hobart, Bart. of Blickling, co. Norfolk. He was one of "Cromwell's peers" nominated to sit in "the other House" of 1658.

^b F. W. Bayly.

^c Taverner Harris.

^d Anne, daughter of Thomas Wentworth, Earl of Cleveland, Dowager Lady Lovelace.

^e Elizabeth, daughter of Sir James Altham, one of the Barons of the Exchequer, married to Arthur Lord Anglesey.

that they talk nothing now but of wageing war with ye King, and
the resolution is concluded on that Westminster Hall must decide
it between the King and them concerneing the town clerk.^a
However, they thought fit first to give his Majesty some warneing,
and therefore some of them attended with a petition at Newmarket
for Princes admission, but could find noe one there that would
introduce them to ye King, soe that they were forced to wait till
the King came forth to walk, and then they delivered it to him in
the feilds, and he ordered them to attend the Ld. Conway for an
answere, which was a very severe reprofe for their ill carriage to
his Majesty both in this and many other affaires; which made them
soe angry, that when they came home they talkd of nothing but of
admitteing Prince forthwith and defying the King. For they say
the charter wch oblidgeth them to have the Kings approbation of
their town clerk was given them since the Kings return, and if
they forfeit that they tell us they are not concernd, they haveing
other charters whereby they hold all their other priviledges in more
ample manner and without any such reserve. But when the time
came they only admitted Prince as deputy, to serve in time of
vacancy; but its supposed they will never otherwise supply y^e
vacancy, thinkeing by the trick to evade the Kings prerogative.
The only man in the town of any note that is true to the Kings
interest is Mr Harris, who is a very honest and very understandeing
man, and, although son-in-law to Alderman Wright, yet acts soe
contrary to him that ye alderman is become a violent and irreconcileable enemy to him, and by his contrivance it is that he is put
by from beeing mayor this year. He is one of the most sufficient
men among them, beeing worth above ten thousand pounds. He
is a very fit man to be town clerk, haveing been bred a lawyer,
but he is not willing to take ye trouble. Sr Thomas Chamberlain,^b
one of ye Deputy-Lieutenants of this county, now lyeth at the point
of death; he will leave 2 daughters behind him, each of wch will be

---

^a Thomas Prince, lately elected town clerk.

^b Sir Thomas Chamberlayne, Bart. of Wickham, co. Oxon. He married Mar-
garet, daughter of Edmund Prideaux, a kinsman of Humphrey. Catherine, the

worth 15000ℓ apeice. I shall take care that Mʳ Guiseᵃ wait on
you before he leave England; he goes from hence on Wednesday;
by him you shall again hear from me.

———

[Oxford, 22 Sept. 1681.]

Since my last I have been further informed that Prince, on his
admission to be pro town clerk, made a very seditious speech to the
town. The summe of it was to represent how ill they had been
treated at Newmarket, with bitter reflections on the King and
Court for it. It seems the linkeboys, those that they call the
black guard, treated them very rudely, calleing them Presbyterian
petitioners and Whiggish dogs, and saluted them into the bargain
with stones and dirt.ᵇ Yᵉ fellow was very large in aggravateing
this, and mentioned them soe often by the name of the black guard,
with such expressions, that he seemd to designe likewise a reflection
by way of comparison on yᵉ schollars; but yᵉ fellows wit could not
reach it. At last he began to tell the townsmen they had indeed
a very gracious King but he had very evill councellors about him,
whereat yᵉ Recorder stopd his mouth and told him if [he] proceeded

elder of his two daughters, was married thrice: to Viscount Wenham, to the Earl of
Abingdon, and to Francis Wroughton, of Heskett; the younger daughter, Penelope,
married Sir Robert Dashwood, Bart. of Northbrooke.

ᵃ See above, p. 44, note ᵃ.

ᵇ The following is an extract from "The Loyal Protestant and True Domestic
Intelligence, or News both from City and Countrey. Printed by Nath. Thompson,
next the Cross-Keys, in Fetter Lane," for Tuesday, September 20, 1681:—

"*Newmarket, September* 13, 1681.—The Right Worshipful the Mayor of *Quin-
borough*, living in *Oxford*, accompanied by some of his Protestant Brethren, the
Aldermen, and other Friends, for want of a convenient Introducer to his Majesty's
Presence, performed that Ceremony one for the other, and presented His Majesty
with a Petition, the Contents of which was, *That His Majesty will be graciously
pleas'd to waive that part of his Prerogative-Royal of His Approbation of their
Town-Clerk, and accept of* Mr. Prince, *who had really qualified himself (spick
and span new in behalf of the Good Old Cause) on purpose for the said Trust,
and was oppos'd by the majority of the Citizens, and Lord Lieutenant of the
County: And (as in duty bound) would pray, &c.*

"His Majesty caused the Petition to be read, and immediately rejected it, well

any farther in that stile he would send him to jayl; which put an end to his speech. However, ye greezy caps cryed out that he should proceed to vindicate the right they had given him, and they would stick by him with their lives and fortunes, which is more then they would tell the King in their late addresse. It is supposed that after all our townsmen will grow fool hardy and admitt him absolutely into the town clerkes place and leave him to try it with ye King, which he promiseth them he will doe. The mayor that they have choosen is a person very much decayed, haveing had two fitts of an apoplexy, which have made him quite unable to doe any businesse himselfe, and therefore he resignes himselfe solely into the hands of Alderman Wright and Pawlin;^a and that they might by this means have ye managery of all affairs in their hands seems to be ye sole end of his beeing made mayor. I find a story here y^t at Colledge's tryal Everard^b and Aron Smith,^c haveing by Alderman Wright hired one Mr Dursleys lodgeings, an attorney in ye town, when they went hence left over his bed their papers of instructions, wherein was set down what they should sware now and what when ye Ld. Shaftsbury come to be tryed with several others . . . .
 . . . .^d them sent immediately to their agent, ye Alderman, to get

perceiving the *pretended* Loyalty and Integrety of the Presenters, who immediately return'd to their Quarters at honest *Bess Pitchers*, where they were suppos'd to be recommended by Mr. *Bull*, the Minister of *Cordwainers' Hall*, in *London*, or some particular Friend of his that was well acquainted there.

"The *Black-Guard* (a Society, perhaps, for its antiquity not to be match'd in any part of *Europe*) as a signal mark of their Gratitude for their kind Reception at *Oxford* in *March* last, waited on their Worships (upon the first notice they had of their Arrival) and secured their Quarters by their continued Guards, and did them the Honour of seeing them out of the Town, following them with lowd Acclamations, *God preserve the King, and His whole Family and Kindred, and keep him safe from the hands of all that are any ways related to the Tribe of Forty-One;* continuing shouting as long as they had any sight of them."

^a The late mayor.

^b Edmund Everard, one of the informers in the Popish Plot.

^c Smith's career was more successful than he deserved. He was Oates's legal adviser during the Popish Plot, and afterwards became Solicitor to the Treasury in 1689, and Chancellor of the Exchequer in 1699.

^d A line lost from decay.

those papers for y^m; which beeing difficult to doe without bringeing himselfe into suspition, Dursley beeing returnd into his lodgeings, after consultation had with his brethren, he went thither as a justice of peace with a counstable to search for treasonable papers, and immediately went to the beds head; which Dursley perceiveing told ye Alderman, if he searched for Everard and Smith[s] instructions, he advised him to goe to the Councill, for he had sent them thither; at wch the Alderman went away in great confusion. I thinke it is by noe means fit such a fellow should be entrusted with authority, who makes use of it to stifle evidence of treason against ye King; for had he found those papers they would have quietly been conveyed to the owners without a words more speakeing of them. Somebody hath lately scattred about the town a Catalogue of Whigs, or those wch he thinkes soe, in every colledge; which hath put us into some disorder, several very honest men beeing inserted among them with ill characters which doe not belong to them. Great search hath been made to find out the author, but noe discovery can be made, wch makes some suspect it may be a bone of division thrown in among us by ye common enemy, whither Papists or Presbyterians I know not. Dr Bathurst and Dr Hall [a] are the two that begin ye list. Our Regius Professor [b] is returned from his northern progresse with his two baronets with him. I am afraid we shall have more of one of them then we shall care for; I mean my countryman.[c] He talkes soe madly that I know not whom to compare him to but Oats, his talke on one side beeing just the same y^t the others is on the other side. It would be rare sport to see them togeather; and perchance it may not be long er we may see it for pence apeice in Bedlam. They . . . .[d] poor rogues

---

[a] See above, p. 13, note [b], and p. 50, note [c].

[b] Dr. William Jane, Regius Professor of Divinity, and Canon of Christ Church.

[c] I think that Prideaux here refers to Sir Jonathan Trelawny. He was elected from Westminster to Oxford in 1668; B.A. 1672; M.A. 1675; D.D. 1685. Bishop of Bristol 1685, of Exeter 1689, and of Winchester 1707. It is uncertain in what year he succeeded to the baronetcy; but he was resident at Oxford at this time, and must be the Sir Jonathan Trelawny mentioned shortly afterwards, at page 102, although his father bore the same Christian name.   [d] A line lost from decay.

nothing but a ridiculous reputation among their own gang of beeing, as they call it, honest fellows, y' is, can take of their beer apace without balkeing what comes to their share. They have filthyly exasperated me, and I am glad I have rap'd one of them on ye fingers for it. It seems it was one Titmarsh, an Anabaptist preacher, that made Colledge dy without confesseing; for, till he came to him, which was the Munday before his execution,[a] he owned all y^t was sworn against him, except Haynes[b] depositions (whom I really beleive a raskal), and seemed very penitent for it; but after this fellow had been with him some hours he grew sullen, would admit none of his former confessors, and soe dyed without confesseing anything further. When any thing else occurs you shall be sure to hear from me; and, if not, you must conclude ye reason is I have nothing worth informeing you.

[Oxford, 25th Sept. 1681.]

Our townsmen still continue in the same humour of disputeing the Kings prerogative with him. Princes speech was made at the election of ye new mayor. If you can remember our Town Hall, there is a large yard before it, and there the rabble meet while the wiser heads of them, wch they call the Common Councill, are consulteing within whom they shall bring out to them; for the Common Councill chuse two and bring them out into a balkony lookeing into the yard wherein the rabble meet, and of them two he which they chuse is mayor of the town. After Baily had been thus brought and choosen mayor, then Prince came forth and began, " Gentlemen, I have something to say to you. You have choosen me town clerk and I will defend your right," and soe proceeded to brag what he would doe against the King (not without some rude reflections) in defence of the town privileges, and then

[a] Colledge was executed on the 31st August.
[b] Bryan Haynes, against whom a charge of plotting had also been laid.

told them how ill they were used at Newmarket, and at last (as his
very words were) he told them indeed he thought the King of
himselfe a very honest man, but he was drawn away by evill
councillors; and then Necessity Holloway,[a] beeing pro-Recorder,
stopd him from proceedeing any farther, not that he misliked the
matter of his speech, but, as he himselfe told me, because he
thought it not soe proper that he should speake soe much in his
own businesse. The way they are resolved to proceed they tell me
is this. Prince is to sue the mayor for admission in the Kings
Bench, and then they say an order must of course issue out to cause
the mayor to give a reason why he doth not admitt him, and then
ye mayor will give the Kings refusal of approbation as the reason,
and crave the judgement of ye Court upon it; and they say they
have it under the hands of the best lawyers in England that the
Court must declare in favour of them, for the charter wherein the
King hath this prerogative of approveing ye recorder and town
clerke reserved to him was granted by this King since his return;
and they make count to cancell this charter and stand to that they
had before. However, it seems theyr courage doth somewhat coole,
for yesterday they went in a full body to the Earle of Angleseys [b]
to crave his assistance in the case; but I suppose all assistance will
come to late in behalfe of Prince after soe seditious a speech. It
seems Alderman Wright is turned out of ye Commission of the
Peace for the town, as well as for the county, on the account of the
story I writ you of in my last. It seems our plenipotentiarys ye
went to Newmarket were likewise very coursely treated at Cambridge; for the innkeeper where they lodged swinged them in their
reckoneing most abominably, makeing them pay five times the
price for every thing they had; and hireing a chamber there to lay
some of their things till their return, which was but 3 days, they

---

[a] Charles, son of Charles Holloway, Serjeant-at-Law; called Necessity, because
"Necessitas non habet legem," he being a barrister but no lawyer.—Wood, Life,
lxxix.

[b] Arthur Annesley, first Earl of Anglesey, Lord Privy Seal, 1673-82; died 1686.

made them pay 20ˢ for it, and, when expostulated with, told them
it was accordeing to the rate gentlemen payd at Oxford when yᵉ
Parliament was here, and therefore they had noe reason to complain; and when they scrupled payment they were in danger of
beeing had before the mayor, but to avoid this they were contented
to pay what was demanded; but all put togeather, and Tompsons
narrative* of their journy in the last Intelligence, is such a heavy
greivance unto them that their great hearts can scarce bear up
under the affliction of it. I hope this will put them upon such
resentments as to make yᵐ loose their charter. Dʳ Hammond ᵇ is
marryed and Jack Benson ᶜ is towards it, beeing got into as bad an
intanglement of love as his brother Sam ᵈ was. I have nothing
more.

- -

[Oxford, 27 Sept. 1681.]

. . . . . . By reason of my late return from Norwich I doe not
as yet understand all the intrigues wᶜʰ have been on foot while I
was absent, but one lately come to my knowledge I cannot omitt
to tell you, although it beeing of 3 weeks date perchance an account
of it might have come to you from other hands. While yᵉ Lord
Lovelace ᵉ had the town of Woodstock solely at his devotion, he
for several years had an horse race there about the middle of
September, and a plate of 50ˡ price was always given by him,

* See above, p. 92, note ᵇ.

ᵇ John Hammond, D.D. Canon of Christ Church; M.A. 1664; B.D. 1679; D.D.
1680; Archdeacon of Huntingdon, 1673.

ᶜ John Benson, son of Dr. George Benson, Dean of Hereford; elected from Westminster to Christ Church 1669; M.A. 1676. He succeeded his father in the Rectory
of Cradley, which he held for thirty-one years; Prebendary of Hereford 1691. Died
1713.

ᵈ Samuel Benson, of Christ Church ; M.A. 1671 ; afterwards Archdeacon of
Hereford.

ᵉ John, third Baron Lovelace of Hurley, 1670-93, the audacious and intemperately
vehement Whig who figures in Macaulay's History.

which drew a great concourse of the gentry thither; but last year,
beeing angry with ye town because they showed respects to the Ld.
Norris,ᵃ by way of revenge he removes the race from Woodstock,
and to collogue with our towns folk, whom he thought more for
his turn, sets up his posts in Portmead; and there last year his 50ˡ
plate was run for, and ye Duke of Munmouth and many of his gauge,
you may remember, were then here. This year his Ldship again
designed to have the same race here, and ye same company promised
to meet him at it, and great dooings there was among the townsmen
in prepareing for the reception of their King James the 2ᵈ; but it
seems his Lordship haveing sent to Alderman Wright to bespeake
ye plate without sendeing the mony, the Alderman would not vouch
for payment, and thereon the goldsmith would not prepare the
plate, and therefore his Lordship, comeing hither to prepare all
things for the time, found the mean affair wonteing; wᶜʰ produced
a kind of a quarrel between his Ldship and ye Alderman. However, all his interest here was not sufficient to gain himselfe trusted
elsewhere for the summe, and therefore, after all his huffeing, he
was forced to uninvite his company and carry away his race horses
again, after that they had been here some time a dieteing for ye
sport; and our blessed townsmen were deprived of the soe much
expected happynesse of seeing the gracious Duke here again. My
last told you of our townsmens goeing to Blechington to the Ld.
Privy Seals. I find the Lady Lovelace was the sole contriver of
this affair, for, our townsmen findeing it necessary since their late
journy to Newmarket to have some friend at Court to favour them
their [sic], she proposed to Wright (who is the cheife governor
here and solely governd by her) the Ld. Privy Seal, and undertook
at the same time to dispose him to it; whereon last Friday out
goes about 20 of them to desire his Ldship to honour them with

<hr>

ᵃ James Bertie, son of Montagu, Earl of Lindsey, became Lord Norreys of Rycote
in 1679, and was created Earl of Abingdon in 1682. Lord-lieutenaut for co. Oxon.
His second wife was Catherine, daughter of Sir Thomas Chamberlayne, mentioned
above, p. 91. He died in 1699.

accepteing of the freedom of their town, and his Ldship readyly
accepted of their offer; and this day is appointed for his comeing
to town, and great preparations are makeing for his reception: for
an account hereof you must expect till my next. The townsmen
take heart mightyly on the Privy Seals acceptcing of their offer
and begin already to defy the Ld. Norris, thinkeing now that they
have got a friend which will be too hard for him, and all their affairs
are to go well for the future by his assistance. Prince promiseth
himselfe now a speedy admission; and in truth they fool themselfes
into a beleive as if the King dared not stand it out with them; soe
considerable a corporation as they take themselfes to be they thinke
is not to be disoblidged; but at worst my Ld. Angleseys interest is
sufficient at Court, they tell us, to over balance ye Lord Norrises.
He is to inform the King aright, and remove those prejudices w^ch
ye evill counsellers Prince complained of have put into him concerning them, and then all is to goe accordeing to their desires. That
which makes the Privy Seal collogue with them at present is a
prospect he hath taken by their applying to him of makeing one
of his sons Burgesse here next Parliament; but, when expectations
come to be performed, I suppose his Ldship will cheat the town of
theirs and the town his Ldship of his; for I am sure they expect
more from him then it will be in his power to effect or for his
interest to attempt; and our fellows are grown soe proud and
insolent, that, if they be not humourd as well as favour, they
will be ready to fly the best man in England in the face. They
threaten ye Ld. Norris at such rate for disapproveing of Prince that
nothing but menaces are in their mouths against him; and they tell
us he shall never more have an interest here, he shall never more
signify anything in this Corporation, and that with such pride and
insolence as if their [*sic*] were noe liveing for his Ldship without
their favour.   Jones[a] and Winnington[b] are their privy counsellers,

---

[a] Sir Thomas Jones, Puisne Judge of the King's Bench, 1676; Chief Justice of
the Common Pleas, 1683; dismissed by James II. 1686.

[b] Sir Francis Winnington, Solicitor-General, 1675; removed 1679.

who speake to them oracles of law and sedition at the same time.
There is constant intelligence kept with that party and those which
are ye governeing men here, especially Wright and Paulin. Could
it be found out and their letters be intercepted, I beleive they would
bring much roguery to light. Sr Thomas Chamberlain's daughters,
of whom I made mention in my former, are both disposed of, one
to Sr Richard Wainman,[a] and the other to Dashwood's son of
London. Another of our students is become a Bar^{tt}, one Throckmorton, who on ye death of Sr Bainam Throckmorton, his unkle,
is now become Sr William,[b] but hath noe estate to support his title.
St Cyprian [c] is now don, and you may speedyly expect the publication of it.

[Oxford], Thursday, Sept. 29, [1681.]

In my last I promised you an account of ye Earl of Angleseys
reception. Accordeing to ye appointment, he was conducted into
the town last Tuesday by the townsmen in great state, and he and
his two sons made freemen of the town. He made a speech to
them, wherein he tooke notice of their disagreeing with the
University, and offerd his service to reconcile them to us, or doe
them any other kindnesse that lay in his power. It seems they
promised him, when they first went to him, that if he would stand
their friend at Court, now the Duke of Buckingham [d] their steward
hath noe accesse there, they would have a burgesses place always
at his service for whomsoever he should recommend; and this it
was that made his Ldship soe readyly comply with them ; and now

[a] Sir Richard Wenman, Bart. of Caswell, co. Oxon.; afterwards fourth Viscount
Wenman.
[b] Sir Baynham Throckmorton, Bart. of Tortworth, co. Gloucester, was succeeded
by his cousin, William Throckmorton, who was killed in a duel in June 1682.
[c] See above, p. 27, note f.
[d] After the dissolution of the Cabal, in 1673, the Duke of Buckingham was distinguished as an opponent of the Court.

they begin to defy the Ld. Norris, they haveing gotten as they thinke soe potent a protection against him ; but I suppose his Ldship will not thinke fit to interfere with any one for their sakes. After he was sworn, a dinner was made ready for him at the mayors, where he was splendidly entertaind. The townsmen have had a Common Councill to consider of ye affront put upon them in Tompsons Intelligence, and have voted it as a scandalous libell against their most honourable Corporation, and an action is ordered to be enterd against him next term. But Tompson is not the only man y^t makes sport with their voyage to Newmarket. Alderman Wright lately goeing before Brazen Nose Coll. a fresh man came out, and spying him past by called after him " Run, Alderman, run; the Black guard are comeing!" which put the alderman into soe violent a passion that he was scarce himselfe all that day after. Whenever he comes, he speakes scurrulously of the King. It seems, when ye alderman was at Newmarket with his petition, the King walkeing in ye feilds met Nel Gwyn, and Nel cald to him, " Charles, I hope I shall have your company at night, shall I not?" With this story the Alderman makes a great deal of worke wherever he comes. He says he had often heard bad things of the King, but now his own eys have seen it. They are mighty at consultation concerneing ye management of their law suit, and doubt mightyly how it will be managed against them, whither the Attorney General will plead against the granteing Prince a mandamus, or let that be granted and after proceed against them with a quo warranto. But which way soever it be, they make mighty shure of their cause ; and all the rabble of y^c town are for liveing and dying by it. Dr Morton * came hither on Tuesday, and on Friday goes for Ireland.

---

* William Moreton, D.D.; Student of Christ Church, 1660. Chaplain to the Earl of Oxford, and afterwards to the Duke of Ormonde. Dean of Christ Church, Dublin, in 1677; Bishop of Kildare in 1681; and translated to Meath, 1705. Died 1716.

. . . . . . Our townsmen are mighty ashamed of their bringeing the Earl of Anglesey hither and the brags they made of what he would doe for him [*sic*, them]; for it seems he utterly refused to be received with any state, and, when ye aldermen and cheife of ye town would have gon out to meet him, he utterly refused to be received in such manner, and told them if any one came to meet him he would return again. When he came into the Council Chamber and was sworn, he told them he thanked them for this respect they had shown him, and he would be glad of doeing them any kindnesse, provided they would make themselfe deserveing of it by beeing loyal to their King and respectfull to the University, for if they stood on ill terms with either of those they would at ye same [time] incapacitate him for doeing anything for them; and in the same manner he proceeded to repriman them for their unworthy behavior both to his Majesty and us, and to show that he did not accept of a freedom to interfere with the Ld. Norris, wch our town politicians thought would be a certain effect of his beeing made free with them. He went the day before to visit the Ld. Norris, and assured him of ye contrary. After his admission he was treated at the mayors, and 5^l allowed by ye town for ye dinner. Our townsmen have taken ye liberty of beeing bold in their talke concerneing several persons of quality at Newmarket, and particularly concerneing ye Lord Conway, whom they reported here to have been drunke all the time they were at Newmarket and 3 days before, and that when they came unto him for their answer he could scarce speake or stand. Sr Jonathan Trelawny hath undertaken to inform his Ldship of it. I would gladly hear what is the effect of it. You would doe well to inform the Secretary of a great inconvenience we here ly under by reason of our beeing over-powered at sessions by the town justices, for, they beeing twice in number to those of ye University, they carry all things that have ye least respect to the University, right or wrong, against it by majority of votes; for the death of Dr Yates and Dr Hyde [a] and the removal of Dr Nicholson [b] hath diminished our number, soe that they have 8 or 9 nine [*sic*] and we not above 5, and of those only 3, that is Dr Marshall,[c] Dr Wallis,[d] and ye Vice-Chancellor,[e] frequent the bench; Dr Bathurst and the Bishop never comeing thither. To remedy this, he cannot doe us a greater kindnesse then to augment the number by putteing in 5 or 6 new ons, and we have enough which are fit for it among ye D^{rs} and heads of colledges. Dr Lloyd [f] of Jesus is a very fit person, and soe is Dr Levet [g] of Magd. Hall, Dr Smith [h] of our colledge, and others that I can mention. If you find such a designe already on foot, as I fancy there may, or that the Secretary may thinke fit such a thing should be don, I desire you would put my kinsman Mr. Guise [i] into the number. He was formerly fellow of All Souls, but now, beeing marryed, lives in town, and hath an estate of his own about 500^l per annum. This his wife thinkes would give him a better reputation in the town, although he wants none as to his parts and learneing, beeing as eminent a person as to this of any of his standeing that, I beleive, may be found in the whole nation, and I have undertaken to endeavour to get it don out of prospect of haveing your assistance with ye Secretary, and shall take it as a great favour if you will undertake ye businesse. I desire your sense of it in your next.

---

[a] See above, p. 76, note *, and p. 29, note ^{f},

[b] A slip of the pen for Nicholas. John Nicholas, D.D. Warden of Winchester College.

[c] Thomas Marshall, D.D. Rector of Lincoln College. Dean of Gloucester, 1681. Died 1685.

[d] John Wallis, D.D. of Exeter College, Savilian Professor of Geometry.

[e] Timothy Halton, D.D. Provost of Queen's College.

[f] John Lloyd, D.D. Bishop of St. David's, 1686. Died 1687.

[g] See above, p. 29, note ^{c}.

[h] Henry Smith, D.D. Canon of Christ Church, 1676.

[i] See above, page 44.

[Oxford, 4th October, 1681.]

Little hath occurr'd here since my last, only our townsmen still persist to threaten the King with war. I find they are animated cheifely by y⁰ faction at London, who designe this as a leadeing chard to all the other citys in England; for at the Kings comeing in they all takeing out new charters had them with the same limitations as to the recorder and town clerke, and if Oxford should carry it against the King you shall find none else will allow it him; which will be as great a diminntion to the Kings prerogative as hath hapned in any Kings time, except the last, when y⁰ Crown it selfe was taken away. Jones and Winnington and Williams,ᵃ with some other of that gang, have made them soe confident of their cause that they already proclaim victory, and talke of nothing else but of burneing their last charter; and last weeke, to show their confidence, they treated one the other in y⁰ greatest profusenesse immaginable. The old mayor at his goeing out and the new mayor at his comeing into office have made two as extravagant entertainments as were ever kept in this place. They brag the King had not the like at Cambridge; but at one of them, before they parted, they had like to have faln a fighteing. They are mighty ashamed they have been soe much deceived in their expectations from y⁰ Earle of Anglesey. Before he came hither they bragd they had now got a friend to support them against y⁰ Ld. Norris, University, and every one else; for they thought their favour soe valuable yᵗ they flaterd themselfes yᵗ his Ldship would [be] engaged with them in all their extravagant pretensions for the sake of it. But it seems now they are of a contrary opinion, and only say they hope his Ldship will procure them an heareing before y⁰ councell; for their lawyers have flaterd them that their cause is soe good that y⁰ King himselfe must give it for yᵐ in spight of his

---

ᵃ William Williams, distinguished at this period for his violent opposition to the Court: but he afterwards made his peace, and became Solicitor-General in 1687.

teeth, if it were once layd open before him. But y⁰ Ld. Anglesey treated them with that distance, and reproved them with that liberty, as may sufficiently let them know he hath very little reguard for them. However, he expects they should chuse one of his sons next Parliament, and I beleive they will; for it seems my Ld. Ansley ᵃ hath utterly lost his interest at Winchester, and it was for his sake yᵗ yᵉ Privy Seal tooke soe much notice of them as he did; otherwise I understand he would not have come nigh them. Sʳ Thomas Chamberlain is dead, and hath left his two daughters 30 thousand pound a peice. Dashwood marryeth yᵉ yongest. He is buryed next Saturday, and I was to have preached his funerall sermon; but they now designeing to bury him at Banbury, there will not be time enough for it, and therefore they have none. My Ld. Lovelace hath been very busy makeing mayors at Woodstock and Wallingford, but hath come of very dully in both places. After he had drunke 3 days with all the rag tag of Woodstock, he found he had gaind soe little to the end he designed, that, to avoyd the disgrace of an open baffle, he tooke horse the night before yᵉ election and rid from them; and at Wallingford they have made an open protest against him yᵗ they will have nothing to doe with him or any that belong to him, and unanimously resolved yᵗ Taverner Harris, a factious gentleman in yᵉ neighbourhood, shall never be choosen to serve in Parliament for their town, because his Ldship recommended him. Prince hath been expostulateing with yᵉ Ld. Norris, and would know yᵉ reason why his Ldship should hinder him, and he hath given him four; two of them I have been told, 1ˢᵗ, that when it was proposed in yᵉ Common Councill to comple-ment his Ldship with a freedom of their town, Prince made a sawey rude speech against it, but this my lord told him beeing personal he did forgive him; 2ᵈˡʸ, yᵗ when yᵉ addresse to the King was proposed in Common Councill he likewise opposed that with a speech altogeather as sawey and rude, and this his Ldship told him

---

ᵃ Lord James Annesley, M.P. for Winchester, succeeded his father as Earl of Anglesey.

he could not forgive; and two other reasons he gave him which as
yet I have not learnt. I suppose another might be the great zeal
he showed at the reception of y[e] D[uke] of M[onmouth], he beeing
the biggest fellow in y[t] affair. He is, it seems, a fellow much
given to speech makeing. In that he made to the townsmen
against y[e] King and y[e] Black Guard, he exasperated y[e] rabble soe
much against Baker[a] y[t] had he been present it is supposed they
would really have torn him in peices; and he hath y[t] autority among
them y[t] his word goes for a law; for at the election of y[e] baylys, two
men of good repute haveing been put up, in whom noe other fault
could be found but that they had voted for Baker, and therefore
the whole cry of y[e] Commons was for them, till at last Prince stood
up and cryed " Noe Baker!" and named two others; and then
the cry immediately turn[ed], " Noe Baker! Noe Wickham!" (y[e]
name of one of y[m] y[t] was first set up), and they w[ch] Prince named
were approved of with general applause, and they are the men that
stand. He is a very silly pragmatical raskal as you may understand
by this, and y[e] best is he is undon by it. I wish all like him could
be soe servd.

Oxf[d], 6 Octob. 1681.

I have received yours, and have been with the Bp. concerneing
the affair you write of, and found y[e] Secretarys letter before him.
He mightyly approves of what I have don, and tells me we shall
be undone without it. He tells me noe one could pitch on fitter
persons then I named, only he would have D[r] Hammond[b] added to
the number. He tells me he will talke with the Vice-Chancellor,
and then answere the Secretarys letter, and recommend the same
persons I named, only adding D[r] Hammond to the number; and he
particularly did let me know he thought it very fit M[r] Guise should
be in the commission, and therefore I desire this kindnesse from you
y[t] you would take care his name be not omitted. That you may

---

[a] Probably Thomas Baker, town clerk in 1685.

[b] See above, p. 97, note [b].

understand the necessity of this, I will tell you one trick they put
upon us last sessions. The mayor haveing unreasonably taken many
licences for ale houses without a legal cause, the excisemen came and
complained to the Vice-Chancellor of it, and remonstrated to him
what diminution his M^{ys} revenue received hereby. Hereon the Vice-
Chancellor takes the redresseing of this into his own power and
licenseth all those the mayor refused; whereon they selld ale as
formerly. But the last session they were indited for it, as selleing ale
without licence, whereon they produced the Vice-Chancellors liceuce;
but our town would not allow y^t to be good, alledgeing the Vice-
Chancellor had noe power to license ale houses, and therefore, the
businesse beeing put to the vote, the town justices on the bench
beeing 9 and the University justices only 3, it was carryed against
the Vice-Chancellor, and the inditement found against all those that
sold by his licences, as if they had sold without any; whereon we are
forced to be at the charge and trouble of getting a certiorari to remove
the businesse to another court, and without soe doeing we shall
never have any thing like justice don us in the plainest cases, and
I thinke plainer case cannot be then this I instance in, and the like
measure we must always expect till we have equal number with
them on ye bench. Pray acquaint the Secretary with this story,
then he will further see ye necessity of doeing what I advised.
This day concluds the sessions. I will at night wait on Dr Marshall,
and from him I shall understand what hath been don there and
give you an account. Our townsmen begin to quarrel now among
themselfes. Their late journy to New Market cost the town 40^l;
at this some of them begin to grumble, and ask ye question, why
they had not reather choosen to have petitioned ye King while nigh
us at Windsor but stay till he was gon to Newmarket which is thrice
as far distant; and on inquiry into this it appears y^t most that went
had businesse at Sturbridge fair, and they choose to carry their
petition to New Market that they might at the same time doe their
private businesse on the publick charge; which discovery makes
great grumbling and muttereing among the inferior townsmen.

The Ld. Lovelace was the first that started it, to be revenged on Wright for not provideing his plate; and it seems, at the same time the Ld. Lovelace sent about y᷃ plate, he sent likewise to the alderman to prepare a lodgeing for the D[uke] of M[onmouth]; but the alderman, beeing somewhat cowd, sent him word that he thought it better for the Duke to tarry away then come; whereon y᷃ Ld. Lovelace came hither himself about it, and then y᷃ alderman plainly told him, if the D. would come, he might if he pleased, but he should not lodge in his house. Hereon his Lordship fell into a passion, and made the discovery I have above mentioned, and hath been very carefull to propagate it among y᷃ inferior townsmen, to make them rebell against their superiors. The Lord Norris is now in town, haveing here a general muster of all the militia in y᷃ county, w᷃ᶜʰ are very well provided and in good order. I scarce beleive any other county in England hath their militia soe well looked after. I suppose now the court are consulteing about the sheriffs for y᷃ ensueing year. I had a brother in law ᵃ served for Cornwall last year; and another ᵇ in Devonshire is afraid this office will fall on him next year, but it will neither be for his interest or the Kings it should be soe. He hath indeed a very good estate, but hath with it y᷃ clog of 8 daughters, 4 of w᷃ᶜʰ he hath late marryed, w᷃ᶜʰ hath cost him 6000ˡ, of w᷃ᶜʰ 1500ˡ is yet oweing; and it will be his utter undoeing to put him into this office. His name is Coffin; he is a very understandeing man and fit for any businesse, but will act too waryly to answere the Kings expectations in such an office. My Ld. Chancellor hath don me the favour to keep him of 5 years. If you could doe me the same kindnesse by Mʳ Secretary, I would be glad not alwayse to trouble the Lord Chancellor about it. The fittest person for the Kings turn in Devon is Sʳ Courtney Pool,ᶜ who you may be sure will never be choosen Parliament man

---

ᵃ William Pendarves, of Pendarves, married Admonition Prideaux.

ᵇ Richard Coffin, of Portledge, married Anne Prideaux. He escaped being Sheriff till 1684.

ᶜ Sir Courtenay Pole, Bart. of Shute, was appointed. He had been Sheriff in 1668. The reference to the chimneys doubtless points to the hearth-tax.

of any place where there are chimneys, and therefore ye King will not loose a friend in Parliament by excludeing him thence with this office; and for Cornwall the only man we have is Mr Arthur Spry,[a] who is a very rich man and sure friend to the King and hath noe interest in any corporation to be choosen their burgesse. When at London, my Ld. Arundel[b] told me he could thinke of noe one fit to be recommended to the King and desired me to help him, and I confesse I was yⁿ at as great a loss as he; but since I have thought on this gentleman, and I thinke there is none like him for the Kings turn.

[Oxford, October, 1681.]

Nothing hapned worth informeing you at our sessions, but only that 2 malefactors were condemned to death (one for killing her bastard and a rogue for cutteing a purse), and the pro-Town Clerke officiated not in his place. It seems ye townsmen doe not keep to their first courage, but begin to be cautious and wary how they give offence, and therefore have thought fit not to let Prince officiate in the place as they first designed, but have appointed another to doe it. The Vice-Chancellor and ye Bp. have had a great consult about the Secretarys letter concerneing ye reneweing our commission, and have agreed to put in Dr Parrot,[c] Dr Levet, Dr Jane, Dr Beson,[d] Warden of New Colledge, Dr Lloyd, and I thinke Mr Guise. The Bp. is very desirous he should be in, but the Vice-Chancellor made an exception that he was not soe proper as beeing only a M^r of Arts; but when I went to him and told him he was not to be looked on as an ordinary M^r of Arts, but as a gentleman which lives in town upon his estate wch is worth 500[l]

[a] He was not appointed. Christopher Bollot, of Bochym, was Sheriff for Cornwall in 1682.

[b] Richard, Lord Arundel of Trerice, an old Cavalier officer.

[c] Charles Perot, M.D. of St. John's College; afterwards M.P. for the University. Died 1686.

[d] Henry Beeston, LL.D. formerly Head-master of Winchester College.

per annum, and therefore sufficient to qualify him for such an office
in any county in England, he semed to be as willing as the Bp.,
but whither they will return his name or noe I can not tell.   I
desire y^t you would give me advice from ye Secretarys, where you
will certainly know; for, if his name be not put in at ye Secretarys,
I will attempt to doe it at the Lord Chancellors, and I hope there
I shall not fail; but if that trouble were saved I should be glad,
and therefore I beg your assistance in it.   I wonder ye Secretary
should say he doth not know him.   He knew him once to doe him
a very great unkindnesse in makeing the Archbp. his enemy,
although he did not designe it.   He is a gentleman of as great
worth and eminency in that way of learneing he hath addicted
himselfe to as any in England, or, I believe, in any other country
in Europe, and on that account is an ornament to the University,
and will er long appear soe to the whole nation.   He is an extraordinary person and I cannot say enough of him, and beside him I
beleive you will find few of his estate to devote themselfes soe
industriously to their studys, or of his parts to make soe good
progresse in them.   And beside, his good inclinations to the Church
doth sufficiently appear in that, in his circumstances and in soe ill
times, he would goe into orders to be rendered thereby ye more
capable of serving it.   I thinke such a man is not to be affronted,
and now his name hath been mentioned on this occasion it would be
an affront not to be put in.   Pray use your interest to effect it, and
if that doth not succeed I will use mine with the Chancellor.   He
is marryed and lives here in the town, and therefore considereing
all his qualifications I know not who can be fitter.   The Secretary
haveing himselfe mentioned Dr Jane, the Bp. thought not fit to
put in either Dr Hammond or Dr Smith, to avoid envy to our
colledge.   Sr William Walter^a already begins to make an interest
to be knight of the shire next Parliament, and will I suppose
without any great difficulty carry it, he beeing a person of general
good esteem in ye county.   Tomorrow I goe to the funeral of

---

^{a} Sir William Walter, Bart. of Saresden, co. Oxon.   He was not returned.

Sr Thomas Chamberlain, where I suppose I shall meet most of the gentry of ye county, and perchance shall be able to inform you of something worth observation from thence. St Cyprian^a is now finished, as likewise a booke of Dugdales of Heraldry;^b it contains ye first principles of it, and the catalogue of ye Nobility and Baronets of ye 3 kingdoms.

[Oxford], Octob. 18th, 1681.

I write you this to repete my request concerneing the information I desired you would give me in my last as to the E. of T.^e It beeing of concern to me to know of him, ye sooner you can satisfy me herein ye greater kindnesse you will doe me. As to Mr Guise, I am well content, for some certain reasons since urged, that he be noe more mentioned; for it seems all ye heads of houses are against it, that a man which is not equal with y^m in academical dignity should be named in ye Kings commission with them. Although I thinke their argument foolish and pedantick, yet, since all of them are against it, I thinke this is a sufficient argument why we should wave it. But Dr Bury,^d Rector of Exeter, hath through inadvertency been omitted, who is really ye fittest person for such a businesse in ye whole University, beeing a man that very well understands businesse and is always very vigorous and diligent in it, and hath been a head of a colledge now 18 years. The Secretary cannot but know him, and in truth it will be an affront to passe

---

^a "S. C. Cypriani Opera recognita et illustrata per Joannem Oxouiensem Episcopum," etc. Oxon, 1682, fol.

^b "The Ancient Usage of bearing such Eusigns of Honour as are commonly called Arms; with Catalogues of the present Nobility and Baronets of England, Scotland, and Ireland." Oxford, 1682, 8vo.

^e Probably Richard Tufton, Earl of Thanet.

^d Arthur Bury, D.D. Student of Exeter College 1638; Rector of Pointington, co. Somerset; Prebendary of Exeter 1660; Rector of his college 1665. He was suspended for a short time, in 1690, for writing a heterodox work, "The Naked Gospel." —*Ath. Oxon.* iv. 482.

him by. I hear noe more town news to inform you. Prince doth not officiate as was first designed, but that province is left to one Mr Kiblewhite, who giveth soe good satisfaction in the management of it y^t I hear ye town is become disposed to elect him into ye place, they haveing already deserted Prince and left him to wage war with ye King upon his own charges. Soe they talke, but when term begins you will see what they will doe. Sir William Walter and Sir Robert Jinkinson^a canvas hard to be choosen Parliament men for ye county next Parliament, and I beleive they will succeed in their pretensions. They are both well known at Court, and therefore I need not trouble you with an account of y^m. We hear here the E[arl] of S[haftesbury]^b desires transportation, and would willingly commute banishment for his life. We are told likewise y^t we shall have part of ye term here, and that ye King intends to visit us again before Christmas; which reports have much amused us. I should be glad to know whither there be any grounds for y^m. Our gate is advanced as far as the top of ye battlements of ye colledge, and there I suppose it must rest till next spring.

[Oxford], Tuesday, Octob. 25th, 1681.

I thank you for your two last, and, if the E[arl] of T[hanet]s affair doth proceed, it will be wholely from that character you give of him. My kinswoman hath an estate of 2500^l per annum, and ye E. is very earnest to be admitted, and, your letters haveing inclined me for it, if my advice be harkned to (as I beleive it will before any other), there shall be no more demur in the businesse. They

^a Sir Robert Jenkinson, Bart. of Walcot, co. Oxon. He was M.P. for the county in William III.'s reign.

^b There was foundation for this rumour. About this time Shaftesbury wrote to Lord Arlington, the Lord Chamberlain, offering, if released from imprisonment, to retire to Carolina, of which province he was part proprietor.—See W. D. Christie, *Life of Anthony Ashley Cooper, first Earl of Shaftesbury,* 1871, ii. 419.

had er this come to a treaty, but that I desired them to be informed first whither this gentleman, haveing lived 20 years in the most vicious court in the world, may not have received those mischeifes w^cb may make the yong ladys condition miserable with him; but since you assure me he is sound, wind and limb, this objection shall put noe further obstruction to it.[a] On Sunday here hapned a very calamitous accident. One Cardonnel,[b] formerly Kings scollar at Westminster and afterward Demy of Magd. Coll. and then Fellow of Merton, there hangeing himselfe at his study door. It seems he was a very fretfull, peevish man, and one of the deepest resentments for ye least seemeing affront that ever I heard of. Beeing, as he conceived, not duely reguarded by ye warden, to expresse his revenge to him, when Burser of the colledge, [he] refused to pay one of his servants wages (as is the custom of y^t college), and, after several sollicitations made to him in the wardens name, at last told the fellow he might be gon and tell the warden he should be hangd if he would, he would pay none of his servants wages. Whereon the warden summoned the fellows to a meeting and informed y^m

---

[a] The Earl of Thanet, however, died unmarried early in 1684.

[b] William Cardonnel, M.A. of Merton College.

"Oct. 23.—Sunday, between 10 and 11 in the morning, Mr. Cardonnell hanged himself in his bedchamber, on his door; discovered by his maid after 12 of the clock; he had only his shirt and night-cap on, and there he hung till between 7 and 8 at night, and then the coroner and jury, coming and seeing him, there pronounced that he was not *compos mentis;* about 11 at night he was buried stark naked in the vestry yard, on the south side of the chancel; he was troubled in conscience for cheating the college of 3*l.* or 4*l.* when he was bursar the year before, and troubled for the warden's misusing him for another matter, as he thought. When he was bursar last Spring, or deputy bursar, [he] sent the gardener to him for money due to the gardener for doing work in the warden's garden. Mr. Cardonnell, not being in a right humour, bid the warden be hanged, he should have no money; the gardener told the warden these words, the warden took affidavit of it, drew up a recantation, which being shown the fellows, Cardonnel at a meeting read it, but this stuck so close to him, that bringing a melancholy fit on him he could never shake it off. In June or August before he threw himself into the water in Magdalen walks to drown himself, but could not effect it."—Wood, *Life,* xcii. The Warden was Sir Thomas Clayton, knt. M.D.

what language Mr Cardonnel had sent him a message in, and put
it to their votes what punishment he deserved; wch beeing unanimously voted expulsion, Mr Cardonnel, to avoyd this, was forced to
signe a submission wch he read on his knees before ye warden and
fellows, wherein he acknowledged his fault and that it deserved
expulsion, and that it was the wardens favour that it was not
accordeingly inflicted on him, and then gave the paper of submission thus signed into the wardens hands; but after reflecteing
on the disgrace, and haveing deeper resentments of it then others
would have had, and apprehendeing that every body contemned
him for it, he endeavonred by all the friends he could possibly make
to get the paper out of the wardens hands; but the warden beeing
obstinately bent not to gratify him herein, although he were told
that this wch hath now hapned might be ye consequence of his
refusal, Mr Cardonnel fell into soe deep a discontent that he hath
endeavoured several times to destroy himselfe; and last Sunday,
about ten in the morneing, he effected it in a most dismal manner
at his study door, where after sermon he was found hangeing in his
shirt.   On end of the rope he tied to a spring lock on ye inner side,
and ye noose comeing to the top of the door, there by helpe of a
stool he put in his head, but however the place was not soe high but
that he was forced to goe to his knees to effect his designe.   The
crowner haveing set on him, he was last night privately without
any ceremony put into a grave in an outer yard belongeing to the
colledge.   In his study were found several directions for the disposal
of his affairs, and on the wals were stuck up in several papers verses
of ye Penitential Psalms; all wch argue it a thing long premeditated.
About a fortnight before he solemnely came to our colledge to take
leave of a brother of his. student here, and told him he intended to
se him noe more; but his brother, apprehendeing the meaneing of
it, prevented soe long his designe; and about a month before he
writ a letter to a friend of his, wch had an influence with the
warden, to desire him to interpose with the warden to get this paper
out of his hands; and this he did intreateing him in the most

earnest manner immaginable (wch shows ye agonys of his mind), for he desired him by all that is sacred, by all the obligations of friendship which he could reckon up, and at last in the words of a dying man, which shows that then he had a designe to destroy himselfe. And would the warden had been soe reasonable as to have granted him his request, I beleive by the help of physick he might have been brought of this designe. The later remedy he hath used all this autumne, but the former beeing wonteing made the other ineffectnal. He was an ingenious man and a good schollar, of about 11 years standeing in the University. It is one of the dismalst accidents that hath ever hapned within ye compasse of my knowledge, and if the warden be not as hard as flint it must stick on him. It was about an halfe year since the warden brought him to this submission. His study was in physick, but however I suppose our whig newsmongers will represent him to be in orders, and make od reflections of it. He was of an unhappy constitution, and y^t brought the dismal destruction upon him. We have another thing hath hapned here very strange. A woman last sessions was here condemned for murdereing her bastard, and, beeing designed to have been hanged last Thursday, on her beeing acquainted with it fell into a sowneing fit and hath soe ever since continued. Two or 3 times she hath come to her selfe, but never remained a quarter of an hour before she relapsed, and it's supposed she will save the hangman the labour, it not beeing likely that she will ever recover. The story of ye E[arl] of S[haftesbury]s goeing to Carolina is soe obstinately beleived here that noe one will be perswaded but that his Ldship petitioned the King to this effect, and all our news letters have had it. The pamphlet intitled " Noo Protestant plot "^{a} is with us, and John Lock is said to be the author of it.^{b} Now term begins,

* " No Protestant Plot: or, The present pretended Conspiracy of Protestants against the King and Government discovered to be a Conspiracy of the Papists against the King and his Protestant Subjects." London, 1681, 4to. It was continued in a Second and Third Part in 1682.

^{b} In a letter written to the Earl of Pembroke, in 1684, Locke denied the authorship of the many pamphlets attributed to him: " I do solemnly protest in the

several causes will be commenced at the Kings bench wch concern
us. Our townsmen sue the King and Tompson about their town
clerk, and some that were disappointed at All Souls last election ^{a}
this term thinke to find releife in Westminster Hall; but we expect
the judges should dismisse that businesse from their court, it not
lying properly before them. We talke here that some part of y"
term will be adjourned hither, and ye sheriffe himself hath reported it.

Since what I have above written concerneing Cardonnel, I
understand there was something of more deep concern then y"
affront he received from ye warden wch made him hang himselfe.
It seems he had lived with ye Earle of Devonshire as præceptor to
his grandson, where, haveing been poisened by Hobs, on his return
hither blasphemy and atheisme was his most frequent talke; of the
guilt of wch beeing at last sensible, this, its supposed, precipitated
him into despair. Beside, he was heard complain he had been
guilty of perjury worse then murder, and y^{t} God could never forgive
him for it. When ye malancholy workd, every thing concurd to
augment it, and all appeared to him in the worst shapes, till this
dismal death became his exit.

[Oxford], Novr 3, [16]81.

Dr Lamphire,^{b} Principal of Hart Hall, last Saturday fell mad
and hath ever since soe continued. Its sayd to be occasioned by
a cold he catched by sitteing up to hear Colledges tryall, wch at
last affecteing his head hath brought him to this condition; but

presence of God that I am not the author, not only of any libel, but not of any
pamphlet or treatise whatever, in part good, bad, or indifferent."—See W. D.
Christie, *Life of Shaftesbury*, i. 261.

    ^{a} For fellowships.

    ^{b} John Lamphire, M.D. sometime Fellow of New College; Principal of Hart Hall
and Camdenian Professor of History.

for my part I attribute it to his gluttony, he being ye greatest
eater that ever I knew. They have bleeded him and used other
remedys, but it seems to little purpose. I beleive his death will
be a speedy consequent of it. The woman still continues in his
[*sic*] trance, soe that now we doe noe more doubt but that [it]
is a trick of hers to save herselfe from hangeing, for it is now 16
days since she first fell into it, and in all this time its pretended
she hath not eat or drunke, but ye impossibility of the thing sufficiently convinceth it. Att All Souls is now the time of their
election. The Archbps injunctions and a mandamus sent thither
by ye King in behalfe of one Sayer, son to the Kings cooke,
causeth great disturbances among them. It seems ye mandamus
past the Ld. Conways office, and by it Mr Booth, his brother-
in-law,^{a} is put by, unlesse it be again revoked. It seems ye young
gentleman acquainted not his Ldship with his designe of being a
candidate for that fellowship, otherwise I suppose he would not
have imbraced anothers interest before his. By next post you shall
have a full account of that affair.

[Oxford, Nov. 5, 1681.]

Our All Souls businesse hath been carryed on with a great deal
of confusion. The truth is, they have been very guilty of selleing
their places, and the Archbp, to prevent this intolerable corruption,
hath gon in a method which ye goodnesse of the end cannot justify,
which hath brought a great deal of trouble upon him. The
principal points controverted between ye fellows and him are concerneing an oath imposed on them, wch they have refused to take;
and its seems the Archbp, findeing he had noe power to impose it,
hath in this particular confessed his error and receded from it; the

---

^{a} Lord Conway married, secondly, Elizabeth, daughter of George Booth, Lord
Delamere. His brother-in-law was Robert Booth, of Christ Church, M.A. 1684;
B.D. 1708. Archdeacon of Durham, 1691; Dean of Bristol, 1708.

other is concerneing an injunction which the Archbp, as their
visitor, hath sent them, requireing them not to fill any place at
their election which shall not be resigned at or before the 22d day
of October; but this beeing directly contrary to their statutes, wᶜʰ
strictly require them to fill all places which shall be void at their
elections, the fellows refuse to pay obedience to it. The former
caused a devolution last year, and the later hath this; for yᵉ Head,
in obedience to the Archbp, refuseing to admit the fellows to vote
except they would take yᵉ oath, their election brooke up without
any conclusion put to it within the time limited, wᶜʰ is the 5ᵗʰ of
November, and consequently was devolved to the Archbp, who, as
impowred by statute, put in 4 fellows by his own autority : but
their right is questioned, and the businesse is now before the Kings
Bench. This year the oath was not proposed, but the injunction of
resigneing before yᵉ 22d of October was still exacted, and therefore,
Mʳ Clerke ᵃ resigneing after yᵉ 22d, yᵉ warden would not propose
any for his place, although a son of yᵉ Earl of Winchelsea ᵇ stood
for it and Mʳ Clerke resigned in his favour; soe that there was
only one vacancy to be supplyed, wᶜʰ fell void by death. For this
one Mʳ Harrington,ᶜ a founders kinsman, appeared, and yᵉ warden
thought himselfe bound by his oath to be for him ; but an allarm
comeing of a mandamus in favour of one Sayer, as I informed you
in my last (although since it appears there is noe truth in it), Mʳ
Finch thought he had as good a title to the Kings favour as any
other, and therefore, sendeing immediatly to London, a mandamus
came hither on Wednesday in his behalfe. But the warden, notwithstandeing that, stickeing firm to Harrington, although yᵉ fellows

---

ᵃ John Clerke, of Christ Church, son of Sir Francis Clerke, of Rochester; M.A.
1671; afterwards Fellow of All Souls. Rector of Ulcomb and Harrietsham in Kent.
—*Fast. Oxon.* ii. 335.

ᵇ Leopold William Finch, fifth son of Heneage Earl of Winchilsea; entered
Christ Church, 1679; B.A. 1681; of All Souls, and M.A. 1685; D.D. 1694. He
became Warden of All Souls in 1686, and Prebendary of Canterbury in 1689. Died
1702.

ᶜ William Harrington, of All Souls; M.A. 1686.

almost unanimously payd their obedience to his Majestys commands
and voted for Finch, yet put in his negative against him; and at last,
because ye fellows would not agree with him to resist the Kings
letter and choose his man, hath devolved the election upon the
Archbishop. Had the warden consented to the fillcing of M^r
Clerkes place as ye statutes absolutely require, both his man and
Mr Finch too might have been provided for; but now I suppose y^e
King will interpose his autority to fill both, and put Mr Finch in
one and Mr Booth in ye other. Dr Lamphire still remaineth mad,
and ye wench in her trance; this beeing ye 18th day she hath been
in it, its sufficiently apparent, and it is a cheat to save herselfe from
hangeing; but this is not like long to hold.

[Oxford], Novemb. 7th, 1681.

You haveing been pleased to promise me your assistance in
behalfe of my kinsman Mr Guise in any thing that could be an
encouragement unto him for his considerable worth, I have an
opportunity now offered to make use of your kind offer in his
behalfe. Dr Lamphire beeing past all hopes of life,[a] his hall, worth
about 60^l per annum, will fall into the Ld. Lieutenants disposal.
If you will be pleased make use of that interest you have to
recommend him to my Lords favour, you will oblidge my friend;
and that is one of the greatest kindnesses you can doe me.

Norw^h, 28 Nov^r, [16]81.

I doe heartyly thanke you for your letter. I am now here
deeply engaged in ye church businesse, which takes up a great part
of my time; otherwise you should er this have heard from me.

[a] Dr Lamphire lived till 1688.

All the news I can inform you of from this place is that the
gentlemen of ye county and my Ld. Townsend^a with them, are
resolved not to make choice of Sr John Hubbert and Sr William
Gleen ^b to be any more k^ts of the shire, or of any other that shall
be against the expedient the King proposed . . . . .

———

Norwich, Dec. 9th, 1681, Friday.

. . . . . . I find my prebendary noe contemptable preferment;
although this were ye worst audit we have had since ye King came
in, yet every prebendarys place hath been worth 100^l this last year,
and it will be oftener 200^l then soe again.   140^l per annum I judge
is the justest computation of ye value of it; but this is an arcanum
among ourselfes; but I speake truth open to you which to another
ought not to be discovered . . . .

Norwich, Dec. 19th, 1681, Monday.

. . . . Our Mayor^c went hence this morneing, being
summoned by a letter from Secretary Jinkins to appear before the
Councel to answere to the complaints of the excisemen made
against him there for putteing down alehouses here. The truth
is, this town swarms with alehouses, every other house is almost
one, and every one of them they tell is alsoe a bawdy house. The
brewers of late, haveing several of them succeeded in the Mayors
office, have increased the number of those houses for their own
advantage ; which proving of very mischeivous consequence to the
place, this Mayor hath set himselfe to redresse it, and, as becomes

---

^a Horatio, Baron, in 1682 Viscount, Townshend.   Died 1687.

^b An error for Sir Peter Gleane, of Hardwick, Bart.

^c Hugh Bokenham, afterwards, 1689-91, M.P. for Norwich.   Prideaux married
one of his kinswomen.

an honest and good magistrate, hath reduced them to a more tolerable number. This vexeing the brewers, they have represented it in the worst colours to the Commissioners of the Excise, and they have made complaint of it to the King in Councill. The Mayor is one Mr Bokenham, a gentleman of good family in Suffolk, and a very good estate, being reputed worth above 15,000^l. He is the gentilest and best behaved man in town, and most sincerely addicted to the Kings interest, and all that are soe in this place have y^t respect for him, that if he should receive any affront it would quite make a turn of ye Kings interest in this place, soe much is he respected here. The Conntesse of Yarmouth[a] and her son, ye Ld. Paston,[b] came last weeke in great state into ye country, and yeasterday were at our church, and I had ye honour to preach before them. This day they treat ye city at their house, about 7 miles from hence, haveing invited all the cheife men of ye town thither. His Ldship hath in severall Parliaments been elected member for this city ; now it seems he declares he will stand for ye county, but it is not expected that he will be able to carry it.

Norwich, Dec. 26, [1681].

. . . . . Ransackeing our treasury I find severall old manuscrip^t , from which I have geathered a very particular account of the foundation and history of our church. Herbert de Lozinga,[c] first Bp. of Norwich, was our founder; he was born in pago Oxamiensi in Normandy, was prior of Fischamps in that country, and was after, by William Rufus, made abbot of Ramsey, and then Bp. of Thedford,

[a] Rebecca, daughter of Sir Jasper Clayton, knt., and wife of Robert Paston, first Earl of Yarmouth.

[b] William Paston, who succeeded to the title of Yarmouth in 1682.

[c] Herbert Losinga, born at Exmes (or Hiemes), in Normandy; Prior of Fécamp; made Abbat of Ramsay by William II. in 1087, and Bishop of Thetford in 1091. He removed the see to Norwich in 1094. Died 1119. He was never Chancellor. Prideaux completed the restoration of his tomb in 1682.

from wch place he translated ye episcopal sea to this city and built ye cathedral here, and was after a long while Chancellor of England under Henry ye First. That I would desire you to inform me is, when he was first chancellor, and when he ceased so to be; of which you will find an account in Dugdales Origines Jurisdiciales, at the end of which is a catalogue of all ye chancellors since ye Conquest; and if you have any bookes of French geography I would gladly be informed what kind of place this Oxam might be which gave birth to him, and likewise ye same of Fischamps in which he was prior. In our manuscripts I find ye name writ differently; one hath it Fiscanum Monasterium, another Fiscamum, and a third Fischamps, ye French name. Pray let me receive your information herein as soone as you can. Y^e defect of bookes in this place makes me trouble you, for I have occasion to be informd herein; for ye truth is, our founders monument being defaced in the late wars, I am again restoreing it, and would gladly be informed in those particulars in order to the contriveing of a new inscription. Our mayor, since his goeing to Londou to appear at ye Councill, hath an estate of 700^l per annum fallen to him, his elder brothers family beeing extinct in [a] child which dyed last week.

Norwich, Jan. 2d, 1681[2].

I doe most heartyly thanke you for ye favour of yours, and ye account you are pleased to give me concerneing Oxam. If there be any such place near Feschamps, y^t is ye place where our founder was born; for he was prior of Feschamps, and in our registers of great antiquity is said to be born in pago Oxamiensi, which some mistakeing have given occasion to Alexander Nevel,[a] and afterward to Bp. Goodwin [b] in his History of Bps., to publish to the world y^t

[a] Alexander Neville, in his "Norwicus," printed at the end of "De Furoribus Norfolciensium Ketto duce," 1575.

[b] Francis Godwin, Bishop of Hereford. "De Præsulibus Angliæ," 1616.

he was born in Oxford. I hope by this you are secured of a faculty place; if soe, I wish you much joy of it, and advise you to thinke of takeing your D^{rs} degree in laws as soon as you can, next Act if I may be harkned to. . . . .

Oxford, 19 Febr. 168¼.

. . . . . I am glad ye account I sent you of Norfolk gives you satisfaction; ye later end of it I huddled over in some hast, and therefore have not so fully and methodically expressed myself therein as I could wish. That which I thinke most proper to be insisted on to the Secretary is the reduceing ye Ld. Townsend and his party to their old principles of loyalty and obedience to the King, which, in ye circumstances ye Ld. Townsend now stands, may easily be effected; for since his letter, which I mentioned, he hath utterly lost himselfe with the Whig party, and they with him by the ill treatment which they gave him hereon, and therefore he now cannot signify much in that country against the King; yet he may doe a great deal for him, because, if he would really declare for the Kings party, he would draw a great many of his friends after him, especially if care be taken to remove their dissatisfaction for the affront they have received by beeing turnd out of the commission, and that can only be don by restoreing them again. This weeke, I understand, is come to London from Norfolke one Mr Townsend, a kinsman of my Lds.; his businesse is to conferre with my Ld. about ye affairs of ye county, to give him a state of them, and consult how his Ldship and his friends shall steer their course for ye future; and therefore I suppose this is the best opportunity to close with what I propose, before this gentleman return into the country to carry my Lds. resolutions and instructions to his party. And I must again tell you y^t one of ye properest remedys to cure the discontents of a great many of y^t county will be to dismisse Dr.

Hilyard[a] and some other of his imprudent pragmaticalnesse from having any thing more to doe in ye county as justices of the peace; for generally all the gentlemen of ye county are dissatisfyed with the D^{rs} carriage, and like it not that he should be among them; and this is sufficiently manifested by y^r publick affronts which are put [upon him] every sessions, and by those of his own party. Last sessions he was inquireing on ye bench very busyly for his man, and one replyed he knew [noe] man he had but his mandamus, reflecteing on his takeing his degree by mandamus at Cambridge on ye Prince of Oranges beeing there. At the same time, papers beeing read which bore date in Olivers time, wherein Sr John Hobard was stild John Lord Hobard,[b] the D^r took the occasion of inveigheing against him for it on ye bench; and one of his expressions beeing " And then it was John Lord Hobard," reply was made by one on ye bench, " And now it seems 'tis John Lord Hilyard." I know not whether I inserted in ye account I sent you that the last session, of 45 inditements wch where [sic] presented there, 30 were ye D^{rs}, and of those one halfe quashed as beeing of matters not inditeable. In a word, his folly and indiscreet pragmaticalnesse have made him intolerable, and others of his profession suffer for his sake, his insolence haveing risen ye odium of ye county not only against himselfe but his gownd alsoe, and he is become hereby ye greatest disturber of ye publick peace y^t is in the county. Pray let it be urged that Mr. Long be taken notice of, he haveing ye best reputation of parts and understandeing of any gentleman in ye county, and if made the Kings, I beleive would be able to do him as good service in y^t county as any one in it, not excepting ye Ld Townsend himselfe. A little care would rout the Whigs in those parts, and now is the opportunity to imploy it. I should be glad to know whither Sr Jonathan hath got the Admirals place in Cornwall, and, if not, which way it is gon. Harry Aldrich is instald,[c] and this day hath obtained a dispensation to proceed D^r in Divinity on

a   John Hildeyard, LL.D. Rector of Cawston.

b   See above, page 90, note a   c   Canon of Christ Church.

his performeing his exercise for that degree only. The Earle of
Northampton [a] and y[e] Ld. Herbert [b] were, at the same time, made
M[rs] of Arts. The Ld. Northampton is at present a member of our
University, but is goeing from us ; and the Ld. Herbert was about
3 years since, and now, comeing occasionally to town, the University
have complimented him with this degree.

[Oxford], Feb. 23, [1682].

I have yours of Tuesday, and know not what to say to your
affair. It is better have the imployment you mention then have
none at all, especially if you are sent soe honourably to it as by
the King himselfe and have his promise of a provision, but to be
always mereteing and receive noe reward is an hard case. This
imployment is not worth medleing with, in my judgment, without
a future prospect of advantage ; if you have any such, it is better
embarke in it then ly idle, but were it my case I would make my
market as good as I could and would not ask lesse then to be
Clerk of y[e] Councill, and old Brown [c] will er long make a place
vacant there ; you can best judge of it. My good wishes I can
put it, but my judgment in cases of this nature is not to be relyed
on, because not versed in y[e] affairs of Court or acquainted how
your circumstances stand there ; only this, I would always lay
down as a general rule, to accept of that which is beneath a mans
expectations rather then have nothing at all. Your cheife point
will be to secure a friend which will solicit for you in your absence
in case an opportunity happen, and next to take care, while in
France, y[t] the faults of the inexperienced ambassador doe not ly at

[a] George Compton, Earl of Northampton; M.A. of Christ Church, 18 February,
1682.
[b] Charles Somerset, Lord Herbert of Ragland, eldest son of Henry Marquess of
Worcester, who was this year created Duke of Beaufort.
[c] Sir Richard Browne, Bart., Ambassador to France in Charles I.'s time; Clerk to
the Privy Council. He was father-in-law to John Evelyn.

your door, for I perceive, in effect, you are to be sent his governor, and often it happens to such y[t] they bear the blame for their pupils fault, whither they can help them or noe.[a] I wish you all the success you can desire or expect in this affair, and the best prosperity in all other.

[P.S.] If it give you not too much trouble, I would desire you to remember your promise of buying me a beaver, such as is proper for a divine, provided not too big ; and get it put into a box and sent to the Oxford carriers either at y[e] Sarazens Head in Snow Hill or y[e] Oxford Arms in Warwic Lane, which y[e] person of whom you buy it of I suppose will take care. If it be not sent away as soon as bought, there will be danger of a change afterward.

Oxford, 12 March, [1682].

Our assizes are ended without affordeing me anything observable to inform you of. Here was very little businesse on y[e] Crown side. Only a poor fellow is condemnd to be hanged for breakeing prison. He was last Michaelmas condemned at y[e] town sessions for cutteing a purse, that haveing it seems been long his trade, for it appeared by his hand he was formerly burnt for it. However, intercession having been made to the King for him, he was repreved in order to transportation; but before orders came concerneing it he broke prison, and, beeing a while after catchd again at his old trade and put into Newgate, our gaylor challenged him as his, and beeing brought hither hath sentence of death passd upon him again for breakeing his prison; and now I suppose, without any further hopes of mercy, he is to prepare for hangeing, he beeing a most notorious

---

[a] It may be gathered from allusions made by Ellis's correspondents (Brit. Mus. Add. MS. 28875) that he was to have had some office under the English Ambassador in France, at this time James Graham, Viscount Preston. He failed, however, to get the appointment, though he appears to have been in Paris early in the year.

rogue, as it sufficiently appeared at his tryall. That which was most observable was a most terrible abhorrence of ye association [a] presented to the bench by the grand jury, and the Ld. Norris beeing present undertooke ye presenteing of it. It is worded at the highest pitch of loyalty and zeal, and in the end of it they promise ye King y^t, whensoever he shall thinke fit to call another Parliament, they will chuse only such as shall be acceptable to the King, and will be for the preserveing the succession of the Crown to the right heir. Levinz sat judge for ye Crown, and Atkings[b] in ye other court. Friday morneing was wholy taken up in giveing ye charge, which was very long, and therefore he made this excuse for it, that there beeing very little busiuesse he had nothing else to entertain ye company with. In his charge he insisted against prosecuteing Protestant dissenters on ye Act of 35th of Queen Elizabeth, and urged some arguments to prove that it was not designed it should be put in execution against them, particularly that of inflicteing lesser penaltys since, which he looked on as disalloweing of those rigorous ones [to be] inflicted by that Act, and told us that it was never but once put in execution, and that was against some of Colchester; which part of his charge gave us here some offence. Aaron Smiths[c] businesse is put of till the next assize, some punctilio in law beeing wonteing for bringeing him to his triall this assizes. We had great expectations of a tryall at the other court between ye Ld. Norris and Brome Whorwood,[d] about their quarrel in the Town Hall at the election of ye Town Clerk. Broom brought an action of battery against my Ld. for beateing him, and my Ld. an action of scandalum magnatum against Broome for calleing him yong fool. But the Bp. of

[a] The association which Shaftesbury was accused of forming for the exclusion of the Duke of York.

[b] Sir Creswell Levinz and Sir Robert Atkyns, Puisne Judges of the Common Pleas.

[c] See above, p. 93, note [c].

[d] Brome Whorwood, of Halton, co. Oxon; sometime of Trinity College; M.P. for Oxford City.

Oxford interposeing spoild the sport and made up the matter between them; for in truth y^r Ld. Norris first began the quarrel, and called Brome old fool before he called him yong fool; and beside it was reather hypothetically then categorically sayd, for my Ld. calleing him old fool, he replyed, "If I am an old fool you are a yong fool," and therefore I thinke his Lordship did very wisely to submitt it to the Bps. arbitration. Whenever there is a Parliament its certain this old knave will never more be choosen here, by reason of the trick he hath put upon his brother representative; for Alderman Wright takeing care of dischargeing the alehouse and paying the bills of their canvas, when he came to Whorwood to be reimbursed his share of it, the old knave told him if he had payed the bills already there was noe need for him to concern himselfe any further, and ye Alderman could not get as much as a fartheing of him for beareing the expences of thre elections for him; and on this account he is out of all expectations here for ye future, and therefore puts in very violently for an interest at Abington. The town are mightyly affrighted with the expectation of a quo warranto, for they haveing repreived a wench condemned here for killing her bastard 4 months without the Kings autority to warrant theyr doeing of it, they all give their charter for gon if the King should come upon them for the forfeiture. And that they should receive any favour herein is what, considereing their carriage to the King, is what they cannot reasonably expect; and I hope his Majesty will thinke soe too. Dr Elliot, an eminent physitian of this place, is lately dead. The Earle of Northampton next weeke takes his leave of the University and goes to travell. I thanke you for ye trouble you are pleased to give your selfe in buying me an hat, but y^r carrier hath not as yet brought him hither.

[P.S.] Pray lets know what is like to become of the charter of London, and w^t use is made of the information I gave concerneing Norwich.

[Oxford], March 14, 1681[2].

I have nothing to tell you further of our assizes but that Jay of Chinnor,[a] wch published ye sermon wherein is made a parallel between ye Earl of Shaftsburys imprisonment in ye Tower and Daniels in the lions den, was presented by the grand jury for it, as beeing a scandalous libel against the Government. John Lock lives a very cunning unintelligible life here, beeing 2 days in town and 3 out, and noe one knows where he goes, or when he goes, or when he returns. Certainly there is some whig intreague a manageing, but here not a word of politics comes from him, nothing of news or anything else concerneing our present affairs, as if he were not at all concernd in them. If any one asks him what news when he returns from a progresse, his answere is: "we know nothing." Last Wednesday our proctors were chosen, Mr Altham is for Christchurch, and Mr Dingley for New College, which had ye choice this year.[b] I should be glad if my Ld. Arrans[c] beeing deputy of Ireland should signify any thing to you. If you goe for France, it will be requisit I send you what mony of yours is in my hands, which may amount to about some 8^l.

[Oxford], March 19th, 1681[2].

. . . . . . It seems we shall have an end at last of [the con]test[d] about ye town clerks place. The town beeing resolved to proceed [in their] choice, and Robin Pawlin, ye canteing preaching attorny

---

[a] "Daniel in the Den, or the Lord President's Imprisonment and Miraculous Deliverance represented in a Discourse from Heb. xi. v. 33. By S. J. Rector of Chinner, in the County of Oxon." London, 1682, 4to.

[b] Roger Altham and William Dingley.

[c] Richard, Earl of Arran, son of the Duke of Ormonde, Lord Deputy of Ireland, 1682-4.

[d] Part of the edge of this letter is torn away.

of our town, is de[signed to be] the man, as notorious a knave as
any in ye county. This whole affair is y^e [contri]vance of Alderman
Wright; and Prince is either to have a summe of mony of this
Pawlin or to officiate for him, and have such a share of ye profits
of ye place: soe that Prince after all will be a gainer. But whither
ye Ld. Norris will be satisfyed with this I know not. The Bp. of
Oxford hath gaind great reputation by composeing ye quarrel
betweeu Brome Whorwood and my Ld., especially with those y^t
were on y^n jury, who were at a losse what to doe in it; and, were
there not an end be put to it this way, it would have made divisions
in ye county. We have had 2 college liveings to dispose of in one
weeke, one in Chesshire worth about 110^l per annum, which is
given to Mr Penny;^{a} and now it appears he hath been marryed
several years to an alewifes daughter at Islip, where he hath been
curat for Dr South. The other is Purton in this county, void by
ye death of Mr Puleston,^{b} worth about 130^l per annum, which is
given Mr Ackworth,^{c} and thereby a very good curacy of ye college,
at Tring in Buckinghamshire, worth 60^l per annum, becomeing
void, it is given to Mr Duke.^{d} It is ye place where Harry Guy
lives, and he gives 20^l per annum, which conduceth to the makeing
up the summe I mention; and this with a students place is a good
preferment, especially since all is payd him in hard mony without
taxes or defalcations. We have another man y^i wants preferment,
one Mr Charles Allestree,^{f} a kinsman of ye D^{rs},^{g} who hath marryed
the most scandalously bad that any fellow hath don I beleive for

^{a} Probably James Penny. See above, p. 10.
^{b} Roger Puleston, M.A. 1661.
^{c} Thomas Acworth, M.A. 1665; B.D. 1683.
^{d} William Duke, M.A. 1670.
^{e} There was a Henry Guy, of Christ Church, M.A. 1663; afterwards Cupbearer
to the Queen and Secretary to the Treasury in 1679.—*Fast. Oxon.* ii. 272.
^{f} See above, p. 36, note ^{a}.
^{g} Richard Allestree, entered Christ Church in 1636; bore arms for the King;
M.A. 1643; was ejected by the Parliamentary visitors. D.D. and Canon of Christ
Church, 1660; Regius Professor of Divinity, 1663; Provost of Eton, 1665. Died
1681.—*Ath. Oxon.* iv. 202.

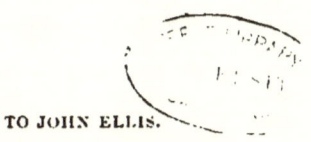

these many years, his wife beeing one Mother Yalden, an old alewife with an house full of children. It is not Alestre, y^c booksellers
son,* whom you may have known, but one whom y^e D^r brought
out of Derbyshire, son to [William Allestree] wch was y^c top of y^e
D^{rs} kinred. He was about 5 years standeing, [and was] a very
gay gentile fellow, proud and insolent to the highest, haveing . . . . .
of his parts, and would fain goe for a man of prudence and wisdom,
and . . . . . . our witts here boid him up mightyly, and by virtue of
their voucher . . . . he went for one of the choicest men of the
town; but at last he [hath lost] himselfe, and his folly hath given
his pride a very deserved reward. [He formerly] was one of my
bitterest enemys, although I never had as much [as an acquain]tance
with him, and I expect er long I shall be sollicited for him for [some
pre]ferment, his condition now beeing such that I beleive he w[ould
hardly] know himselfe. Its one of ye greatest disgraces that hath
h[appened to] our college a long while, and we are mightyly pelted
with ye jeers [of our neigh]bours about it; but if we must defend
the follys of all that [belong to us] we shall have enough to doe.
Where J[ohn] L[ocke] goes I cannot by any means learn, all his
voyages beeing so cunninly contrived; sometimes he will goe to
some acquaintances of his near y^c town, and then he will let any-
body know wheie he is; but other times, when I am assured he
goes elsewhere, noe one knows where he goes, and therefore the
other is made use of only for a blind. He hath in his last sally
been absent at least 10 days, where I cannot learn. Last night he
returnd; and sometimes he himselfe goes out and leaves his man
behind, who shall then to be often seen in y^c quadrangle to make
people beleive his master is at home, for he will let noe one come
to his chamber, and therefore it is not certain when he is there
or when he is absent. I fancy there are projects afoot. To-morrow

* James Allestree or Allestry, son of a bookseller of the same name who suffered
great losses in the Fire of London; Scholar of Westminster; elected to Christ Church,
1672; M.A. 1679. Died 1686.

Dr Busbys benefaction^a is proposed in Convocation, but I beleive it will be rejected, ye generallity of y^r University beeing against it.

- - - - - - -

[Oxford], Sunday, Octob. 8th, 1682.

I have y^r favour of your [letter to] acknowledge, and especially for the information you give me as to the Earle of Ossory, and ye small likelyhood of my haveing any assistance from him in ye affair I last writ to you of.^{b} I find I shall be necessitated to put myselfe upon a competition whenever the place falls, and therefore would strengthen my interest soe beforehand as not to fail of successe when ye time comes, whenever it is. I shall have but one competitor, wch is Mr Huntington,^{c} and perchance not him; however, it is good to provide. At present ye good D^r is again in perfect health, and God long preserve him soe. I find he takes it very ill of Mr Secretary Jinkings, that, he being Arabic Professor, he should put such a slight upon him as to send his Arabic letters to another to translate; and in truth ye passing him by is an affront upon him, and every one here consters it soe, for it is, in effect, telling ye world y^t he thinkes the D^r insufficient for the work, otherwise he would not set another upon that businesse wch is properly his, as beeing professor of that language. And the indignity appears ye greater in that he should imploy soe egregious a donce in it as Hyde;^{d} for

---

^{a} See above, p. 59, note ^{a}.

^{b} Prideaux refers to the Hebrew professorship, which he anticipated falling vacant by the death of Dr. Pocock. The Doctor, however, did not die till 1691.

^{c} Robert Huntington, entered Merton College in 1662, and became Fellow. Chaplain to the English Factory at Aleppo for many years; D.D. 1683; and, in the same year, Master of Trinity College, Dublin. Bishop of Raphoe, 1701; in which year he died. See also above, p. 39, note ^{a}.

^{d} Thomas Hyde, son of Ralph Hyde, Minister of Billingsley, in Shropshire, began Oriental studies under his father. Entered King's College, Cambridge, in 1652, and was encouraged in his studies by Abraham Wheelock, the famous Orientalist, who

what is this but to prefer him before him as to skil in that affair, and, in effect, call the D^r doter? for noe one y^t hath common sense and but the hundredth part of that skill the D^r hath been noted to have in that language but must doe better then Hyde, who doth not understand common sense in his own language, and therefore I cannot conceive how he can make sense of anything that is writ in another. And beside, he hath ye least skil in this language of any that pretend to it in the University; in the Persian language he can doe something, as haveing been bred to it when young, to correct as much of ye Polyglot bible as is in that language when in ye presse. This place affords noe news. The sessions was kept here this week, but I hear of nothing don at it worth observeing. Dr Lloyd ^a was last Friday admitted Vice-Chancellor, but I doubt how he may acquit himselfe of it; he is an honest good man, but of a temper too mild for a governor; but time must show him.

———

[Oxford], Oct. 24th, 1682.

I doe heartyly thanke you for yours and am glad you are still in London and hope y^t I shall find you there 3 weekes hence, about wch time my Norwich concerns call me that way. I were told you had your dispatch for Ireland ^b and were accordingly gon thither, but your last hath let me know ye contrary, and I please myselfe mightyly now in the hopes I have of seeing you before you goe thither I am sorry Mr Seamour ^c hath left the court, for I promised myselfe a friend in him, and have reasons to thinke I

made him one of the correctors of the Polyglot Bible. In 1658 he entered Queen's College, Oxford; M.A. 1659; D.D. 1682. Keeper of the Bodleian Library, 1665; Archdeacon of Gloucester, 1678; and Professor of Arabic, in succession to Dr. Pocock, in 1691.—*Ath. Oxon.* iv. 522.

^a The Principal of Jesus College
^b Ellis received at this time the appointment of Secretary to the Commissioners of the Revenue of Ireland.
^c Perhaps Henry Seymour, one of the Gentlemen of the Bedchamber.

should not have been deceived.   This place affords nothing worth
telling you, all things going with us very quietly.   M[r] Walls[a]
of our college is lately gon from hence to be chaplain to the company at Hamburg. an imployment worth 300[l] per annum; and this
I procurd for him by my interest with the Dean of Glocester,[b] who
was commissioned by the company to elect the man.   John Lock
lives very quietly with us, and not a word ever drops from his
mouth that discovers any thing of his heart within.   Now his
master is fled,[c] I suppose we shall have him all together.   He
seems to be a man of very good converse, and that we have of him
with content; as for what else he is he keeps it to himselfe, and
therefore troubles not us with it nor we him.

Norwich, Nov. 15th, 1683.

I have received, in this place, your kind letter, and am sorry I
am in a place w[ch] affords me nothing to maintain a correspondence
with.   For y[r] publick news, that you have from better hands; and
from hence nothing will be worth informeing you.   About a fortnight or 3 weeks hence I shall be again in Oxford.   I have lately
lost my ffather,[d] who, having lived to an exceeding old age, dyed
in the most happyest circumstances of it.   He hath left me a very
good yonger brothers estate, whereby I may be enabled, come what
times there will, to support my selfe.   I am affraid you find Ireland
a kind of banishment.   I wish you had an equivalent in England.
I hope, at least, some occasions may er long call you over, and

[a] See above, p. 49, note [a].

[b] Dr. Thomas Marshall, who had himself been Preacher to the English merchants
of Rotterdam and Dort during the Civil War. He preceded Prideaux in the Rectory
of Bladen. See also above, p. 103, note [c].

[c] Shaftesbury was in hiding at this time; but he did not actually leave England
till the 28th November.—Christie, Life of Shaftesbury, ii. 452.

[d] Edmund Prideaux, of Padstow, died 25 October, 1683.

whenever that happens you shall not go back againe without my seeing you, for I shall thinke it worth my while to come to London on purpose. I am glad Dr Huntington is soe well liked; he is a very worthy person, and I sent a letter by him to you for this purpose, that you might be acquainted with him. . . . .

[Oxford], March 19th, 1683[4].

. . . . . The city haveing resigned their charter, expect as a reward of this to have [new privileges] granted them, to wch purpose they have had a petition before ye council, but, objections being put in thereto by our agents, the whole petition and every clause of it was rejected. In this affair Sr Lionel Jinkins was our best friend, and argued our case with a great deal of zeal for ye University interest. Y^e debate concerning this lasted 2 hours, a full councill being present. Dr Bourchier,[a] our law professor, begins to grow very infirm. I know not why you should not secure his place; it is worth 100^l per annum, and ye duty is very little wch is to be don for it. Pray think of it, for your commission, I understand, is not like to last long, and it is good to have a refuge in England. I suppose your provost will stick by what he hath, for if he expects better I fear he will be deceived; for our great men doe not care to humour those that are candidates for their favour, and, if that doth not please him wch is already given him, it will scarce please them ever to give him anything else. As to y^r Hebrew lectorers place, whenever it falls I must appear for it, but I know not whither it may not be best for my interest to wish a disappointment, because now I have ye same income with quiet wch then I must have with trouble and envy. My prebendship and students place are worth more y^n a canonry of Christ Church; and all this must be left if ever I obtain that; whereby I have this

---

[a] See above, p. 6.

advantage, that if I am disappointed I shall not at all be concernd
for it. But yᵉ good old Dʳ is yet in good health, and God grant he
may soe long continue.

Oxford, Aug. 6, 1684.

I have yʳ favour of two of yours to acknowledge. Both of them
came to my hands at Woodstock, but now I am again at Oxford.
Our Act ended here with yᵉ expulsion of both yᵉ Terrefilii, but that
hath not put an end to yʳ bussle wᶜʰ we are now in on two
account[s]; yᵉ one is yᵉ concern of yᵉ whole University, yᵉ other of
a private college. Yᵉ University concern is about yᵉ town carter.
It seems, to induce them to surrender it, yᵉ Earle of Abington
promised them yᵉ addition of several new grants, and in order
thereto a petition was presented to yᵉ King in councill concerneing
it, wᶜʰ contained 5 points; but, yᵉ University apprehendeing that yᵉ
King by granteing it would prejudice us, they presented a counter
petition in answer to it, and upon a full heareing in councill yᵉ
town petition was rejected in every point. This was about 5
months since. But yᵉ Lord Abington, not acquiesceing in it,
hath ever since been imploying his interest in yᵉ town behalfe
to doe us all yᵉ prejudice he can, and acts very vehemently and
pevishly in the thing, and soe yᵉ businesse now stands; but we do
not doubt our interest herein, and I hope er long I shall be able to
give you an account of our good successe. The other affair is
concerneing Magd. Coll. Yᵉ divinity lecturer beeing dead, yᵉ
college proceeded to an election, and by a great majority choose
on Dʳ Bayly [a] into yᵉ place, at wᶜʰ Dʳ Smyth,[b] formerly Sʳ Joseph
Williamsons chaplain, beeing yᵉ senʳ, thinkes himselfe aggreived,
because at yᵉ colleges petition yᵉ Bishop of Winchester made an
injunction yᵗ all offices and lectures should be disposed of accordeing

ᵃ See above, p. 6.   ᵇ See above, p. 47, note ᶜ.

to seniority, supposeing ye persons capable. Upon this ye D^r makes his appeal to ye Bishop, and upon a full hearcing y^r Bp. determines in favour of Smyth, and orders ye college to proceed to a new election and make choice of Smyth. Y^e college refuses to submit to this sentence; hereupon ye 9 seniors are put out of commons; herenpon ye college addresse to ye D. of Ormond, and by him present a petition to ye King for redresse; and y^r Bp. hath been served with an order to proceed noe further herein, the King haveing appointed to have ye hearcing of it himselfe, and there it now rests. In ye meantime Dr Smyths party, wch are only two, have presented a libel of accusation to y^r Bishop against their head.[a] The crimes they accuse him of are cheifely corruption in selleing of places, and knavery in falsifying ye college register in a thing that was enterd there by order of King and councill on ye decision of a former controversy in Dr Peirces[b] time heard before ye councill, while I suppose you were of ye University, wch beeing much to the infamy of Dr Peirce, when he sould his headship to the present man, it seems one part of ye bargain was that he should race all this out of ye register, as he should have an opportunity of so doeing; and accordingly, to make good his promise, this honest man, findeing ye whole to be contained within two pages, pasts them both togeather and soe made y^r whole disappear. They are now at Farnham about it, but what ye result will be I know not. What we have now don at ye presse ye Gazet hath er this told you. Dr Brady[c] hath lately published altogeather several tracts he formerly published against some antimonarchical antiquarys, and in ye preface promiseth us ye 1st part of his long talked of History of England to be published in Michaelmas term. He hath been long a searcher

[a] Dr. Clerk.

[b] Thomas Peirce, D.D. President of Magdalen College, 1661-72. Dean of Salisbury, 1675. Died 1691.

[c] Robert Brady, M.D. Master of Cains College, Cambridge " An Introduction to Old English History, comprehended in Three several Tracts," &c. London, 1684, fol. The first volume of his "Complete History of England" to Richard II. was published in 1685.

after English antiquity and pretends to have made great discoverys. What they are we shall know when his book comes forth. There is a booke lately published by some of ye foreigne seminarys against ye Bp. of Winchester [a] in answere to his lately put forth against ye papists, in wch the old man is dealt very rudely with. Drayden hath published a translation of Maimburgs History of ye League, as he tells us at ye Kings command.[b] Judge Windham [c] beeing dead, its talked Roger North, ye Keepers brother, will succeed him. But for such sort of news I refer you to ye news papers you have publick with you. My house [d] will be coverd by Michaelmas, and when it is habitable I shall fix my residence in it to ye end of my days. I wish you good health and all things that can be good in that country.

Oxford, Nov. 12th, 1684.

I have lately received ye favour of yours and am glad you are in health, and wish with that you had all the other satisfactions you can desire, especially a good establishment in England, wch I wish, in some respect, for my own sake, that I might have soe good a friend within reach sometimes of enjoying you. But time and opportunity will, at last, I hope, bring all things to passe that may be for your full content. The publick accounts you have of news

[a] Dr. George Morley. The book referred to is "A Revision of Dr. George Morley's judgment in matters of Religion, by L. W. *Permissu Superiorum*," 1683, 4to. written in answer to the Bishop's "Several Treatises" against the Church of Rome.

[b] "The History of the League, written in French by Monsieur Maimbourg. Translated into English according to His Majesty's command. By Mr. Dryden." London, 1684, 8vo.

[c] Sir Hugh Wyndham, Puisne Judge of the Common Pleas; died at Norwich, 27 July, 1684.

[d] At his living of Bladen-cum-Woodstock, to which he had been presented by Lord Guildford in 1682.

from England sufficiently inform you how all things goe with us.
Whiggism goes down a pace, and y[e] punishments of sedition and
treason fall very heavy upon those that have soe boldly been guilty
of it in the late licentious times. You have an instance of it, lately,
in Papillion,[a] who is gon to his brethren into y[e] Marshalsea for
10,000[l]. Our friend John Lock is likewise become a brother
sufferer with them. As soon as y[e] plot was discovered, he cun-
ningly stole away from us, and in halfe a years time noe one
knew where he was. At last he began to appear in Holland,[b]
and the last account we had of him from thence was, that he
had consorted himselfe with Dare of Taunton,[c] and they two had
taken lodgeing togeather in Amsterdam. We have been told
orders have been given at Court to inquire after him; however, y[e]
Bishop is resolved to know where he is, or put him out of beeing
student of Christ Church, a citation being fixd up in the Hall to
warn him to appear and give an account of his absence on y[e] 1st
day of January next; but it is supposed he will reather chuse
forfet his place by still absenteing then venture his neck by
comeing any more within reach of y[e] Kings justice. It seems
he transacted all affairs with West,[d] and, therefore, as soon as he
was secured, he thought it time to shift for himselfe for fear West
should tell all he knew. When West was first taken he was very
solicitous to know of us at the table who this West was, at w[ch]
one made an unlucky reply, that it was y[e] very same person whom
he treated at his chambers and caressed at soe great a rate when

* Thomas Papillon, an Exclusionist: one of the directors of the East India
Company. He had stood for the representation of one of the City wards, but his
election had been thwarted by the Lord Mayor, Sir William Pritchard; whereupon he
brought an action, and obtained the temporary arrest of the Mayor. Pritchard then
sued Papillon for false imprisonment. The trial took a political complexion, and
Papillon was cast with 10,000l. damages.

b Locke fled to Holland at the end of August of this year.

c Thomas Dare, afterwards slain in a quarrel by Fletcher of Saltoun, in Monmouth's rebellion.—See Macaulay's *History of England.*

d Robert West, barrister, implicated in the Rye House Plot. He gave evidence on
Lord William Russell's trial.

College was tryed here at Oxford, wch put ye gentleman into a
profound silence : and the next thing we heard of him was that
he was fled for the same. I have taken up your bill of 50^l of y^e
Bp., and soe there is an end of that affair. We hear ye Duke of
Ormond ^a is speedyly to be succeeded in his government by y^e
Earle of Rochester; it seems Halyfax ^b cannot be treasurer till he
is gon. How ye Duke of Ormond will like this, you best know
that are on ye place with him. I have a kinsman, one Mr William
Morice, a lad about 16 years old, who last week ran away from
his ffather, Mr John Morice,^c a merchant in London, with whom
he was an apprentice to his trade; he apprehends he is gon into
Ireland, having traced him as far as St Albans. If he should
chance to come thither, and any accident should bring it to your
knowledge, I beg ye favour of you to secure him and send his father
an account of it, whom a letter will find if directed to him only by
ye title of merchant, in London. Perchance if you should send to y^e
Custom House he may be there seased if this arrive first, or at least
there an account may be had of him. If you can any way hear of
him and secure him, it will be a favour for wch I shall be very
thankfull to you. I am now goeing for Norwich, where I shall
tarry till Candlemas; in ye meantime, if you thinke fit to favour me
with a letter, I desire you would be pleased to lodge it with M^r
Edmund Prideaux,^d merchant, in London, a brother of mine, who
will know always where to send to me. The Bp. of Winchester
beeing dead, Bath and Wells ^e succeeds him; but ye wealth of all y^e

^a The Duke of Ormonde was succeeded, after a short government by Lords
Justices, by Henry Hyde, Earl of Clarendon, as Lord Lieutenant of Ireland.
Lawrence Hyde, Earl of Rochester, was Lord President of the Council, and soon
after Lord Treasurer.

^b George Savile, Marquess of Halifax, Lord Privy Seal, succeeded Rochester as
Lord President.

^c Prideaux's aunt Elizabeth married Sir William Morrice, knt., of Werrington,
co. Devon, sometime Secretary of State. John Morice appears to have been the
second son of this marriage.

^d An elder brother, a Smyrna merchant.

^e Peter Mews, translated to Winchester, 22 November, 1684.

bishopricks in England canuot be sufficient for yᵉ prodigality of
that man. He is head and cars in debt, and now he has grown
higher in preferment he will alsoc advance in his expenses and I
fear in his debts too. It seems yᵉ King hath a mind to provide
himselfe of a good hous in his way to Winchester. Yᵉ Morleys
began to murmur mightyly at the Kings soe often calleing at
Farnham, and asked some that told the King again whither his
Majesty did intend to make yᵉ Bps. house alwayse his inne, at wᶜʰ
yᵉ King was much offended and never after called there. He dyed
very scandalously, haveing in the time of his last sicknesse filled up
all his lease[s], soe that the 3 last weeks of his life the nephews
received on this account above 20,000ˡ, and they would let yᵉ old
Bp. scarce have time to say his prayers for fear he should dy before
he had seald and signed as many leases as they contracted for.
But I hope a way will be found to call them to an account for it.
Bath and Wells lys between Kenᵃ and Parker,ᵇ and he that fails of
it will have Norwich, where yᵉ Bp.ᶜ lyes a dying.

London, Nov. 22d, 1684.

That you might know how concerns stand betwixt us I have
herewith sent you your account. Your bill of 50ˡ was not payd
till November, because yᵉ debt yᵉ Bp. had transferd upon me on
that account was not then payable. In my last I writ to you
concerning a kinsman of mine fled from his friends into Ireland.
If you light upon him it will be a great favour. His father seems
irreconcileable unto him, but my brother that is a merchant here

ᵃ Thomas Kenn, D.D. Prebendary of Winchester, consecrated Bishop of Bath and
Wells 25 January, 1685.
ᵇ Samuel Parker, D.D. Archdeacon of Canterbury, made Bishop of Oxford
17 October, 1686.
ᶜ Anthony Sparrow, Bishop of Norwich, died 19 August, 1685, and was succeeded
by William Lloyd, Bishop of Peterborough.

will take care of him, and therefore, if he be seased, pray send him account of it. A letter directed to him by y° name of M' Edmund Prideaux, merchant in London, will be sufficient. I beg your favour in this affair, but desire not to give you much trouble; for the young man in his circumstances doth not deserve that any one should be much troubled concerneing him, only I would desire, if possible, to retrive him from absolute ruin. Lock is expeld by y° Kings speciall command.[a] It seems there is a most bitter libel published in Holland in English, Dutch, and French, called a " Hue and Cry after y° Earle of Essexs murther," w°h is layd at his doores. Burnet is turned out of y° Rolls[b] for preacheing a very reflecteing sermon on the 5th day of November last. The argument that gave y° offence was he made a great deal of doe about a curse w°h King James should lay upon all of his posterity that should imbrace y° Romish religion. He is a troublesom knave, and it is well the pulpit is thus rid of him. On M[onday] I goe for Norwich. There I shall be glad to hear from you.

Oxford. July 9th, 1685.

I have received yours, and accordeing to your order have payd your brother[c] 5l. Your former makeing me hope I should speedyly see you here made me deferre writeing, least my letter might come too late to find you in Dublyn. Our rebellion is now over, Monmouth and all his party beeing routed. Instead thereof we have now got a standeing army, a thing the nation hath long been

[a] See the correspondence between Sunderland, as Principal Secretary of State, and Bishop Fell, printed in Lord King's *Life of John Locke*, 1830, i. 278.

[b] Burnet was appointed Preacher at the Rolls Chapel in 1675. Soon after the date of the above letter he retired abroad.

[c] Welbore Ellis, elected from Westminster to Christ Church, 1680; M.A. 1687; Prebendary of Winchester, 1696; D.D. 1697. He became Dean of Christ Church, Dublin; and Bishop of Kildare in 1705, and of Meath in 1731. Died 1734.— Welch, 189.

jealous of; but I hope y⁰ King will noe otherwise use it then to secure our peace. The war now from y⁰ feild I suppose will passe into y⁰ roads, w⁰ʰ we must expect will a while be infested with the remainder of those rogues. You will have a more exact account of these transactions from London then I am able to give you from this place. Our good Bp. is faln very ill, and I fear will not long last. We begin already to be sollicitous who may be his successor. I beleive it may be your tutor,[a] and I am of an opinion he may not be soe unfit a man as some apprehend. The Bp. of Chichester[b] is lately dead and y⁰ sea of Peterborough is vacant by y⁰ translation of Bp. Lloyd to Norwich. Trelawny will be a Bishop somewhere before all those vacancys be supplyed, its supposed at Bristol,[c] the Bp. of that place beeing to be translated to Peterborough. We have noe Act this year, altho y⁰ greatest number of Doctors that I ever knew in all facultys, especially in divinity. The rebellion hath been y⁰ occasion of this intermission. Dʳ Stillingfleet hath lately published a booke worth your seeing, containeing an historicall account of y⁰ British Church before its suppression by y⁰ Saxon invasion.[d] I shall doe your brother all the service I can, but I beleive my time in the college will now be short, especially if y⁰ Bp. dyes. I have now been long enough here to begin to be weary of a place where now almost every one is my junior, and therefore have resolved to retire to my liveing and fix for good and all there; and in order hereto I have hearkned to proposals that have been made to me of marriage, and because they are such as are very advantagious. I have already got soe far as y⁰ sealeing of articles, whereby I have secured to myselfe 3,000ˡ; but after y⁰ death of y⁰

---

[a] Woodroffe.

[b] Guy Carleton, died 6 July, 1685.

[c] Jonathan Trelawny was consecrated Bishop of Bristol, 8 November, 1685. John Lake, the present Bishop, was translated, not to Peterborough but to Chichester. Thomas White, Archdeacon of Northampton, succeeded to Peterborough.

[d] Edward Stillingfleet, Dean of St. Paul's. "Origines Britannicæ, or Antiquities of the British Churches." London, 1685, folio.

ffather and mother, whose only child y° gentlewoman is,[a] I beleive there will be at least 1,500[l] more. I little thought I should ever come to this; but abundance of motives have overpowred me, and therefore I have yeilded to the circumstances of my present condition, wch would neither be convenient nor comfortable to me without this resolution. Altho they are very few who I have yet communicated this to, I cannot conceal it from yourselfe. I doe not ask your advice herein, because it is too late for it; neither doe I your opinion, because you cannot judge of it without knoweing all my circumstances, wch it would be too long for me now to tell you.

━━━━━━━

Oxford, Nov. 12, [1685].

I thanke you for y° favour of yours, and especially for your advice in reference to my affair, but what to resolve on after all I know not. I am offered, in exchange for my living and sine cure (wch both togeather are not worth me 120[l] per annum), a living in Norfolke [b] worth 220[l] per annum, in a quiet place 15 miles this side Norwich, and, if times prove well, I may also have one of y^r city livings wch may be worth me above 100[l] per annum more, soe that with my Prebentship I can settle myselfe there in ecclesiastical preferments of 450[l] per annum income; and, beside, in that countrey I am to have an estate of 80[l] per annum with y° gentlewoman I am to marry, and, with the money I have to bestowe, I can there purchase an estate, now offered me, of 250[l] per annum, more by 60[l] per annum then I can purchase for y° money elsewhere; wch being put altogeather, here will be an income of 800[l] per annum, wch I shall never be able to arrive to elsewhere. As to Dr Pococks place, I have no expectations of it, y° Earle of Rochester

---

[a] The lady was Bridget, daughter of Anthony Bokenham, of Helmingham, co. Suffolk.

[b] Saham-Tony, into which Prideaux was inducted, 8 June, 1686. He afterwards, p. 149, estimates the value of the living at 120l.

haveing engaged to get it for his kinsman,[a] and I have now noe
friend that hath interest at Court soe much as to ask this for me,
much lesse to obtain it against soe great an interest as that of y[e]
Ld. Treasurers; besides, I am not fond of y[e] place; I begin now to
be desirous of quiet, w[ch] cannot be enjoyed in such a place, where
a man must continually ly open to censure and envy. Soe plen-
tyfull a fortune as I can establish myselfe in in Norfolk will
be sufficient to supply me with all things w[ch], in this world, I
need desire, and that with quiet is, in my judgment, infinitely
preferable to y[e] trouble and vexation w[ch] usually attend greater
preferments. Besides, I have this further temptation to goe thither,
because it is y[e] pleasantest countrey in England, beeing all open and
dry; the only inconvenience is y[e] want of good bread, but, this
proceedeing from a cause w[ch] any one may remedy that will, I
beleive I shall not stick much at this. If I aggree with S[r] William
Godolphin [b] for his estate in that county, I beleive it will determine
me absolutely to fix there; and, since it will place me only 30 miles
further from London then now I am, I hope I shall not want
frequent opportunitys of seeing my friends there. My thoughts
are much averse from aspireing to high places. I see nothing but
trouble and vexation in them, and therefore, to tell you y[e] whole of
my heart, there is nothing w[ch] I doe soe much desire in this world
as to be fixed in a station once for all, where I may have as little
trouble as possible besides that w[ch] is y[e] duty of my profession, and
from whence I may noe more remove till I dy. And the offer that
is made me sutes very much with my desires as to this particular.
However, I shall resolve nothing till I come to Norwich, and then
I will take my resolutions as I find things there to answere my
expectations. I shall be glad to know when you designe for
Ireland,[c] or whither you tarry to accompany y[e] Ld. Lieutenant.
The Irish seas afford but a bad passage in winter, and therefore I

---

[a] Thomas Hyde. See above, p. 132.
[b] Sir William Godolphin, created a baronet in 1661. Died unmarried, 1710.
[c] Ellis was on a visit to England at this time.

shall not be very easy till I know you are over them. I wish you good successe in your designes of settleing at London, but shall by noe means advise you to lay out any money for a place wch is not freeholt, because of ye changes that may happen.

—

Norwich, Octob. 27th, 1686.

I am to beg your pardon that it hath been soe long since I wrot to you. The truth is, I have been a long while in an unsetled condition, but now have fixed my selfe and all my concerns in this place, and shall be glad of a line or two to know of your health. Before I left Oxford I thinke I acquainted you how our accounts stand, and shall be answereable for what remains due unto you as you shall direct. Your brothers [a] interest beeing soe great at court I should thinke it might be made use of to gett you an establishment in England, soe that you might be no longer confined to a place where I fear all things may run into confusion. We live here remote from ye center of affairs and in a great deal of quiet; only fears from London sometimes allarm us here, but I still hope it may goe much better with us then we thinke or doe deserve. Our Dean [b] is here with us, and goes not to London because under his Majestys displeasure, but I hope that affair er long may be over. We have got here a very excellent person for our Bishop, wch is a great comfort unto us. I shall be glad to know of your health and how affairs stand with you.

[a] Philip Ellis. He was kidnapped by the Jesuits from Westminster School, and was brought up at St. Omer, and is said to have been afterwards accidentally recognised by means of his Westminster nick-name of "Jolly Phil." He became a Benedictine monk, and was chaplain to Mary of Modena, Queen of James II. He retired abroad after the Revolution, and was made Bishop of Segni.—Welch, 164.

[b] Dr. Sharp. The cause of the King's displeasure was a sermon preached by Sharp in St. Giles's-in-the-Fields, of which he was Rector, against the pretensions of the Church of Rome.—See Macaulay's *History.*

It hath been soe long since I have heard from you that I begin
to fear I must loose your correspondence. I confesse we are now
at a great distance; however I should be loath onr old friendship
should be forgot. Your brother beeing now a great man at Court,
I have been expecteing that by his interest a translation might be
procured for you to some place in the English Court as advantagious
to you as that you have in ye Irish, and I hope some time or other
it may be don, that I may have my good friend again where I may
sometimes have ye happinesse of enjoying his conversation. Things
looke cloudy upon us here, and ye matter of ye Declaration[a] hath,
I fear, put ns much under the Kings displeasure. However, I
thanke God we still live in quiett, and, if God continues that, we
may be content patiently to bear all things else. At present we
are only hurt in imagination, and our greatest torment is our fears
of what may after happen; but I hope they will prove to be only
fears and nothing else. I hope when you come into England you
may think Norwich worth your seeing, when you have a friend
here that would soe heartyly make you welcome. I have now
lived here 2 years in great content, it beeing ye most delightfull
city of any I have seen in England for a man to live in, especially
in our distrinct, wch hath all sorts of conveniences to recommend it
to our satisfaction. There is still some money due unto you from
me, and it hath layn in London for you now near these 2 years,
but it beeing ye last acconnt I am like to make with you I would
gladly have your full discharge when it is payd you, and therefore
I hope your occasions may er long call you to London, and then
all things shall be made even between us. I confesse I am ye more
cautious because ye last 15^l I payd you had like to have been lost
through ye death of your kinsman to whom it was to be payd, and
I only ow it to Mr Pitts negligence in omitteing to give him y^e

---

[a] The Declaration of Indulgence was published on the 4th April.

bill when he ought that it was not. Pray favour me to lett me
hear from you when you have leasure, and you will very much
oblidge,[a] etc.

[Norwich], June 7th, 1691.

I should be glad to hear whether you have taken my advice in
applying to D[r] Sharpe[b] in reference to your brother,[c] and what
successe you have had in it. He is a generous, free spirited man,
and would deal well with a chaplain, and in his station will be able
to advance him. But as to y[e] other person you mentioned[d] (whom
I thoroughly know), all is y[e] contrary. He hath nothing in his
gift fitt for your brother to accept, and, if he had, he is a close
designeing man that will reguard little but what tends to his own
or relations interests, and I would by noe means advise any friend
of mine to list himselfe under him. Whatever y[e] Church may be
advantaged by others of y[e] new promotion, I expect it will be very
little by him. He is indeed my old friend and acquaintance;
however, it grieves me to se this diocesse sacrificed to his secular
interest, he beeing one that will by noe means answere its needs,
and I thinke there is noe diocesse in England needs a good Bishop
more then this. You see the London ministers gett all y[e] preferments, and therefore, if possible, fix your brother there, and I
assure you, as y[e] world now goes, a curacy is better then a liveing,

[a] This letter forms part of Birch MS. 4194 in the British Museum, and was
published, with the other letters contained in that volume, in the *Ellis Correspondence*, edited by the Hon. G. A. Ellis, London, 1829, ii. 47.

[b] The former Dean of Norwich, now Archbishop of York.

[c] Charles Ellis, the youngest brother, elected from Westminster to Cambridge,
1681; B.A., 1684; M.A. of Christ's College, 1688. He was appointed chaplain to
the Earl of Pembroke.

[d] The Bishop of Norwich, who is here referred to, was John Moore, D.D. of St.
Catherine's Hall, Cambridge. He had been chaplain to Lord Chancellor Finch;
Prebendary of Ely, 1679; Rector of St. Austin's, London, 1687, and of St. Andrew's,
Holborn, 1689. He became Bishop of Norwich, 23 April, 1691, in the room of
Dr. Lloyd, deprived. Translated to Ely in 1707.

for, all country commoditys beeing soe low and taxes soe high, all liveings that depend upon prediall tiths are fallen more then halfe in value. I assure you ye liveing I now live at, although in common reputation 120^l per annum, and soe it was when I first took it, is not now worth 40^l per annum clear of all charges, and therefore, till ye world be better, I would by noe means advise you to putt your brother into such a liveing as would forfeit his fellow-ship, but reather to begin in some imployment that might be consistent with it and make way for further provision; and in order to this I could not direct you better then to ye Archbishop of York, and I should be heartyly glad to hear you have had any successe with him.

Sabam near Watton, June 15th, 1691.

I have yours, and am heartyly sorry you mist ye opportunity of speaking to ye Archbp. of York. Had you don it I am sure you would have succeeded, but now ye opportunity is lost, and I know not when you will have such another, for by this time to be sure he is provided. Noe wonder you can get nothing for yourselfe when you are soe bad a sollicitor.^{a} All that I can doe now is to send you ye enclosed to ye new Bp. of Bath and Wells,^{b} with whom I have a much better interest then with ye Archbp. of York. I desire you would deliver it to him as soon as he comes to towne, for to be sure he will be immediately besett, and ye first application usually hath y^r best successe. He can provide for your brother better y^n ye Archbp. I doe heartyly wish you successe one way or other, and will endeavour it myselfe as far as I am able.

---

^{a} Ellis left Dublin early in 1689, and did not retain his place at the Irish Treasury after the Revolution. Towards the close of the year he became Secretary to the young Duke of Ormonde, the same office he had held in his father the Earl of Ossory's household.

^{b} Richard Kidder, Dean of Peterborough; nominated Bishop of Bath and Wells, 13th June, 1691. He was killed in the storm of the 26th November, 1703.

Saham, June 17th, 1691.

I write you this only to acquaint you I have wrot by this post to ye Archbp. of York of your brother, and I think you would doe well to wait on him to know ye result of ye matter what can be don for him. I hope you will find successe for him either one way or ye other; I heartily wish it you.

Saham near Watton, in Norfolk, Octob. 12th, 1691.

I doe most humbly thanke you for y^r favour of yours. I have been a while from home, otherwise you had been troubled from me er this. As to Dr Pocooks place, it was offered me and I refused it, and that for two reasons: the first is, I nauseate that learning, and am resolved to loose noe more time upon it; and the 2^d is, I nauseate Christ Church; and, further, if I should goe to Oxford again I must quit whatever I have here, and ye advantage would scarce pay for ye remove. But my main argument is, I have an unconquerable aversion to ye place, and will never live more among such people who now have ye prevaileing power there. I should be glad to be assured you are at the same lodgeings, for I will send you a bill for y^r remainder of your money in my hand, it beeing now in London for you. I am glad you have placed your brother as you mention; ye Earl of Pembroke hath good liveings in his gift, and if they fall he can provide for him. Our Dean ^a tells me that you have got now an imployment; ^b I should be glad to wish you joy of it, if I knew what. It seems you had him always with you at your coffee house, and I wish you had him there still for any good he doth at Norwich, for ye truth is, he is good for nothing

^a Henry Fairfax, D.D. Fellow of Magdalen College. Dean of Norwich, 1 Nov. 1689. He is best remembered by his bold opposition to James II. in the affair of the election of the President of Magdalen in 1687. He died in 1702.

^b Ellis was about this time appointed one of the Commissioners of Transports.

but his pipe and his pot, and we are wretchedly holpd[a] up with him.

[P.S.] S[r] Robert Baldoc[b] that was judge in King James's reigne is lately dead.

I doe most heartyly thank you for y[e] favour of yours, w[ch] were more then ordinaryly welcom for y[e] sake of y[e] good news they brought. Till this happy turn our Jacobites were come to that height of confidence to talke openly that now all was their owne, and some of them suspended their payment of y[e] taxes; and at y[e] bishops visitation at Norwich, w[ch] was the 3 latter days of Whitsun week, the Jacobite clergy would not own his jurisdiction and refused to appear; but on Sunday night y[e] news comeing to us of y[e] victory,[c] they came all the next day and made their submission, and I hope now they will have y[e] witt to carry themselfes better, and if they doe not that y[e] government will have y[e] courage to call all such to an account. For in the strength of such a victory the King may now begin to act accordeing to his own measures. I remember, when last at London, I was with one of y[e] deprived Bishops, who seemed as confident of goeing again very speedyly to his bishoprick as I was of goeing home again, but I thank God he is like now to be disappointed. I perceive the French King and our Jacobites deceaved each other; he made them believe wonders he would doe for them, and they made him believe as much that they [would] doe for him. I hope they will now be both unde-ceived, and an end be put to that great confidence w[ch] was between them. I have for 3 years been exceedeingly troubled[d] at Ipswich

---

[a] Perhaps the same as " halped—crippled," which appears in Halliwell's *Dictionary of Archaic and Provincial Words.*

[b] Sir Robert Baldock, Puisne Judge of the King's Bench in 1688.

[c] The battle of La Hogue, 19 May, 1692.

[d] As Archdeacon of Suffolk, which office Prideaux had held since 21 December, 1688.

with an untoward clergyman there, one Alexander.[a] He was
lecturer of the towne, a place very considerable, but, beeing turned
out for his misdemeanour in y[e] beginneing of the revolution by the
towne on whom he depended, he got another church in y[e] towne,
although of little or noe value, and there did nourish such a faction
and division in y[e] place, and was soe closely stuck to by y[e] Jacobites,
as beeing looked on a martyr for that cause, that he had almost
undon y[e] place in setteing the people togeather by y[e] cars. I had
autority enough of my side to have routed him, and will enough
to doe it, but found him backd by men of that power both in
church and state that I durst not meddle with him for fear of
draweing them upon myselfe, but reserv'd the case for y[e] Bp., his
authority better enableing him to encounter him. But the truth is,
I found his Lordship as cautious in the matter as myselfe, and the
mischiefe must have gone on to y[e] utter undoeing of this place, but
that this Jacobite designe, God be thanked, hath delivered us from
him. It seems he, beeing an agent imployed to give y[e] party
warneing to be in readynesse, put on a tinkers habit with a
snapsack on his back, and soe went on foot through all Essex; but
in one place beeing discovered, where he had been too free of his
talk as to y[e] designe on foot, he was followed to Ipswich, and there
seased on and layd in jayl for treason, w[ch] putes an end to the
whole controversy.

Sabam near Watton, in Norfolk, June 27th, 1692.

I have yours of the 16[th], but it came not to my hands till last
Friday, for I was absent at Ipswich on a visitation. I there had y[e]
whole of Alexanders affair. He was lect[ure]r of that place, but
was turnd out about 3 years since for several misdemeanours. To
revenge himselfe for this, he hath lived in y[e] towne ever since,

[a] Thomas Alexander, appointed Lecturer to the Corporation in the church of St.
Mary Tower in 1687.—Wodderspoon, *Memorials of Ipswich*, 1850, p. 375.

made a party there big enough to put the place into a flame ever since. At first I interposed with my autority to quench it, but findeing him backd by the then Archbps. of Canterbury and York, whom he had made beleive that he sufferd for ye cause of the Church, I thought it best to let it alone, and soe it hath stood ever since, and the towne and he have been at law ever since; but on this advantage I suppose they will be too hard for him, for one of ye main reasons why he was turned out was his busy opposition to y^r present Government, especially in one sermon which they say was ye cause of y^r mutiny of ye Scotch souldiers ^{a} that quartered there about 3 years since, wch I suppose you may remember; and his present misdemeanour is a grand confirmation of that argument. The true story of his doeings in Essex is, he came to Keldane ^{b} in a gray coat and pair of bags on his back, wch it seems by some was improved into a tinkers budgett, and lay there two days to wait for a coach to goe for Ipswich. In the interim he makes it his endeavour to make his landlord a Jacobit; tells him King James was a comeing; that if he would not declare for him him now he would be glad to doe it two months hence, for he was a comeing; that they were sure of ye major part of ye fleet; and a great deal more to this purpose; and that he had 3 horses ready to be imployed in his service, whereof one was kept in London, and ye others elsewhere. However, it will be that advantage to ye towne of Ipswich to gett rid of him that, in case he will quitt that place and create noe more disturbances there, ye Bp. hath undertook to intercede for him; and I should be heartyly glad ye cause would fall this way. He is a fellow of parts, but imploys them mostly to doe mischiefe. The Bp. hath finished his visitation and is again gon to London, but it was little more then pro formâ, for ye truth is, in our present case of unsettlement the. times will not bear

---

^{a} The mutiny of the regiment which now ranks as the First Regiment of Foot, in 1689. It was almost entirely composed of Scotchmen. The story is graphically told by Macaulay in the eleventh chapter of his *History*.

^{b} Kelvedon.

doeing more. The Act of Toleration [a] hath almost undon us, not in increaseing ye number of dissenters but of wicked and profane persons; for it is now difficult almost to get any to church, all pleadeing ye licence, although they make use of it only for ye ale-house. There must be a regulation in these matters, and yet it will be difficult to gett a parliament sober enough to doe it. Phanaticisme hath got ye prevalency in corporations, and ye gentle-men must humour them this way or else they will not be chosen.

Saham, July 18th, 1692.

I doe most thankfully acknowledge the kind favour of yours. And as to ye Toleration Act, unlesse there be some regulation made in it, in a short time it will turn halfe the nation into downe right athiesme. I doe not find it in my archdeaconry (and I believe it is the same in other places) that conventicles have gained anything at all thereby, but reather that they have lost. But the mischieve is, a liberty being now granted, more lay hold of it to separate from all manner of worship to perfect irreligion then goe to them; and, although the Act allows noe such liberty, the people will under-stand it soe, and, say what ye judges can at ye assizes, or ye justice of peace at their sessions, or we at our visitations, noe church-warden or counstable will present any for not goeing to church, though they goe noe where else but to the alehouse, for this liberty they will have; and some have made the mob nowadays too much our masters to be contrould. The regulation I would desire is, that all that goe to any conventicle allowed by the Act be registred, and, as long as they are, be incapacitated for all offices of state according to ye proposall of Mon^r Fagels letter,[b] for nothing is more un-

---

[a] Passed in 1689.

[b] The reply written by the Grand Pensionary Fagel to a letter from James Stewart, on the views of the Prince of Orange with regard to James II.'s Declara-tion of Indulgence. The English version was prepared by Burnet, and published with the title, "A letter to Mr. Stewart, giving an account of the Prince and Princess of Orange's thoughts concerning the Repeal of the Test and Penal Laws." Amster-dam, 1688, 4to.

reasonable then that those that are against ye government should
have any hand in the management of it, because such will be always
endeavouring for the subversion of it. But one thing I observe
is, that in my archdeaconry none of ye conventicle preachers have
taken ye oaths,ᵃ and I am told it is soe in most parts of England
besides, soe they are ready for King James whenever he returns.
Our Bps tarrying at London out of his diocese is, he hath marryed
a wifeᵇ and cannot come? She hath a big belly to lay downe, and
his Lordship must be at her labour; but when that is over, then he
comes downe with all his family and settles among us, and that
will be, he tells us, about ye end of ye next month. Here is an od
story sent me from Norwich. The summe of it is, 2 gentlemen
haveing been abroad negotiateing K. James's affair in this diocese,
met accidentally on Hartford Bridge, 2 miles from Norwich, in
the Suffolk road from thence, and it being in an open place, they,
thinkeing noe one present, began to talke of their affairs and what
each had don, and particularly mentioned that before harvest was
in they doubted not King James would be in England, and many
other things of this affair. But it seems at last the[y] espyed a
chimney sweeper lying downe with his tool near enough to
overhear all they sayd, whereat on drew out his pistol to dispatch
him, but the other not consenteing they left him bound till a cart
came by and unloosend him. Hereon he hath been with the
Mayor of Norwich and one Major Haughton and made affidavit
of all that past; but if there be any thing of it noe doubt an
account will be sent to London.

ᵃ The Toleration Act provided that the penal statutes against nonconformity
should not extend to such as took the Oaths of Allegiance and Supremacy and subscribed the Declaration against Transubstantiation.

ᵇ Bishop Moore's second wife, Dorothy, daughter of ——— Barnes, of Sadbergh,
co. Durham, and relict of two husbands: Sir Michael Blacket, of Newcastle, and Sir
Richard Browne, Bart.—Blomefield's *History of Norfolk*, iii. 591.

[Norwich], Nov. 27th, 1693.

I have two of yours to thank you for, and I had not been soe
tardy in acknowledgeing the debt but that I tarryed to have
wherewith to make a return, wch ye countrey is not soe fertill of as
ye city. Out of Suffolk I have full assurance that ye recorder of
Oxford is sent thither of purpose to promote ye great designe in
hand. He is a stranger to that countrey, and on his first comeing
thither came with ye keeper[s] [a] letter and ye interest of ye Feltons [b]
to back it to make him recorder of that towne.[c] He calls himselfe
a lawyer, and yet doth not practice; he seems to be a very fair
conditioned good-tempered man, and thereby ye better capacitated
to wheedle; but those that send me this character of him have not
enabled me to tell you his name, but I have expressly wrot to be
informed of it. I have been told alsoe of a person of quality that
hath made a tour this last summer through that whole countrey at
ye gentlemens houses for this purpose; soe we see they turn every
stone for their designe, without considereing they serve none by it
but the King of France; and indeed I have been lately told by a
very intelligent person that he is well assured that abundance of
those that seem fierce Republicarians are in reallity fierce Jacobites,
and that they openly promote this designe for noe other end but
that it is ye likelyest to bring about what they would really have.
Whenever there is a new parliament, the knights of ye shire for
Norfolk will be Sr Henry Hobart and Sr Roger Potts,[d] and for
Suffolk Sr Samuel Bernardiston and Sr Jarvis Elways, all stiffe
Republicarians; but I hope most of ye burroughs will provide better.

[a] Sir John Somers, Lord Keeper, 23 March, 1693.

[b] Baronets of Playford, co. Suffolk.

[c] Charles Whittaker, Serjeant-at-Law, was appointed Recorder of Ipswich in
1692. The Recorder of Oxford was Sir George Pudsey.

[d] Sir Roger Potts, Bart., of Mannington, co. Norfolk; Sir Samuel Barnardiston,
Bart., of Brightwell, co. Suffolk; and Sir Gervase Elwys, Bart., of Stoke, co. Suffolk.
With the exception of Sir R. Potts, they were all returned in the Parliament of
1695.

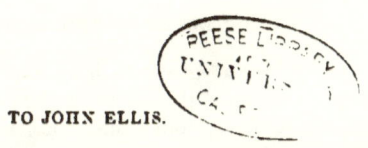

I am now at Norwich, where yᵉ Dean behaves himselfe more like a beast theu ever, and is so obstinate and perverse in his own humours (wᶜʰ are indeed intolerable) that there is noe endureing of him. I find he is much in with the party, without considereing that if they prevail they will take his deanery from him; and indeed, if that were all the hurt they would doe, it would be noe great matter. The Ld. N[ottingham] beeing now out,ᵃ I suppose all that were put into imployment by his means will follow yᵉ same risk, wᶜʰ makes me concerned for you. I shall be glad to know what will be yᵉ event in this matter. I confesse, were I worthy to advise you, I should be desirous you still keep your place, although it be by temporiseing with them you cannot like. If yᵉ Government stands, things must revert again to yᵉ interest of those that now seem to be undermost, and my Ld. N[ottingham] will be in place again; for I looke on it only as a trick to suit yᵉ exigencys of yᵉ times that yᵉ King is forced to humour those men, and if once yᵉ cause be removed yᵉ effect of it will be soe alsoe.

[Norwich], Dec. 4th, 1693.

I doe most heartyly thank you for yᵉ favour of yours, and am exceedeing glad of the carrying of the 2 points you mention. Yᵉ next offer will be yᵉ abjuration oath;ᵇ if that goes, as I cojecture it will, I must out, for I cannot take it; for I am told yᵗ [the] contents of that oath are, that there lys noe obligation upon us from yᵉ oaths taken to King James, and that King William is lawfull and rightfull king of this realme. As to yᵉ first part, I think none can stick at it that have sworn to King William and Queen Mary; for certainly we cannot ow allegiance to King James and

---

ᵃ Daniel Finch, second Earl of Nottingham, Secretary of State, 1689-93, and again in 1702.

ᵇ An Abjuration Bill was introduced in 1689, but was not passed. Nothing further was done.

them too; at least allegiance to King James must be suspended as long as they are on ye throne, and soe swearing allegiance to them hath certainly put ye other allegiance out of doores. And as to lawfull, I should not stick at that; for King William and Queen Mary, beeing invested by those who had ye lawfull power to doe soe, are certainly lawfull King and Queen. But ye word rightfull is that I cannot goe over; for that is to swear to King Williams title. Not y^t I have anything to say against his title, but that it may be good as far as I know; but before he can have a right and title, King James must have lost his, and of this we must be well assured before we can swear to ye right of ye other. Soe that it draws in this whole question, whither King James was rightfully deposed; wch dependeing upon ye knowledge of soe many circumstances, matters of fact and matters of law, wch private men can never have a clear inspect into, it is impossible one of us, who are strangers to ye whole action and know nothing of it but by news letters and news talk, can be so well assured of it as to swear to it. This is my sense of ye matter, and, as I apprehend, must be ye sense of all others that will consider it. You would doe me a great favour if you could send me a copy of ye oath as proposed last sessions; for I have many relations in ye House, and if ever this matter comes to bear I would send them my sense of it. For a prince, that makes his way to a throne by y^r sword, to make ye people swear to his title seems to me a very strange imposition; and indeed it is, I think, what noe wise prince would doe for care not to have their titles sifted, be they what they will; and if King William will have swear to his title (for I hear his heart is in it), he must allow us to examine into it. Perchance some people will not see a distinction between lawfull and rightfull; but nothing is more clear then y^t a man may be a lawfull possessor where he hath noe just title. The thing may be made out as to government in a very familiar instance; for in all governments there are two things, 1st, the power of governing, and 2dly, ye power of investeing with it. The power of governeing in all corporations is in ye Mayor; y^e

power of investeing him with this is either in ye Recorder or ye old Mayor, as the charter placeth it. Now in case they that have ye power of investeing swear in a Mayor that had not ye majority of votes in ye election, its certain that his beeing thus invested by those that had the lawfull power to doe it makes him ye lawfull Mayor, though he hath noe title to the office; and all that by their corporation oath are bound to be obedient to ye Mayor must, by virtue of that oath, pay their obedience unto him, till by law ejected; and soe, to apply y^c matter to ye King, there is ye power by wch he governs and ye power of investeing him with it. That the states of y^c kingdom have this latter, I reckon all sides will allow as a thing indubitable, and therefore, they haveing invested King William, I take it for certain this makes him ye lawfull K. But whether ye states did this rightfully still remains a question wch I wish may never be proposed to be examind. Its certain many that the oath will be imposed upon can never doe it soe far as to make a satisfactory judgement upon it.

[P.S.] The B. you mentioned in your last is B. enough.[a] Mr. Hodges,[b] whom you knew at Christ Church, is the man that puts these notions into him, who imbibed them from Shaftsbury, whose chaplain he was. He leads here a very od kind of life, drink beeing his whole trade, which he takes down without measure, and is thereby become ye scandal of ye whole countrey; and his exceedeing ruffe and provokeing carryage to all men makes all forward to propagate his fame. Last Saterday there came hither a very scurrilous pamphlett against my Lord Nottingham; what ye title of it is I know not, but it begins with an addresse to ye King, and ye purport of it is to show that that lord and others of his partys have betrayed ye King in every thing wherein they have been intrusted, and ye drift of [it] is to perswade ye King that he cannot

---

[a] I suppose that this is a not very complimentary reference to the Dean.
[b] See above, p. 34, note [d].

safely trust any that bore office either under King James or King Charles ye 2^d. This pamphlet was sent to severall persons with a cover haveing neither name nor any other writeing.

———————

[Norwich], Dec. 11th, [1693].

I have ye favour of yours, and by a letter from another friend ye names of all the pensioners. I am of opinion this discovery will soe blast that party that we have noe need to fear any thing from them this sessions. The Dialogue between Whig and Tory[a] is with great eagernesse dispersed here, and all that's sayd in it goes for gospell amongst too many. The poison is soe takeing that I think it needs an antidote. We are here at a miserable passe with this horrid sot we have got for our Dean. He cannot sleep at night till dosed with drink, and therefore, when in bed, his maine businesse is to drink with him till he hath his dose; and it beeing his way to keep a man only for ye time of his residence and then dismisse him, he hath spread his fame soe through ye whole countrey that nothing is more scandalous; for his servants, whom he thus dismisseth, goeing into other familys, tell all, especially one, a leud fellow enough, beeing intertained by one Mr. Earle, a drinkeing leud gentleman of this countrey, to be his butler, gives there a most horrid account of his old M^r ye Dean; and when ye leud ones there meet togeather to drinke, one of their chiefe entertainments is to have ye butler come in and tell all his storys of ye Dean of N., wch represent him one of ye greatest beasts in nature. And indeed his carriage in busjnesse represents him as much a brute as his man can a beast, for he acts by noe rules of justice, honesty, civility, or good manners towards any one, but after an obstinate, selfe-wild, irrationall manner in all sorts of businesses, whereby he disoblidgeth every one that hath

[a] " A Dialogue betwixt Whig and Tory, alias Williamite and Jacobite, wherein the Principles and Practices of each Party are fairly and impartially stated." 1693, 4to.

any thing to doe with him. He hath after a most unreasonable
manner disoblidged every one of the prebendarys except Hodges,
and nothing will satisfy him but to be an absolute king over us.
He comes little to church and never to ye sacrament, though
we have a sacrament every Sunday; and as for a booke, he looks
not into any from ye beginning of ye year to ye end. His whole
life is ye pot and ye pipe, and, goe to him when you will, you will
find him walkeing about his roome with a pipe in his mouth and a
bottle of claret and a bottle of old strong beer (wch in this countrey
they call nog) upon ye table, and every other turn he takes a glass
of one or ye other of them.^{a} If Hodges comes to him (for scarce
any other doth), then he reads Don Quixot, while ye other walkes
about with his pipe as before, and this is noble entertainment
between them. Certainly ye preferments of ye Church were never
designed for such drones; and yet these two fellows have about
300^1 per annum each, and never did it a farthings worth of service
in their life, professeing nothing else but to live idlely and feed
their bellys upon what they have. Hodges indeed is noe drinker
as ye other, for his body cannot bear it; but although nothing is
more mean then he, either in his birth or his merit, yet nothing can
be more proud and conceited, or possibly can have a more
despicable thought then he hath of the businesse of his profession,
and, to tell ye truth, he is not made for it. Once in a year he will
offer to preach, but, his sermons beeing most on end ye translation
of his morall philosophy lectures at Oxford, as soon as ye people
see him in ye pulpit they all get out of church. Nothing could be
more humble and complaisant then this fellow was all the time of
ye 2 late Kings, when he was obnoxious on ye account of his M^r,
Shaftsbury,^{b} or can there be any thing more proud and insolent
then he hath appeared ever since this government began. But
I hope after all their point will not goe. This discovery of

---

^{a} One recalls Addison's two bottles of wine in the long library of Holland House,
if Addison may be compared with Dean Fairfax and port and sherry with claret
and "nog." ^{b} See above, p. 34, note ^{d}.

pensioners[a] I reckon will breake yͤ reputation of yͤ party, especially if it be persued with 2 or 3 pamphletts, wᶜʰ I heartyly wish for. The late Archbp. would be buried in yͤ churchyard and by a Nonjuror.[b] Dͬ Trumball,[c] his quondam chaplain, performed that office for him. His library he gave to Emmanuel College in Cambridge,[d] whither he sent it before his death. The reason of his beeing buryed in the churchyard, I am told, was noe other but to ly among his relations who are buryed there. A friend of mine wrot me from London yͭ yͤ E[arl] of N[ottingham] may be Secretary again if he will, and [yͤ] E[arl] of S[hrewsbury's] refusall[e] haveing put yͤ King out of all his measures and much exasperated him against that party who assured him yͭ E[arl] would accept of yͬ place, severall of our members went out of this countrey prepared to fall upon the church this sessions; but now, I hope, we shall escape their malice this bout. Our Bp. will never accept of Dublin;[f] he acts here as wise and cunning a part as possibly a man can doe, and will make his fortune any where, and therefore you may be assured he will never leave England. I find the Republicarians in these parts openly sedulous to promote atheisme, to wᶜʰ end they spread themselfes in coffy houses and talk violently for it, and Dͬ Burnets Archaiologia[g] is much made use of by them to confute yͤ account yͤ Scriptures give us of yͤ creation of yͤ

[a] Pensiouers of the Court of St. Germain.

[b] William Sancroft, the deprived Archbishop of Canterbury, was buried in the churchyard of Fressinfield, co. Suffolk, on the 27 November. "The day before he breathed his last, he received the sacrament from Dr. Trumball, who had formerly been his chaplain and who was a nonjuror. Dr. Trumball came there accidentally that day: he had intended to receive it from the ejected minister of Eye, Mr. Edwards."—D'Oyly, *Life of Sancroft*, 1821, ii. 63.

[c] Charles Trumball, of Christ Church, B.C.L. 1670; D.C.L. of All Souls, 1677.

[d] He had been Master of that college.

[e] Charles Talbot, Earl of Shrewsbury, at length accepted office in the following March, and was created a Duke.

[f] Dr. Narcissus Marsh was translated thither from Cashel.

[g] Thomas Burnet. "Archæologiæ Philosophicæ, sive doctrina antiqua de rerum originibus." London, 1692, fol.

world, and other books are alsoe dispersed for this purpose, and ye number of their proselytes I am assured is great. You see where licentiousnesse and confusion at last end.

— — ——

[Saham], Dec. 25th, 1693.

I am sorry things are soe as you represent; but there is an overrulcing Providence wch often blasts the designes of ye wisest Ahitophels. The Government seems now to be brought to a kind of anarchy; nothing can long stand upon such a bottom of confusion; we must again tack about to our old constitutions or be lost. The late Archbp. ordered himselfe to be buryed in the churchyard, next his ffather and mother. Y^e directions wch he gave for ye other parts of his funerall (for those he concerned himselfe about before he dyed) were that he should be carryed in his coach to the churchyard and from thence by his servants to his grave, and to be layd into it by two of his nephews, both Sancrofts, whom he made his heirs and hath left between them about 600^l per annum. He was buryed by a Nonjuror, but not Dr Trumball, but Mr Edwards, formerly Vicar of Eye in ye neighbourhood, a wretched dull duncyeall fellow. Trumball was there a little before to administer ye sacrament to him, and that gave occasion to ye mistake. This is not ye Trumball that you mean,^{a} who is minister of Whitney near Oxford, but a brother of his about your standeing, 1st a Commoner of Christ Church and afterwards Fellow of All Souls. He was chaplain to ye Archbp. and by him preferred to ye Rectory of Hadley in Suffolk, ye best living in his diocesse, computed to be worth 300^l per annum, wch he still holds, notwithstandcing his refuseing ye oaths, and

^{a} Probably Ralph Trumbull, of Christ Church, M.A. 1663.

dayly officiates at it, another being instituted in trust for him; but his other liveing of equal value in Essex, alsoe given him by ye Archbishop, he is dispossessed of. The Archbp. left 1000¹ to be distributed among the Nonjurors, accordeing to ye discretion of the late Bp. of Norwich,ᵃ who lives at Hogsdon and now takes on him to be ye head of ye party. He hath long been their treasurer, and all gift money for their support is deposited with him. While I was at Norwich, a soldier was their shot to death for deserting; but all the effect it had was to make 30 more desert before night, and one in ye boldest manner possible; for, ye regement beeing draw[n] up at ye execution, as soon as it was over, in ye face of them all, he lays down his sword and gun and away he runs. Ye officers on horseback rod after him with all ye speed and diligence they could, but he outslipd them all and got clear away. Our brutish Dean is again got to London, and I suppose you find him at ye coffehouse. He carrys away with him ye generall odium of ye place. Such a man certainly was never before advanced to such a station, and yet he complains he hath not higher advancement, that a bishoprick was not given him to reward his meritts; for he thinks noe meaner of himself then that he was the person that put ye crown on this Kings head, and he hath ye vanity and folly to say soe. However, it seems they have promised him ye Deanery of York, if it be true what he says; but to my knowledge ye Archbishop of York hath that mislike of him that he will hinder him if possible from comeing thither. But ye other Archbishop ᵇ hath a kindnesse for him. One good quality he hath among others, that he will ly abominably, and hath very scandalously been convicted of it in many instances. I cannot expect my Ld. N[ottingham] will any more meddle with the government while in this posture, but when it tacks about again, wch it either must or break, I expect he will then again come in to ye chiefe management of affairs. It seems some of ye other side are out too,

---

ᵃ Dr. William Lloyd.   ᵇ Dr. John Tillotson.

if it be true what hath been wrot me of Monmouths[a] beeing
discarded. It was Lovelace[b] that was in Suffolk upon y[e] designe
last summer, but, since y[t], death hath put an end to all his mad
attempts. His marrying of his daughter to S[r] Henry Johnson
was y[e] occasion that brought him thither. We have a young
nobleman of .our country that now makes his first start in
London, that is y[e] Lord Townshend;[c] he is about 20 years old,
and hath been bred at Eaton College and Kings College in Cambridge; he tooke his leave of the latter about a month since and
is now at London. We are made to hope well of him; but
London is y[e] place that is to try him, and y[e] company he first gets
into is that w[ch] will either make or mar him. For, as yet, we
may reckon him as rasa tabula; a twelvemonth hence we shall
better see whither good or evill is to be wrot thereon. His estate
is about 6000[l] per annum, and in very good condition, without
debt or charge upon it; y[e] seat is y[e] best on this side London, as
beeing in y[e] best part of Norfolk for pleasure or health, and y[e]
house a very good and stately ffabric, distant about 10 miles from
Lyn and 20 from Norwich. Beside him we have noe other nobleman in this country but y[e] Earle of Yarmouth, who at present
lives very obscurely and yet increaseth his debts. His mother,[d]
who made a great bussle in King Charles y[e] 2ds time, now boards
in a thatched house; and, altho there she keeps up her pride to y[e]
heigth by suffering noe one to sett at meat with her and many
other vain formalitys, yet with difficulty enough finds money to
pay for her board, and hath made her landlord soe weary of her

[a] Charles Mordaunt, Earl of Monmouth, afterwards Earl of Peterborough, First
Commissioner of the Treasury, 1689-90; Lord of the Bedchamber; and one of the
Council of Nine appointed by William to act during his absence from England.

[b] John, third Baron Lovelace. His daughter Martha, afterwards Baroness
Wentworth, married Sir Henry Johnson, a shipbuilder.

[c] Charles, second Viscount Townshend, Ambassador at the Hague in the reign of
Queen Anne, and Secretary of State under George I.; K.G.; Lord Lieutenant of
Ireland, 1717.

[d] See above, p. 121.

as to make use of all the civil ways he can to gett rid of her; but she will understand none of them, not knowing where next to goe. Her son gives her noe respects or holds any correspondence with her, tho she lives not above 2 miles from him. The greatest family next ye lords, and I think before them both for antiquity an[d] estate, is the Barneys, wch is now expireing; the present possessor,^a though left 7000^l per annum and 50,000^l in money and stock on his estate, having squandered all away and yet never lived like a gentlemen in this life. He hath been infatuated to a vile expensive whore, and she hath been ye broad ditch that hath swallowed all; and by her help he hath advanced the charge upon ye estate soe high that next Easter Term, by decree of Chancery, ye morgagees enter all, unlesse he can find a chapman in ye interim to purchase ye estate. My Lord N[ottingham] offered at it, but I gave him those reasons against medleing there that he did not proceed.

--- --- ---

Norwich, April 8th, 1696.

We are now in ye midst of our [assizes]. Y^e judge^b dischargeth himselfe as much to ye generall satisfaction of ye countrey as ye last did to ye generall dissatisfaction. The D. of Norfolk^e hath [sent] downe an association subscribed by himselfe in a forme made up of that of ye House of Lords and House of Commons togeather, wch hath put ye countrey to doe ye matter over again after it had in a

---

^a Richard Berney, second son of Sir Richard Berney, Bart., of Reedham, co. Norfolk. He succeeded to his father's estates and fortune, his elder brother being disinherited. "He was high sheriff in the fourth year of William III., and died *s. p.* having sold the family seat at Redham and spent very nearly his whole estate."— Blomefield's *Norfolk*, xi. 128.

^b Sir Edward Ward, Lord Chief Baron.

^c Henry Howard, twelfth Duke of Norfolk.

manner gon through every parish before.[a] The city you see have
made a scisme and sent up two formes, one from ye Mayor and
common councill men, and ye other from ye weavers, who are
indeed a distinct corporation of themselfes. That wch made y^c
scisme was y^c word "revenge." Mr. Robert Cooke,[b] who is y^c
wealthyest man in ye city, and a weaver himselfe, and alsoe a con-
venticler, was ye person that made ye exception, as beeing one of y^c
aldermen, and, on ye debate of y^c matter among them, it was
carryed by a great majority to leave out ye word "revenge," and
put instead of it ye word "punish," as y^t wch expressed all that y^c
Parliament could mean by ye word "revenge." But a letter
comeing from Sr Henry Hobart[c] about it put y^c weavers upon a
project of associateing by themselfes in a forme wch contained y^c
word "revenge;" and this they chiefly did because they were made
believe y^t y^c more zeal they showed on this occasion ye better they
should carry their bill for ye prohibiteing Indian silks and Bengalls;
and Sr Harry Hobarts letter haveing put this into their heads they
run away with it like mad, and noe one durst gainsay them. However, they beeing a corporation by themselfes, the thing may passe
well enough. The sheriffe at our assizes for this countey is S^r
James Edwards.[d] How he came by his estate I have formerly told
you. He makes profuse wast enough of his money, but doth it
with soe ill a grace that it gains him nothing [but to] make him y^c
more ridiculous and [ill]bred. He is as ridiculous silly fellow as
ever I saw in my life. The small pox beeing got into y^c jayl
hinders severall of y^c criminalls from beeing [tryed], soe they must

[a] The "Association" in defence of the King after the discovery of the assassination
plot was subscribed in Parliament and throughout the country in February and
following months.

[b] Mayor of Norwich in 1693, and one of the founders of Cooke's Hospital in
that city.

[c] Sir Henry Hobart, of Blickling, Bart., at this time M.P. for Norfolk. He was
present at the battle of the Boyne with William III. Died from a wound received
in a duel with Oliver Le Neve, 1698.

[d] Sir James Edwards, of Reedham Hall, Bart.

ly till next assizes. The gentlemen have made y" fullest appearance
upon ye grand jury that hath been seen here a long time, and, were
it not for ye small pox, there would have been more, and show a
great heartynesse in y^r interest of the government. But I hear
there are some about this town that prate very desperately, and I
am told it hath been muttered among them as if ye thing might
yet be don, but I cannot fix it on any and hope it may be noc
more then what reports have made it by additions from those whose
hands they have gon thorough. However, I wish ye King would
take care of himselfe; for there is such a generall mutter through
this countrey of many that fear it, and some that hope it, that still
some desperat attempt may be made upon his person by ye remainder
of those villains who first designed it. But it is what I confesse I
can make nothing of; and perchance it may have noc foundations
at all besides ye bare apprehensions of people, accordeing as they
stand affected either one way or the other. The Bps. haveing
agreed on a form in wch ye clergy are to addresse to y" King on
this occasion, I have this day sent it into Suffolk; but, although
it be in ye moderatest terms possible, I doubt severall will refuse
to subscribe it. The judge endeth ye assize to-morrow and will be
in London on Saterday.

—— .

Norwich, Ap[ril] 10, 1696.

Our assizes are now finished; seven malefactors are sentenced
to death, four for house robbeing, two for highwaymen, and one
for clippeing. Others as guilty were discharged, contrary to the
directions of ye judge, by an over-kind jury; and some remained
untryed, because sick of ye small pox. It would have made a very
bloody assizes had all had sentence of death that deserved. The
judge discharged himselfe exceedeingly well. The main cause
tryed before him was between two clergymen about a woman;
one whose name was Williams marryed her, and Dean, who was

ye other, claimed a precontract and sues Williams for damages last
assizes, where, on his produceing ye contract and severall love letters
from ye woman, he obtained a verdict for 200¹; whereon Williams
undertakes to prove Dean guilty of forgery, and this assizes y^e
cause was tryed. The judge allowed eight hours for ye heareing
of it, and ye jury found ye cause for Williams, severall very notorious
acts of forgery haveing been proved against Dean, who hath indeed
all along been a very raskall; and hereon he is run away. They
say he is gon to London to sue out a pardon; but its pitty but y^t
such a villain should be left to ye law. If he comes to your office,
he is not a person that deserves any favour.

[Norwich], April 15, 1696.

The account wch is given in one of ye prints, called y^e " Post
boy," of the Association of this place gives ye governours of this
city great disgust; ffor ye truth is, every word of it is false,
and it foully reflects upon them. Y^e whole spring of that contrivance I told you in my last, and indeed, considereing ye notion
wch those had of the word " revenge " who were soe zealous for it,
there was good reason for ye altereing of it. For they declared
they meant thereby that, in case ye King was kild, they would draw
their swords and cut ye throats of all ye Jacobites, and that by virtue
of the Parliaments Association they were bound thereto; wch extra-
vagancy deserved to be discountenanced and disowned; for should
ever ye case happen, wch God forbid, every man shall be a Jacobite
whom ye rabble shall think fitt to plunder and abuse. Next Friday
our seven condemned criminalls are to be executed. They are stout
fellows all of them, but as hardned villains as ever I heard of in my
life. All that those ministers who assist them can doe to make
them sensible of their condition availeth nothing, [and] those few
minutes they have left they spend in the heigth of loudnesse and
frolick. The Mayor hath ordered ye town clerk of ye city now in

London to prosecute ye writer of y^e " l'ost boy " for slandering
them in his print, unlesse he will discover the intelligencer that
sent him ye news from hence, and then they will right themselfes
of him here on the place. The truth is, whoever wrot that account
to him was a very impudent lying fellow, and by one passage I
perceive intends a reflection on me, as if I influenced the city to y^e
alteration; whereas nothing is a more constant rule with me then
never to meddle with any of their concerns, and indeed I very
seldom goe among them. Our close is as it were a town of
itselfe apart from ye city, separated from it by walls and gates.   I
acknowledge I have as great a share of their respects as any of my
profession perchance that hath ever lived among them, but I take
care to have nothing at any time to doe with them but in my profession, and in this they have my pains constantly gratis. I am
affraid we shall have but a lame return from ye clergy to whom we
have sent our Association to be subscribed; it is a very moderate
forme, and I have sent this argument with it into my archdeaconry:
that the ready subscribeing of it will be ye surest way to prevent an
harder forme from beeing imposed on us.   I have taken all ye care
I can to induce all, where I am concerned, to comply.   I need not
trouble you with a copy of ye forme; I suppose you have it at
London.

——— ———

Norwich, April 17th, 1696.

This day ye sentence was executed upon those desperate villains
who were condemned at ye last assizes; and their last effort had
something [in] it more then ordinary. Those that brought them
their coffins conveyed to them therein arms, provisions, and other
things, in order to an escape; wch haveing got, they knockd of
their irons and made an attempt to breake out, but, not beeing
able to succeed, they tooke possession of ye dungeon, into w^{ch}
there was only one narrow passage, and there stood severall days

upon their guard. But this morneing, by help of ye soldiers that quarter here, they forced ye place and tooke ye malefactors, whereon one of them immediately tooke poison, to prevent ye execution, but by poureing oyle into his mouth they made him cast it up again, soe he lived long enough to be hanged with the rest. They were seven desperate sturdy villains, and we are well rid of them. When they came to ye gallows they did lament that they had been deceived by some at London, who fed them with promises of pardon, and soe dyed in a manner by surprise without makeing any use of ye time wch they had between sentence and execution. Yesterday ye Thanksgiveing day was kept here in a more then ordinary manner, the Mayor being willeing to doe more then ordinary to relieve himselfe from ye slur cast upon him about ye Association by ye weavers and their correspondent, ye writer of y^e "Post boy." Next May day they chuse a new Mayor; ye man next in order, and who will certainly be chosen, is one Mr Bikerdike,[a] who is ye most intelligent person of ye whole body.

[Norwich], April 24th, 1696.

There is this morneing gon from hence towards London one Dr Bambridge, a physitian of this place. His businesse is to sollicite Mr Tasboroughs discharge, in order to wch he is to apply to ye D[uke] of N[orfolk], with whom he is very dear whenever his Grace comes hither. I have many years looked on him as a very dangerous person. His practice cannot be worth him 40^l per annum, and yet he lives at ye rate of 400^l per annum, without any visible estate. Everybody looks on him here as a great mystery. Most will have it that he lives by ye trade of a stallion; but noe one can tell where he should have trade enough this way to maintain him as he lives. For my part I have looked on him for

---

[a] Nicholas Bickerdyke, Mayor of Norwich, 1696.

those ten years to have been a spy for y² papists. I am sure he
acted for their interest strenuously in y² late reigne, and is continually with them now, and is their servant on all occasions. But
as to religion, he hath none but that wch will best serve his interest.
Some one put in an information against him to the Councill table
since this plot broke out, but y² D[uke] of N[orfolk] got him
of. One part of his instructions are, I hear, to know what informations are against Mr Tasborough, and from whom. If M^r
Tasborough be discharged, I wish it may be on condition that he
leave this place, where he hath don a great deal of mischiefe. His
businesse here is looked on to be to manage the correspondence of
y² party in receiveing and sendeing all letters, for wch they have
messengers of their owne. Two of them were observed to have
been here on y² breakeing out of y² plot, and, as soon as they had
y^r news of it, immediatly took horse and rod away. Sr Robert
Yallup,[a] Sr Christopher Calthrop,[b] and Sr Nicholas Lestrange,[c]
yesterday, upon summons, appeared at the sessions and had y² oaths
tendered to them; but all refused. Y² latter payd his 5^l and found
security accordeing to law, but y² other two refused both, and soe
are committed. Sr Robert Yallup is y² greatest knave in nature,
but y² other two very honest gentlemen. Sr Nicholas Lestrange is
a man of parts, virtue, and prudence, but cannot at present conforme
to y² takeing of y² oaths; but Sr Christopher Calthrop a man of
strong zeal and weak judgement and totally bigotted to Torisme,
but one whom I reckon a harmlesse man and noe otherwise
inclined to show his affection to y² cause he is in but by suffering
for it; and he seems in his present acteings to court suffereing. I
am of opinion that y² Government, as to him, would best serve its
interest by dischargeing him.

---

[a] Sir Robert Yallop, of Bowthorp, Kt.
[b] Sir Christopher Calthorp, of East Barsham, K.B
[c] Sir Nicholas Lestrange, of Hunstanton, Bart.

[Norwich], Ap. 29 [1696.]

S' Christopher Calthrop and S' Robert Yallup still chuse to continue in custody rather then give security to y' Government on their second refusall of y' oaths. What y' later means by it noe one knows, unlesse it be that he thinks y' plot would still take effect, and therefore he would by his suffereings y' better recommend himselfe to King James on another revolution; for he is as great a knave as lives, that hath noe reguard either for oaths, religion, or any thing else but what will best sute with his interest. But the other is a very religious, sober, good man, but of a very weake judgement, wch misguides him into this folley to court suffereings, because he thinks he is in y' right cause. I am of opinion that y' Government cannot better serve its interests, in reference to this gentleman, then by ordereing him to be discharged; for he is a quiet, harmlesse man, who will never doe any hurt, but may by his suffereings raise a needlesse odium among y' people who have an opinion of him; and indeed, noe government getts any credit by prosecuteing such men barely upon the account of a misguided conscience. I wish you would be pleased to move y' matter; for y' dischargeing of this gentleman would more afflict y' party here then y' suffereings of ten such as Yallup are, one of their chiefe braggs beeing that he is a confessor in their cause. The papists all came to towne at y' same time those gentlemen did upon their summons, but findeing what course was taken with them, upon consult among themselfes, all went home again and did not appear, whereon another summons is gon out to call them again on Thursday sennight.

[Norwich], May 4th, 1696.

Last Friday M' Bikerdike was chosen mayor of this city, who of all the aldermen we looke on to be y' ablest to bear such an office, though not yᵉ ablest in purse; but he is an honest and a very understandeing man, and hath always carryed himselfe decently. The Jacobites put up one of their party against him, one Mʳ Workhouse,[a] but lost it by a very great majority. The two knights still continue prisoners in yᵉ under-sheriffs hands for refuseing to find bayl. Mʳ Tasborough hath lately lost his wife, while in jayl. She had been a great brandy drinker, and that, with yᵉ small pox, hath set him at liberty from her, however else he stands hamperd. I hope, when discharged from his confinement, he will be oblidged to leave this place. We have good hopes we shall be able to bring Sʳ Nicholas Lestrange to take yᵒ oaths; he is one of yᵉ worthyest gentlemen of the countrey and a very fitt person to serve in parliament, and, would he qualify himselfe for it, would certainly be chosen for yᵉ countey. Next Thursday yᵉ papists are called yᵉ 2d time to make their appearance to take yᵉ oaths. If they come not then in, yᵉ county troup will be raised to fetch them in prisoners.

— · ·· ··

[Norwich], May 16, 1696.

I doe most heartyly thank you for yᵉ continuation of your great favour in still sendeing me yᵉ news. I shall not be here to receive it the ensueing fortnight, for I goe into Suffolk next Tuesday, and doe not return again till yᵉ end of yᵉ week following. I have yᵉ Association sent from yᵉ Bishop subscribed by all yᵉ clergy of my archdeaconry, but now they have put us to all this trouble I hear it is not to be presented, because it agreeth not with yᵉ form of yᵉ Act of Parliament. But, since the Act doth not concern us in that matter, I should think however this should be received. But we have a Bp. who takes as little notice of his diocesse as if he were not concerned in it at all, or can I say this diocesse is any more

[a] Samuel Warkehouse, Mayor of Norwich 1698.

the better for him then ye diocesse of Carlile. He will be sure to take care of himselfe, and that is all I find he minds. He was, it seems, to have preached one of ye Lent sermons, and ye Archbp. of York the Thanksgiveing sermon at Whitehall; but he exchanged with his friend, to have ye opportunity on that occasion to recommend himselfe by y^t performance for ye bishoprick of Ely, wch its supposed will be vacated on Mews death ^{a} by ye removall of Patrick ^{b} thither. But whither his sermon may deserve it ye world is to judge, for it seems it is printed. Our old mayor ^{c} now lys a dying. His disease is a perpetuall thirst after brandy, wch he loveing better then his life must even pay it down for ye purchase, as all such doe who habituate themselfes to this sottishnesse.

Norwich, June 1, 1696.

I am now returned again from my Suffolk journey, where I found all things very quiet. Ye long struggle wch hath been between the two partys in y^t countrey is now totally at an end by ye absolute victory wch ye Whig party hath got over ye other. For they have not only carryed all ye elections from them in ye last Parliament, but have alsoe made them criminalls for opposeing them, haveing brought indictments of riot against them at ye last assizes on this account, and by a packd jury (5 of wch were ye members chosen, who came down from the Parliament of purpose for this job) caused ye bills to be found against them, wch hath sent ye other party to London with a petition for a noli prosequi; but those persons who were thus used (and some of them are ye worthiest gentlemen of ye countrey) are exceedeingly soured against ye Government on this account, wch by noe means tends

---

^{a} Peter Mews, Bishop of Winchester, lived to 1706.
^{b} Simon Patrick, Bishop of Ely.
^{c} Augustine Briggs, Mayor of Norwich in 1695, died in 1704.

to ye Kings interest, or doe I find any one pleased with it but
Sr Robert Rich ^a and his gang. Our mayor is like again to recover
since sequesterd from ye brandy bottle. I find ye difficultys about
ye coin to presse hard everywhere all ye way I came, but I hope
the mint will take care speedyly to remedy this inconvenience.^b

---

The enclosed contains what I [have] ^c to say of Sr Christopher
Calthop's case. I think it proper to acquaint you in [this] paper
apart that S^r H[enry] H[obart']s moveing ye Councill again against
him is a [m]atter of peevish malice not to be countenanced ; for
ye originall of it is [a] quarrell between their familys, and S^r H.
would fain bring in the Government to revenge it for him. In
ye last Parliament of K. Charles ye 2ds r[eign], wch was held at
Westminster, the Whig party, you may remember, made a great
struggle to get into ye House, and Sr John Hobart, ye father of
Sr Henry, set up here to be knight of the shire, but, after all y^e
interest he could make and many thousands spent in ye canvas,
Sr Christopher Colthrop, without any great struggle, by the
interest and reputation he then had in his countrey, carryed it from
him ; and this it seems must be remembered against him to this
day. I wish Sr Henry, instead of prosecuteing his neighbours,
would think of paying his debts, wch he takes noe care of, but
useth his privilege to protect him, to the doeing of great prejudices
to some of his creditors. Here is a lady of one of ye best familys
in ye countrey who hath all her fortune in his hands, and he hath

---

^a Sir Robert Rich, of Rosehall, co. Suffolk, Bart.

^b In accordance with the terms of the Recoinage Act, all clipped money was
called in and was now being replaced by the new milled coinage. A mint was set
up at Norwich.—See Macaulay's account of the state of the coinage, in chapter xxi.
of his *History*.

^c This letter and the following, its enclosure, have been much injured by damp.

not payd her any interest these severall years, whereby she is put
to great hardships for her subsistence. The case of severall others
of ye like nature will come against him next sessions, and I
hope the House will not think fitt to protect him in such unjust
practices. He stays at London to agent for ye party; he heads all
their malicious devices, and I believe, if he carrys on this humour,
he will at last have enough of it. Most men have too many follys
of their own of this sort to gratify ; he need not make himselfe a
tool to other mens irregular passions herein; perchance it may be
his turn, sometime or other, to bear as much as he now acts. But
how much soever he delights in ye office, it is certainly ye worst
any man can be imployed in. My Lord Archbp. of Canterbury,
who is a Norfolk man by birth, knows Sr Christopher Colthops
case as well as I doe, and, I am sure, hath ye same sentiments of
it. As to Yallups case, there is this difference between his and
Sr Christopher Colthrops, that ye one is a gentleman of ye greatest
integrity in ye countrey and ye other ye most defective of it; S^r C.
refused ye oath only for the sake of his conscience, the other hath
none at all; and Sr C. hath lived quietly under ye Government, and ye other hath been a very turbulent enterprising knave
against it, as I have formerly acquainted you, in his caballeing at
ye Goat Tavern, where he constantly, at 4 in ye afternoon, used to
meet with all ye principall Jacobites in this place, and there be
with them in a private club with doores shut for ye most part till
9 at night every Saterday, and this he continued to doe till about
Christmas last. It began to be soe much taken notice of, that they
were forced to discontinue their meeting, and ye plot breaking out
a little after put an end to it. The whole reason of his refuseing
to give security, as far as I can learn, is to fling an odium upon
ye Government from ye ill practices of ye Clerk of ye Assizes, who,
beeing a very great knave, did it seems put some hardships upon
gentlemen who were suretys for others in defaulteing their appearance, although they did appear perfectly, to advance his own gain;
which Yallup laying hold sayd he durst not [trust] ye Government

with his friends, and therefore would not ensnare them in a surety
for [him, for] he was sure, right or wrong, they would suffer for
it. I am sorry there was foundation for his charge and I could
wish it might be prevented for ye future, but whither his refuseing
to give security for this reason (and this is all I hear he alledgeth)
is a thing to be well resented by ye Government, I leave it to them
whom it belongs to to consider.

                                         [Norwich], June 22^d, 1696.

. . . . . . As to Sr Christopher Colthrop, he is a very innocent,
sober, religious gentleman, [but is exceed]cingly enslaved to a
scrupulous and weake conscience. If he were [to be executed]
to morrow for not takeing the oaths I am well assured [he would
die] with chearfullnesse reather then submitt thereto.   I never
saw ye g[entleman] in my life; but I know his character well, and
by ye best information I [can] gett I cannot discover that he hath
in ye least been either openly turbulent or . . . . privately
designeing against the present Government, but lives quietly at
home.   And to put such a man upon suffereings, who would be
glad to bear them, would be to give ye cause too great a reputation
and ye party an argument to value themselfes upon.   And, had
you not heard how they began to bragg of their confessor, I should
not have writ you my opinion in his case; and that opinion wch I
sent you I am still of, that ye Government would gratify ye party
too much in letteing this gentleman suffer for their cause, and
cannot better serve its own interest then by thus disappointeing
them of what they would be glad of.   And besides, there are a
great many in this countrey with [whom] Sr Christopher Colthrop
hath a great reputation for his integrity and [honest] conversation,
with whom ye Government would create itselfe [a great] odium by
detaineing him in prison, as long as there is nothing else against

him but his refuseing to take the oaths. If there be anything else
against him (wch I never could learn), I have nothing to say. Let
Sr Henry Hobart alledge· it, and ye Lords of the Councill will see
what is best to be don. I will be noe advocate for such who
cannot at least live quietly under the Government that protects
them. But if Sr Christopher Calthrop hath don soe (as I am well
[assured he] hath), the makeing him suffer all that he is willeing
to suffer for not takeing ye oaths will serve for nothing else but to
draw a needlesse [odium] upon ye Government, and give ye party a
confessor to brag of and va[unt them]selfes upon. Besides, he
hath this further to alledge in his case: when he was summoned to
appear at the sessions he obeyed ye summons and made his
appearance, and then, on his not beeing able to comply with
takeing ye oaths, he was committed accordeing to statute. But y^e
papists (and we have [some as] dangerous enemys to ye Government as any in England) beeing summoned at ye same time,
although they refused to appear and stood in conte[mpt of the]
law, are let alone and nothing don to them. If Sr Christopher be
[detained] in prison for not takeing the oaths, why should they
escape? And if they escape, why should he be detained? This
would be to open some mens mouths in calumny against ye present
Government, as if papists found more favour under it then
protestants. If Sr H. Hobart will have Sr Christopher be re-
committed, I think ye papists ought to be committed alsoe. I
think them much more criminall and much more dangerous enemys
to ye Government. Besides, I have thus much further to say of
Sr Christopher, that I am well assured he hath that aversion to
popery that he will never be brought to have anything to doe with
those that professe it. But in short his character is, he is a very
religious, sober [honest] gentleman, that will suffer ten thousand
deaths reather then [doe any]thing wch he thinks amisse; but
beeing of a weak judgement [he is soe] prepossest of ye illegality of
takeing ye oaths to his present Majesty that it is not all the world
can turn him, and there is noe suffereings wch can be devised w^ch

he would not patiently submitt to reather then doe this thing.   If
the Government hath a mind to give ye party y^r reputation of
haveing such a confessor to suffer for them, he is totally fitted to
answere their desires and serve their interest in this particular.
[But how the Government can] serve itself herein I cannot see.   I
am sure he [will doe] it noe hurt to be let goe home, and that he
will create it a great de[al of need]lesse odium to be kept in prison.
Besides, there is this further to be con[sidered], that he is low in y^e
world and a great part of his estate in his hands, [soe that, if he]
be kept from lookeing after it now harvest draws nigh, it m[ay
doe great injur]y unto him; and I am sure it can doe noe Go[vern-
ment any credit] to create any that live under it such hardships.
[In accordance with] the mercy wch I have observed in his Majesty
[I scarce think that] it would be most agreable to his mind to
confine [him reather the]n to discharge him; ffor his crime is
nothing else but a m[isguided conscien]ce wch can not be rectifyed.

[P.S.]   There is this further to be sayd in Sr Christopher
Calthrops case, that ever since ye statute, wch oblidgeth those that
cannot take ye oaths not to keep'an horse above ye value of 5^l, he
hath punctually complyed with it, as he alsoe hath with all other
circumstances wch ye Goverment hath thought fit to put men in his
case under.   This I am well informed of from those who are
thoroughly acquainted with his way of liveing, and persons of that
integrity that I durst rely on their informations; and his generall
character is, he is one of the most inoffensive men that lives and
delights in nothing soe much as to doe good to all he can.   The
countrey is now in expectation of ye assizes and what judge shall
[have] ye circuit.   The Lord Chiefe Baron g[ave soe ver]y great
satisfaction on his last beeing here ^{a} that it is y^e generall h[ope of y^e
cou]ntey that he would come this circuit again, and it is y^e same
fo[r Suffolk, as] I understand from y^e High Sheriff of that countey

See above, p. 166.

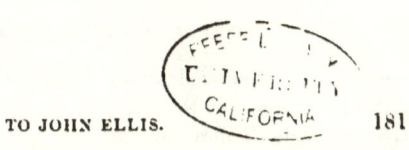

who dined with [me last] week. The Government cannot more effectually secure its reputation and [credit] with yᵉ people then by furnisheing the benches of judicature with such men to administer justice unto them. He hath yᵉ character with us to be yᵉ fairest hearer of causes that ever came yᵉ circuit.

[Norwich], July 20th, 1696.

I am sorry yᵉ matter of Sʳ C. C. did raise such a storme; but some men delight in mischiefe, and such seldom fail at last of haveing enough of it upon their owne heads. Here hath been of late sculkeing in this towne the Archbp. of Glasco,ᵃ to whom yᵉ Jacobites of the place did much resort. I wish here be not more mischiefe a breweing, for that party beginns again to be very confident and insolent. The Archbp. is now at Yarmouth and there much caress'd as I hear. Sʳ John Barker,ᵇ one of yᵉ burgesses of Ipswich, lys in a very languishing condition, not like to recover. His death, I believe, will reconcile the towne and bring them all again to be of a piece, wᶜʰ hath been in perpetuall feuds for these seven or 8 years last past. I intend, if I can, to perswade my Lᵈ Huntingtowr ᶜ to stand there in case of a vacancy, who is a very sensible man, and with great prudence manageth all affairs that he putts his hands unto, only, haveing come to an incumberd estate, that frugality and spareing way of liveing wᶜʰ his circumstances at first made necessary hath habituated him to that wᶜʰ, now he is out of those circumstances, is downright stingynesse. For he, haveing now cleared his estate of yᵉ vast debt wᶜʰ he found

---

ᵃ John Paterson, Archbishop of Glasgow, 1687; ejected soon after the Revolution.

ᵇ Sir John Barker, of Grimston Hall, co. Suffolk, Bart.

ᶜ Lionel Tallemache, Lord Huntingtower, son of Sir Lionel Tallemache, Bart., and of Elizabeth Murray, daughter of William Earl of Dysart. He became Earl of Dysart in 1697. His mother married, secondly, John Duke of Lauderdale.

upon it, may very well afford to live accordeing to his quality.
After his mother ye Dutchesse of Lauderdale, and his mother-in-
law ye Lady Wilbraham, he will have better then 3000[1] per
annum. For Sr Thomas Wilbraham[a] had only two daughters to
inherit his estate, wch was large. Mr Newport marryed one, and y^e
Ld Huntingtowr ye other. He lives most on end near Harborough
in Northamptonshire; but ye principall seat of his family is at
Helmingham, 7 miles from Ipswich. Here hath lately been in
this place one that calls himselfe Archbishop of Glascoe.[b] The
papists did not appear at ye sessions; they say they will return
them convict at ye next assizes. I should be glad could I see it,
for then ye University would have the disposall of their liveings,
wch now they give to ye worst men they can find. The difficultys
about money still grow more presseing. Mr Hodges beeing here
hath received an invitation from Mr Lock, to desire a visit from
him, in terms that bespeaks him a dying man.[c]

[Norwich], Aug. 24, [1696].

We have had here a long assizes, it haveing continued from
Saterday last was sennight till this evening. On ye Crown side
there have been two condemned for murder and one for clippeing
and coineing. Att ye other bar y^r most remarkeable cause hath
been between two clergymen, Dean and Williams; ye later about 3
years since marryed a widdow whom we reckoned worth 1500[1];
y^r other pretends a contract and sues Williams upon it, and this
time twelmonth had a verdict and 200[1] damage. Hereon Williams

---

[a] Sir Thomas Wilbraham, of Woodhey, co. Chester, Bart., married Elizabeth
Mitton. He had three daughters: 1. Elizabeth, married Sir Thomas Myddleton;
2. Grace, married Lord Huntingtower; and 3. Mary, married Richard Newport,
Earl of Bradford in 1708.

[b] This sentence is struck out with the pen.

[c] Locke died in 1704.

pleads Dean to be guilty of forgery in forgeing y⁰ sayd contract
and severall other love letters produced to prove that contract, and
upon a long tryall of 9 hours last assizes Dean was found guilty
of y⁰ forgery; but he having obtained another tryall, it was this
assizes tryed over again, and it tooke up a whole days hearing,
and y⁰ jury were locked up a whole night, and at last, through y⁰
obstinacy of one man, the forgerer was acquitted, though his guilt
manifestly appeared to every stander-by at y⁰ tryall, and y⁰ Judge
yesterday at dinner, when 1 dined with him,ᵃ fully expressed
himself as to Deans guilt; and indeed he is as ill a man as any
of his profession in the country, and the other as honest a man.
This affair hath made much noise and is not yet at an end; there
will be another tryall about it. Sʳ C[hristopher] C[althorp]s
affair is much talked of. Sʳ Roger Potts,ᵇ one concerned against
him, would have perswaded a gentleman to have wrot to Sʳ C. C.
to render himselfe prisoner again at y⁰ assizes, for, sayd he, this
may prevent a great deal of trouble in Parliament; for it seems
Sʳ H[enry] H[obart] threatens he will bring this matter into
Parliament. However y⁰ Lord Cheife Justice Treby ᶜ at this
assizes hath judged in effect his commitment to be illegall, as
really it was; ffor he was committed for not findeing security on
his second refusall of y⁰ oaths, whereas the first was before y⁰ act
of pardon and pardond by it, and, if pardond by it, it cannot
certainly operate to make a second offence; for, in that it is
pardond, it must fall under oblivion and not be any more remembred, and therefore certainly must not be brought into any
reckoning in order to make a second offence; and when this
was pleaded this assizes, in behalfe of Sʳ Nicholas Lestrange who
had given security in the same case, that he was illegally put upon
it because y⁰ first offence was pardoned, the judge allowed the
plea and discharged him. However, y⁰ Duke of Norfolk, who is

ᵃ These five words are struck out with the pen.
ᵇ Sir Roger Potts, of Mannington, co. Norfolk, Bart.
ᶜ Sir John Treby, Chief Justice of the Common Pleas.

now here, talks that there will be an order of Councill again to
recommitt S[r] C. C.; and if such a thing should be moved, I wish
it might be granted, and let those men who trouble themselves
soe much in this affair take y[e] shame of it; ffor y[e] illegality of his
commitment will be manifested, whenever an opportunity shall be
given for it. The D. of N. brought down one M[rs] Lane, his mis,
with him, who made a great show here; however he faild of his
main purpose, w[ch] was to entertain himselfe with y[e] ladys; for,
when he had made great preparations for a ball, none would come
to it, which gave him y[t] offence that he sayd he would never make
one here more; and I think it is time for him to leave it of, when
all that have any reguard to their reputations think it scandalous
to accept his invitations. Our mint doth not yet work, and y[e]
difficultys about y[e] coin grow worse and worse. S[r] John Barker
dyed Friday last was sennight. It is not yet known, or as far as
I can hear as much as conjectured, who will stand for the place.

[Norwich], Sept. 16, 1696.

Here hath been this week 4000[l] brought into y[e] m[int.   On]
Friday a trick was played them by a goldsmith, w[ch] shows how
[such ro]gues sharp upon y[e] kingdom. He, haveing saved all y[e]
broad hammerd money that came to his hands w[ch] would hold
weight, brought it in for y[e] sake of y[e] 6[d] per ounce advance,
whereby he got 2[s] in y[e] pound more then it would goe for in tale;
and the summe he payd amounteing to 80[l] his gain herein will be
8[l]. The officers of y[e] mint refused not to receive it, saying their
commission was to refuse none; but this is a knavery I think
should not be tolerated, for its a gross abuseing of y[e] publick. The
D[uke] of N[orfolk]s wh. is still in y[e] countrey, and carryeth
herselfe here as such cattell use to doe, without shame or modesty.
I goe next Tuesday for Suffolk and shall not return till 10 days

after; and therefore you may be pleased, after Saterdays post, to suspend your favour of sendeing me your news till I acquaint you of my return.

[P.S.] At the closeing of their bookes this night at ye mint, the summe above mentioned of clipd money brought in to be recoined is excreased to above ten thousand pound.

- - - -

Norwich, May 14, 1697.

I thank you for ye kind acceptance of y^r booke I sent you.^a I know not whether it might not be a presumption in me to present one of them to Mr Secretary; ^b as beeing your friend, I would gladly show him my respects, and as haveing been ambassador in Turkey, perchance such a booke might not be unacceptable unto him. However, I durst offer at it noe further than to leave you master of ye matter, to doe as you should think fitteing; and, since you have thought fitt to present it to him, I hope I made noe wrong step in this tender of my respects unto him. I had much adoe to get it printed, for it lay a year in towne before any bookeseller would venture on it. I am just now returned from Suffolk to here. I find nothing remarkeable, but that a gentleman of ye countrey hath lately martyed one sister of his late deceased wife and whored another. He is a man of 1000^l per annum; however, I am resolved he shall not escape my censure. Things continue every where quiet as yet, but I scarce think they will endure another yeare tax. The

---

^a This was Prideaux's new work, " The True nature of Imposture fully display'd in the Life of Mahomet." London, 1697, 8vo.

^b Sir William Trumbull, Kt., Secretary of State, 1695-7. He entered St. John's College; B.C.L. of All Souls, 1659; D.C.L. 1667. He was sent Envoy Extraordinary to France in 1685, and was Ambassador to Constantinople, 1687-91.—*Ath. Oxon.* ii. 229.

barley tax much pincheth this countrey. Dr Smyth,[a] one of our prebendarys, lys a dying; he is a very old man, beeing about 85, and of that vigour, till this sicknesse, that he never felt any indisposition or decay before, but to all appearance was as strong a man in every particular as any other at 40. But his disease beeing ye stone in ye bladder, there can be noe remedy for him but death, and I scarce think he can outlive this week. He was first taken while preacheing ye last fast sermon; then, it seems, ye fibers breakeing by wch it was held, it fell upon ye neck of [the] bladder, and hath put him into that disorder that every morneing I expect his death; he hardly escaped ye last night. His successor will be one Mr Rowell,[b] who marryed a cosin german of ye Lord Chancellors,[c] a raw yong fellow; but, his kinsman haveing ye disposall of ye benefice, that is enough to entitle him to it. This last weeke a new mayor was chosen for this city, and the choice fell upon one Mr Goodwin,[d] a very honest, quiet, good man, but not soe fit for businesse, and I hope there will be none for him to doe. The last mayor hath approved himselfe the wiseth man in ye city. I haveing occasion to send to severall registrys in England to get some ancient proceedeings in ye Ecclesiasticall Courts to [be] transcribed out of them, I desire you would doe me ye favour to give leave that they may be sent in a cover to you; otherwise the charge will be very hard upon me.

—   —

[Norwich], May 28, 1697.

Dr Smyth, one of our prebendarys, dyed last Tuesday. He was a very vigorous old man, and, although past 80, had the strength of

[a] Dr. William Smyth, Prebendary of Norwich, 1670-97.
[b] Not so. Dr. Smyth's successor was Richard Brodrepp.
[c] Lord Chancellor Somers.
[d] Laurence Goodwin.

a man of 40; but, beeing taken with an inflamation of y[e] bladder, y[e] chirurgion who searched him gave his judgement positively that he had a very great stone in his bladder, w[ch] misguideing his physitians, they gave him over as desperate; but when opend after his death the mistake appeard, and, had it not been for this mistake, he might easyly have been cured and lived many years more. I am now come to be y[e] senior of our church save one, it beeing y[e] 17th year that I have been here prebendary. All this countrey continues very quiet, and money is now as plentifull among us as ever, and trade begins to grow as brisk. My bookseller writes me that he hath already sould of one impression of my booke and is now on a second edition. I have by me a systeme of the Mahometan divinity, w[ch] is y[e] oddest stuffe that I believe you ever saw; but to ad this will double y[e] bulk of y[e] book, w[ch] will not be for y[e] booksellers profit now paper is soe dear. This would make that booke compleat. Perchance paper may be cheaper by that time y[e] 2[d] edition is of, and then it shall be ready to be inserted into y[e] 3[d]. The life of Mahomet I find is a novelty that makes y[e] booke acceptable. The expectation of a peace is in every bodys mouth, and all very greedyly run after y[e] news to se how it proceeds; and indeed y[e] taxes are now sufficiently heavy to make them weary of y[e] war.

[Norwich], June 4th, 1697.

All this countrey is filled with very malancholy storys in reference to our present circumstances. They represent Jamaica lost, Aeth[a] taken, the King and y[e] Duke of Bavaria parted in a feud never to be reconciled again, and that King William is deserted by all y[e] confederates and left to shift for himselfe, it

---

[a] Ath, in Hainault, surrendered to the French 26 May.

beeing certainly agreed by them to make a peace without him;[a] that, unlesse y[e] House of Austria doth consent to such a peace, the French are strong enough immediatly to possesse themselfes of all Flanders and Catalonia; and that we are to be sacrificed to prevent it. If this be our case, it is bad enough with a vengeance. I should be very sorry to see cause to believe any of it; but, were our circumstances well, I scarce think men would be thus bold with y[e] Government in representeing its case in such a manner. However, as far as it is false, I would be glad to have it authentically refuted. Nothing else from hence worth your knowledge.

[Norwich], June 14, 1697.

I thank you for y[e] favour of yours. The Jacobites here grow higher than ever; but an accident hapned last Thursday w[ch] I believe will cut their combes a little. It beeing the Prince of Wales's birthday, about 16 of them met at a tavern to drink his health, and among others there was one Captain Ogilby, who had formerly been a captain in Dumbartons Regiment, and hath some years sculk'd here with a certain widdow woman of this countrey that kept him to serve her purposes. He, with one Doedale and Ryley, two Irish papists, and one Caps, a papist of this towne, were y[e] last that left y[e] bottle. At 12 they broke up and went all 4 home together; on y[e] way, Doedale and Ogilby quarrelleing, y[e] later was run thorough and is since dead. Doedale is fled, but y[e] other two are still on y[e] place, and I thinke in law must answer for y[e] fact, for they are proved all 4 to have had their swords drawn, and y[e] other two fled y[e] streets as soon as Ogilby fell. I am told an ejectment hath been left at S[r] H. Hobarts house for 8000[l], w[ch] will reach a great part of his estate. I have been informed out

---

[a] The Congress of Ryswick was sitting at this time, and at length, after long delay, signed the treaty of peace on the 11th of September.

of Suffolk that ye dissenters there are busy upon some designes relateing to their interest, against ye next Parliament. I have sent to have it sifted into, and, if there be any thing in it, you shall have an account of it. One of our aldermen, a very rude huffeing fellow, was on Saterday condemned by ye Court of Aldermen to ye stool of repentance for abuseing one of his brethren, that is, to beg his pardon publickly before ye Court in a forme prescribed him, and subscribe his hand to it in their publicke register to stand upon record; and next Weduesday is assigned him for ye day, on penalty of beeing expelled out of his aldermans place. He is a proud insolent fellow and rich, so the city is in expectation what he will doe. If he refuseth it, as by his temper I suspect he will, there will be work for ye lawyers.

Norwich, Nov. 8, 1697.

. . . . . . The Jacobits are here full of expectations of some great matter, I know not what, unlesse it be ye designe of another assassination. They [st]ick not to say, as I am told, that within an halfe year there will be a whole change in our affairs, notwith-standeing ye peace and all . . . . .[a] When I [was last in] Suffolk, [I] met there an account of a letter from St Germains wrot by Dr Taylour,[b] a protestant divine, that now attends K. James's Court, wherein, telling ye Jacobites here in England of the great con-sternation wch was at St Germains on ye approach of ye peace, he sayd that ye French King comeing thither assured K. James soe far of his interest beeing safe, notwithstandeing ye peace, as gave full satisfaction; and therefore he perswades those to whom he writes to stand firme to their principles and not desert ye interest they were

[a] Injured by damp.
[b] Ralph Tayler, of Trinity College: M.A. 1673; D.D. 1686.

in upon any rumours they might hear, for ye peace would be noe
way to their disadvantage. But ye point on wch they [rely] is a
secret locked up soe close as not to be communicated to any. I
gave ye Archbp. immediately an account thereof, and, as far as I
know, ye letter is commun enough among ye party to be [true];
it is wrot under ye cant of a master of a college and his fellows,
but soe plain as the riddle may be easyly seen thorough. This D^r
Taylor took his degree of D^r of Divinity at Oxford ye same time I
did, and all along seemed to be a very good honest man; but, beeing
bigotted to Jacobitisme, I think he tooke ye right way to goe out
of ye protection of that Government wch he would not submit to,
and, would ye rest of y^m doe ye same, it would be a good riddance.
However, I am assured from one that is very intimate with ye popish
party that they are prepareing an addresse to K. William, to assure
him of their quiet submission to his government, and to crave his
favour and protection to them. But it seems our protestant Jacobites
are of ye worse temper of ye two.

Norwich, Nov. 15, 1697.

This night is spread all over this towne a generall rumour that
the King is kild in Holland by [one] of his guards. It comes by
ye way of Yarmouth; but, it beeing a generall rule with us here
never to believe Yarmouth news, we give not any credit to it; but
ye party that would have it soe grow very confident hereon. I pray
God we may hear better news another way of his safe arrivall on
English ground. Should ye thing be effected, wch God forbid, I
cannot see how that party could serve themselfes of it. Y^e villany
of ye fact must exasperate ye nation to such a degree as to make
their case worse than ever, and, instead of bringeing about y^e
restoration of K. James, put it at a greater distance than ever.
I have observed that ever since the peace hath been concluded

that party hath talked of something to be don wch would doe their businesse however, and that within an halfe an year we should see it.

[Norwich], Sept. 30, 1698.

I am now returned from my Suffolk journey. While I was there ye Earl of Orford ^{a} came to Orford to influence ye election of a mayor there, and was expected at Beccles this week at Sr Robert Riches, who was makeing preparations for his reception when I was there last Munday. Sr Robert came to my inne to visit me, and overpowered me with his civilitys, and of these I find he is very liberall to other people in his good moodes; but, when his passion takes its turn, he vents that in soe unreasonable a manner, even upon ye same persons, that I find he hath scarce any interest but among ye dissenters, who in that corner have noe other support but what they have from him. There is one Le Pell,^{b} an officer in the Danish auxiliary that came over here, who hath catchd a yong heiresse in my archdeaconry worth 15000^1, and he not worth 5 groats. Y^e yong woman indeed was noe beauty, but was reckoned to have witt and discretion; but she miserably betrayed ye want of the latter in this particular. Her name was Brookes. Mr Whitacre,^{c} Recorder of Ipswich, who served for that place last Parliament, I find hath soe far lost himselfe in that corporation that he will scarce ever recover himselfe there againe. The Ld.

^{a} Admiral Edward Russell, Earl of Orford, 1697-1727.

^{b} Nicholas Lepel, afterwards Brigadier-General. The lady whom he married was Mary Brooke, daughter of John Brooke of Rendlesham. The notice of the marriage is of interest, for the issue of it was Mary Lepel,
—— " Youth's youngest daughter, sweet Lepel,"
married in 1720 to John, Lord Hervey. From Prideaux's words we may gather that her beauty came from her father, her wit from her mother.

^{c} Charles Whittaker, Serjeant-at-law, Recorder of Ipswich. He was also M.P. in 1701. See above, p. 156, note ^{c}.

Paston [a] is like to be chosen at Thetford in y[e] place of S[r] Joseph Williamson,[b] who hath let that corporation know that he intends to serve for Rochester. His letters to that corporation in y[e] behalfe of Sloan were in a more than ordinary strain in his favour, calleing him in every line his dear Sloan, and telleing them that they could not be kind to him if they were not soe to his dear Sloan alsoe. However, that corporation getts but little credit by this choice. The Dutchesse of Grafton hath been with her son,[c] y[e] yong Duke, at Euston Hall ever since July; but this next week she goes for London.

[Norwich], Dec. 29th, 1699.

I doe most heartyly thank you for y[e] favour of yours and y[e] account w[ch] you gave of M[r] Neves case;[d] but I find he hath other sentiments of it. All y[t] he expected from y[e] Court he reckons is already granted him in makeing his friend M[r] Lombe[e] sheriffe of y[e] county; and now he is fully resolved to come over next assizes

---

[a] Charles, Lord Paston; died before his father the Earl of Yarmouth.

[b] Sir Joseph was elected in the Parliaments of 1695, 1698, and 1700, for Rochester as well as for Thetford; and the latter place was represented by James Sloane, Lord Paston, and Thomas Hanmer successively in his stead. Sloane also sat in the Parliament of 1698.

[c] Isabella, daughter of Henry Bennet, Earl of Arlington, married Henry Fitz-Roy, Duke of Grafton, who died in 1690. The young duke was Charles, their son.

[d] Oliver Le Neve, of Great Wichingham, co. Norfolk. Prideaux refers to his fatal duel with Sir Henry Hobart. "In 1695, he [Sir H. Hobart] was again elected to serve in Parliament for the county, and always behaved like a man of honour in that post, but being disappointed of his election in 1698, and resenting some words said to be spoken by Oliver Le Neve, Esq. (which Le Neve denied under his hand), a challenge was given, and a duel ensued, in which Sir Henry passed his sword through Neve's arm, and Neve ran his into Sir Henry's belly, of which wound he died the next day, being Sunday, 21 August, 1698."—Blomefield's *Norfolk*, vi. 402.

[e] Edward Lombe, Sheriff for Norfolk.

and take his tryall, assureing himselfe that he [will only be found guilty] of manslaughter, for wch he will submitt to [a verdict]; but I . . . . .ª for I know not how he can be cleared of y" murder . . . . duel and kild in it. The D[uke] of N[orfolk] hath been here; and some will have it that his only businesse was to fix Dogget ᵇ and his players here, who have now their stage up at yᵉ Dukes place, and are helping all they can to undoe this place, w^ch, on yᵉ decay of their weaveing trade, now sinks apace. But I suppose his Grace had some other designe in this journey than for yᵉ sake of those varletts. Yᵉ only caballeing designe here is for a new election; for it is resolved to think of neither of yᵉ old ones any more, and I find they are at a losse whom to fix on [for] yᵉ new. Mʳ Windham ᶜ I reckon will be one, who is a yong gentleman of a very considerable estate in this countrey, but, haveing had an Italian education, is all over Italiz'd. that is, an Italian as to religion, I mean a down right atheist; an Italian in politics, that is a Commonwealths man; and an Italian I doubt in his moralls, for he cannot be perswaded to marry. He is about 25 years old, of a tolerable good understandeing and an estate of 4000ˡ per annum. His mother and yᵉ Lord Townshends mother were sisters, both beeing daughters of Sʳ Joseph [Ashe],ᵈ I reckon [this was part] of what was caballed on this journey. One night of his beeing here . . . . one of his lethargic fits, and I doubt he is not yet . . . . Our new barᵗ, Sʳ Richard Allen,ᵉ makes all yᵉ steps he can to get out of yᵉ

ª This letter is injured by damp.
ᵇ Thomas Dogget, founder of the Dogget coat and badge.
ᶜ Ashe Wyndham, of Fellbrigg.
ᵈ Sir Joseph Ashe of Twickenham, Bart. His elder daughter, Catherine, married William Wyndham; his younger daughter, Mary, married Horatio, Visconnt Townsend.
ᵉ Richard Anguish succeeded to the property, and assumed the name, of his uncle, Sir Thomas Allin, of Blundeston, Bart. He was created a baronet of Somerleyton, co. Suffolk, 14 Dec. 1699. He married Frances, daughter of Sir Henry Ashurst.

[phanatic] interest now Sr R. Rich is dead, and his lady is as earnest in it as he. He hath refused to stand a[t] Dunwich upon the phanatic interest; and yet I doe not find ye gentrey are very forward to give any reguard to him. My thanks to you for all favours.

Norwich, Jan. 11, 1699 [1700].

The Duke still continues here under regimen for his health, wch is soo very bad that his physitian told me he was tantum non apoplecticus. His lethargy is grown to that hieght that he in a manner continually sleeps, and one night he had a fit out of which they difficultly awaked him. This drove him to ye doctor, who hath bleeded him 18 ounces, blistered him, and purged him, and tells him, if he will follow rules, he will undertake to put him to rights again, but, if not, an apoplexy will soon knock him off. It was with difficulty that he prevailed with him to be bleeded; and he had not prevailed at all, but that, after the D^r had done talkeing with him about it and without any successe, a gentleman that stood by entering into discourse with him told him that he was sorry the Duke would not be perswaded by him, and feared he would have reason to repent of it. At this ye D^r answered lowd enough for ye Duke to hear him, "Repent! there will be noe roome for that, for, if he will not be advised by me, an apoplexy comes next wch will give him noe leasure to repent, for then he goes all at once, and an end will soon be made beyond ye remedy of physic and repentance." At this his Grace was startled, and then became resolved to submitt to blister, bleeding, and purgeing, wch hath very much relieved him; [but if he continues] to live on at this rate, and I doe not find he takes any . . . . . .^{a} soon again

* Words lost from damp.

recover his strength, and I take it for granted he will not . . . . .
In case this happens,[a] a new Lord Liuetenant must be thought on
for us, [and] y⁰ choice of y' Lord Townshend is soe obvious that
I think y' Court cannot misse it; for nothing else can be acceptable to the countey, or, in truth, doe y° King any service in it.
The chiefe man of y⁰ opposit faction to that w^cb now prevails is
M' Walpole,[b] who was guardian to y' Lord Townshend; if he be
Ld. Liuetenant, all y' Dukes party will come in to him as one man,
and Walpole will bring him in the other [party, and, if] he doth
not, you may be assured Walpole himselfe will joyne with him;
and, beside him, there is not a man of any parts or interest in all
that party. To pitch on him I reckon will be a certain expedient
to remove all manner of divisions out of this countrey; and ever
since y⁰ old Lord Towshend, for some discontents at Court, joyned
with S' John Hobart, y⁰ father of S' Henry, this countrey for now
25 years hath been continually harassed with them, and I think
it would be a great happinesse to be rid of them. It is now y⁰
Sessions week, and if y⁰ Duke gives himselfe the liberty, w^cb is
usually taken at such meetings of y⁰ gentrey, I know not how far
it may goe to y⁰ carrying him of the stage. I intend, God willing,
to be in London y⁰ beginning of the next month.

--- -

[Norwich]. May 9, 1705.

The Norwich cause[c] is now goeing up to the Councill, the
freemen haveing delivered a petition to y⁰ Lord Townshend, to
be presented to y⁰ Queen and Councill, against the Mayor and

---

[a] The Duke lived to 1701. Lord Townshend afterwards became Lord Lieutenant.
[b] Robert Walpole, father of the statesman. Charles Lord Townshend married
his daughter Dorothy.
[c] "In 1704 there were great disputes about electing an alderman in the room of
Augustine Briggs, Esq., deceased, for the great ward of Conisford and Berstreet.
The court swore Benjamin Austin, who was displaced in 1706 by Thomas Dunch,
who had the majority at the election, and obtained a mandamus to be sworn in
Austin's place."— Blomefield's *Norfolk*, iii. 431.

Aldermen, for depriveing them of their rights; and the Lord Townshend hath undertaken that it shall be delivered. The case is thus. One Mr Briggs, an alderman, dying ye 3rd of August last, there appeared candidates in that ward for his place Mr Dunch and Mr Austin. Mr Dunch beeing a sturdy Whig and a fellow of notable parts and understandeing, the Mayor,[a] who is a sturdy Tory, resolved to doe all he could to keep him out; and therefore, although the elections in such cases used to be made within 10 or 12 days, the Mayor deferred it till ye middle of ye last month, hopeing in all this time to make sure of a party to keepe Dunch out; but it hapneing to work ye contrary way, Dunches party grew by ye delay, and he was chosen by a great majority. Whereon ye Mayor and his party in the Court of Aldermen claimed a right of approveing the alderman chosen, and they would not approve the election of Dunch, but rejected him, giveing him for their reasons of soe doeing that he was a turbulent, malicious man, and of uncivill behaviour in conversation; and ordered ye ward to chuse again. The ward met and chose Dunch again, but, notwith-standeing, the Mayor hath sworn in Austin, takeing, I suppose, all ye votes given for Dunch to goe for nothing. Hereon Dunch hath served a mandamus upon the Mayor out of the Kings Bench, and there ye point now is. I find none of their charters can justify their claim to an approbation. They have an instance in their books of an alderman once chosen by ye ward and disapproved by ye Court of Aldermen; but all their charters seem to be quite ye contrary, that ye Mayor is to swear in whomsoever the ward chooseth. This is like to creat a great ruffle here, and I take it Blofield[b] will certainly be flung out for beeing of the Mayors party in this matter. I was apprehensive of it some time since, and tooke notice to Blofield of it; but his over-confidence in his party made him neglect ye advice I gave him.

---

[a] Peter Thacker.   [b] Thomas Blofield, M.P. for Norwich.

Norwich, June 25th, 1705.

A rumour hath been here for some time that you have of late been under some trouble;[a] although ye experience wch now I have had for near 40 years of your untainted integrity doth give me full assurance that nothing of that wch is sayd can stick upon you, yet to be assured from yourselfe that all is made clear will be a great satisfaction to me.   I beg this favour of you.

--- --- ---

Norwich, July 11, 1705.

I am very sorry you have suffered that trouble and damage wch you mention.   Whatsoever may have brought this misfortune upon you I can never think otherwise of you than I have always known and experienced for so many years, and I hope you will see clear this matter as to maintain your reputation as fully and as intirely with every body else as you always must with me ; for, whatever becomes of your place, I would advise you by noe means to give up ye reputation of your integrity, but vindicate that to ye utmost you are able, that, although you are not in ye same post you were, yet still you may be looked on as ye same honest man.   There beeing few I have had more friendship from than from yourselfe, I cannot but be very much grieved at this misfortune wch hath hapned to you, and I assure you I bear my share with you in it.

--- --- ---

[a] Towards the end of May of this year Ellis resigned his appoiutment of Under-Secretary.   He seems to have fallen under the displeasure of his chief, Secretary Hedges, for some breach of duty; though the particular cause cannot now be ascertained.

Norwich, Nov. 26, 1707.

I acquainted you in my last with ye case of ye Yarmouth petition, wch I am much concerned to oppose; because it lays a great incombrance upon my estate. To hinder its progresse, I have drawn the enclosed petition to be subscribed by myselfe and others who will be damaged by it; but, beeing ignorant of the stile and usuall forme in wch such petitions are addressed to ye House, the favour wch I beg of you is, that you would put it into due forme where it [is] defective, and put the stile of addresse soe as it ought to be, and then send it me back again, that I may get it wrot out fair and subscribed, that soe it may be lodged ready to be presented, if their [sic] shall be an occasion. But I am of opinion that, when it becomes known that a counter petition is ready, the petition will never be at all presented; for I think it cannot stand against the reasons which we offer against it. I humbly beg your pardon for this trouble wch I give you.

Norwich, March 31, 1707[8].

I doe very much thank you for ye favour of yours, and am glad that the Scotch plot [a] is over. I reckon ye Court plot for confoundeing the Ministrey and the City plot for the breakeing of the Bank and ye East Indy Company are all branches of it, wch argues it to be a very deep layd designe, and I doubt we doe not yet see halfe way into the bottom of it. I wish it doe not hereafter break out in some other mischiefe. I am of opinion people will be willing enough to overlook ye Queens mistake in the matter of the Ministry,[b] provided the Admiralty be better provided

[a] The futile attempt of the Chevalier St. George to effect a landing in Scotland.
[b] The dismissal of Harley, which had taken place in February.

for ; but ye generality are soe excccdeingly dissatisfyed with ye present management of that, that they will never cease clam-oureing till that great trust be in other hands. And, indeed, I wonder at the indiscretion of those counsells wch influence the continueing of the Prince in such a post, where he is only to bear ye blame of other mens miscarriages.[a] Had the Bank broke when ye run was made upon it, I must have broke too, for I had then 4000[1] in it ; but I have now disposed of it to ye purpose for wch it lay there. I hope I shall never again have the occasion of running such an hazard. I reckon ye matters that have been of late transacted will, on this baffle, have a great influence on this next election. I wish it doe not carry the Whig interest too high, for that is best when well ballanced. I durst not trust them when paramount; whenever they are soe, I am affraid they will be makeing dangerous attempts. I pray God all things may goe well at last; at present I think we are much unjointed.

<hr />

Norwich, Sept. 13, 1708.

. . . . All that I can tell you from hence is, that now taxes begin to come very heavy; and the reason is, that rent comes heavyer from the tenants; and, when ye land lord receives nothing, how can he pay anything? The failure of the countrymans trade is ye cause of this. We are now upon a very tickelish point abroad. If this campaigne doth not succeed soe well as to force the French to a peace next winter, I am affraid we shall not be able to find ffunds for another year. The event shows our victory at Oudenard[b]

* Prince George of Denmark held the office of High Admiral, and was assisted by a Council. Slight changes were made in the Council both in April and June of this year.

b Fought on the 15th July. The only action of importance during the rest of the campaign was the repulse, by General Webb, of the enemy who attacked him in great force at Wynendael on the 28th September.

was noe great matter, and we are not strong enough to have any
prospect of gaineing another, and without gaineing another I doubt
ye campaigne may end to our disadvantage. Our new bishop[a] is
gon again to London; he hath set himselfe in here in a very good
interest in his diocesse, beeing generally as much in every mans
good opinion as his predecessor was in the contrary. He hath been
at great expense about his house, w^ch, from a very ugly one, he
hath made very convenient and handsom; but it is likely to cost
him severall hundred of pounds before he hath don. The Earle of
Yarmouth is as low as you can imagin; he hath vast debts, and
suffers every thing to run to extremity; soe his goods have been
all seised in execution and his lands extended, soe that he hath
scarce a servant to attend him or an horse to ride abroad upon, and
yett cannot be perswaded to take any method of putteing his affairs
into a better posture, wch they are still capable of, if he would set
about it. But ye Lord Townshend florisheth much among us, for
ye whole countey is absolutely at his beck, and he hath got such
an ascendant here over everybody by his courteous carriage that he
may doe anything among us what he will, and that not only in the
countey, but alsoe in all the corporations, except at Thetford, where
all is sould. Y^e election there is among the magistracy, and 50
guineas for a vote is their price. One Mr Baylis,[b] a stranger, was
their last chapman, to whom they say they have sould themselfes
much dearer; for it hath cost him 3000[l] to get a return from
thence for the next Parliament, and that is but a litigious one, for
Sr John Woodhouse[c] will be a petitioner against him.

---

[a] Charles Trimnell, Prebendary; Bishop of Norwich in succession to Dr. Moore,
23 Jan. 1708. Translated to Winchester, 1721.

[b] Robert Baylis.

[c] Sir John Woodhouse, Bart., had represented Thetford in several Parliaments.

Norwich, July 11. 1709.

I thank you for your kindnesse to my nephew. He did not let me know of this intended ramble till he was ready to be gon, and therefore it was too late for me to diswade him from it. I know not what advantage it can bring him, and I am affraid it may doe him a great deal of hurt. My opinion hath been that it would be best for him to marry and settle at home upon his estate, wch is better than 1000^l per annum; but ye young man hath an ambition to make himselfe somewhat greater than a countrey gentleman, and, to give him his due, he hath a capacity for any thing, had he had an education suitable to it; and this it is he hopes to mend by travelling. I hope the new commotions in France may make it necessary for that Crown forthwith to make peace upon the pre-liminaries agreed, and thereby prevent the fatigues, wch otherwise our army must be harassed with, in carrying on a siege in a wet season.[a] My Lord of Norwich is now thoroughly recovered and gon into Suffolk to complete his visitation. Mr Clerk [b] is now here and speaks gratefully to me of your respects to him. He is a person of great learneing and integrity, and I hope he will answere in all things else. His greatest preferment, in beeing made Rector of your parish, is in that hereby he is emancipated from the Bishop of Ely,[c] whose service and ways he was heartyly weary of. That man hath lately made one Dr Canon [d] a Prebendary of his church, on contract to marry his daughter ; and it is hard to say wch is the greatest fool of the two in this matter. Canon is about 50 years and a very infirme man, beeing exceedingly troubled with y^e

---

[a] The allies invested Tournay in June, and finally reduced it in September.

[b] Samuel Clarke, of Caius Coll., Cambridge; B.A. 1694; M.A. 1698; S.T.P. 1710; Rector of Drayton, co. Norfolk; of St. Benet's Wharf, London; and of St. James's, Westminster; died 1729.

[c] Dr. John Moore, translated from Norwich in 1707.

[d] Robert Cannon, D.D.; Prebendary of Ely, 1709; Dean of Lincoln, 1721; died 1722.

falleing of ye gut, wch usually takes him up all the morneing to get it up; and she is a yong sanguine girle of about 24. That he should at all marry in such a case and such an one as will be sure to loath him, or that y^r other should marry such a daughter to such a man, is a folly on both sides wch is not to be accounted for, and must end ill on both sides. I reckon the wedding is about this time. Canon is a favourit of ye Lord Treasurer,[a] as haveing been tutor to his son at Cambridge, and, to give him his due, is a man of worth and learneing; and I suppose his father-in-law expects, on this bottom, to raise him in the Church, perchance to a bishoprick. He is already Archdeacon of Norfolke, Prebendary of Ely, and Chaplain to Chelsey Hospital. I hear Dr Robinson is sent for over to be Bishop of Chichester,[b] and I hope he will be a very fit man for it; and his interest with the northern protestants may be of great use to unite them with the Church of England. Should ye present Archbp.[c] hold out a year longer, perchance by that time he may be thought of as a fit person to succeed him; and, if he should hold out soe long, I would hope by that time ye man now talked of may [be] soe truely represented to ye Queen as not to be approved of by her for that station; and I hear there are many at work to convince her of it, and that she is dayly told something or other by those about her to this purpose. The Professor of Divinity at Oxford[d] hath lately marryed a wife out of this countrey, and it is a very scandalous match; however, he became drawn into it. She is the daughter of one Coll. Venner, son to the famous Venner[e] that was ye head of the Fifth Monarchy

[a] Sidney, Earl of Godolphin.

[b] The new Bishop of Chichester was Dr. Thomas Manningham, Dean of Windsor, Dr. John Robinson succeeding him as Dean; and became Bishop of Bristol, 1710; Lord Privy Seal, 1711; and Bishop of London, 1713.

[c] I suppose that Dr. Sharp, Archbishop of York, is referred to; but he lived to 1714.

[d] John Wynne, D.D.

[e] Thomas Venner, one of the leaders in the insurrection of the Fifth Monarchy Men in London, January, 1661. He was taken and executed.

men. This man served ye Venetians in the Morea, and was there a Coll. He, beeing in Holland when K. William came over, engaged with him in that expedition, and had a regiment in Ireland, and was entrusted with ye government of the hospital of ye army; but, beeing for his falsenesse in the management of that trust broken and discarded, he hath retired into this countrey and hath lived here several years, but with ye worst reputation that you can imagin in all respects, and is one of the most ill-looked fellows that ever I saw in my life, for he had occasion once to appear before me when on publick businesse, and this was ye only time I ever saw him. But you cannot be a stranger to this mans character, and such an alliance cannot be to the credit of ye Professor; and they tell me it is as bad on ye mothers side as on ye fathers, who is daughter to one Dr Gardiner (as they call him), one that practiseth physick in Covent Garden. The Christ Church men, I apprehend, will make work with him upon this marriage.

I thank you for ye favour of yours and the trouble wch you are pleased, on my request, to take on you of disposeing of ye two books I sent you.ª I beg your pardon that I thus presume on you; your many favours in other matters have encouraged me alsoe in this to rely npon you. I am glad what I have in this book published gives you satisfaction. I doe not expect soe to come of with others, because I goe not ye usuall way in driveing this matter to those hieghts where it cannot stand, though I hear the Archbp. likes it well. Another part was intended when I begun, wch would

---

ª This is probably Prideaux's work, "The Original and Right of Tithes," the publishing date of which is 1710.

be much larger than this, but God hath been pleased to disable me from proceedeing any further by ye calamity wch is since fallen upon me. I am sorry ye clergy doe soe much embrace Sachevarells cause. I wish it may not provoke the Parliament to vigorous methods against the whole body. John Dyer tells me y^t ye 54th Psalme was sung in most of the church[es] in London on ye Sunday, in wch were preached ye sermons wch you mention. By ye present proceedeings of the French King, I suspect he depends upon something to be don in favour of his cause, wch is as yet in ye dark, perchance some secret plot to be executed between this and the beginneing of the next campaigne; otherwise he acts not with his usuall wisdom in continueing the war in such circumstances as cannot promise him any successe in it. As to the King of Sweden,^a I reckon it would be to the advantage of Christendom were he dead, for otherwise he will be always disturbeing it[s] peace as long as he shall live. I find in ye news papers that ye Earle of Dorset hath marryed Mrs Collier,^b who is ye daughter, I am told, of one Coll. Collier, that was killed in King Williams service in ye last wars. I have a curiosity to know who this gentleman was. My reason for it is, one Collier, that had been a page to the Prince of Orange and afterwards one of his guards, came into Cornwall, beeing then in poor condition, and marryed a poor kinswoman of mine that had been a servant in my fathers house. This same man came over with King William and was a Coll. in his army, and was afterwards kild, I think, a[t] Steenkirk. He used often to come to my brother in London while he livd. When you favour me with your next pray give me a line about this matter.

---

^a Charles XII.; killed in 1718.

^b Lionel Cranfield Sackville, seventh Earl, afterwards Duke, of Dorset, married Elizabeth, daughter of Lieut.-General Walter Colyear, a younger brother of the Earl of Portmore. General Colyear lived to 1717.

Norwich, July 7, 1710.

Dureing these unsteady times I doe not expect any news from you, but as long as I live I should be glad to hear from you. My case grows worse and worse, and there is noe remedy for me but by cutteing; and, on full advice had upon my case, I am told I cannot bear that operation, but that in all likelyhood I must dy under it. If soe, to put myselfe upon it is nothing lesse than selfe murder, and for that I cannot answer to God, who gave me my life; and therefore I must be content to bear my burden as it is, and it is heavy enough.[a] We are here in great confusion upon the convulsions that are above, and there is generally a damp upon the spirits of all men that wish well to their countrey. Our war against France hath been carryed on with great successe, and, now we are almost come to the harvest when we are to receive ye fruits of it, its now snachd out of our hands by our own madnesse; and, as far as I see, we are as far from a peace as we were 7 years since, at least such a peace as will be beneficiall for England. We have in our contests at home don more for France this year than we have don against them with all our victorys; and, if we goe on at this rate, they will carry their point at last, and popery and slavery must be our lot. Although I am going out of the world, I cannot but lament the mischiefes that are like speedyly to happen to this nation, if we tread on the same measures y^t we now seem to be running into. This will be lamented by those who are now its chiefe instruments, when it will be too late for them to remedy it.

— —

---

[a] However, he underwent the operation and was cut for "the calamitous distemper of the stone," as he tells us in his Preface to the *Connection of the Old and New Testaments*.

Norwich, Sept. 29, 1722.

I thank you for your last, and am glad to find by it that your case is much better than mine   As to Dr John Clark,[a] his case is thus; about 30 years since Dr Fairfax, then Dean of Norwich, put one Mr Richardson to be Minister of the parish of the Close, with a permission to serve it once a fortnight. This I then protested against as contrary both to former usage and to the service of God Almighty, and have ever since many times expressed my dislike of it, and have as often promised that it should be remedi'd whenever it should fall in my power. About a year since, Richardson dying, Dr Clark applyed to me for the place, and would serve it no otherwise than Richardson did. But, not being able to comply with him herein, I did put another in the place. This is the whole reason of his quarrel with me.   I told him I denyed him nothing but what I would deny to a brother or a son; that I thought the obligation for doeing the best for Gods service to be greater than any obligation whatsoever for ye acting contrary thereto, and neither his brother nor his father think I did otherwise than my duty herein. As to publick affairs, this countrey is now become the scene of action; this town is in a general mutiny about the election of a sherif;[b] our two cheife Ministers of State are both Norfolk men;[c] and Layer,[d] who is lately sent to ye Tower, is also of this country, and a viler wretch scarce lives in it. No one that knows him will think him fitt to be trusted with the secrets of any plot, or to be relyed on in any evidence he shall give

---

[a] John Clarke, of Caius Coll Cambridge; B.A. 1703; M.A. 1707; S.T.P. 1717; Dean of Salisbury, 1728; died 1757.   He was brother of Dr. Samuel Clarke mentioned above, p. 201.

[b] The Sheriff for Norfolk for the year 1723 was Gresham Page.

[c] Charles Viscount Townsend and John Lord Carteret became Principal Secretaries of State in 1721.

[d] Christopher Layer, concerned in the Jacobite plot of this year, was sent to the Tower 20 September.   He was tried and condemned in November, and was executed in the following May.

about it. He went indeed last year into Italy on pretence of transacting some affairs of my Lord London-Derry [a] with M[r] Knights,[b] and then he saw y[e] Pretender, and was admitted by him to audience more then once; and of thus much he has several times bragged in company, and said enough hereof to be hanged for it; and, if this comes to be his lott, scarce anyone here will be concerned for it. The time of the setteing of the Parliament now approaching, I wish all things w[ch] are for y[e] honour of y[e] King and y[e] good of the country may be transacted in it.[c]

---

[a] Thomas Pitt, Lord Londonderry.

[b] Perhaps Robert Knight, Treasurer of the South Sea Company, who had escaped abroad the previous year.

[c] This letter is written by an amanuensis.

INDEX.

Westminster: Printed by Nichols and Sons, 25, Parliament Street.

REPORT OF THE COUNCIL

OF

THE CAMDEN SOCIETY,

READ AT THE GENERAL MEETING

ON THE 3RD MAY, 1875.

THE Council of the Camden Society elected on the 2nd May, 1874, deeply regret the loss of

The Right Hon. LORD ROMILLY.

Lord Romilly did not take an active part in the operations of the Society, yet the benefits he conferred upon historical literature in throwing open the Public Records to Literary and Historical inquirers, and in directing the compilation of calendars and other means of help for those who deserve aid by doing their best to help themselves, are of such a nature as to render it impossible that the Members of the Camden Society will ever forget the debt which they owe to him. It is undeniable that but for Lord Romilly many of the most valuable of the publications of the Society would either never have been issued at all, or would have been issued in a sadly incomplete state.

The Council have to regret also the loss of

BARON VAN DE WEYER,

whose valuable help as a Member of the Council during many years merits the warmest recognition on the part of the Members of the Camden Society. Baron Van de Weyer also kindly undertook to edit for the Society a Collection of Despatches of the French Ambassadors. This, however, want of time prevented him from carrying out—a cause of much regret to the Society.

And COLONEL CAREW,

from whose library some books of great value have been already printed, and by whose courtesy copies of other MSS. have been taken which the Council hope in the course of time to be able to issue to the Society.

The Council are sorry to have to add the following List of Members who have died within the last year:

RICHARD ALMACK, Esq., F.S.A.

W. BLANDY, Esq.

JOHN BOOTH, Esq.

BENJAMIN BOND CABBELL, Esq., F.R.S., F.S.A.

SIR STEPHEN R. GLYNNE, Bart., F.S.A.

MISS MARIA HACKETT,

SIR JOSEPH HAWLEY, Bart.

W. E. WALMISLEY, Esq. and

CHARLES WINN, Esq.

The following are the books for the past year:

I. Account of the Executors of Richard Bishop of London, 1303, and of the Executors of Thomas Bishop of Exeter, 1310. Edited by the late ARCHDEACON HALE and the Rev. T. ELLACOMBE, M.A., F.S.A.

This volume is full of curious details on the household and ecclesiastical furniture of a Bishop of the 14th century.

II. Wriothesley's Chronicle of England. Vol I. Reigns of Henry VII. and Henry VIII. Edited, from a MS. in the Library of Lieut.-General Lord Henry Percy, by W.D. HAMILTON, F.S.A. In addition to the information offered by the Chronicle itself, Mr. Hamilton has printed in the Appendix the original official records of the trial of Anne Boleyn, never hitherto printed or quoted in a copy by any historian.

III. Papers relating to the Quarrel between Oliver Cromwell and the Earl of Manchester. Edited by the late JOHN BRUCE, F.S.A. and PROFESSOR MASSON.

This volume gives information about the proceedings of the Earl of Manchester and Cromwell from the Battle of Marston Moor till after the second Battle of Newbury, as well as the arguments on both sides in the dispute which arose out of those proceedings.

The books for the year 1875-6 will probably be—

I. The Camden Miscellany Vol. VII. (Just ready.) Containing, 1. The Boy Bishop. Edited by the late J. G. NICHOLS, F.S.A. and DR. RIMBAULT. 2. The Speech of the Attorney-General Heath in the Star Chamber against Alexander Leighton. Edited by the late JOHN BRUCE, F.S.A. and S. R. GARDINER. 3. The Judgment of Sir G. Croke in the Case of Ship Money. Edited by S. R. GARDINER. 4. Accounts of the Building of Bodmin Church. Edited by the Rev. J. J. WILKINSON, M.A. 5. The Mission of Sir Thomas Roe to Gustavus Adolphus. Edited by S. R. GARDINER.

II. Letters of Dr. Prideaux, Dean of Norwich. 1674-1722.

III. The Autobiography of Lady Anne Halkett. Edited by the late JOHN GOUGH NICHOLS, F.S.A.

Amongst the papers in the Miscellany the Society will find more memorials of the work of their late Director and of Mr. J. G. Nichols. The Boy Bishop occupied his thoughts much in his later years, and, if it did not appear long ago from his own hand, it was because in his search after absolute perfection he had such difficulty in contenting himself with work which seemed admirable to others. In this same way he has left behind him an almost infinite stock of notes on the Life of Lady Anne Halkett, (a pious lady of the days of the Commonwealth and Restoration,) some of which are so slight that no one can now hope to interpret them, or even to guess at the intention with which they were made.

In the letters of Dr. Prideaux the Society will have a most amusing sketch of life at Oxford and in the country during a most interesting period. The chatty writer will probably be a favourite even with those who usually look upon the Society's publications as too dry for their reading.

The Council having at several meetings debated the question of the advisability of disposing of the surplus stock of the Society's Publications belonging to the First Series of Publications, instead of paying an annual charge for storage, &c. it was at length resolved that some arrangement should be come to whereby the Society might realize some benefit for its funds, instead of expending a portion of its yearly income in providing house-room for stock. It was thought, however, that previously to any sale taking place to the trade of the stock in question, it would be courteous and just to the actual Members of the Society to give them a chance of completing their sets of the Society's publications, should they wish so to do; and a list of the publications was made at revised prices, so that the Members should have any volumes they required at a cheap rate. This list has been circulated by direction of the Council amongst the Members, and as soon as the results for which it was issued shall have been accomplished, steps will be taken for disposing of the remaining stock.

By order of the Council,

SAMUEL R. GARDINER, *Director*.
ALFRED KINGSTON, *Hon. Secretary*.

REPORT OF THE AUDITORS.

We, the Auditors appointed to audit the Accounts of the Camden Society, report to the Society, that the Treasurer has exhibited to us an Account of the Receipts and Expenditure from the 17th of April 1874 to the 31st of March 1875, and that we have examined the said accounts, with the vouchers relating thereto, and find the same to be correct and satisfactory.

And we further report that the following is an Abstract of the Receipts and Expenditure during the period we have mentioned :—

Receipts.	£	s.	d.	Expenditure.	£	s.	d.
To Balance of last year's account..	520	7	10	Paid for printing 500 copies Accounts of the Bishops of London and Exeter.......................................	66	6	0
Received on account of Members whose Subscriptions were in arrear at last Audit	32	0	0	Paid for printing 500 copies Wriothesley's Chronicle, vol. I..	84	16	6
The like on account of Subscriptions due on the 1st of May, 1874......	248	0	3	Paid for Miscellaneous Printing............................	6	18	0
The like on account of Subscriptions due on the 1st of May, 1875.. ...	18	0	0	Paid for delivery and transmission of Books, with paper for wrappers, warehousing expenses (including Insurance)	22	5	2
To one Composition in lieu of Annual Subscription	10	0	0	Paid for paper	46	3	0
One year's dividend on £466 3 1 3 per Cent. Consols, standing in the names of the Trustees of the Society, deducting Income Tax..	13	17	6	Paid for binding	68	8	0
To Sale of the Publications of past years...................................	70	8	6	Paid for Transcripts of Instructions to Sir Thomas Roe : Documents for Appendix to Wriothesley's Chronicle ; Justice Croke's Judgment; Whitelocke Memorials ; Index to Williamson Correspondence	35	3	0
To Sale of Promptorium Parvulorum (3 vols. in 1)	3	2	0	Paid for postages, collecting, country expenses, &c. ...	3	1	11
				By Balance	582	11	6
	£915	16	1		£915	16	1

And we, the Auditors, further state, that the Treasurer has reported to us, that over and above the present balance of £582 11s. 6d. there are outstanding various subscriptions of Foreign Members, and of Members resident at a distance from London, which the Treasurer sees no reason to doubt will shortly be received.

Henry Hill.
George F. Smith.